Friends, Lovers and other Indiscretions

Fiona Neill is a features writer for *The Times Magazine* and author and creator of its hugely popular 'Slummy Mummy' column. After working abroad for six years as a foreign correspondent in Latin America, she returned to the UK to become assistant editor at *Marie Claire* and then *The Times Magazine*. Brought up in Norfolk, she now lives in London with her husband and three children. Her first novel, *The Secret Life of a Slummy Mummy*, was a *Sunday Times* bestseller and international rights have been sold worldwide across twenty-four countries.

Praise for *Friends, Lovers & Other Indiscretions*

'Neill had a huge hit with *The Secret Life of a Slummy Mummy*, her hilarious take on modern motherhood. This is every bit as funny, and packed with observations of wince-making accuracy . . . Superb entertainment' *The Times*

'Fiona Neill's comic novel is an investigation into modern marriage . . . Neill's characters are so cleverly depicted, you feel as if you've met at least one of them before' *Vogue*

'A comical look at the trials and tribulations of modern marriage' *Daily Express*

'There is something of Bridget Jones's hopeless-but-adorable quality about Lucy . . . Neill's hilarious depiction of the manifold daily perils of stay-at-home motherhood is so convincing that it soon looks like the most challenging job in the world – and Lucy is all the more sympathetic simply for staying afloat' *Daily Telegraph*

'An intelligent and funny look at modern parenting' *Eve*

'This will have you laughing out loud with empathy' *Star Magazine*

'Hilarious' *Sainsbury's Magazine*

'The chaotic tale of the hapless Lucy will strike a chord with any woman who hasn't quite mastered the art of being a domestic goddess' *InStyle*

'Neill bucks the chick-lit trend with prose that's clever and endearing, and frazzled parents will love the way she nails the sticky, hair-pulling mania of domestic life' *Washington Post*

'A sharply observed comedy . . . her writing burbles along effortlessly. Her comic timing is excellent' *Boston Globe*

'Neill's diverting domestic farce reminds us that the most remarkable aspect of enduring love is its patience and complexity' *People Magazine* (US)

Friends, Lovers
and other
Indiscretions

Fiona Neill

arrow books

Published by Arrow Books 2010

4 6 8 10 9 7 5 3

First published in Great Britain in 2009 by Century

Arrow Books
Random House, 20 Vauxhall Bridge Road,
London SW1V 2SA

www.rbooks.co.uk

Addresses for companies within The Random House Group Limited can be
found at: www.randomhouse.co.uk/offices.htm

The Random House Group Limited Reg. No. 954009

A CIP catalogue record for this book
is available from the British Library

ISBN 9780099502890

The Random House Group Limited supports The Forest Stewardship
Council (FSC), the leading international forest certification organisation. All
our titles that are printed on Greenpeace approved FSC certified paper carry
the FSC logo. Our paper procurement policy can be found at:
www.rbooks.co.uk/environment

Typeset by SX Composing DTP, Rayleigh, Essex
Printed and bound in Great Britain by
CPI Bookmarque Ltd, Croydon, CR0 4TD

For Felix, Maia and Caspar

Tell all the Truth but tell it slant –
Success in Circuit lies
Too bright for our infirm Delight
The Truth's superb surprise

As Lightning to the Children eased
With explanation kind
The Truth must dazzle gradually
Or every man be blind –

Emily Dickinson

'Tell me what company thou keepst and I'll tell thee what thou are'

Cervantes, *Don Quixote*

1

Until eleven o'clock that morning in late February, Sam Diamond had considered himself a reasonably happily married man. It was his thirty-ninth birthday and every year since they had met, Laura had sprung a surprise on him. Admittedly these had become less inventive since they'd had children, and he always suspected she might be engaged in one-upmanship with his mother, but nevertheless he counted himself fortunate to be married to a woman who still went to such effort on her husband's birthday.

Of course Laura's attempts at dissimulation were undermined by his inability to resist looking in her diary to find carefully compiled lists in neat black writing of potential presents, possible restaurants and surprise dinner guests. But Sam was good at feigning astonishment and he found Laura's transparency reassuring, proof of her certainty about where their life was heading.

Today though was different. There had been no notes anywhere. No hints from their children about what their mother might have planned. No clues from friends. So when the babysitter arrived at ten o'clock in the morning greeting him with a knowing smile and Laura explained they were leaving the house for the rest of the day, he had allowed his imagination to run wild: this was going to be a big one. She was carrying a bag, large enough for toothbrushes and underwear, Sam noted, but too small for spare clothes. He inspected it hopefully. It was the one she used to carry her medical journals and neurological kit. As far as he could see, there was nothing that suggested work inside: no patella hammer, no tuning fork or copy of the *British Medical Journal*. On top he was pleased to note the back cover of a book, because this suggested they would be away for some time.

If he had looked carefully he would have realised the book was called *Mating in Captivity*, and that might have tempered his expectations. Although Laura was a prolific reader, and had for a short while joined a book club until it clashed with her on-call duties, self-help was something she usually avoided. But Sam was in an optimistic mood because he knew unquestionably that they were heading for a hotel, possibly for the rest of the day, but probably for an entire night. To his mind, the reason she had brought a small bag was that she didn't want to spoil the surprise for him. Besides there was no need to wear anything in bed in an anonymous room in the sort of hotel that had white fluffy dressing gowns on the back of the bathroom door and adult channels on television. Undoubtedly when they got in that bedroom, the first thing they would do was have sex, an event that hadn't taken place under their own roof for five months and six days.

Sam now counted the days of sexual austerity in much the same way that his teenage self notched up conquests. It suddenly occurred to him that Laura probably hadn't considered contraception and he literally stopped in his tracks. Perhaps all this was nothing more than another elaborate ploy to trap him into having a third child. He spotted a chemist on the other side of the Earl's Court Road.

'What's wrong?' asked Laura, nervously twisting a strand of hair around her finger.

'I need to get one or two things,' Sam said, raising an eyebrow.

'We're going to be late,' she insisted, tugging at his arm.

'Hotels don't generally allow you to check in until after midday,' Sam said knowingly.

She watched him with her steely grey eyes. They were the most astonishing thing about Laura. The sun was behind her and in the morning light they were pale and limpid, as though she had emerged from a strange, Tolkienesque spirit world. Her long fair hair, cut twice a year in the same style, her discreet nose and generous mouth with its single coat of strawberry-flavoured lip salve were like familiar friends, taken for granted over the years. They all spoke of Laura's grounded nature. But even after a decade, her eyes still surprised Sam. She pulled out a pair of sunglasses from the bag and put them on and became ordinary again.

Obviously, she didn't want to give the game away. Or at least she didn't want the possible ulterior motive for such subterfuge to be exposed so quickly, certainly not before his unwitting, enthusiastic sperm had engaged with her ovum. He smiled at Laura's transparency and, heartened with thoughts of what lay ahead and his foresight in derailing her master plan, Sam felt benevolent. He took her hand and was surprised when she gripped his own tightly in response. Laura was never fragile.

Sam sucked in his paunch, a habit he had recently adopted when he found himself talking to an attractive woman or the type of man who noticed that you could now press at least half a finger into your stomach before meeting any significant resistance. Even the children commented on its doughy softness. It needed boundaries, Sam thought to himself. Like Nell and Ben. In five years people might say he looked good for his age. Right now he resembled a Labrador going to seed, with his patchy hair, rebellious stomach and watery eyes. But this was one of the many advantages of being married. The act of love was no longer a qualitative undertaking and that was a relief. Laura wouldn't flee the hotel room when he undressed. Nor would she require any elaborate foreplay. Or have unrealistic expectations of his recovery rate.

He half wondered whether the same man who used to sell grass in the cul-de-sac opposite the tube station more than twenty years ago might still be there. But perhaps this was a bad idea since nowadays dope was so strong it would either make him paranoid and therefore unable to perform, and he couldn't risk that happening again, or more likely it would fill him with torpor. Because the only urge that competed significantly in Sam's mind with the desire to have sex was the desire to sleep.

He wondered at the sheer optimism of the human spirit that every Friday he and Laura went to bed convinced this would be the night that they would get eight hours of uninterrupted sleep, followed by a lie-in the next morning, and a couple of days to unwind properly before stepping out on the treadmill again on Monday morning. What force of will did it take to believe at the end of each week that the weekend would be recuperative? They must be delusional.

He thought about this morning. His birthday. Sam had woken up and with quiet jubilation discovered there were no interlopers in the bed. No dogs, no cats and, most significantly, neither of their children. He noticed through a half-open eye that one of Laura's breasts had escaped from her T-shirt and was casually lying just inches from his mouth. He reached out to touch her and Laura sighed with a noise that resembled pleasure. This was good, thought Sam. Very good. Conditions like this were rare.

But as he closed his eyes and reached for the nipple with his tongue, he felt a pain inside his left nostril so searing that all he could see was red froth. His brain bubbled as it struggled to process what had caused this agony. It was a high-pitched, sharp pain that lasted less than thirty seconds, but was intense enough to make Sam retch over the side of the bed.

'What the fuck was that?' asked Sam, clutching his nose.

'Don't swear,' said Laura, as Ben sobbed in her arms. 'Ben was hiding at the end of the bed. His finger went up your nose.'

'It's like that bit in *Carrie* when the hand comes out the grave,' stumbled Sam, still in a state of shock. Even though the finger had lingered for no more than a few seconds, it felt as though it had penetrated his nasal cavity so far that cerebral fluid might start leaking out through his nose. He felt for blood, but there was none.

'Poor Ben,' said Laura, stroking her four-year-old son's tangled curly hair.

'What about me?' asked Sam. 'What about me? What about me?'

*

At what age did men stop waking up in the morning with a desire for sex? Sam now wondered. When their nitric oxide levels dipped, another voice in his head answered smugly. Sam recalled once mentioning this to his oldest friend, Jonathan Sleet, in the pre-Viagra era, knowing that he was uniquely suggestible to this kind of fact. Jonathan had gone out and bought laughing gas in the mistaken belief that nitric oxide and nitrous oxide were one and the same thing. His girlfriend – there had been so many before Hannah that Sam couldn't remember which one it was – was unimpressed and left him the same day.

A half smile curled round Sam's lips as he remembered this but it quickly turned into a grimace as he considered work. Once he had been impressed by the wealth of knowledge accumulated during the course of his career writing medical dramas. For a while he even acted as an amateur GP for their friends. No longer. There were a finite number of diseases and accidents and these had been exhausted in the first five years that he had written for *Do Not Resuscitate*. Since then the storylines had become more and more fantastical. One of his more recent episodes had been about a female doctor who had plastic surgery to look identical to her sister so that she could find out whether her husband was having an affair with her sibling.

'God, who dreams up this stuff?' muttered Sam wearily. A moratorium on television hospital soaps should be declared. Even if it would leave him unemployed, he would be doing a service for the rest of mankind. And he was never going to get a job writing for *Grey's Anatomy*. Not now. It was like writing songs for Barry Manilow and thinking you could turn your hand to opera. Perhaps he should become a paramedic instead. He could put all his knowledge into action. Or become a neurologist, like Laura. Although she was exhausted by her job, at least it had some purpose.

He should articulate his crisis to Laura. That was Jonathan's recommendation. Laura was a phlegmatic woman with practical solutions to problems. She always had been. Even when they were students, Jonathan pointed out. But Sam didn't want to take advice on how to handle his wife from Jonathan and he couldn't bear to disappoint Laura more than he already had. She had married a man that everyone had tipped for early success and here he was still in the same job seventeen years on, circling forty with the certainty that the best was probably not yet to come.

Today, however, none of this mattered. He could put aside such preoccupations and enjoy the moment. This was something he used to be good at. He was alone with his wife, without their children, on a Saturday morning in central London and he couldn't remember the last time that this had happened on a weekend. The possibilities seemed endless.

They were walking down the Earl's Court Road, a place neither of them had visited, as far as he was aware, for more than a decade. It was remarkably unchanged, Sam thought benignly. The dried vomit on the pavement was more likely to belong to teenage binge drinkers than Australian backpackers and the bucket shops selling cheap flights to far-flung places had mutated into respectable travel agencies. But as it had years ago, the road still held the promise of escape. He pulled Laura close to him.

*

Surprised that Sam couldn't sense the depth of her retreat, Laura allowed the arm to enfold her. If he noticed her hesitation, he didn't mention it. It was ironic that he seemed more positive this morning than he had for months. Either he had no idea of what was about to come to pass or he was more skilled in the dark arts of deception than she had anticipated. All aspects of his personality needed to be rescrutinised in light of her recent discovery. It was an exhausting prospect.

She wondered how they appeared to other people. Did they look like a married couple who still enjoyed sex with each other? Or the kind of people whose relationship had morphed from easy passion into indifferent companionship, when sex became like incest? At least they weren't dead in the water yet: all lines of communication were still open and this was an achievement. Even if they could no longer read each other's signals.

It occurred to Laura that if the contours of their relationship were blurry to her, then they almost certainly were to other people. As far as all their friends were concerned, she and Sam were rock solid. But no one knew what lurked inside a marriage other than the two people involved and if you scratched the surface of any relationship hard enough you would surely draw blood. Relationships were like amoebas, continuously changing form. Their only certainty lay in the fact they would evolve into something else.

The same could be said of friendships. Laura didn't stop to consider this, however, and by the time she did months later, things between them all had altered in ways that she could neither have anticipated nor understood.

She wondered fleetingly whether she was doing the right thing but wouldn't allow the thought to take shape in her mind because it might deter her from her course of action. She had to be resolute. If she wanted to confront the truth she needed to be strong, for both her and the children. As soon as she thought this, her eyes started to well with tears. There was something about the need to be strong that always made her cry. Was it having children that had made her more fragile or was it because she was the wrong side of thirty-five, in the foothills of impending hormonal meltdown? She searched in her bag for the *A–Z*, hoping that Sam wouldn't notice her mood. He was always so nice when she was upset and if he was kind it would make things worse.

Instead she imagined Nell and Ben playing at home and the stab of guilt that she wasn't there was comforting in its familiarity. Ben would be in the dog basket pretending to be Nell's pet, a lead fastened to the loop in his jeans, or they would be playing their new game, one Laura hadn't yet witnessed, where Ben became Nell's slave and did everything she demanded. It was an unrealistically harmonious vision because together they were as volatile as a sixth-form chemistry experiment.

Away from her children, it was easy for Laura to idealise family life. A frozen image of herself sitting at the kitchen table, stirring cake mixture with one arm and holding a third baby in the other, often came to mind when she should have been writing up notes in between patients. This still life had evolved over the years as more and more detail was sketched in. There was a green-and-white gingham tablecloth, a vase of picked flowers, and the baby was wearing a Fair Isle cardigan as it guzzled from an enormous milky breast. The nipple was big and brown and unnaturally large. As Laura closed her eyes in her warm, airless office she would almost smell the sweet stickiness of the scene.

Reality was less saccharine. Only this week, Nell, just seven years old, had asked why they needed another child, because quite frankly (this was her favourite new phrase) she would have a much easier life without Ben. Laura tried to explain that she would be lonely, that she wouldn't learn to share, and when Nell persisted, she finally said that when Sam and she were old and infirm, she would appreciate having someone else around to share the responsibility.

Then that same afternoon, when Laura was beginning to wonder whether Nell might be right, she had taken them for their MMR injection at the local surgery. Sam had decided to come at the last minute, claiming he needed a break from work, even though Laura could see his screen was blank. He stood nervously by the clinic door as the young practice nurse approached to administer the booster. For a moment, Nell was utterly calm and then just as Laura assumed everything was fine, she gave a blood-curdling scream that made the ends of Laura's toes curl. Sam managed to calm her down. It was to him Nell turned when she was hurt, Laura noted with resignation, as she focused on Ben, who was rooted to the ground. The nurse prepared the second syringe, held it up to the light and gently pressed the stopper to check that there were no air bubbles. She stepped towards Ben and bent down to put the needle in his arm. Suddenly Nell dashed forward, placed herself between Ben and the syringe, and demanded that she be given the injection instead.

'Don't hurt my little brother,' she sobbed, 'please don't hurt him.' Ben was astonished. For being so selfless, the nurse gave Nell a small plastic magnet that she had admired and then stuck the needle in Ben's arm.

'That was proof of your love,' Laura had told Nell in amazement afterwards.

'Don't be ridiculous, Mummy,' said Nell dismissively. 'I wanted the magnet.'

The only benefit of this sudden unexpected diversion in her life was that for the first time in years, Sam had become a priority again. It reminded Laura of the uncertainty that defined the intensity of the early days in their relationship when the unknown outweighed the known, before Sam's virtues became his vices. Instead of worrying about her children (Nell's school, Ben's eczema, their refusal to eat vegetables) she thought about Sam, observing his mood, analysing his movements, and reading in between the lines of their conversation. Laura held Sam's hand tightly as she glanced down into her bag and started to flick through the pages of the *A–Z*.

'Tell me the name of the hotel. I might know it,' he said cheerily.

She winced. How could Sam think, given the state of their ongoing financial crisis, that they would part with hundreds of pounds to spend the night in an elaborate hotel on the fringes of South Kensington? They walked past a corner shop that sold international newspapers from a neatly stacked pavement stand: *Le Monde*, *El País*,

Süddeutsche Zeitung. But there was only one headline '*Crise Bancaire*', '*Crisis de Liquidez*', '*Kreditkrise: Geld Zerstört die Welt*'. Sam walked by, oblivious.

He was as impervious to the global economic downturn as a Russian oligarch, thought Laura, trying to curb her annoyance. He didn't notice that it cost £20 more to fill up the car, or that their mortgage payments had increased, or that Laura had switched from Sainsbury's to Lidl to do the weekly shop. When Janey had announced she was pregnant a couple of months earlier, in the shadow of the collapse of Northern Rock, her recently acquired boyfriend, Steve, a hedge fund manager, had swiftly accepted their congratulations and turned the conversation away from the contraceptive crisis to the credit crisis. He muttered about 'the shadow banking system', and 'dark unregulated corners' of the finance sector and warned them that no traders would touch Lehman's stock any more. Sam had dismissed his concerns, saying he was trying to impress Laura and make his job sound more interesting than it really was.

It irked Laura that she minded so much that the financial burden rested on her shoulders because for years this was what she thought she had wanted. She had argued with her mother that her generation was reinventing the domestic landscape. She was part of the first generation of neurologists where men and women were equally represented at work, Laura had proudly informed her. Sam would pursue his creative ambitions, manage the domestic front line and she would make money. Except that neither of these ambitions had been fully realised: Laura had decided against private practice to augment her NHS salary and Sam still watched *Match of the Day* while she hung out damp laundry at ten thirty in the evening. Now it felt less like revolution and more like death by exhaustion.

'It's a house somewhere on the south side of Stanhope Gardens,' explained Laura vaguely, turning the map around in her hands trying to work out which way was north.

'We'll find it,' said Sam confidently, taking her hand again and pulling her closer.

'You smell of burnt plastic, Sam,' murmured Laura, pulling away without releasing his hand.

'I'll have a bath when we get there,' he apologised. 'Maybe we could share one.' Laura didn't say anything. 'I'm sorry about the kettle.'

'It doesn't matter,' said Laura. 'It was a good job that Nell went into the kitchen when she did.'

'I can't understand why I keep doing that,' Sam said, shaking his head. 'I'm so distracted at the moment.'

'We can talk about it later,' suggested Laura. 'It's just a kettle.'

But it was more than a kettle. It was a symptom. Sam had put the electric kettle on the gas hob three times in the past two months. Twice she had received a phone call from the school saying that no one had arrived to pick up the children. At first she had run through the medical possibilities. Causes of Amnestic syndrome: Alzheimer's, head injury, herpes, solvent abuse, tumours, arsenic poisoning, alcohol. Although it was true that Sam was drinking more, it was not a complete explanation. Then, when she was searching for a number in his mobile phone, she found the text messages and her suspicions were confirmed by what she had already seen on their computer. There was no neurological condition: he was having an affair.

This was what happened when men turned forty. There was a mother in Nell's class. A year ago she happily attended the nativity play with her husband, dabbing her eyes at the appropriate moments when her daughter was on stage as a sheep. This Christmas her daughter was promoted to Mary to facilitate the transition to a new stepmother. Laura saw her in the crowd. She was a carbon copy of the first wife, just twenty years younger. All you had to do was listen to the new Radiohead album, as Sam did with alarming frequency, to understand the principles of classic male midlife maelstrom. Laura berated herself for being so slow to grasp the nettle but at least she had taken action now.

And so it was that, holding hands, they arrived outside an anonymous white stucco house with a small sign beside the doorbell that read 'Marital Therapy Unit'. For a brief optimistic second Sam thought that maybe they were going to an urban spa for exhausted parents. As they waited by the door another couple emerged. The man was so tight-lipped that the area around his mouth was white. His wife was clutching a soggy handkerchief to her nose and pulled a pair of large sunglasses from her handbag. For a moment they caught each other's eye. Sam, who was naturally affable and prone to making friends, opened his mouth to introduce himself. Instead she looked at him in horror and they scurried up the road.

'We're not like them,' Sam wanted to say, but he was so discombobulated that the words wouldn't come out of his mouth. Instead there was a series of long, incomprehensible sounds, as though his voice had been slowed down.

'If I told you, you would have refused to come,' said Laura, by way of apology.

Sam checked his watch. It was three minutes past eleven.

2

'So why are you here, Sam?'

The question hung in the air. Laura waited for her husband to respond. When he didn't, she tried to speak but instead of words a fine dust of digestive biscuit came out of her mouth and she began to cough. The woman sitting opposite didn't look up and continued to write down their names at the top of a blank page of an A4 spiral pad. While she waited for Sam to reply she underlined their names several times. Laura noticed, as she picked up her second glass of water, that she had written them in capital letters, something that made her uncomfortable, as though it inflated the problems she wanted this woman to diminish. Also, she was writing in pencil, which of course should have made the problems seem more ephemeral than if she had written them in indelible ink, but instead it made Laura doubt her professional credentials. The pencil was blunt and the end chewed. The only person in Laura's life who wrote in pencil was Nell and she was seven years old.

On the other side of the notebook, also written in pencil, were notes from the counsellor's previous session. Laura could see two words in capitals and underlined several times. *Things to work on*, it said. *FOREPLAY. FANTASY.* It was not what Laura was expecting. And this was not territory she intended to explore. She realised that she hadn't considered what she might be asked, only what she wanted to tell. Anyway, this was their first meeting. The main challenge would be getting Sam to talk or even remain in the room.

Laura crossed her arms and then her legs and carelessly drew spirals in the biscuit dust, willing Sam to say something, hoping that he hadn't seen the notes belonging to the previous couple. She picked up another digestive biscuit and began nibbling around the edges, then put it down on the plate again. Aware that her body language might appear defensive, she uncurled her legs and leant back into the oversize sofa. It was so deep that her legs couldn't bend at the knee. Perhaps it was intended to infantilise its occupants, or at least disable them, because once she had sunk back into the soft cushions, Laura realised she didn't have the energy to move again. She was stranded. And although the pastel blue made her feel a little queasy, Laura was surprised to discover it wasn't an unpleasant sensation.

Sam was sitting further along, right on the edge, his back turned to her. She didn't want to catch his eye because he was already so incensed with her that even a glance could be misconstrued as a further act of aggression. But she could smell him. He smelt of burnt plastic and the inside of aeroplanes. She wanted to tell the counsellor how he had put the electric kettle on the gas hob and caused a minor kitchen fire, in case she thought this was something sinister. But mostly because it might be relevant.

Laura swallowed the water too quickly, began to cough again, and then drank more. The woman looked up. When she saw Laura was trying to decipher her writing, she folded the notebook back on itself, and pushed it towards the couple.

'I like to be completely open,' she said smoothly. 'The notes are just to remind myself what has been discussed so that we can pick up threads the following week.'

'Very sensible,' said Laura, nodding her head a little too vigorously so that the glass of water slopped over her jeans. She decided that having been caught in flagrante, it was best to be open about what she had seen. 'I can't imagine we'll get on to fantasy and foreplay until the fifth week.'

Laura thought she heard Sam groan but she was too busy trying to extricate herself from the unexpected turn in conversation to consider how the unfolding scene might impact upon him. The woman didn't say anything.

'Or maybe sooner,' said Laura in a bid to demonstrate her pliancy. 'I'm open to all options. We both are, aren't we, Sam? Although I'm sure we're way more boring than the couple with the, er, homework.'

'You're not here to entertain me, Laura,' the woman said. She wasn't smiling but nor was she angry, Laura decided. In fact, she was completely inscrutable.

'Now, Sam, perhaps you want to tell me why you are here?'

On balance, Laura decided, it was best that Sam was being questioned first. Although the need to unburden herself had become almost unbearable, now that she was here, with not just the opportunity but the expectation that she would reveal everything, she knew absolutely that she had made the wrong decision. It would have been far better to have confronted Sam at home. But she'd needed to get here, to be shut in this room with this total stranger to know. Life was too often like that. You didn't know whether you had done the right or wrong thing until you had declared your hand.

She had run through this plan so many times in her head that somehow it felt as though it would never become a reality. Even when she told Sam this morning that they were going out alone to celebrate his birthday, she half believed it was true. Laura pulled out a piece of paper from her back pocket and began fanning herself. The glass of water was already empty. Laura realised that although the premise of this whole ill-conceived operation had been the need to have total control, in fact she had lost all possibility of directing proceedings.

'So why are you here, Sam?' The woman patiently repeated the question, uncrossing and crossing her legs again. Sam couldn't help noticing that her tweed skirt, in neutral colours but a little on the tight side, had started to ride above her knee to reveal a hint of thigh. He had been staring at the herringbone weave of the tweed for so long that his vision was blurred. He wondered fleetingly whether she ever slept with any of her clients and rapidly concluded that the essential ingredients of domestic free-fall – bitterness, reproach and pain – probably made both parties unattractive. It was lack of knowledge about people that made them sexually interesting. The depth of detail he knew about his wife's best friends – Hannah's post-partum haemorrhoids, Janey's irritable bowel – definitely neutralised their sexual potential, even in the dog days. He roused himself. He was, he correctly concluded, in a state of utter shock.

'Why am I here? Now that's a very interesting question,' he began. 'Do you mean in specific or general terms?'

'Specific, of course,' muttered Laura beside him.

'Laura, it's important to let your husband answer questions for himself,' the woman insisted.

'Do you mean in the French philosopher sense or the inquisitive toddler sense?' Sam asked. 'Actually, I've got no idea why we are here. In fact I'm stunned. I thought we were going out because it's my birthday.'

Laura felt a brief stab of guilt but she was distracted by Sam who had started to lurch towards the middle of the sofa. When he reached an uncomfortable angle somewhere around thirty degrees, he started to tilt his head slowly to one side and began to stare fixedly at a label on the left lapel of the woman's jacket, trying to read what it said. The woman, trained in the art of mimicking gestures to make people feel comfortable, obligingly did exactly the same and the two of them stared at each other, heads to one side, like puppets that had lost a string.

'It's upside down, Lisa,' said Laura politely, pointing at the label. 'Your name is upside down.'

Lisa looked down, peeled off the label, and tried to stick it back the right way round but it had lost its adhesiveness. So she began to use the palm of her hands to roll it into a ball. When it was small enough she put it on the table and Sam picked it up and pushed it into the bottle of water that he had brought into the room with them. It floated.

'Do you know that Lisa is an anagram of sail?' he said.

'I think, Sam, that you are feeling a little passive aggressive,' said Lisa calmly. 'I'll go and make us all a cup of tea, Sam, and we can try again when I come back. Do either of you take sugar?'

'Yes,' 'No,' said Sam and Laura simultaneously. The door shut and they were alone.

'Why are you being so antagonistic?' whispered Laura. 'It's not her fault.'

'I can't believe you are even asking that question,' said Sam. 'But in the spirit of shared confession, I have to say, Laura, that until two hours ago, I thought that you had booked a babysitter on a Saturday morning so that we could spend some quality time together. I thought you might be springing the sort of surprise that Jonathan is so fond of: a weekend in Prague or even a cheap B&B off the Earl's Court Road. I just can't believe you've done this. I'm incredulous. Lost for words.'

'Well, it's partly because of Jonathan that we're here,' muttered Laura. She was wrestling to find a way of explaining what she had done that might put her in a positive light. Or at least might provide a logical explanation.

'What has Jonathan got to do with all this?' Sam demanded. 'I've known about you and him for years. It's ancient history. No need for an exhumation now.'

'What are you talking about?' asked Laura, taken aback by his line of questioning.

'I know that you had something going years ago,' he said dismissively.

'Are you accusing me of sleeping with your best friend?' asked Laura, outraged. 'Is that what you think this is about?'

'Well it would have to be something sufficiently dramatic to justify clandestinely organising for us to see a marriage guidance counsellor on my birthday,' responded Sam, his composure partially regained by his success in wrong-footing her.

'I can't believe you've assumed that for so many years without saying anything,' said Laura eventually.

'It wouldn't have bothered me that much anyway,' said Sam, waving his hand as though swatting away a fly. 'He slept with virtually every woman he met. Discrimination was not his strong point.'

'You mean you wouldn't have cared if I had slept with your oldest friend?' replied Laura, trying to work out exactly how the accusation of infidelity had turned on her. Perhaps it was part of Sam's wider strategy to try and vindicate his own indiscretion.

'It's irrelevant.'

'You don't care who I've slept with?'

'I can't believe that I am the one on the defensive here.'

'I'm astonished,' said Laura finally. It was the quietest argument they had ever had.

'How can you say that after what you've done to me?' hissed Sam. 'I'm in a state of utter turmoil: skin pale, brain confused, sweating like a pig and probably tachycardic. Your blood-pressure machine would be pushed to its limits.'

'Funny how you can remember that but forget about the kettle,' Laura pointed out, trying to conjure anger that she didn't really feel. She was struck by the absurdity of their situation. They were as captive as the goldfish swimming aimlessly around the tank on the bookshelf opposite them.

And fish had the advantage of a three-second memory span. Sam would remember this forever.

She should have consulted Hannah. She had known Sam even longer than Laura because Jonathan and Hannah had frequently used Sam's house in Oxford as a weekend retreat away from the eye of Jonathan's possessive girlfriend, when they were both students at Manchester. Laura's first insights into Sam, long before she met him, were based on Hannah's descriptions of Jonathan's scruffy, creative, sweet-natured childhood friend. Their eldest son, Luke, was conceived in Sam's bed during their last year at university and born just after they graduated in July 1990. Hannah would have advised Laura what to do. She would have given an honest opinion if Laura had asked.

Equally, she could have called up Janey and met her for coffee. Lunch was out of the question because Janey worked so hard. Janey, mistrustful of anything that smacked of therapy, would have warned her against this plan of action. She would have told her that Sam was too chaotic for duplicity and that he adored Laura for being all the things he wasn't. But Laura had never spoken to Janey about the underbelly of her marriage. Until Janey met Steve early last year, the dynamic of their friendship had been Sam and Laura providing Janey with relationship advice over the kitchen table late into the night. To expose any of their weaknesses might have been discouraging. Besides, neither Hannah nor Janey would understand how it felt to live with the humiliation and uncertainty of infidelity. Laura was flying solo.

'Why are we whispering?' asked Sam.

'Because I'm afraid there's a two-way mirror and that she's observing how we interact when we are on our own together,' sighed Laura. 'I feel as though I've got a walk-on part in a wildlife documentary.'

'There is more meaning and mutual understanding in exchanging a glance with a gorilla than with any other animal I know,' said Sam, doing an almost perfect impersonation of David Attenborough, as he edged towards Laura, lunged and pushed her down on to the sofa. 'If you have sex with me now, all is forgiven. Then they'll really get their money's worth.'

'You are so infuriating,' said Laura, rubbing her chin where his stubble had scratched before pulling herself up into a sitting position. But she was relieved that Sam hadn't entirely lost his sense of humour.

'How can you say that when you have launched this full-frontal assault?' questioned Sam, sensing a moment of weakness. 'Laura, just tell me, why are we here? Because if I could understand that, Laura, then I might be a little more responsive to the woman in the tweed skirt.'

'It's complicated,' she said.

Laura had vowed never to be one of those women who checked her husband's mobile phone. But once her suspicions started it was like trying to salvage a piece of knitting that had come adrift from its needles. Everything had to be unpicked in order to start again. On V. just don't do it, there's no going back with that stuff, the most significant exchange of texts between Jonathan and Sam had started. Not sure I can resist, Sam's text back had read. Will it be painful? Sam had asked

Jonathan a week later. No pleasure without a little pain, Jonathan had written back. Does Laura have any idea? said another. Absolutely not, Sam had responded. Didn't realise you were a man with so many secrets, Jonathan texted back. The evidence was overwhelming.

'If you can't provide me with some reasonable explanation of why we are throwing away eighty quid an hour —' Laura heard Sam say.

'A hundred, Sam, if you include the babysitter . . .' she unthinkingly interrupted. Laura liked to be precise about things.

'If you can't rationalise that to me in the next five minutes, Laura, then I'll have a tantrum that will make Ben's seem devoid of any passion,' said Sam, a mock-dramatic tone entering his voice.

'Will you do that thing, Sam, where you lie on the floor and scream and pretend to be a deadweight?' Laura smiled for the first time.

'I will, and more,' said Sam.

'Why do you suppose Lisa uses our names so many times in a sentence?'

'In order, Laura, to create a sense of familiarity, to force us to concentrate, Laura, so that we unveil the inner workings of our marriage to a complete and utter fucking stranger, Laura,' he replied, but his tone was ironic rather than angry.

'I agree it's all a bit surreal,' she conceded. 'But I think there are questions that need to be addressed.'

'You know, I thought we had reached a fairly happy plateau in our marriage,' sighed Sam. There was a long pause. 'Apart from the sex issue, of course.'

'We shouldn't talk about our relationship unless Lisa is here,' said Laura, without conviction.

'Don't be so absurd,' replied Sam. 'We've spent thirteen years dissecting our relationship and now we can't discuss it without the presence of someone we've known for less than fifteen minutes?'

'She needs to witness our arguments,' said Laura, 'in order to know how to proceed.'

Laura got up and walked towards a bookshelf beside the large gilt mirror opposite the sofa. They had been asked to take off their shoes before they went into the meeting room and underfoot she was vaguely aware of a carpet thick enough to make her feel as though she was wading. How odd to have such an impractical carpet in such a public space. She began to calculate how many people in an average day might walk across it to sit on the same sofa where Sam was currently marooned. Possibly as many as a dozen. The thought made her want to put her shoes back on. It was like staying in a hotel and considering how many people had used the mattress before you. When she reached the bookshelf she noticed that each shelf was lined with a thick piece of foam and when she glanced back at the table that separated Sam and her from Lisa she saw that the under-side of the table was also similarly swaddled. It made Laura feel as though they were in a padded cell.

Despite the awkwardness of this encounter, Laura felt strangely elated. She liked to be in control of her emotions and for the first time in weeks she felt as though Sam was on the defensive. She was enjoying his discomfort. She began inspecting the books in front of her. Laura noted the underside of the shelf was also clad in foam. She was about to mention this to Sam but became distracted by the titles.

Men Are from Mars, Women Are from Venus, Stop! You're Driving Me Crazy, Why Men Lie and Women Cry, Why Men Don't Listen and Women Can't Read Maps, How to Train Your Husband to Do Exactly What You Want Him To. She took the last one off the shelf. On the cover was a performing seal.

'I don't want to be married to a performing seal,' she said vaguely, flicking through the book.

'Well that's one thing on our side right now,' said Sam. 'Although I'm considering all career alternatives.'

He wanted to continue, but Lisa had come back in the room. She closed the door slowly and meaningfully. Sam took it personally, as a reproach for his lack of co-operation.

'I think perhaps we'll let Laura start this part of the session,' said Lisa, smiling sweetly in an effort to placate him. 'I brought sugar for you, Sam.'

Bright-eyed and bushy-tailed, thought Sam. If she had a tail to wag she would. He wished he could summon similar feelings of enthusiasm for his own job and wondered whether he could become a marriage guidance counsellor. What was it about your late thirties that made you start behaving like a small child again? Astronaut, train driver, farmer. Career paths last considered when he was Ben's age had become options that needed to be seriously analysed. Any job that gave him space in his head to think and a regular wage packet at the end of the week was worth considering. They were running out of money and Laura was fed up with the responsibility of being the main bread-winner.

'She who bakes the bread should not make the bread,' he said out loud, repeating something that Jonathan had mentioned to him recently.

'Sorry,' said Lisa. 'Did you want to add something, Sam?'

'No, I was just thinking out loud,' he said, smiling inanely.

'This is what I mean,' pointed out Laura, sounding hurt rather than angry. 'He's talking about making bread. He never listens to me. Not even here.'

'It might be helpful if you shared your thoughts with us, Sam,' said Lisa. She was trying to draw him back into the conversation.

'I was imagining our children growing up and telling their friends how their career path was defined by the poverty of their childhood,' said Sam. 'I have a vivid image of Nell, working as a corporate lawyer, telling her colleagues how she woke up one night and found her father stealing money from her piggy bank to pay the mortgage and how this was a defining moment in her decision to join Freshfields.'

'You didn't do that did you, Sam?' asked Laura.

'She didn't wake up,' Sam reassured her. 'Actually, I was wondering whether I should become a marriage guidance counsellor.'

'You couldn't. You get too distracted,' Laura said, 'or you'd want to use it as source material for something you're writing.' Of course Laura was right. She generally was about the practicalities of life. They didn't call neurologists the philosophers of the medical profession for nothing.

'So are you under financial pressure?' asked Lisa, pleased

that he had not only added something coherent to the discussion but seemed willing to join in the debate. 'Because that can put a lot of pressure on a marriage. It's especially bad for the male sex drive. It depletes testosterone. How is your sex life?' Laura felt her back stiffening.

How long do you need to know someone before you can legitimately ask this question? she wondered. Twenty minutes simply wasn't enough. In many cases, even twenty years was too short. Of course, before she got pregnant, Janey could not have a conversation without alluding to the fabulous sex she was having with Steve, but it was not something Laura generally discussed with her other married friends and not something she planned to explore with Lisa.

'Well, since you have brought up the subject,' Sam interjected, 'I can categorically say that it is crap. That our four-year-old son is like a human contraceptive. That I haven't been this sexually frustrated since I was a teenager. That sometimes I think I might never have sex again. And that is all I have to say on the subject.'

'And you, Laura?' said Lisa. 'Do you feel the same?'

'Yes, except possibly more tired,' mumbled Laura, at once taken aback by Sam's honesty and relieved at the economy of his description.

Sam felt vaguely sorry for Lisa. Although he considered himself a man in touch with his emotions, this did not extend to exposing the foundations of his marriage to a complete stranger. Not even the dull financial aspects, although actually his bank balance was far from boring, it was too exciting, and certainly not his testosterone levels.

He began in his head to deconstruct their relationship.

But it was reduced to dull chronology. He had met Laura for the first time in 1990 when they were both twenty-one years old. Their relationship started five years later. They got married when they were twenty-eight and three years later Nell was born.

It was difficult to move beyond this morning's traumatic turn of events. How could he have been so unaware of what Laura was planning? When their babysitter had arrived at ten o'clock, he had imagined only pleasurable things. How many people are hand in hand when their wife reveals to them that their marriage is under such strain that she has booked a babysitter so that they can attend marriage guidance counselling?

'So how did you meet?' asked Lisa, picking up her pencil again.

'At a party,' said Laura. Lisa wrote this down.

'No, we didn't,' interrupted Sam. 'I sat next to you at dinner when I came to stay with Jonathan in London.' There was a long silence.

'Laura, perhaps you want to explain to Sam why you are here?' said Lisa eventually.

'I think he's having an affair,' said Laura slowly, watching Sam closely. She felt no urge to cry. Instead it was like pulling the trigger of a gun. For a moment afterwards, Laura felt nothing but sheer exhilaration. These were the only words that needed to be said in this room. She watched Sam to gauge his reaction but he couldn't say anything. Instead his mouth opened and shut like a goldfish's. Laura concluded that he was staggered that she had uncovered his intrigue with such ease and was now unmasking him in such a public way. She had been right after all.

'What makes you think that?' said Lisa, breaking her own rule and speaking for Sam.

'There are a number of things,' said Laura, pulling out a sheet of paper from her handbag. It was covered in her neat looped handwriting. She studied her notes. 'On the nineteenth of October and a dozen times after that I noticed that he had been looking up fidelity on the Internet. This made me suspicious. Mostly I was hurt that he felt so frustrated in his marriage but couldn't share this with me. The best-case scenario was that he was struggling with his conscience over something and seeking advice.'

'And the worst case?' asked Lisa, taking careful notes of this conversation.

'I thought he might be searching for an Internet site where married women and men arrange to meet up for sex.'

It felt so good to reveal herself, to lay everything out coherently, that she almost forgot how it might impact on Sam. There was a long silence. Lisa stared at Sam expectantly. It was like a game of tennis, he just needed to return the serve.

'And did you consider why else I might be looking up fidelity?' asked Sam finally.

'Because you are so distracted by this woman whose name begins with V that you can't work and instead of finishing that script, you spend hours trawling the Internet for advice that condones your affair,' said Laura. She was pleased with how she was articulating this part of the process. Sam was horrified. He sat back against the sofa, his head shrinking into the cushion at the back. Men never expect to be discovered. The way the left and right sides of their brain work in isolation might heighten their ability to compartmentalise, thought Laura. But women will always be ahead when it comes to instinct because they can switch between the two.

'Then there were the messages from Jonathan,' she continued, buoyed by the way she had managed to confound Sam. 'I know her name begins with V. And I know that he was advising you not to get involved with her. And I know that you did.'

When she finished she felt exhausted. Her face was hot and she began fanning herself with a leaflet that she found on the table. *Sexual healing: how to lose your inhibitions*, it read. She threw it down quickly.

'I think we should think about a trial separation,' she suggested to Lisa.

'I think perhaps we should listen to what Sam has to say first,' said Lisa. 'Unless you want to leave this for the next session? Perhaps by then, Sam, you will find it easier to contribute.'

'I can't wait a week to have my say,' Sam panicked.

'I know what he's going to say,' Laura explained. 'Men always have elaborate alibis.'

'Married couples have this tendency to second-guess each other's reactions to things,' said Lisa.

'Not me,' interrupted Sam. 'I thought I was married to someone fairly predictable. Now I won't ever take anything for granted again.'

'Breaking trust is a terrible thing,' said Laura. 'I just don't think that I can come back from that. I want to know who V is. I thought it might be Victoria, you've always held a torch for her.'

'Victoria,' said Sam, genuinely taken aback. 'Why in God's name if I was going to be unfaithful, would it be with her? Give me credit for having some imagination. I wouldn't just go and have sex with the last woman I slept with before you. And it wasn't a serious relationship, she was one of Jonathan's cast-offs. It was a sympathy thing.'

'Your sympathy lasted almost four years,' Laura pointed out. 'Strictly speaking you slept with her while you were with me.' She noticed that Lisa was writing this down.

'Is that what all this is about?' asked Sam, relieved that no matter how left-field this hypothesis might sound, at least it stacked up to a plausible catalyst.

'So you're not denying it?'

'I'm simply saying that if I was to go off with another woman it would be for purely sexual reasons, with absolutely no strings attached.'

'So V is a prostitute?' said Laura. This hadn't crossed her mind and she was unsure whether it made her feel better or worse. 'I read something that said ten per cent of married men sleep with prostitutes but I never thought that you would be that . . . that . . .'

'Organised?' replied Sam.

'That's a whole different issue,' retorted Laura.

'I think we need to hear from Sam,' Lisa interrupted. The tone of her voice was exactly the same. It depressed Laura to think her situation was so un-unique. Every day Lisa sat in this room listening to other couples outline similar stories. Every day she offered similar possibilities of redemption.

'Did you ever consider, Laura, apart from the reasons that you outlined — and I have to say that you have shown so much imagination I think you're in the wrong job – did you stop to consider that there might be a legitimate reason for me looking up fidelity on the Internet? One that might be related to your father?'

'My father?' said Laura, as it dawned on her for the first time that this might be even more complicated than she had anticipated. 'Oh my God! Why would he tell you?'

An image of her father back in the late seventies, wearing a white tennis shirt with a faded red collar, tucked into shorts that were slightly too short, sprung to mind. He was pleading with Laura's mother to stop washing his squash kit every day. Laura was sitting at the kitchen table doing homework watching as her mother repeatedly washed her hands. She would turn on the tap, hold them under the hot water for twenty counts, smother them with Fairy Liquid for another minute and then clean them rigorously with a nail brush until the knuckles started to bleed. Her father would leave the house, his shirt and shorts almost transparent after another session in boiling water. She couldn't blame her father for seeking solace in the arms of another woman, but why would he wait until he was seventy?

'Your father isn't having an affair,' said Sam quickly, fighting the urge to punish her. 'There's another thing I thought I would never have to say to you. I was looking up fidelity on the Internet because your father said that I should show a bit of responsibility and buy a life insurance policy.'

Sam paused for dramatic effect and held out his mobile phone.

'Call him if you don't believe me.'

Laura shook her head in defeat. She knew Sam was telling the truth. To her credit, even Lisa was taken aback. They were no longer following the script. The middle classes were always unpredictable. No matter how many times they came in with their careful clothes and wide-ranging vocabulary full of adjectives to describe their emotional state, their problems were never formulaic. There was always some hidden drama that took them beyond the normal range of possibilities.

'I've got the paperwork at home. I still haven't sent it off,' said Sam.

'Oh God,' said Laura, knowing he was telling the truth.

'And as for V,' said Sam. 'I can see how the text messages might have appeared, but it was code for vasectomy. I know that you really want to have a third baby but I really don't and I was sounding out Jonathan to see whether he thought it would be unforgivably underhand of me to have my tubes snipped behind your back. I'd got it all worked out, but he said it was a bad idea. You can phone him too if you like. Or you can wait until we see them in a few weeks.'

Jonathan was a less reliable alibi than her father but Laura couldn't face calling him. It might stir memories of a different kind.

'Please don't tell Jonathan about this,' she said weakly.

'You know, I spend a lot of time trying to think up plot-lines but I could never have elaborated something like this,' said Sam. 'Perhaps we should do a job swap for a while.'

'I'm so sorry,' said Laura, for whom apology was normally a long-drawn-out process.

'Can we go now?' asked Sam, getting up from the sofa and helping himself to a digestive biscuit.

'What about your next session?' enquired Lisa, removing the packet from the table.

'I don't think we'll need one,' said Laura, following Sam out of the door.

'I think what you really need is a bit of time together. A holiday alone without your children, some quality time,' called Lisa, who liked to have the last word, as they left the room for the first and last time. 'You need to have a good time together.' Laura could see that she was writing that in capital letters at the end of her notes.

'What do you think, Sam?' Laura asked.

'A holiday sounds good to me,' he replied.

'Are you very angry?' asked Laura, as she closed the door behind them.

'Yes,' said Sam, who was gripping his fists so tightly that his knuckles were white. 'But it's just one of a range of emotions.'

'How else do you feel?' asked Laura politely.

'You sound like that woman,' said Sam. 'But yes, I can tell you that as well as incandescent fucking rage, I also feel slightly flattered that you think I'm leading such an exciting clandestine life, and there is also a sense of relief.'

'Relief?' repeated Laura.

'Because you owe me big time and long term for this one,' said Sam, more benignly than he really felt. 'You reap what you sow.'

Much later Laura thought more about this comment. She considered it scientifically at first: could the essential essence of a relationship be irrevocably altered by such a jolt, in the same way an injury to the brain could change someone's personality? Certainly, if none of this had happened, they wouldn't have agreed to the holiday. And ultimately it was the holiday that was their undoing. Laura understood that what she had done had changed the natural order of things. But it wasn't clear to her until much later that in trying to resolve one crisis, she had unwittingly precipitated another.

3

Janey Dart heard her BlackBerry ring but decided not to answer. Her juniors would have to learn to take decisions without her soon enough, and it was a good test of her will to resist its siren call. She sat on the floor marooned in the middle of an almost perfect circle of detritus, all of which needed to be dealt with by the following morning. If anyone wanted to know exactly what was going on in her head at that particular moment when Sunday afternoon melted into Sunday evening, all they would need to do was examine the seemingly random series of objects that encircled her. It was the banal fragments of life that always proved the most revealing.

She closed her eyes and forced herself to remember each item that lay on the floor. She might be seven months pregnant but she was determined not to succumb to the infamous woolly fog. Her job depended on her eye for detail and memory lapses were not something that she could afford. When she opened them again she was pleased to discover that her memory hadn't betrayed her: everything was as she had imagined it.

Beside her were two uneven piles of legal briefs. The smaller was a riot of fluorescent pen with carefully highlighted passages in different colours and small yellow stickers filled with neat red comments in thin spidery handwriting. The pile on her right, taller and precariously balanced, was ominously monotone and demanded her immediate consideration. It was the books, however, spread spine down beside the cluster of aromatherapy candles and list of songs to be played during childbirth, that won the competition for her attention. The takeover of a Spanish company by its German counterpart was a deal that inspired envy among her colleagues, coming amidst fears of an economic downturn. But it could no longer compete with the ongoing debate in Janey's mind between the benefits of the baby-care regime offered by Gina Ford and the more benign methodology outlined by Tracy Hogg, although if she thought hard enough she could no doubt find cultural parallels.

What Janey couldn't understand was why there was no consensus on what exactly was the best regime for a newborn baby. Surely enough people had used these books to know that? And surely enough babies had been born to draw up some rudimentary ground rules? A piece of paper outlining the pros and cons of the two rival systems sat beside her in the centre of the circle. She was confident that by a process of careful analysis she would arrive at the correct conclusion. She had already rejected the option of all three of them sleeping in the same bed for a couple of years because open-ended breastfeeding wasn't a possibility for her: sleep was a priority if she had any hope of deconstructing Spanish law again twelve weeks after the baby was born. Besides, that free-range approach reminded her too much of her own childhood. Organisation was the main weapon in the armoury of any working mother.

PRIMIGRAVIDA,' it said in big red letters on the hospital file beside her age. It seemed like a reproach: another professional woman trying to defy the laws of nature by having her first baby after the age of thirty-five.

Janey hadn't meant it to be this way. And actually, as she tried to pull her left leg over her right thigh to sit cross-legged and straight-backed, a position that the antenatal yoga teacher said would allow the baby room to stretch and would ease Janey's heartburn, she still couldn't believe how fate had pivoted on its axis. Because at the point where she was finally reconciled to her single, childless status, she had met Steve and within six months had discovered she was pregnant. She had felt as irresponsible as a teenager when she told Sam and Laura and, despite their effusive congratulations, she could sense disappointment. Less because of the pregnancy and more because of her new boyfriend. Steve wasn't in the script her friends had written for Janey. He didn't look right. He didn't sound right. Most significantly, he wasn't Patrick.

Using her stomach as a lectern, Janey picked up *The New Contented Little Baby Book*, rested it on her belly, and read a couple of pages outlining the typical timetable of a six-week-old baby. It was more demanding than her diary at work. But if she applied the methodology correctly she apparently could turn her baby into a predictable and rational human being within weeks. She highlighted a couple of passages and marked pages with yellow stickers until the book resembled the legal document biked around earlier in the day. Then she picked up the remaining pages of the brief and began work again.

Janey's twenty-eight-year-old junior, the very together Rosemary Dunhurst (she politely asked Janey not to use the diminutive), had probably spent the best part of the night in the office to complete the document that she was now defacing. Some of the juniors shared lines of coke in the toilet to make it through the night, but not Rosemary. She knew that if she was to make partner by the age of thirty-two and be in a position to have a baby by thirty-five, then she couldn't allow anything to derail her ambition. And learning to get by on four hours' sleep was a useful skill for any woman who hoped to survive either a legal career or motherhood.

Janey often thought about Rosemary because the younger woman's more unpleasant traits reminded her of her former self. She could remember viewing pregnant colleagues with a similar combination of acid emotions: pity at their lack of foresight over the pitfalls of pregnancy and excitement at the possibility they might not come back to work. If they did return, she was dismissive of problems with unreliable nannies and husbands who expected their wives to shoulder the entire domestic burden, despite the equality of their working hours. What did you expect? she wanted to tell them. And don't assume I will pick up the slack. Now she viewed them with new-found respect, trying to compensate for her former lack of empathy.

She could feel Rosemary's hot scrutiny as she searched for any signs of vacillation over Janey's intention to return to work exactly twelve weeks after the baby was born. She might have interviewed her for the job, but Janey expected no loyalty. Female partners at the magic circle of elite City law firms were no longer a rare breed, but once they had babies they were in sufficiently short supply to be on the endangered list. Rosemary would wonder whether testosterone would win over oestrogen. Would Janey continue to hack it as a partner, where fourteen-hour days were the norm and her new baby would be a luxury weekend accessory sandwiched between legal briefs, or would she head for the less glamorous but saner hinterland to work as a PSL? To Janey it was obvious that she would continue to run with the wolves. Soft options were anathema to her and even the phrase Professional Support Lawyer left the bitter taste of failure in her mouth.

That decision made, she had switched her focus to instructing her secretary to watch out for any attempts to steal clients while she was away. Since her company had merged with a couple of European law firms a few years ago, loyalty was a quaint anachronism, even among fellow partners. It was each for himself, especially when the newspapers talked of nothing but recession and crisis in the American banking system. Steve had come home late on Friday night explaining that he was trying to unravel his positions with Bear Stearns. The American bank was close to collapse, he said.

Janey struggled with a couple of complex paragraphs involving the transfer of share options but was interrupted by the doorbell. It rang in a long demanding drone. She waited for Steve to come upstairs, knowing that if she heaved herself up she might never go back to the piles on the floor. Then she remembered that he was in the office in the basement, scrolling through iTunes in his effort to put together the perfect playlist for childbirth. It was among the multifarious tasks that he had set himself before her due date in ten weeks' time. It meant that she ran the risk of giving birth during a Phil Collins track, but there were plenty of years ahead to inoculate their child against Steve's taste in music.

As she pulled herself up, using the sofa as ballast, Janey decided quite spontaneously to opt for Gina Ford: the draconian regime would compel her to leave the doorbell to ring if people called at times of day when mother and baby were meant to be resting, or doing pelvic-floor exercises, or reading legal documents. Besides, although she had put the years of hedonism firmly behind her, there might be a temptation to re-engage when the shroud of sleep deprivation descended and she was no longer in her right mind. She liked the idea of structure. That was one of Steve's attractions.

Once upright, she slouched in all her splay-legged clumsiness towards the front door. Pregnancy turned even the shortest journey into an odyssey. Just as she reached the intercom, her BlackBerry, at the centrepiece of the circle of admin in the vast open-plan kitchen, began to trill again. She eyed it reproachfully.

'Hello,' she panted into the intercom.

'It's me,' replied Laura, equally breathlessly. 'Can I come in?'

Janey could tell from the limited exchange and the scuffling noises on her doorstep that Laura wasn't alone. She also knew that whatever brought Laura here on a late Sunday afternoon probably didn't involve a short conversation. She forced a smile and opened the door.

'Something's happened,' Laura said simply, her lower lip trembling. Her long fair hair was flat from the rain and hung dejectedly across her face, like a wonky curtain.

Janey felt a stab of self-reproach at her lack of generosity. She recalled historical acts of kindness: Laura inviting her to move in with her and Jonathan, their second year at university, after her mother unexpectedly took off for India, forgetting to leave Janey any money; Laura telling her to ignore everyone else and follow her own instincts when Janey decided to give up history and study law the following year; Laura introducing her to Patrick at a Christmas party at Jonathan and Hannah's house after she had started her job and was complaining that the long hours meant she would never find a boyfriend. Then Janey remembered the awful evening when she came home from work to discover that Patrick had packed up his share of their flat with surgical precision and left for Afghanistan without saying goodbye. It was Laura who had arrived with a couple of bottles of wine before Janey had even called her. In the difficult months after Patrick's departure, Janey had spent more nights than she cared to remember sleeping on the sofa bed in Sam and Laura's sitting room.

'Come in, all of you,' Janey said, weaving warmth from these threads of memory. 'It's not often I get to see you on a Sunday.'

'Children's tea,' Laura babbled nervously, waving a plastic bag of anaemic chipolatas in one hand and a bag of white bread rolls in the other. Nell and Ben stood either side of her, like praetorian guards, looking serious. Laura glanced down at the sausages sitting stiffly in her hand. They were affectionately entwined but frozen fast. That is how my skin must look, she thought, comparing their mottled, sallow complexion with her own. She found herself envying their stillness and inconsequential existence. 'Where's your nearest radiator? I need to defrost these.'

Laura often spoke in this staccato fashion when she was with Nell and Ben. While at work she had the luxury of finding the right words to attach to a diagnosis: 'The symptoms of multiple sclerosis can sometimes be alleviated, but not cured, with the right combination of medicine and physiotherapy,' she might say. Or, 'There are some indications that the very dopamine stimulators prescribed for Parkinson's disease might cause unpredictable personality changes, like compulsive sexual behaviour or gambling.' Back home, however, it was essential to economise on words if there was any hope of finishing a sentence, because otherwise you would be besieged by interruptions. Children could topple a conversation without even using words.

'It's all underfloor heating,' said Janey apologetically. 'But I can sort them out in the microwave.'

'I thought your fridge would be full of seeds and folic acid,' said Laura, releasing the sausages and rolls. Then she knelt down on the floor to rummage in a dark green handbag. It was fat with promise. Janey was intrigued as Laura opened and shut various compartments, reaching deep into its inner recesses.

All this was now relevant to her. She would soon be initiated into the mysterious rites of the post-natal handbag and it was essential to absorb this detail for future reference. Laura pulled out a couple of pairs of children's pyjamas, two mobile phones and a packet of crayons before growing impatient and tipping the entire contents on to the floor. Chunks of rice cake tumbled from inside followed by tinier crushed particles that floated on to Janey's legal documents. The front page of a medical paper wafted to the ground. *Parkinson's and memory loss*, it read. On the front Laura had written a single sentence: *A memory is a stored pattern of connections between neurons in the brain.* Janey smiled, reassured that whatever the nature of the crisis, it wasn't distracting Laura from work. A few drops of thick red liquid began dripping from the bag.

'Is that blood?' asked Janey nervously, as the dripping became more rhythmic.

'Don't be ridiculous,' laughed Laura.

'I thought it might be your work bag,' said Janey, with relief.

'It's tomato ketchup,' Laura pointed out as the bottle finally tumbled to the floor. A glutinous red puddle immediately started to obscure the title of the Gina Ford book. The lid must have come unstuck during the journey.

Nell bent down to pick it up. At seven, she was old enough to understand that it was embarrassing to turn up unannounced on her godmother's doorstep on a Sunday evening with a leaking bottle of tomato ketchup, even if she couldn't articulate why. She held the lidless ketchup at shoulder height so that Ben couldn't reach it, until she realised that one of her carefully braided plaits had sunk inside. She pulled the bottle away and put the end of her hair in her mouth and sucked at the ketchup.

'Daddy isn't here because he's working,' Nell said seriously, in between sucks. 'I think he's missed another deadline. So we thought we should leave him in peace and come to see you and Steve.' Janey could hear Laura's voice in Nell's words. Ben was tugging at Nell's arm as she spoke.

She took him by the hand and stared at Janey with a serious expression. Nell was a child who never ate a whole packet of sweets all at once and who kept her piggy bank on the highest shelf in the bedroom in case of a rainy day. She never took advantage of the au pairs who sometimes lived in the tiny spare bedroom of their house in Kensal Rise during the summer holidays. She corrected their English and showed them where the washing powder was kept. She was self-contained, her teachers said. Janey carefully took the ketchup from her hand and gave her a hug. Nell allowed herself to be enfolded and rested her head on her godmother's stomach.

'Mummy,' asked Ben, as he eyed the ketchup. He knew he was losing ground to his sister. 'Can you take guinea pigs to Hamster Heath?'

'Oh God, I'm sorry, Janey,' said Laura, using a finger to mop up the ketchup before wiping it on to the medical bulletin. The contented little baby on the front cover of Janey's book was now an unhealthy red colour, as though it had caught measles. Remember never to carry tomato ketchup in your handbag, thought Janey. That was a pretty straightforward rule of thumb. As the stain spread Janey felt a wave of anxiety. If this happened to Laura, most meticulous of friends, then what hope was there for her? Janey recalled Laura's bedroom at their home in Fallowfield twenty years earlier: the skeleton in the corner, complete down to the tiniest finger joint; the way she could tell what day of the week it was by observing the packet of contraceptive pills that sat on Laura's bedside table; and how Laura would call her parents at exactly the same time every Friday afternoon. She remembered a moment a couple of months after she moved in with Laura and Jonathan, when the drug squad had raided the club Jonathan was helping to run in the city centre. Laura was the only person he wanted to talk to and the only one capable of calming his jangly nerves. She was conscious back then, as she was now, that people felt safe with Laura.

'I know what you're thinking,' said Laura, without waiting for an answer. 'You're thinking, "I'll never do this when I'm a parent,"' she continued, holding the ketchup up to the light to see how much was left inside. 'But everyone does. I said I'd never let them eat meals watching television. I vowed to use a reusable nappy service. No pizza. No tomato ketchup . . . the road to parenthood is potholed with broken principles.'

'Mummy,' Ben insisted. 'Can you take guinea pigs to Hamster Heath?'

'Or chutney to Putney?' Nell brightly interjected, glancing between Laura and Janey, trying to read their silent exchange.

'It's Hampstead Heath. Nothing to do with hamsters,' said Laura, absent-mindedly stroking Ben's hair with ketchup-stained fingers. A clutch of blond curls stood stiffly to attention.

'Or guinea pigs?' questioned Ben.

'But it's got lots of lycopene,' said Laura as she tried to give Nell what she hoped was a reassuring smile.

'You could take lycopene to East Sheen,' suggested Nell, trying to be helpful. 'That's where Granny and Grandpa live.'

'What's a lycopene? Is it like a chinchilla?' asked Ben. 'Can you take it to Hamster Heath?'

'So you don't need to feel guilty,' babbled Laura. 'Because lycopene is an antioxidant, and antioxidants prevent cancer and there is more lycopene in tomato ketchup than almost any other food.'

'Mummy, have you brought my spellings?' asked Nell.

'In the side pocket of the bag. I've brought this for you,' said Laura, holding out a small bottle of almond oil.

Janey realised that at least a couple of strands of this conversation were directed at her and that she needed to pick out these threads before they were forever obscured by some new diversion. But keeping up was challenging, not least because when Laura was addressing her she wasn't necessarily looking at her. Ben approached and slipped his hand into her own. It was hot and sticky.

'Janey, we saw an actual hedgehog on Hamster Heath,' he said seriously.

'An actual hedgehog?' repeated Janey, struggling to pick him up.

'Actually running around in circles,' stressed Ben, putting out a hand to push her face towards him, 'round and round.'

'In circles?' said Janey, as she wiped her cheek.

'Maybe it had missed a deadline, like Daddy,' Nell suggested.

'It's to massage your perineum,' said Laura, pressing the bottle of almond oil into Janey's hand. 'To make it work with you not against you. It's good to have an elastic perineum. Not in general. But for childbirth. To avoid tearing.'

'Er, thanks,' said Janey, as she put Ben back down on to the floor.

'What's a perineum, Mummy?' asked Nell.

To Janey's relief, Nell and Ben headed towards the kitchen island and began running circuits around it. She imagined Steve downstairs, flinching at the thuds overhead. He would be worrying about the scratches and skid marks that the cleaning lady had tried to scour from the wood with disastrous results after their last visit. There were still blond patches from the bleach. Janey hadn't cared. She had been relieved that the floor finally showed some signs of history. She felt its censure when she came home from work at midnight to find it buffed and polished to perfection.

'Why are you so out of breath?' Laura asked.

'All the running around,' Janey said vaguely, sweeping her hand around the huge room.

'Sorry,' mumbled Laura.

'Serves me right for having such a big kitchen,' said Janey unthinkingly. Since she had moved in with Steve after discovering she was pregnant, she was always trying to justify the luxury of her domestic arrangements. The cleaning lady; the laundry service; the five bedrooms; the garden that required a lawn mower; and the sitting rooms that inspired Nell to ask why her godmother had moved into a museum. She resolved to stop apologising. It wasn't as though Laura drew comparisons or even commented on the gulf between their financial realities.

'I've become a fat cat,' she muttered to herself.

Besides, it was ridiculous to apologise when this was what she wanted. Money had been the major incentive in her decision to become a corporate lawyer. Janey had seen her own mother struggle to bring up two children on the lean proceeds from selling paintings produced on the commune in Lyme Regis where she was brought up. Her father had abandoned her and his children for another woman after her mother had agreed to his argument in favour of an open marriage. Thenceforth his financial contributions were sporadic and only followed demeaning letters from her mother requesting help. Janey wanted a big house. She wanted to buy privacy and silence and the things she had never known as a child. On the commune everything was discussed from her first period to her first boyfriend. She didn't want to be tribal. She wanted a wet room. A bathroom with two sinks and a house with a long staircase separating the different parts of human need so that desire could be confined to the bedroom, appetite to the kitchen and ablutions to the bathroom. We are defined by our childhood, thought Janey, and hers was defined by penury. Unlike Sam and Laura, she didn't have the luxury of principles. Her salary enabled her to buy not just a flat for herself but also, finally, a home for her mother. She would never be financially dependent on a man, not even one as solid as Steve.

'Sam and I are in crisis,' said Laura, when she was convinced the children were out of earshot.

'In crisis?' repeated Janey, struggling to make the transition to adult conversation.

'I thought he was having an affair,' explained Laura. She summarised her reasoning: the text exchanges between Sam and Jonathan; the number of times he had googled fidelity on the Internet; the coincidence of V possibly being code for Victoria. But even as she outlined the evidence, exaggerating some of the strongest elements, Laura realised that she sounded off balance. Actually she reminded herself of her patients. Particularly those who read up about their symptoms on the Internet and then came to her clinic convinced they were harbouring an incurable neurological condition that another doctor had missed.

At the end, almost as an afterthought, she added that she had tricked Sam into visiting a marriage guidance counsellor.

'I can't believe you did that,' said Janey finally. She sounded less shocked than impressed, as though she had discovered something new and important about Laura that merited close attention.

'V stood for vasectomy,' said Laura finally. It was important to stress this part last to counterbalance the more unhinged elements of her behaviour. 'Are you surprised?' she questioned, when Janey didn't say anything.

'By both of you in equal measure,' said Janey diplomatically, adding that she understood why Laura might have jumped to the wrong conclusions but couldn't really grasp why such a drastic response was required. Even as she said it, she knew it was untrue: Sam's behaviour was entirely in character. He buried problems like a dog buried bones. It was Laura who surprised her.

'Can you believe that Sam was going to have a vasectomy behind my back when he knows how much I want to have another baby?' asked Laura.

'You would have found out,' said Janey, intuiting that Laura wanted to discuss this part of the crisis first.

'Mummy, quite frankly, we're really hungry,' Nell shouted from the other side of the room.

'Sausages are almost ready,' Laura said seriously, as she

gripped Janey's arm. 'Where's the microwave? Do you mean from the scar?'

Janey was confused.

'Mummy, I'm hungry,' Ben repeated.

Janey's head began to ache. She pressed her index fingers into her temples and began to massage.

'Do you want to cook the sausages in the microwave?' Janey asked.

'How would I know?' questioned Laura.

'Well, the children are hungry and that seems a pretty good indicator,' said Janey.

'I mean, how would I know if he'd had a vasectomy?' Laura asked.

'The tight pants would have given him away,' smiled Janey, relieved that she could finally answer a question.

'What are you talking about?' asked Laura.

'After the operation men have to wear extra-tight Y-fronts to hold everything in place,' explained Janey. 'If Sam started wearing extra-small pants you would have known something was up.'

'But what if I didn't and I spent the next couple of years having sex all the time in the hope of having a baby when it was physically impossible?' said Laura.

'Then Sam would have reached a state of affairs that most men can only dream of,' said Janey. 'A lot of inconsequential sex.'

'Mum, we're hungry,' said Ben.

'Let's talk while they eat tea,' Janey urged.

The problem with minimalism is that it just isn't absorbent enough, thought Laura, as she went in search of the microwave. She contemplated the kitchen island in wonder. It was as long as a landing strip. It was longer than their entire house. If they moved it to the home that she shared with Sam and the children then its end would rest somewhere in their garden, possibly against the end wall. Six adults could lie out on it head to toe and still there would be room for the newspapers at the end. But its length meant they had the luxury of a thirty-second conversation when the children reached the far end, before they were interrupted by the noise of four feet clattering back across the red-oak floor and round the other side.

One of Janey's gadgets was beeping for attention. Laura could hear it but she couldn't see where it was coming from because everything was hidden in cupboards and shelving units and the children were making too much noise. The only visible sign that anyone lived in this kitchen was a small row of bottles behind the sink: folic acid, evening primrose oil, vitamin C. The plaintive whine continued. Was it the coffee maker? The dishwasher? Or the bread machine? Or the microwave? She drifted up and down the wall of storage occasionally opening a cupboard. Each machine must have its own call, like birds, marvelled Laura, who didn't own a microwave because it would have taken up too much space.

She opened a cupboard to the right of a huge double sink and was dazzled by the straight rows of white cups and plates. The handles were all pitched at exactly the same angle and nothing was chipped or stained. The cutlery drawer was almost a metre wide. Knives, forks and spoons were all obediently lined up. The spoons neatly lying on their sides reminded her of the previous night when Nell and Ben had both woken and got into bed with them. Laura blamed herself for her children's slack sleeping habits. She had once read that the children of working mothers woke more in the night, because they wanted to spend time with their parents, and even though she knew this was the sort of dodgy research that her colleagues would have torn apart, she couldn't forget its insinuation when the children crawled in during the night.

She had lain awake on her side for hours, a dessert spoon squeezed between two teaspoons, running through events at the marriage guidance counsellor's. She remembered the awful moment when she realised that she had got everything wrong and Sam's exhilaration at her mistake. It was the look of a man who scented freedom.

Laura had slept for less than four hours. She caught a glimpse of her reflection in a large carving knife. Is that really me? she thought, pulling the knife out to examine the face peering back at her. She ran a hand along her forehead, tracing a finger through the lines. Age didn't necessarily bring wisdom. It just brought more confusion. Wrinkles were nothing more than increasing tension between the conflicting urges to laugh and cry.

Laura thought of her own cutlery drawer, of knives that could never be found when she needed them; of food that had congregated there over the years until it formed a community of its own; of tiny pieces of Lego, Polly Pocket and stones from the garden that Nell had hidden there from her brother. And Sam's corks from his late-night attempts to hit slippery deadlines.

She noticed Janey lifting a shutter to reveal a stainless-steel microwave and watched her take out six flawlessly cooked sausages, remove a perfectly sharpened bread knife from the drawer and neatly slice open the bread rolls. She called Ben and Nell on to a couple of stools on the other side of the island and they complied immediately. Janey told them that if they were good, they could put the tomato ketchup on.

'Can I just say, Laura, that if you consider the situation coldly, nothing truly awful has happened,' said Janey, urging Laura towards the sofa at the other end of the kitchen. 'It would have been worse to be right. Now it's just a question of doing a few mea culpas. In a couple of weeks, you might even be laughing about it.'

'Sam is never going to want to have another child,' said Laura, as she sat down, shaky-voiced. 'That's worse than an affair. In fact you could argue that if I'd uncovered an infidelity, then he could have shown remorse by agreeing to have a baby. Now, there's no hope.'

Janey tried to follow the logic of her argument but each time she came up against the irrationality of Laura's position. The last time she saw Sam he had emphatically told her that they hadn't the time, the money or the space for a new baby.

'Isn't two children enough?' said Janey gently.

'Enough for Sam. Not for me,' Laura responded. 'The maternal urge is utterly visceral.' Laura articulated an argument that Janey would have torn apart in a court of law. She wanted the chance to have time with a third baby that she didn't have with Nell and Ben. She wanted to breastfeed for a year. Fill her freezer with cubes of organic fruit purée. Bake cakes. Make soups. Do baby yoga. Baby massage.

'You could argue that you've prevented a crisis,' interrupted Janey. 'A vasectomy is pretty final.'

'Lawyers can always argue things from all angles,' muttered Laura.

'He hasn't had an affair and he hasn't had a vasectomy. That's not a double negative, it's a double positive,' said Janey.

'What about the element of betrayal?' said Laura. 'And the fact that I know so little of what's going on inside his head?'

Sitting straight-backed and cross-legged on the sofa, Janey struggled to lean over her stomach to put a hand on Laura's shoulder. 'He didn't do it,' said Janey gently.

'If I hadn't uncovered the trail of deceit then it might have happened,' argued Laura.

'He should have told you,' agreed Janey. 'But all relationships have secrets. Otherwise there would be no mystery.' She stopped to organise a series of cushions around her.

'And did I mention that for years he assumed that I slept with Jonathan and never bothered to ask me whether I did?' asked Laura, as though she was just remembering this part of their exchange.

'Perhaps he thought there was nothing to be gained from that knowledge,' said Janey. 'The trouble with being a scientist is that you want answers to everything. But some questions aren't worth asking. Enlightenment and wisdom are not the same thing. In fact sometimes it's wiser not to be enlightened.' She took a slurp of chamomile tea before saying, 'So did you?'

'Did I what?' replied Laura.

'Did you sleep with Jonathan?' Janey questioned. 'No smoke without fire and all that. I've wondered the same thing. You were very close.'

'I can't believe you're asking that too,' said Laura.

'Well, it wouldn't alter anything, would it?' asked Janey. 'It would just be a dim historical memory. A shadow.'

'I think it might have made things a little uncomfortable with Hannah,' conjectured Laura.

'I've been known to find myself round a dinner table chatting to the wife of someone I slept with years ago,' joked Janey. 'No one comes to a relationship without history any more.'

'But not with your closest friends presumably?' asked Laura. 'Just peripheral types.'

There was a long pause.

'Well, not necessarily,' said Janey, regretting the way this conversation had burst its banks.

'Did you ever sleep with Sam?' asked Laura impetuously, immediately wishing she hadn't asked the question. She didn't want to know the answer and she didn't want the burden of implied reciprocity that this confession demanded. But she already knew from the expression on Janey's face that the answer was yes.

Now it was Janey's turn to look serious. She licked her teeth with her tongue and ran her hand through her dark hair. Pregnancy hadn't really changed her face, thought Laura. She still had the air of a rather beautiful boy with her short bob and fringe and awkward angles. Patrick had once described her as postmodern and said that she looked as though she had been made in a hurry. Janey had joked that she almost certainly was, because her mother couldn't really remember when exactly she had been conceived. Everything about her was big, her shoulders, her lips, her forehead, her legs. It was as though someone had forgotten to edit her.

'I assumed you knew,' said Janey, knowing that Laura hadn't.

'Why did you never say anything?' asked Laura in astonishment, wondering whether this knowledge would have changed anything.

'I assumed Sam had mentioned it and you had decided it was irrelevant. Which of course it is. Was, I mean,' said Janey, fiddling with the edge of a cushion.

Ben had climbed on to a stool and was messing around with the lights at the other end of the room, turning the dimmer up and down, to experiment with different combinations. He found the switch for a wall light where Janey was seated and turned it up high so that the spotlight beamed uncomfortably on her face.

'You're under interrogation,' he shouted. Janey was relieved to see that Laura was smiling.

'The urge to reveal is greater than the urge to conceal. Isn't that what Jung claimed?' said Janey, as the bulb dimmed so low they were bathed in light from the street lamp outside.

'Not in Sam's case,' said Laura.

'It happened years ago,' said Janey. 'Maybe Sam forgot. We were both pretty wasted. All long before you got it together.'

'Had you met Patrick?' asked Laura, struggling to digest this unexpected piece of information. She wasn't sure how to react. She had just discovered that her husband and one of her best friends had once slept together, and that felt as though it should be significant, not least because neither of them had ever mentioned it. Yet weren't there entanglements in her own past that Laura preferred to forget? And so she didn't say anything because it felt less dangerous that way.

'He never knew,' explained Janey. 'We've all behaved badly. That's what your twenties are about. Regrets for what you've done.'

'And your thirties?' asked Laura.

'That's when you regret what you haven't done,' smiled Janey.

'So what are your regrets?' questioned Laura.

She looked up, realising that Ben had fallen quiet. She was relieved to see Nell still sitting on the stool, intently picking off the crust from the bread roll and rolling it into small balls around the edge of her plate. She was rhythmically swinging her bare legs backwards and forwards. Laura called Ben and he answered with a contented grunt from the other end of the room. This degree of concentration would normally have made Laura immediately suspicious because it suggested a dangerous level of intent. Instead her attention was drawn to the staircase leading down into the basement, where she could see Steve coming up the stairs in bare feet.

'I don't regret sleeping with Sam, if that's what you mean, but with Patrick there are too many unanswered questions,' said Janey.

'Hello, Laura,' Steve said in surprise, as he came into the room. 'What brings you and your two small children here on a Sunday evening?' He searched for Nell and Ben but they were below his line of vision.

'I'll explain,' said Janey soothingly.

'How's work? Is the credit crunch biting?' Laura heard herself ask as she stood up to greet Steve. He was an imposing presence, even in bare feet. His feet were enormous, his toes as long as Laura's fingers. Less flat-footed than fat-footed, thought Laura. He was wearing a white shirt so bright and wrinkle-free that it made Laura's eyes smart. Janey had once told her that Steve chose shirts in plain colours to show off the perfect delineation of his upper torso. Perhaps he needed public exposure of his gym routine to inspire trust in those who invested in his business. Laura wondered whether people were more likely to hand over their money to someone whose body spoke of rigorous 6 a.m. sessions in the gym than someone who had given in to middle-age spread and a couple of glasses of wine with lunch. She was conscious that he was talking to her.

'. . . so the market falls haven't really eaten into our gigantic gains of the last year or so,' said Steve languidly, 'although of course we're all affected to some degree by the tightening margin terms from the banks. It's getting tougher and tougher to finance our portfolios.'

'What exactly is it that you do?' Laura heard herself ask. He was gratified by her question.

'Convertible bond arbitrage,' said Steve. Laura looked at him blankly. 'Well, in simple terms what we do is lower the risk of holding bonds by short-selling linked equity. It's all driven by statistical analysis. The computer defines the model and we do what it says.'

'Gosh,' said Laura, 'how does that work?'

'The computer uses statistical arbitrage to find small

mispricings in shares and then we short or long it. Actually, Laura, since you're here and I'm reasonably sure that you've got no interest in my work, I'd really appreciate your advice about something else,' he said.

Laura stared at him, wondering what he was about to ask. She knew his appearance was a cue for them to leave.

'Do you think for the pushing stage you want something rousing in a Queen, "We Are the Champions" mode, or something a little slower? I was thinking of "I can feel it coming in the air tonight". What do you think?'

'Not rousing,' said Laura, who was watching Ben walk across the room, wide-legged like a cowboy, waving something that resembled a tube of toothpaste.

'And I'm anticipating that the pushing stage will last no more than three-quarters of an hour. Do you think that sounds about right? There seems to be some divergence in the books,' he continued.

'I've sealed the holes,' said Ben triumphantly.

Laura walked towards him and prised the tiny tube from his hot sweaty fist. Two of his fingers were firmly stuck together.

'Like a mermaid,' said Nell, in awe, getting down from the stool to admire Ben's webbed fingers.

'What holes?' demanded Laura. He led her proudly to a neat row of electrical sockets at the end of the room. Each was carefully filled with superglue.

On the way home, Laura put on Dr Seuss for the children and considered what she had just learnt. Of course it shouldn't matter that Janey and Sam had once had sex. It was simply a newly unearthed historical detail, she told herself. Its significance lay in the fact that Laura had never known. And because this piece of information remained firmly ensconced in her frontal cortex on the slow drive home to Kensal Rise and continued to dominate her thoughts when she went to bed, Laura completely forgot to tell Janey that Steve had overheard their conversation.

'What I can't understand,' said Steve, after they had left, 'is why Laura couldn't come alone.'

'Because Sam missed another deadline and needed to work,' explained Janey.

'Sam misses deadlines like other people skip meals,' said Steve. 'If he's missed one, can't he just miss another?'

'Laura thought Sam was having an affair,' explained Janey, hoping the drama of this statement would cauterise this line of questioning.

'Sam isn't organised enough to have an affair.' Steve laughed dismissively.

'In fact he was planning a clandestine vasectomy,' Janey continued, anticipating this would elicit greater sympathy.

Steve digested this information and then cleared his throat. 'Why are your friends so emotionally incontinent?' he asked. His tone was more curious than angry. 'Why can't they just deal with things on their own? Why do they have to talk everything over? You can't live life by committee.' He sat down on one of the kitchen stools and flicked through the back section of yesterday's *Financial Times*.

'The sub-prime market has collapsed and they're worrying about stuff that hasn't even happened,' said Steve, scribbling notes on a piece of paper.

'Do you feel as though there are three of us in this marriage?' Janey teased, as she switched on the kettle to brew another cup of chamomile tea.

'Four actually,' said Steve. 'There's Hannah too. This is the first weekend she hasn't called you. And when the baby arrives I'll slip even lower down the list of priorities. Do you think your tea would relax me?'

'Maybe if you had it intravenously,' said Janey, leaning over to hug him. But her burgeoning stomach meant that she could only rest her forehead on his chest. He shifted sideways on the stool and patted her head affectionately.

'They're our friends,' Janey tried to explain.

'They're your friends.'

'Friends are the new family.'

'You don't sleep with relatives.'

Janey put a hand on her stomach as the baby started its contortions. She could feel a small pointed heel hammering below her ribcage. She took a deep breath before adding, 'Patrick was a legitimate boyfriend.'

'That was most definitely a pregnant pause,' laughed Steve, putting his hand on her stomach.

'I can't abandon my friends. Anyway, they're enjoying the process of getting to know you,' she said.

'Don't be absurd. They disapprove of me,' said Steve, handing over the piece of paper to Janey. 'They think I'm an uptight money-grabbing capitalist.'

'Well you are,' replied Janey standing beside him, examining the hieroglyphics on the piece of paper. 'What's all this?'

At the top of the page were three identical overlapping circles and at the bottom there were two overlapping circles and a smaller lone one on the far side of the page.

'This', explained Steve in a serious tone, 'is a Venn diagram illustrating how our lives are intertwined with your friends'. The one at the bottom is to demonstrate how life could be if we could break away and leave Sam and Laura and Hannah and Jonathan to their own devices.'

'This is a joke, right?' said Janey.

4

In some respects it would have been easier if Sam was having an affair, thought Laura, as she chased a cherry with a cocktail stick around an exotic alcohol-free cocktail in the bar of Jonathan's restaurant a few weeks later. Jonathan and Hannah had hastily arranged a going-away dinner at Eden to celebrate their move from London to the country. Except that the gathering smacked of being an after-thought, because they had moved out of their London home in the autumn, and Jonathan still spent more time in London than in Suffolk. But in the middle of March, any excuse to celebrate was welcome. At least an affair would have provided a logical explanation for his behaviour over the past six months. Laura's instincts would have been vindicated and the session with the marriage guidance counsellor would have seemed an act of rational self-preservation, rather than one of folly.

Now she found herself in emotional no-man's-land. Sam clearly didn't want to talk about what had happened, because that would entail a thorough dissection of what was going on in his head. Instead he looked down at her, Buddha-like, from the moral high ground. Laura would have welcomed recrimination and argument because it might have forced him to reveal himself. But Sam's central philosophy had always been that a problem buried was generally a problem resolved. Besides, it had long been his belief that the fact he cried when United won a match was proof that he was a man in touch with his emotions.

Laura caught sight of herself in the long mirror that stretched behind the bar and the discovery that her breasts were riding high in perfect equilibrium made her sigh with pleasure. Buying underwear she couldn't afford from Agent Provocateur during her lunch hour was undoubtedly the female definition of a midlife crisis. It had been Janey's parting suggestion as she ushered Laura and her disgraced children out of her home.

'It's one of those guilty female secrets,' Janey whispered.

'A clandestine bra isn't the same as a clandestine vasectomy,' Laura had insisted.

She looked down at the purple and black lace edging as she took a sip from the cocktail. Janey was right: knowing that you were wearing a bra that was both perfectly engineered and utterly seductive was soothing to the soul in a way that drinking a cocktail that promised to boost energy and reduce stress simply wasn't. She imagined a neurological experiment in which electrodes were attached to the brains of women shopping in Agent Provocateur to see exactly which parts of their limbic system lit up when trying on diaphanous underwear.

She hadn't planned to follow Janey's advice. Although Janey believed in retail therapy like some people believe in God, Laura was an agnostic shopper. But then two things had transpired at work that day to persuade her she needed a break from her normal routine. Laura always went into the waiting room to find the people attending her clinic because that initial glance, when they were unaware of her presence, provided valuable diagnostic clues. She had spotted her first patient trying to pull herself out of a plastic green armchair, using a shelf for support. She was that type of middle-aged woman who had given up hope with her appearance. Her mud-coloured skirt had a crooked hem and she was wearing a man's blue anorak with a broken zip. Using two walking sticks, she shuffled across the floor towards Laura.

The woman had come to ask for a medical certificate that would allow her to collect incapacity benefit. At least a couple of patients every week fell into this category and the challenge was to winkle out the fakers. But the letter from the GP and a thorough examination convinced Laura that the woman clearly had a neuropathic disorder.

Her last patient was an elderly woman suffering from that combination of confusion and forgetfulness that pointed to an easy diagnosis of the early symptoms of dementia. Mrs Viner told Laura that she was baking cakes through the night because she had become one of the main suppliers for the M&S luxury patisserie section and couldn't keep up with demand. Delusion was a key component of dementia and Laura had written to the GP suggesting that perhaps her family should partially indulge her fantasy during the day by pretending to buy her cakes, and then administer a course of sleeping tablets to ensure that the nocturnal baking habit ceased.

When she left St Mary's at midday to go and buy a sandwich at M&S, Laura decided in half-hearted amusement to study the cake section. And there she had seen a whole counter dedicated to Mrs Viner's very fine home-baked cakes, as endorsed by Nigella Lawson. Then at the queue by the checkout she saw the same woman who could barely walk into her clinic briskly and efficiently moving objects from her basket on to the counter. She was wearing a completely different outfit. Laura didn't say anything. She hoped for a moment that perhaps the condition only affected the nerve endings in her legs but as the woman hurtled out of the shop, buoyed no doubt by thoughts of the certificate that sat in her handbag, there was no doubting the fact that Laura had been had.

The underwear was pure indulgence. It was a sop to compensate for the chain of bad decisions she had made over the past few weeks. Because Laura knew that even going to Janey's house was a bad idea, although it had made her feel better at the time. Turning a nebulous problem between her and Sam into a talking point among friends was a mistake: it made it more tangible.

The sensual interior of the shop smoothed the rough edges of her soul and for half an hour, while shop assistants wearing little more than underwear urged her to try bras as meticulously designed as Concorde, Laura stepped outside herself. She talked about lift, plunge, depth of cleavage and the absolute importance of perfect fit as though these were of primordial importance to the outcome of the rest of her life. She compared silk with satin, the pros and cons of underwiring, and assessed with mathematical precision the ideal ratio between Lycra and cotton.

Now wanting to be distracted from these guilty thoughts, she picked up a copy of *The Times* that someone had left on the bar. There was nothing but headlines about US recession and the collapse of the sub-prime mortgage market and Laura felt it was a subliminal message of reproach to her for spending almost £150 on underwear. A hotel in South Kensington wouldn't have cost much more, she calculated, and it could have led to another baby. That is what she should have done. She consoled herself that Sam would never discover the cost of the underwear because the upside of living with someone who had no idea how much money was in his bank account was that there was never any recrimination over expenditure.

She forced herself to read the financial pages in case she had to sit next to Steve at dinner. Then she could ask him if his hedge fund was overleveraged, if it had any exposure to the secondary debt market, and whether, in his considered opinion, the BRIC economies were indeed decoupling from the US. Toxic debt, leverage without limit, liquidity cushion, systemic failure. The language of finance was not so different from the language of illness.

Laura needed to be prepared, because, on previous form, she was absolutely certain that Steve would ask nothing about her life, beyond a few cursory enquiries about Nell and Ben. He might present her with an electrical bill for repairing the sabotaged plug sockets. He almost certainly wouldn't ask about the paper she had written on the links between dopamine stimulators and compulsive gambling among Parkinson's patients. Although, from everything Janey had told them about his sexual appetite, he would probably appreciate a vicarious meander around Agent Provocateur. Steve was mostly insulated from the world, cushioned by his vast house with its array of Banham locks and high-quality upholstery, and his bespoke suits, made somewhere like Jermyn Street.

If she had known twenty years ago that her contemporaries who worked in the City would earn bonuses ten times her annual salary, would that have changed her decision to become a doctor and marry a scriptwriter? wondered Laura. If Sam had earned a regular salary, their life could have been so different. As it would if Laura abandoned her principles and cut back on her NHS work to do private practice. The mortgage wouldn't hang over their house like a dark cloud; they wouldn't have to toss up between the cost of piano lessons for Nell and football for Ben; nor pretend that a week in Cornwall every summer was way more exciting than going trekking in the Masai Mara. Even in her current slump, the thought made Laura smile, because Sam's relationship with money was so precarious that she didn't even reveal her pin number to him. He was someone who could accidentally cause the collapse of the entire banking system.

She blamed his parents. Sam's father was a painter whose abstract paintings of the flat Suffolk landscape enjoyed a brief period in fashion in the mid seventies. One even sold for more than £10,000, a fact he recounted every time they went to stay with him. But he was incapable of saving money. Sam's mother, a potter, was equally profligate. So Sam's childhood resembled recent graphs of the FTSE 100 index, with its wild fluctuations and lack of consistency. There were short-lived peaks of extravagance. These periods were defined by holidays abroad and a one-year stint at a local private school, where he met Jonathan. The troughs were longer and deeper. Sam transferred to the local state school and didn't leave Suffolk for two years. During the lean times, he frequently ended up eating at Jonathan's home.

As Laura turned to the business pages, wondering if they would reveal how she and Sam might be affected by financial Armageddon, she heard a familiar voice a couple of bar stools away from her. Jonathan had arrived. A ripple of energy surged through the restaurant. Laura peered over the newspaper and saw that he was talking to someone. She decided not to interrupt. It was always interesting to see how other people behaved in their work environment because it was a world generally inaccessible to those closest to them. And in any case, his back was turned to her.

The waiters and waitresses had assumed an almost regal air. Trays seemed to be carried at a slightly higher angle, noses too. Drinks seemed brighter and fizzier. Behind the bar, the lanky Polish bartender began polishing the counter and snapped orders to his underlings to check all glasses for blemishes. Eden had an open-plan kitchen and the kitchen staff now seemed to move so swiftly their outlines became blurred. At the rotisserie counter, where organic lamb and pheasants were roasted, flames had to be dampened.

Jonathan changed the molecular structure of the air around him. It wasn't just that he moved more swiftly than anyone else. It was more that he displaced the existing energy with his own high-octane version. There were some people who made you feel more alive, as though you were a wittier, cleverer and more interesting version of yourself when you were with them, and Jonathan was one of these. He invigorated people and made them believe they were of consequence. When he left there was a sense of emptiness. This was in part a feeling of loss at no longer being the object of his attention, but mostly the discovery that the version of themselves that emerged when they were with

Jonathan retreated just as quickly once he had disappeared. Jonathan, Laura decided, was an addictive personality.

Laura could see that he was talking to a young woman. She imagined she was one of the waitresses from the restaurant. It was impossible to age people nowadays, but Laura hazarded a guess that she was somewhere between twenty-five and thirty-two. She was pitched in the wonderful world that women inhabit for a short period as the years of self-doubt evaporate and the years of invisibility beckon. She definitely had no children. She trod too lightly for that. Laura tried to imagine Nell at that age and wondered what nuggets of wisdom she would try to impart to her daughter.

That was the age at which her parents had warned her of the perils of buying a flat with someone like Sam. Sam, they agreed, had a lovely temperament, but lived with his head in the clouds. Her mother advised her to try and find someone like Jonathan, who had drive and ambition, and could give his wife the option of not working and staying at home to look after her children. Laura gently explained that her attitudes belonged to a different era. Her mother's relationship with the kitchen sink was not one she wanted to replicate. She told her parents that she would always want a career and that Sam was the most talented person she had ever met. And largely, she still believed that.

The girl started to laugh and Laura noted that she had short dark hair and was wearing a denim miniskirt and black leather jacket. Pure Notting Hill, Laura concluded.

'Are you waiting for someone?' she heard Jonathan ask in the lull as the Goldfrapp track ended.

'An Internet date,' the girl replied, 'set up by an agency

that does socio-economic profiling to match people up.'
She checked the piece of paper in her hand. 'Are you per
chance Duncan Harris, creative director of one of Britain's
leading advertising agencies?'

'Do you wish I was?' asked Jonathan.

Laura smiled at his gall.

'I'll let you know when he turns up,' the girl replied
flirtatiously. She was gorgeous, Laura thought. Not someone whose ego needed propping up with an Agent
Provocateur bra.

'Where did you arrange to meet him?' Jonathan asked.

'Julie's,' said the girl. 'At eight o'clock.'

'Wrong place, right time,' Jonathan replied, giving her a
couple of directions.

'Why don't you give me your number in case he doesn't
work out?' she asked Jonathan.

Laura took a sharp intake of breath. The girl's
confidence was extraordinary. 'Unless you're attached, of
course. I don't do married men.' That was pretty definitive,
thought Laura, gratified by the idea of solidarity between
women of different generations.

'I'm very available,' Laura heard Jonathan say, as he
wrote down his number and email address on a piece of
paper. Laura felt her face go hot. Jonathan started to say
something else but Laura couldn't hear the end of the
sentence because the barman had turned up the music. The
girl leant towards Jonathan's ear and whispered something
that made him laugh. Then she got up off the red leather
bar stool and left without turning back.

Laura admired the bounce in her bobbed hair and
wondered whether she should go after her to say that her

husband was godfather to Jonathan's eldest son. But even as the thought passed through her mind, she knew it was ridiculous. Instead she stirred the cocktail vigorously, wishing she had ordered something alcoholic. A small dollop of blueberry, kiwi and yogurt landed on the bare skin above her open-necked black shirt and slid coldly down to rest on the new bra. She caught it with her finger and wiped it on the edge of the bar. The barman noticed and immediately came to wipe away the smear. He didn't say anything but gave a disdainful shake of the head. Laura barely noticed, returning to the stirring. Perhaps she misheard Jonathan and he had said he was unavailable. Sometimes just two letters could mark the difference between sinking and swimming. More likely it was part of a game. Jonathan could never resist an opportunity to flirt. And on current form, Laura's instincts about sexual attraction were not to be trusted.

So she decided on impulse that the best course of events was to acknowledge what she had overheard. She put down the newspaper and leant over the bar stool that was separating them to tap Jonathan on the shoulder.

'What was all that about?' she asked, raising an eyebrow. 'Old habits dying hard?'

'I will stop at nothing to attract the punters,' said Jonathan, getting up off his stool to come and kiss her on the cheek. 'She might bring her date back here for dinner. And that's what it's about. Bums on seats. Especially at the moment.' He didn't flinch.

'You sounded so convincing,' continued Laura.

'Laura, I'm a very busy man,' said Jonathan. 'And girls like that are too complicated.'

'So are you suggesting that if you had sufficient time and came across a sufficiently uncomplicated woman then you might be tempted?' asked Laura.

'No,' said Jonathan.

'She was gorgeous,' conceded Laura.

'The sort of girl to turn your heterosexual head?' he teased, gesturing to Laura to follow him towards a table in the far corner of the restaurant. 'Lucky Sam.'

Laura shot a look at him. She wondered just how much Sam had told him. Jonathan and Sam saw each other often enough, probably once every two weeks, which wasn't bad going for two men scraping forty with four children between them. Although of course Jonathan's children, Luke and Gaby, were almost adults. But by the time Sam got home from those evenings with Jonathan, Laura was generally in bed asleep or Sam wasn't making sense, and by the next morning, with the scramble to get children to school and herself to work, the previous evening seemed like ancient history.

You wouldn't make a comment like this about a man if you knew he hadn't had sex for more than six months. Although Sam had clearly discussed the vasectomy question with Jonathan, perhaps he hadn't painted an accurate picture of the sexual landscape it inhabited, or its role in defining that landscape, barren and empty as it was. To Laura's mind you could draw a graph that would perfectly illustrate the inverse relationship between her desire to get pregnant and Sam's desire to have sex.

'Have you seen Sam recently?' asked Laura. The words came out louder than she intended. Jonathan strode confidently in front of her, occasionally stopping to greet someone at another table. She was no longer the focus of his attention. His sheer height always drew comment, but inside Eden, at the heart of his territory with its low ceilings and burnished yellow lighting, he seemed to consume the space around him. He was still a well-made man, Laura conceded. His nervous energy and cycling habit meant he remained as wiry as he had been when she first met him in her late teens. The chaos of black curly hair was perhaps a little greyer, but thick enough that if she was to run her hand through the top, it would quickly become entangled.

'Yes,' said Jonathan hesitantly, long after the question was asked.

Finally they reached the table. Jonathan urged Laura to sit in the corner so that she would have the best view of the restaurant fanning out before her and instructed her to save the space opposite her, while he went to speak to the manager. The table was laid for six. She picked up the menu. Berkshire pig, Whitstable oysters, Aylesbury duck, Bath chaps with Tewkesbury mustard . . . She admired the drawings around the edge of the menu, recognising them as copies of illustrations from Mrs Beeton.

When Jonathan had announced nine years ago that he was going to set up a restaurant with impeccable environmental credentials to produce British dishes, with seasonal ingredients sourced locally, critics had laughed in his face. They said the Eden menu was too restrictive, the idea of a national cuisine risible, and the environment a minority issue. His friends had questioned the wisdom of someone who couldn't really cook setting up a restaurant at all. Jonathan explained with absolute confidence that Hannah would devise dishes and develop menus, and he would be responsible for its day-to-day running. After all, he had run a chain of six Café Europa restaurants in London more or less since he left university. His environmental credentials were questionable, born of pragmatism rather than idealism. Laura had filled him in on the essentials of composting, recycling and sustainable energy. The Toyota Prius, the offsetting of air miles and the obligatory wind turbine on the roof of their home in Queen's Park came easily later. Now Jonathan was seen as a visionary, someone who had resurrected ancient British cuisine and harnessed it to contemporary environmental concerns. Bath chaps, pease pudding, pickled mackerel were all reinvented for Eden. He was about to publish a cookery book and had almost finished shooting his first television series. It was an example of the transforming power of utter self-belief.

Laura started to fiddle with the cutlery. She noticed that the same drawings on the menu were etched into the fork handles. To her mind, Jonathan's transformation still seemed faintly ridiculous. But no less ludicrous than Hannah's sudden decision in the middle of last year to up sticks and move to the farm in Suffolk that belonged to Jonathan's father. Even now, Laura shook her head in disbelief. It was a dramatic and utterly baffling decision. Hannah was an urban person whose idea of a rustic idyll was wearing a pair of Cath Kidston oven gloves. But she was the one who insisted they should move to Suffolk permanently and swap their house in London for a small flat where Jonathan could live during the week. It was Hannah's idea to farm some of the livestock and vegetables to supply Eden.

This move unsettled Laura more than she liked to

admit, not least because it marked the geographical loss of old friends, but on a more irrational level because it was a quandary stolen from her and Sam. She was the one destined to live the rural idyll. The roles of Tom and Barbara belonged to Sam and Laura, not Jonathan and Hannah. For more years than she cared to remember they had had long discussions about whether Sam and Laura should leave London in search of a bigger house and better schools. Then Hannah and Jonathan had unexpectedly hijacked their plan.

Jonathan appeared carrying a couple of vodka and tonics and sat down opposite her, looking at the neat lines of knives and forks that Laura had constructed from the cutlery.

'So why are you so early?' asked Jonathan, moving everything back into place.

'I came straight from work,' said Laura.

'What about your guilty working-mum complex?' asked Jonathan. 'All that quality time you need to pack into the hour before bedtime? The fifteen minutes of free play with each child against a backdrop of classical music, followed by bath time, and individually tailored bedtime stories with appropriate educational themes. Isn't that what goes on behind the twitchy curtains of Kensal Rise?'

'Behind the John Lewis blinds, thank you very much,' said Laura. 'Anyway, it's Sam's turn tonight. At least until the babysitter arrives.'

'I admire your democratic parenting principles,' Jonathan commented. 'I'm just relieved they weren't in vogue when mine were young.'

Jonathan saw Laura glancing down at her watch. The others would be here soon.

'You look tired, Laura,' said Jonathan.

'You mean I look old,' said Laura, unconsciously stroking the furrow in her brow.

'Tired,' Jonathan reiterated. 'Do you fancy a quick line, just for old times' sake?'

'Don't be ridiculous,' laughed Laura.

'You want to know what I know, don't you?' questioned Jonathan so gently that Laura became worried about what he might reveal. 'You want to know whether in between my bouts of chronic self-indulgence, Sam gets to articulate worries he might have about his own life when we see each other.'

'So does he?' Laura quickly asked. She leant against the red leather back of the chair so that she could watch the expression on Jonathan's face.

'I'm not such a selfish bastard,' he said reproachfully.

'That's not what I meant,' said Laura. 'He doesn't talk to me about what's going on and it would make me feel better if I knew he was at least communicating with someone. He works all the time and there's never anything to show for it.'

'It's all going to be fine, Laura,' insisted Jonathan. 'That much I know.'

'You've got to give me more than that,' said Laura firmly. 'There's a direct correlation between his output of words and his intake of alcohol.'

'Well at least it's a positive relationship,' Jonathan pointed out.

'Except he always seems to be writing but never managing to finish,' said Laura. 'It's like watching someone pedal very fast without a bicycle chain.'

'If I tell you what I know, you must promise not to say anything to Sam,' said Jonathan, unthinkingly stroking Laura's hand. 'And absolutely no more therapists, life coaches or self-help books.'

'I'll never do anything like that again,' Laura promised. 'I just want to know what's going on so that I can help Sam subconsciously. I understand that whatever the problem is, he needs to be the one who sorts it out.'

Even as she said it, Laura knew this wasn't true. And if Jonathan had been observing her, instead of glancing down at his BlackBerry to read a message, he would have noticed Laura's eyes narrow and realised she was lying. Because although the circle they had trodden around each other had widened over the past eleven years since Laura had married Sam, Jonathan and Laura had spent enough time together in their early twenties to understand the full vocabulary of each other's gestures. In fact sometimes words confused things. But Jonathan was too engrossed in the possibilities opened up by the email to consider this.

'First up,' began Jonathan, putting the BlackBerry face down on the table. 'He absolutely doesn't want to have another child.' He turned to face Laura and saw a shadow pass over the perfectly grey eyes that had caught his attention when she first met him at Manchester.

'I know that,' said Laura. 'And I won't do it as long as he feels like that.'

'He also thinks you resent him for not earning enough money,' said Jonathan. 'He thinks you'd like to work part-time but don't want to admit it to him because you're worried he would feel bad about himself.'

'That is partially true,' agreed Laura.

Relieved by the logic of the discussion so far, Laura allowed herself a moment of reprieve to gaze around the restaurant. She wondered what the couple opposite were discussing so intently and would have been surprised to know they were trying to decide whether she was Jonathan's wife. They had that easy manner bestowed on some couples by years of marriage, the elderly lady insisted to her husband, who in turn reasoned that it was a sense of familiarity a brother and sister might enjoy. As members of the culinary cognoscenti, they were excited to recognise Jonathan, but both agreed they had never seen a photo of his wife in the paper. They wouldn't know that Hannah shunned the limelight while Jonathan sucked up the attention like a needy child.

'And he loathed his job,' said Jonathan.

'Why the use of the past tense?' asked Laura.

'This is the big one,' said Jonathan, holding Laura's hand in his own. 'Sam left his job about three months ago. Or rather his job left Sam.'

'What do you mean?' asked Laura, not wanting to understand what Jonathan was saying.

'They asked him to write an episode about an outbreak of Ebola in the hospital in *Do Not Resuscitate*,' said Jonathan. 'Initially Sam refused because the premise was so absurd and so they suggested that perhaps it was time for him to consider other options.'

'They fired him?' asked Laura.

'Not exactly,' said Jonathan. 'Sam came round to the idea but his plot involved every major character contracting the disease and dying.'

'So they binned it?' asked Laura.

'No,' said Jonathan, 'they decided they loved it and it was an ideal way of wrapping up the show with a bang. *Do Not Resuscitate* is no more. It's not even on life support. Sam killed the characters. And he wrote himself out of a job. They're screening the last episode in the autumn.'

'But why didn't he tell me?' Laura asked, as she picked at her cuticles. Jonathan winced. The past collided with the present. He remembered Laura biting her fingers until they bled when he asked questions from her *Clinical Medicine* textbook during their second year at Manchester. Over that year, Jonathan would frequently arrive home from a club in the early hours of the morning to find Laura sitting at the kitchen table leaning over her well-thumbed copy of Kumar and Clark. Prevented from sleeping by the chemical cocktail slipping round his bloodstream and understanding that Laura's need to pass exams was far greater than his own, he would insist they move to the sofa and then happily spend a couple of hours firing off questions until both of them fell asleep with exhaustion.

'He knew you'd be paralysed with worry,' explained Jonathan, placing his hand firmly over her own to prevent the biting. 'And he wanted some time to work on something else without any pressure.'

'Another hospital drama?' asked Laura.

'Something of his own,' said Jonathan.

'Money has been landing in his account every month,' said Laura, still disbelieving the situation. 'And he's been leaving for work every morning.'

'I've been paying him,' said Jonathan calmly. 'So that he didn't have to ask you for money. And he's been writing in my office here.'

'You can't bankroll Sam.'

'I'm not. I've offered him a job. He's going to help out with Eden while I'm away filming the rest of this TV series. He just needs a bit of time to finish this script first.'

'He can't work for you,' said Laura, struggling to absorb the full impact of Jonathan's revelation.

'Why not?' asked Jonathan.

'He already feels totally inadequate beside you,' said Laura. 'Can you imagine what it's like living in the shadow of your success?'

'I think that's your problem, not Sam's,' said Jonathan quietly. 'He doesn't compare himself with me because he doesn't want to do what I want to do. Sam is only competitive with himself. It's his failure to achieve his own goals that makes him feel bad. It's not a status thing or a financial thing. It's personal. And perhaps you should consider what it's like living in the shadow of your success.'

'I'm just a jobbing doctor,' said Laura.

'Laura, you're a respected neurologist,' said Jonathan. 'Everyone knows that you keep the whole show on the road. I understand why you pretend that Sam pays for stuff, and why you never want to talk about your job so that you don't embarrass him. I know about the research that gets written up in those magazines, the way you pay for his credit card bills. You don't have to pretend with me.'

Laura could see Sam trundling towards them wearing a long overcoat that he had bought in a second-hand shop years ago. He waved and smiled at them, happy to see his wife and oldest friend deep in conversation, oblivious to its content. They were too far away to notice the shadow pass across his face as he saw Jonathan remove his hand from

Laura's. Laura wanted to get up and hug him but her body felt frozen, as though it shouldn't expend any energy that her mind could usefully use to process the implications of what Jonathan was saying. The idea that Jonathan might tell Laura about his deceit wouldn't occur to Sam because he was keeper of too many of Jonathan's secrets. Besides, the big news that Jonathan had to tell Laura only concerned them tangentially. And Sam imagined that was what they had talked about.

'There's another thing,' said Jonathan quickly, before Sam was in earshot.

'I don't think I can absorb any more,' said Laura.

'I thought you might want to know that Patrick is back. Maybe you should let Janey know too.'

5

'What I really want to know,' said Jonathan, smiling up and down the table a little later, 'is why asparagus makes your piss smell so much?' He attempted to make eye contact with everyone, but the question was really directed at Laura, because Jonathan, who was not prone to self-analysis, was concerned about Laura, who most certainly was. Sam's arrival had prematurely derailed their conversation and Jonathan knew that unlike him, Laura wasn't good at sudden emotional gear shifts and needed to be discouraged from introspection.

Jonathan would have been surprised to know that precisely at that moment, far from worrying about the new problems he had carelessly sown before her, Laura was transfixed by the thought that this was the first time she had seen Sam and Janey together since her recent discovery about their secret coupling all those years ago. They happened to be sitting next to each other on the opposite side of the table, allowing her plenty of opportunity to observe them at close quarters. In her heavily pregnant state, Janey looked like a ripe fig about to burst its skin. Her elbow leant comfortably against Sam's forearm as she scanned the menu.

However much it shouldn't matter, this knowledge cast

their relationship in a different light. It explained the easy intimacy between them and the way they occasionally bickered with each other. Sometimes it was difficult to imagine people having sex, but Janey and Sam didn't require a huge leap. Laura was seized by an image of them, limbs entangled, tussling over who should go on top.

She felt irrationally grateful to Janey for giving her something to think about that transcended her other worries. Unemployment, vasectomies and ill-advised trips to marriage guidance counsellors crept back into the shadows as Laura focused on the implications of this historic entanglement.

'It's the asparagusic acid,' said Sam. 'Do you know you can also use it to treat urinary tract infections?'

'Sam, you should retrain as a homeopath,' said Janey enthusiastically.

'That would be the maximum expression of my impending meltdown,' replied Sam drily.

'You're too young for a midlife crisis,' insisted Janey.

'Apparently men have them at forty and women at fifty,' replied Sam.

'And what are the symptoms so I know what to watch out for with Steve?' Janey asked, only half joking.

'Buying sports cars, having affairs, deciding you want to become an acupuncturist, and taking up triathlon,' explained Sam blithely.

It struck Laura that this was the first time they had all got together in almost six months and now that Jonathan and Hannah were no longer living in London, these events would become even more infrequent. Of course there were new friends, parents from school to whom they were connected by the coincidence of living in the same area and having children the same age, and work colleagues who had become woven into the fabric of domestic life. But the wondrous thing about seeing friends who knew you long before you had children was that they provided a thread to the person you used to be. They were bound historically. And that was comforting in these choppy times.

She wanted to work out exactly when Janey and Sam might have slept with each other. Laura couldn't decide whether Janey had met Sam before her. Then she remembered a weekend during their last year at university, when she had gone back home to visit her parents and Sam had visited Jonathan in Manchester. He had slept in her bed, Jonathan casually announced when she arrived back at their flat on Monday morning.

'My relationship with hygiene has evolved since I tested you on bacterial infection,' Jonathan had joked, as he dutifully stuffed Laura's sheets into the washing machine. Janey was in the kitchen cooking breakfast at midday. She was beating eggs in a glass with a fork. They existed on a diet of scrambled eggs through that year and Laura still ate them reluctantly. Jonathan's issues over cleanliness never really extended to washing up and the saucepan was caked with a fine crust of dried egg built up over months. It was good to challenge the immune system, Laura comforted herself.

'I wish you'd been here to meet Sam,' Jonathan had said at one point. Laura remembered Janey's hand circling ever faster around the glass and drops of egg slopping over the edge. Nothing more. Then other images collided in Laura's mind, jostling each other for supremacy. She remembered knocking on Jonathan's door late one night and discovering him in bed with his English tutor. But she couldn't recall why she had wanted to wake him up at two in the morning.

Then she thought of an evening in 1990, the year after they left Manchester, when Jonathan came over to Laura and Janey's house in Shepherd's Bush with a small bag of cocaine for the first time. Hannah had stayed at home with Luke, who was just a couple of months old, and Jonathan had arrived with Sam and his new girlfriend, Victoria, a pale willowy girl who didn't leave Sam's side. After the first couple of lines, Janey forced Laura to get out her stethoscope, because she thought she was about to have a heart attack. As Laura held it to Janey's chest, telling her to breathe in and out from her diaphragm, Sam complimented her on her calm bedside manner.

'I'd want you on my ship if it was sinking,' he said.

There was a Laurie Anderson song playing in the background. Quirky lyrics, Laura remembered, something about pineapples and school buses. Jonathan had introduced them, explaining to Sam that Laura was a medic and might be able to help him with plotlines for the new job he had just secured writing scripts for a medical drama. Even then Jonathan was trying to help organise Sam's life. She remembered Jonathan describing Sam as one to watch.

Laura should have said then that she had met Sam before. It was a fact that seemed irrelevant at the time, but gained importance over the years, when it became apparent that they disagreed on something both regarded as significant. Their first conversation had taken place during a house-warming party at Jonathan and Hannah's a couple of months earlier, just before Luke was born. Laura had decided to stay up all night and go straight to her A&E shift at St Mary's from their flat in Notting Hill. She had gone upstairs to the bathroom to splash water on her face and found Sam waiting outside, leaning against a wall covered with an Ordnance Survey map of London. He was obscuring Battersea Park.

She recognised Sam from photos Jonathan had shown her. When she walked past him to reach the bathroom, he had asked her about the map and she told him that Hannah had put it up in lieu of wallpaper. Sam had made a joke about the pressure of being twenty-two and having a friend the same age who already had a baby, owned his own flat, ran a successful business and had opinions on how his house should be decorated. Then Victoria had appeared and steered him back downstairs.

Over the years, the fact that they couldn't agree when they first met had turned from a standing joke into something more bittersweet. Sam could remember his first conversation with Janey (a description of a week spent with her mother and brother when she was a child on a Rajneesh commune in Suffolk near Sam's parents); his first conversation with Hannah (how to spot someone who was going to try and leave Jonathan's restaurant without paying); and his first encounter with Jonathan (Sam positively identified a magic mushroom in the school playground). But he couldn't remember this encounter with Laura.

When Laura thought about this now, she realised that this was probably because she had fallen in love with the idea of Sam, long before she had met him. There were the stories that Jonathan told about them growing up together in Suffolk. Funny tales of hopeless endeavour to win the girl they wanted, camping trips that ended ignominiously after they scared each other witless recounting the plotlines of horror stories, and foul-tasting dishes that Jonathan cobbled together from ingredients found in the hedgerow.

But it was a short story written by Sam for a university magazine that had sealed their fate. Laura found it underneath a pile of newspapers the day after Sam's first visit to Manchester. It was smeared with jam, butter and cigarette ash, cast aside by Jonathan, who had clearly forgotten its existence. Laura had picked it up and read it. It was a simple account of a girl meeting her half-brother for the first time. She couldn't believe that a twenty-one-year-old could write with such confidence and emotional insight. When she met Sam, her mind was already made up, although it was another five years before he finally managed to extricate himself from the relationship with Victoria. The problem with falling in love with the idea of someone is that of course reality rarely matches the fantasy.

Was that the first time Janey met Patrick? Laura tried to remember. She could remember Patrick staying in the flat with them on a number of occasions but was he there that same weekend? Did Sam take Patrick with him? The chronology of how Patrick blended into their life was hazy. But Laura was grateful for the lapse because she knew it meant that as far as her neural pathways were concerned, meeting Sam was the more significant event. The memory of that initial encounter had become a long-term memory, a permanent connection between the neurons, whereas the encounter with Patrick was conveniently deleted.

Who you slept with in your teens and twenties seemed irrelevant at the time but gained currency as time passed, decided Laura. Some provided historic fuel to current fantasies, others demonstrated nothing more than a worrying lapse of judgement. Considered chronologically, however, they provided a timeline that told you something of people's essential nature. The archaeology of relationships was obviously worth excavating. Apart from her own, of course, which should remain deeply buried.

Laura then considered the fact that both Janey and Sam had erroneously assumed that she had slept with Jonathan, and wondered whether now, as they sat in Eden, they were observing her in a different light in view of this mental decoupling. She suddenly felt claustrophobic. Could you know the same people for too long? she wondered. Could you have too much history? Steve certainly thought so and perhaps, Laura begrudgingly conceded, in part he was right. She imagined a future where Sam worked for Jonathan and their lives became entwined in the same way as they were in their twenties and the thought made her gasp for air.

'When Hannah has finished making the new beds we'll be able to give customers fresh asparagus within a day of harvest in late August. No other restaurant can do that,' said Jonathan, as he urged them to start the meal with a large plate of early asparagus covered in lemon and olive oil.

'And nor can we because the asparagus season finishes in mid June,' said Hannah breezily. 'You can bend a lot of things to your will, Jonathan, but not asparagus.'

'You must make acquaintance with the Jersey Royals, Laura,' said Hannah, leaning over the empty space between the two of them as if to impart an important secret. 'Spring is their time of year.' For a moment, Laura thought she must be talking about some new friends that she and Sam hadn't yet met. But when she looked down at the menu she realised Hannah was pointing at the list of vegetables.

'It's the seaweed fertiliser that makes them taste so good,' continued Hannah. 'But I love them because they are the first potatoes of spring.'

Hannah had arrived late on the train, carrying nothing more than a large handbag as luggage. It was three months since Laura had last seen her and she had changed in ways that were subtle when taken in isolation, but significant when considered in the round. Laura inspected the fingers tapping the words *Jersey Royals* and was amused to see hastily clipped fingernails with mud caked underneath. She turned Hannah's small bony hand over in her own and saw the palm was stained with a complex network of tiny muddy channels. It felt rough to the touch. Her face was windburnt and a few freckles had emerged around her nose. Unruly eyebrows made her lids appear heavier. Her hair was darker and longer than Laura had seen it in years. She had put on a little weight, adding a few curves to her naturally angular form. In Laura none of this would have resonated. But in Hannah the contrast was too great to ignore.

'Am I looking a bit agricultural?' she asked Laura in a teasing tone. 'Jonathan says I'm channelling *The Good Life*.'

'Definitely more Felicity Kendall than Penelope Keith,' confirmed Laura. But it was her essence that had altered, thought Laura. There was a fluidity to her movements that suggested a certain languid contentment. Laura wanted to question her more closely but she knew that the best way to elicit information from Hannah was to pretend not to be too interested. Hannah wasn't aloof, as Laura had initially assumed when she first encountered her. It was more that she liked to tell rather than be asked. Laura watched her contemplating Sam and wondered whether she had known about Sam and Janey for years and never said anything. Or perhaps she had never known.

'And before you start worrying about their carbon footprint, I should tell you that we offset the air miles from Jersey,' Jonathan teased Laura.

'The most interesting thing about asparagus is that only forty per cent of people can smell it in their piss,' said Sam. 'To the rest it's odourless, and the Chinese can't smell it at all. Maybe it has something to do with your blood group.'

'That is amazing,' said Janey. 'I wonder if it smells different if you're pregnant?'

'Perhaps we should conduct an experiment later,' suggested Jonathan. 'If you all deliver a urine sample we can examine the empirical evidence.' It was the sort of thing that years ago he might have persuaded them to do. And he would probably have pursued the idea further, because it would have been interesting to mention during interviews, fitting as it did with his image as someone with unrivalled knowledge about the quirks of British ingredients, had Steve not arrived.

Everyone apart from Laura stood up and made a fuss of Steve because they understood he was there under duress. Even Janey got up to give him a very public long kiss on the lips, explaining that they had both been working so hard they hadn't seen each other for three days. Laura remained seated because she thought that instead of making Steve feel welcome, the exuberance of the greeting underlined his outsider status. He sat down between her and Hannah and Laura thought she saw him gritting his teeth.

'Good of you to come. Especially given what's going on in the markets,' said Jonathan, trying not to sound gleeful. 'Must be an uncomfortable time for you Masters of the Universe.'

'In fact we have had our best two days ever,' said Steve, smiling at him. 'Most of our positions were held on the assumption there would be a downturn.'

'Oh,' said Jonathan, a little deflated.

'Even in these choppy waters, I can make more money on one trade than you make in an entire year,' teased Steve, ignoring Janey's kick from under the table.

A decade ago Jonathan had regarded people who worked in the City with a mixture of pity and derision for their lack of imagination in their choice of career and their long hours. When Janey announced she was becoming a corporate lawyer he had laughed in her face and accused her of selling out. The role models back then were Sam and Laura, who both had vocations for doing something motivated by loftier aims than the urge to make money. Jonathan, chameleon by nature, could claim a foot in both camps. Now, in their late thirties, with their mortgages covered and pension plans already overflowing, Steve's and Janey's choices seemed almost enlightened. They could probably retire within a decade.

'We have this amazing computer system that predicts

the market for us and it's made us almost £80 million in less than forty-eight hours,' said Steve. 'Of course we provide the analysis and feed in the stats but it's impressive nonetheless.'

He took off his jacket to reveal an expensive white shirt beneath. There was barely a wrinkle in its smooth surface and no signs of dried sweat under the armpits. Either Steve didn't sweat or he kept a spare shirt in the black leather briefcase that he insisted on putting between his feet underneath the table. He leant forward towards Janey and stuck out his arms, palms upwards in supplication. They stared at each other with a half smile as Janey took each wrist in her hand, traced a few small circles at the point where arm becomes hand, and then carefully removed each cufflink. Laura looked away, as if embarrassed to be witnessing such an intimate scene. It was a proprietorial gesture, directed, she guessed, at Sam.

'Turn down the heat a little or we'll all get burnt,' said Jonathan, raising an eyebrow as Janey adjusted her husband's shirtsleeves, rolling them up in careful turns until they sat just below his elbow. 'Shall we order?' he suggested.

'I think I'll have the mushroom risotto,' said Laura, snapping the menu shut with what she hoped was a persuasive finality. Ordering at Eden could be a protracted affair.

'Me too,' said Janey, with similar conviction.

'What about the baby, darling?' questioned Steve. 'What does the book say about fungi?'

'Mushrooms are fine,' said Janey, stroking his arm with one hand and her stomach with the other.

'You can't go wrong with a St George's mushroom,' said Jonathan approvingly. 'And you're in luck because they're a couple of weeks early this year.'

He approved of their choice, Laura realised with relief. There would be no further discussion of ingredients, no dissecting the recipe in order to urge them towards something that he really thought they should try.

'What if a rogue toadstool finds its way in?' asked Steve. Laura's heart sank.

'They come from a really reliable source in Herefordshire,' said Jonathan.

'The only one they resemble is the deadly fibrecap,' said Hannah, overcome with the urge to show off her mycological knowledge. '*Inocybe erubescens*. And they don't come out until later.'

'Sounds lethal. Just not worth the risk,' said Steve.

'So what would happen if you ate one?' asked Laura, her curiosity surpassing her appetite.

'Excessive urination, vomiting and diarrhoea. Slowing of the heart. Constriction of the lungs. It's the muscarine,' explained Hannah enthusiastically. 'But they're hardly ever fatal.'

'How reassuring,' said Steve sarcastically.

'And there's an antidote,' chipped in Sam. 'We did an episode in *Do Not Resuscitate* about a mass poisoning in a restaurant. You can treat it with atropine, which is really fascinating, because it's the same toxin you find in belladonna. So if you eat a deadly fibrecap followed by deadly nightshade, you should be fine.'

'Maybe I'll have the seared pigeon breast instead,' said Janey.

'Heartburn,' interrupted Steve. 'Why don't you have a piece of cod?'

'Cod,' said Jonathan abruptly. 'No one should eat cod any more. It's practically an endangered species. We don't even have it on the menu.'

'It's hardly like eating a polar bear,' laughed Steve.

'How about some albacore tuna?' Jonathan suggested. 'I've got some in the fridge. It's approved by the Marine Stewardship Council.'

'Too much mercury,' said Steve.

'The calf's liver then,' said Jonathan to the waiter.

'Too much vitamin A,' said Steve apologetically.

'Then the gurnard it is,' said Jonathan. 'The pregnant lady will have the gurnard. And her husband will risk life and limb with the mushroom risotto. Bankers are too used to playing it safe.'

'I'm not a banker,' spluttered Steve. 'I manage a hedge fund. They're very different jobs.'

'How so?' asked Laura politely. 'I've never really understood the subtle differences between you City folk.'

'They're all arrogant, but in different degrees,' muttered Jonathan. Steve either didn't hear or chose to ignore him.

'We're more imaginative,' said Steve, leaning expansively back in his chair. 'Bankers are wage slaves like everyone else, private-equity people gamble with other people's money, but we're the 007s of the financial world. We put our money where our mouths are.'

Laura coughed, as was her habit when embarrassed by something that someone had said or done.

'Do you know what plant family asparagus belongs to?' asked Hannah. Steve appeared taken aback. He was used to his conversation being indulged. He shrugged his shoulders.

'I couldn't possibly hazard a guess,' said Steve, who didn't like getting things wrong.

'It's a type of lily,' said Hannah triumphantly. 'A recipe for cooking it appears in the world's first cookery book in 200 BC. Imagine, people have been cooking asparagus for more than twenty-four centuries.'

'That's twenty-two centuries,' observed Steve pedantically.

'Well, it's a long time, anyway,' said Hannah. 'East Anglia is one of the first places it was grown in the country. The soil there is very alkaline.'

'I used to eat it a lot when I was at Cambridge,' said Steve. Hannah caught Laura's eye. Since he had first appeared on the scene with Janey, they had taken to timing how long into a conversation it would take him to mention his degree from Cambridge. This was possibly a new record.

Sam looked across at Hannah with a mixture of awe and disbelief as she continued to eulogise about asparagus. She had an amazing ability to throw herself into different ventures with utter enthusiasm and then extricate herself with barely a blush a few months later. When her children were small she had dabbled in photography, then for a brief period taught piano before undertaking a horticultural course. All of these had been done to such a high standard that she could have turned any of them into a full-time career. Then a decade ago, when the children were older, to everyone's surprise she had helped Jonathan to set up Eden. She had an extraordinary ability to reinvent herself. It should have given Sam belief in the possibility of change; instead it exhausted him.

'The male asparagus are more fertile than the female . . . we're sowing from seed in a couple of months . . . the same bed can last twenty years,' she said. 'Can you imagine, I will be almost sixty when we need to change it again. It's like relationships: you have to get things right from the start, otherwise the cracks start to appear later. The beds take three years before they start to be productive.'

'Is that your secret with Jonathan?' Steve asked benignly.

'Well, we're not a very good example of that, are we?' she smiled back. 'He was going out with someone else when I got pregnant with Luke.'

Sam's eyes felt heavy. He could feel the lids bearing down so he stared at Janey in an effort to focus on something that might force them to stay open. This was the price you paid for lunchtime drinking, he realised. But his script was almost finished and a drink with Jonathan provided useful punctuation to the day. He found himself entranced by the sight of Janey's stomach rising and falling beside him and resisted the urge to lean over and rest his head on the enticing mass for a few moments. The baby would surely kick and that was something that always made him feel squeamish, as did the sight of Janey's belly button protruding through her T-shirt. Why did men hate that so much? Was it because it reminded them of the umbilical bond with their own mother?

He continued to stare at Janey's stomach, as though it could provide him with answers to the unfathomable. There was something primeval about pregnant women. It wasn't simply their size. It was their animal-like instinct, the way they craved strange foods, their ability to discern different flavours and their animal sense of smell. They were steeped in ancient mystery. That was their power.

An image of him lying in bed with Janey suddenly came to mind. He would lie down beside her and Janey's soft presence would soothe the parts that the alcohol couldn't reach. Then he would sleep without waking up for an entire night. If he tried to explain this desire to anyone they would assume it had a sexual edge. But Janey had long ceased to be the object of Sam's sexual fantasy, least of all in her current state. Listening to those conversations she used to have over the kitchen table with Laura late into the night had killed off that possibility. God, he even knew, improbable as it seemed, that Steve was master of the clitoral orgasm. Perhaps that was why she had married him. There had to be some compensations. If she had married Patrick it would have been so different.

'Anyone who knows me well understands exactly why I favour matrix over classic methods,' Steve was telling Hannah. For a moment Sam thought he was referring to some sexual technique. Then he realised he was pontificating about the benefits of different business models for managing large corporations. Steve licked his top lip several times with his tongue and Sam considered its flaccid pointed pink tip in a new light.

'So what's your news?' Janey asked Jonathan in an effort to steer the conversation on to safer terrain.

'Well, I'm in the middle of filming my first TV series,' said Jonathan.

'Which is why I never see him,' interrupted Hannah, without sounding very concerned.

'Is it about your discovery of British cuisine?' asked Steve. Jonathan ignored the thinly veiled disdain.

'It's about places in Britain which spawned classic ingredients and recipes,' he said, smiling benignly.

'That sounds fantastic,' said Janey enthusiastically. 'Where have you been so far?'

'I've done knobs in Dorset, tarts in Bakewell and chaps in Bath,' said Jonathan blithely. 'Where are you from, Steve?'

'Tewkesbury,' said Steve.

'Then I'll do you too,' said Jonathan, with a wry grin as he reached over to touch Steve's arm. Steve leant back in his chair and pulled his hand sharply away from the table, knocking over a small bowl of salt in the process.

'His wit's as thick as Tewkesbury mustard,' Jonathan said, licking his finger and sticking it in the salt. 'Falstaff in *Henry IV*. It's one of our oldest sauces.'

'Then he's doing Stilton in Leicestershire, salt in Maldon, pork pies in Melton Mowbray, and the last Aylesbury duck producer,' explained Hannah proudly.

'Are the children missing you?' Laura asked Jonathan.

'It's a toss-up whether they're more resentful about my absence or about moving to Suffolk,' said Jonathan. 'But there are some compensations, including one I'm hoping my friends might benefit from.'

Everyone looked up from the big plate of asparagus that had arrived in front of them.

'I want to invite you all to come on holiday for a week to celebrate my fortieth birthday in July,' said Jonathan, smiling benevolently around the table.

'That's a very generous offer, Jonathan,' said Laura a little too quickly. 'But we've already got plans.'

'Have we?' asked Sam, sounding surprised.

Laura stared at him hard, sending a subliminal message about the precise cost of their mortgage, the exact limit of their overdraft facility, and how utility bills had increased over the previous three months. Did he not remember they were debating between buying a new set of tyres for the car or painting window sills whose layers had peeled back to the wood? How could he imagine they could afford to go on holiday with the people gathered around this table?

She considered the reverse alchemy in relationships, where the traits that made Sam so beguiling when she first met him gradually lost their allure and became the very characteristics that infuriated her most. His relaxed attitude was shorthand for laziness; his hedonism a by-product of retreat from the world just when she needed him to be fully engaged with it; his lack of concern over their financial situation a mark of irresponsibility rather than liberation.

'It's all expenses paid,' said Jonathan jocularly. 'A magazine has offered to send me and a group of my closest friends to do a piece about cooking and friendship to coincide with the start of my television series. But that shouldn't affect us too much. They'll send a journalist for a day and then leave us alone. The highlight involves me cooking a meal for you all.'

'But how are you going to do that?' Laura asked incredulously.

'I'll fudge it,' said Jonathan. 'And that's why I want you guys there, because I know you won't stitch me up.'

'Well in that case, I'm in if you're in?' Sam said, hoping for affirmation from Laura. She nodded her head with a tight smile. 'Maybe we could leave the children with your parents?'

'That sounds great,' Laura said, knowing that she was cornered.

'Can I bring the new baby?' asked Janey.

'Absolutely,' agreed Jonathan.

'So where are we going?' asked Steve. 'I'm not sure we'll be able to travel very far with a young baby and I need to be within BlackBerry range.'

'An island,' said Jonathan mysteriously. 'An island so remote that you can only reach it by boat.'

'A Greek one?' suggested Laura, trying to muster enthusiasm.

'Corsica?' proffered Janey hopefully.

'You can fly to Corsica,' Steve pointed out.

'The Isle of Coll,' said Jonathan with self-satisfaction.

'Where's that?' asked Sam.

'It's in the Inner Hebrides,' said Jonathan triumphantly.

6

Each time she checked to see whether Nell and Ben were asleep in the back of the car, Laura's right shoulder protested. She wriggled the joint around in the socket resolving that next week she would go and make an appointment with a colleague in the physiotherapy unit and get a shot of corticosteroid. Otherwise she would end up with a frozen shoulder. But the chances of the children falling asleep so early in the evening were as remote as the Suffolk landscape unfolding either side of the A12. She stared out the window, hoping for ten uninterrupted minutes in which she could tease out the details of Sam's professional freefall, without revealing what she already knew. Laura understood enough about the relationship between the mind and body to know if only he could talk about this, then the knot in her shoulder would unravel. Just last week she had seen a patient whose neuropathic disorder was apparently cured by the purchase of a washing machine.

'A watched pot never boils,' advised Sam, as he headed up the dual carriageway. Behind the wheel he was everything he wasn't in other parts of his life: decisive, aggressive and ambitious. *The Cat in the Hat* finished on the CD player. For the fourth time. It was now seven o'clock and Sam had negotiated with Nell and Ben that if they all recited Dr Seuss together one last time without any mistakes, then he could switch to Radio Four to catch the headlines. Laura questioned the wisdom of listening to the news in front of her children. She argued that Nell and Ben should be protected from early exposure to the vicissitudes of human nature, worrying that it might make them grow up anxious and nervous about the world they lived in. Like her mother, she thought, but didn't say. Sam said that apart from headlines about rape, paedophiles and murder, it didn't matter what they heard. Mostly they didn't notice and if they did, it was generally positive that they began to learn about the reality of other people's lives, because it might give them some perspective on their own. Laura deferred to Sam, as she often did in parenting matters, because he spent more time with Nell and Ben and that had undermined her power of veto.

There had been riots in Tibet. J P Morgan wanted to lower the price it had offered to buy Bear Stearns. Shares in Lehman Brothers had dropped sixteen per cent, but everything was apparently fine. 'Our liquidity position has been and continues to be very strong . . .' someone was quoted. Unlike ours, thought Laura, who had opened her bank statement just as they reached the A12.

'Do you know it's the vernal equinox today?' Sam asked Nell and Ben. He never talked down to his children, Laura thought with admiration, as she heard him patiently start to explain how just twice a year everyone in the world had exactly twelve hours of darkness and twelve hours of light.

'Equinox means equal night and day,' he said. 'From

today, the North Pole will start pointing towards the sun again. Easter always comes on the first Sunday after the full moon of the equinox.'

'And so do the chocolate eggs,' said Ben.

'And so do the chocolate eggs,' Sam reassured him.

There was a short silence. Laura knew Ben was processing this information.

'Mummy,' said Ben eventually, 'when I was an egg did you keep me in the airing cupboard? And if you did, why didn't I melt?'

'Human beings don't lay eggs,' said Laura, turning round to face Ben. He was still young enough that his cheeks resembled hamster pouches and his face was all pouting lips and saucer eyes. She reached into the back, ignoring her screaming shoulder joint, and drew a gentle line with her finger down his face from the top of his forehead to the end of his nose. He closed his eyes with satisfaction.

'Ben, I know how we were made,' Nell announced authoritatively. Ben looked at her expectantly. 'I've seen it on television. Mummy and Daddy circle each other. They move closer and closer, then one of them bites the other to show interest,' Nell began, 'then they release slime, more slime than you can possibly imagine, and they start to wind themselves around each other tighter and tighter for about an hour. When they are as entwined as my plait, Daddy's sperm visit Mummy and then Mummy's sperm visit Daddy. And that's how we were perceived.'

'I told you David Attenborough muddied the waters,' Sam murmured to Laura. 'You've got to sit down with her and explain.'

'There's never time,' muttered Laura, as she turned

towards Nell. 'That's the way leopard sea slugs do it, Nell, but human beings are –'

'Quicker,' said Sam. Another spasm gripped Laura's shoulder.

A little later, Laura picked her way round the unfamiliar bedroom in Hannah and Jonathan's Suffolk home, wearing nothing more than underwear and a pair of uncharacteristically high heels. Nell and Ben were in bed, possibly asleep, in a room down the corridor. Sam had dutifully read them *The Cat in the Hat* (their choice, not his), weighing up the advantage of being able to recite it with his eyes closed against the disadvantage of not being able to miss out chunks to speed up the process.

Sam leaned back on the rather small double bed and took the opportunity to observe Laura at close quarters. Her stomach was full and round and looked pleased with itself, as though relieved to have escaped from the top of the rather stern pair of knickers that she had pulled on a few minutes earlier. It moved with her body and the general effect was one of pleasing synchronicity, although he knew she wouldn't agree.

He might have forgotten the first time they met, but he could recall the first time they slept together with significant detail. He recalled how Laura's body was soft and undulating and seemed to ripple beneath his touch. Afterwards she walked round the bedroom naked, unselfconsciously picking up her clothes, allowing him to consume her all over again. It was impossible to avoid comparisons with Victoria, who was all bones and harsh angles. Bumping against her pelvis was a bruising experience and made Sam worry she might break up into little pieces.

Laura's breasts, contained nowadays in bras that spoke of assiduous engineering rather than the perky attention-seeking that characterised the early part of their relationship, were pushed firmly together, jostling for supremacy. Sam had always liked voluptuous women and he enjoyed the way that his wife now occupied her body with such authority. What man wanted straight lines when he could have contours? he wondered. He relished a body that had perspective. Her shape embodied the essence of her personality. Laura's solid form spoke of a grounded nature. Neurotic women were nearly always thin, he concluded. And right now, more than anything in the world, Sam needed someone strong enough to pull him to shore.

'What's up?' asked Laura, when she realised he was staring at her from the bed. She smiled down at him and then continued her careful exploration of the bedroom. Her face was fresh and rosy, so quintessentially English that it made Sam smile. Without lipstick her lips were exactly the same colour as her nipples. He was surprised he hadn't noticed this before.

'Looks good,' said Sam appreciatively.

He thought more about the unfamiliar ensemble Laura was wearing. He had never had much interest in the contents of his wife's underwear drawer and it puzzled him that despite the enforced intimacy of more than a decade of marriage, there were so many things about her that had become more mysterious rather than less. There was her astonishing behaviour over the marriage guidance counsellor of course, but that was clearly an aberration. Most of the changes were more domestic: voices on the answer machine that he didn't recognise; dinner with couples whose names he couldn't remember by the time he made coffee; new friends who appeared at their home with unfamiliar children in tow. It struck him that Laura spent more time with people he didn't know than she did with him.

It also occurred to him as he stared at her body in the dappled evening light that whilst he was very familiar with its individual components – the way the skin puckered above her navel or the constellation of freckles on her forearm – it was a very long time since he had appreciated it as more than the sum of its parts. In fact, since they'd had children, he couldn't remember the last time that he had seen her in this languid state of unselfconscious undress. She was usually in perpetual motion, feverishly throwing clothes on and off, worrying about being late for everything. Even in sleep she moved restlessly around the bed, never waking in the same position. Laura never had time to herself, Sam thought guiltily.

Now she walked slowly, lifting each foot a little higher than necessary, in a way that was studious rather than coltish, trying to find her new centre of gravity. He liked the way that the shoes made her walk because it was both unfamiliar and made her more vulnerable than she really was. Although of course Sam would never say so to Laura, there was a part of him that secretly relished what she had done: the way she had attempted to unmask him was spectacular. And it had curtailed a number of awkward conversations. There had, for example, been no mention of having another child for more than three weeks and surely that was a record. He leant over to write a few notes in a black notebook that sat on the bedside table beside a bottle of vodka.

'I'm thinking about spare bedrooms,' Sam lied.

'And our lack of one?' Laura questioned, raising an eyebrow.

'How they are like spinster aunts,' Sam replied, ignoring her comment. 'Lonely and neglected for most of the year and wheeled out only on special occasions wearing shabby clothes and smelling of lavender water.'

That wasn't what he was thinking about, but he was right, thought Laura, glancing at an old wooden clock on the mantelpiece to discover it was time to go downstairs. Even though it was the beginning of spring, and the window had been open all day, the room was musty and airless. It spoke of a different era: one where en suite bathrooms didn't exist and sinks were called vanity units and counted as impressive addenda to guest bedrooms.

There was just one picture, hung too high on the wall on the other side of the room opposite the window, which meant that the reflection from the sun on glass made it impossible to appreciate. In any case it was lost amidst the jungle of floral wallpaper in pink and avocado green. The curtains and even the lampshades were made in the same fabric. Hannah had warned her that this was the only room that hadn't yet been repainted, but insisted they sleep there because it had the best view over the garden.

'There are no more spinsters any more,' said Laura, who was now facing him, applying mascara without a mirror, a habit that made Sam wince because she nearly always poked herself in the eye.

'That sounds like a line from a Stranglers song,' said Sam.

'And that reminds me,' said Laura. 'Please no competitiveness over music trivia. It's so tedious.'

'But we enjoy it,' protested Sam. 'It makes us feel young. Makes me remember a time when everything was possibilities instead of responsibilities.'

'It makes the rest of us feel old,' muttered Laura.

'You can't censor my conversation,' said Sam, taking another long drink from the glass on the bedside table.

'But you censor mine,' Laura persisted, waving the mascara in the air for emphasis.

'What don't I let you talk about?' asked Sam bemusedly.

'How much you are drinking, for example?' she said, staring at him solemnly.

'I'm drowning my sex drive rather than finding another outlet for it,' he joked. 'It's a heroic gesture.' She ignored him and continued.

'Why, for example, you were so comfortable with the idea that your wife once slept with your best friend; whether we should go to church so that our children can get into a better school; how you were considering a clandestine vasectomy,' she began, using a different finger to emphasise each point. 'Mostly why you spend so much time locked away in your office every evening without anything to show for it.' There was a long silence.

'Do you know that we are conforming to a national stereotype here?' said Sam, who had discovered over the years that many arguments could be diverted by asking questions. Laura looked puzzled and stuck the mascara wand into her eye.

'Oh God,' she winced in pain. Sam's eyes began to water in sympathy.

'Couples have more arguments on public holidays than any other time of the year,' Sam continued, pouring himself another generous slug of vodka from the bottle on the bedside table. He picked up a magazine. It was an old issue of *Vogue* that fell open on a page with a brief profile of Jonathan and a review of Eden shortly after it had opened.

'This isn't an argument. It's a discussion,' said Laura, trying to divert the black stream of mascara flowing down the side of her left cheek.

'"Is there anything Jonathan Sleet can't do?"' Sam read out the headline to Laura.

'Cook?' suggested Laura, who was busy trying to remove lumps of mascara from her eye.

'"His instinctive approach to English cuisine and use of seasonal produce is unrivalled. He should be given national-treasure status,"' read Sam.

'It's incredible that no one rumbles him,' laughed Laura. 'It's because of Hannah. Without her, he couldn't make it work.'

'He'd just find someone else who could,' said Sam unthinkingly, before pouring himself another vodka and tonic. 'One of Jonathan's greatest skills is surrounding himself with people who compensate for his weaknesses.'

'How do we fit into that scheme?' asked Laura.

'Our insecurity heightens his sense of security,' said Sam. 'That's why we're here. We make Hannah and Jonathan feel better about themselves.'

*

It wasn't always that way, thought Laura. When she was introduced to Jonathan, during their first year at Manchester, it was because he had cut off the tip of his finger with a bread knife. Someone from his house came in search of a medic and Laura half-heartedly agreed to take a look because she was the only one in her flat still awake at two o'clock in the morning. She had an exam the following day and reluctantly closed the chapter on Gram-negative bacteria to head over to Jonathan's flat.

She found Jonathan standing against the kitchen wall looking pale and dreamy. Blood from his finger dripped rhythmically on to the floor. Janey stood beside him drinking a glass of water so quickly that it slopped over her purple top. They stared at her, their pupils fully dilated, and Jonathan tried to give her a hug. His thick black curls were so long and the beam from the light so pale that it looked as though he was wearing a large woolly hat.

Their kitchen was a complete mess. There were dirty plates and cups stacked high in the sink, half-empty saucepans on the cooker, and a pile of dirty laundry beside the washing machine. If she looked hard enough, she could probably find Gram-negative bacteria here, thought Laura, her mind still in her textbook.

She instructed Jonathan to hold his finger above his head and he meekly obliged, telling her that he loved her. When the blood stopped dripping, Laura led Jonathan towards the sink, warning him not to touch anything, because she wanted to clean the wound. The tip of the finger hung by a small thread of flesh and Laura thought she could knit it back together with some careful bandaging. Janey observed from beneath her long black fringe and Laura admired her cheekbones and porcelain skin. Laura assumed they were brother and sister. After this, Jonathan decided that he needed Laura in his life, and even though she was initially a reluctant recruit into his close-knit group of friends, Jonathan insisted that they live together during their second year.

As she now meandered towards a large mahogany chest of drawers at the other end of the room, the sort that always stick and smell of mothballs, Laura wanted to tell Sam that they shouldn't be here. Last-minute invitations only worked when they were extended in a spirit of spontaneity that made everyone feel youthful again. Jonathan's late-night phone call to Sam suggesting they come and stay for a couple of days over Easter was born of more adult emotions involving a complex chemistry of sympathy and guilt.

Laura could feel Sam's gaze on her back and knew that he either wanted to talk about something related to the script that she was meant to know nothing about or to have sex. Neither was an attractive prospect right now because both subjects had become so complicated. She closed her eyes momentarily and imagined the web of synapses that had formed in her brain to deal with these two conflicting strands of her life. They would resemble balls of wool, she decided, their ends so entangled that no one would be able to unravel where one started and the other ended.

Sexual dissatisfaction was a mysterious disease because it was invisible to the naked eye, which made it difficult to diagnose in other people. You could only feel it yourself. And articulating its symptoms only made it worse. Which made it a virtually incurable condition. Engaging in Sam's deceit that he was still working for *Do Not Resuscitate* was more immediately challenging.

She half wondered whether his failure to find professional fulfilment had also killed her own sense of ambition, as though any further success might throw them irrevocably off balance. She thought of a name for this peculiarly twenty-first-century condition: 'Subliminal professional empathy,' she muttered angrily to herself.

So when she grabbed the handle of one of the small top drawers in the heavy mahogany chest, she used more force than she intended to pull it open. Instead of sticking, however, it escaped so swiftly that both the drawer and its contents spilled on to the floor. Laura realised that Hannah had covered the sides with either soap or candle wax to make them open smoothly, a gesture that spoke volumes of her attention to detail.

'What are you doing?' asked Sam loudly. The noise had made him jump and he had banged his temple on the carved oak headboard.

'Clues,' said Laura. 'You can tell a lot about people from what they keep in their spare bedroom. It's the stuff they forget to censor.'

He sat up straight to see what she had unearthed. On the floor lay a packet of brand-new handkerchiefs, still in their plastic wrapping, a bundle of menus from one of the restaurants Jonathan used to manage, a half-used bottle of Anaïs Anaïs perfume, a foreign newspaper, and a half-empty packet of themed condoms. Laura noticed that only the red ones were left. *Hot mint* it read on the side.

'Who would benefit from a mint-flavoured condom?' Laura asked, and then immediately regretted the question because Sam might insist that the only way to really discover was to try one.

'Someone with bad breath?' he suggested, as she threw it over to him for closer examination.

'Amazing to think Jonathan and Hannah are still at it after all these years,' said Laura thoughtfully.

'But why wouldn't they stick to their own bedroom?' asked Sam.

'Maybe they find the anonymity of the room creates the right atmosphere?' suggested Laura.

'If you're proposing that a bedroom decorated in a style associated with the mid seventies might reignite your libido, then we should redecorate immediately,' said Sam. 'You, me and Laura Ashley could be an explosive combination.' He was only half joking.

'It's not the decor, it's the fact it's a neutral room with no history,' she explained.

'So it's about the size of our house,' Sam retorted. Nowadays it seemed all their arguments were circular, ending as they usually did with Laura bemoaning their two-bedroom terraced house on the wrong side of Kensal Rise. 'I thought we'd banned any further discussion over that issue.'

'That's not what I meant,' said Laura, who was now kneeling on the floor putting everything back into the drawer. 'What I mean is that if you are somewhere unfamiliar you're not reminded of the things that distract you when you're at home. You don't have that situation where you're having sex and you see a crack down the wall and think the house might have subsidence and then you remember you haven't renewed the building insurance.'

'Is that what you think about when we have sex?' Sam asked in disbelief. 'Subsidence?'

'I don't lose myself in the moment, if that's what you mean,' said Laura. 'I don't lack the will, just the energy, the opportunity and the desire. And I don't think Laura Ashley would help.'

'That's quite a lot of obstacles,' responded Sam.

'It's got nothing to do with you,' she said. 'I'm just too tired. I don't want to have sex with anyone really.'

'Well that's deeply reassuring,' Sam said, his tone laced with a little more sarcasm than he intended. 'I'm getting a little fed up with the narcissistic relationship I have developed with myself, although the muscle tone in my right bicep is formidable.'

'But it's not just me is it, Sam?' asked Laura intently.

Sam didn't reply. Sometimes he wondered if he would ever have sex again. With anyone. Because although Laura used to consider him a catch, she didn't any more, and the idea that other women might find him attractive was not one that had occurred to him until the debacle at the end of February. He smelt of failure and there was nothing more repellent to a woman.

He couldn't even justify his existence by claiming that he was entertaining people any more. When he was out at night with people he didn't know, he had stopped describing himself as a scriptwriter, because it sounded more glamorous than it was, at least at the level he was pitched. His job was now as predictable as an accountant's, without the benefit of similar financial remuneration. So he now told people that was what he was, because it tended to stop a conversation in its tracks, the male equivalent of saying you were a stay-at-home mum.

Sam sighed deeply and sank further into the bed. If he lay still for long enough he might simply disappear into its doughy welcome, never to emerge again, weighed down by the burdens of life. He felt consumed by the bed in a way that was reassuring to someone with so many uncertainties. He imagined himself as a piece of plasticine being moulded and pressed into the mattress until he became part of it. It was a strangely relaxing image, aided by the three vodka and tonics he had consumed since the children had gone to sleep.

That was the beauty of old friends. You could drink alone in your room before dinner or fall asleep on the sofa afterwards without anyone thinking you were either unsociable or alcoholic. They were like old pieces of furniture: they might have flaws, several in Jonathan's case, but at least their fallibilities were familiar and the patterns of their imperfections predictable.

Having put back the drawer, Laura walked over to the lonely picture on the wall. The height of her heels brought it level with her nose. It was an old black-and-white photo of a group of people in their late twenties on an old canal boat. It must have been taken from a bridge because the photographer was looking down at them all. The composition of the image was perfect. They all appeared connected even though no one was obviously touching each other and most were looking away from the camera. But that only added to the atmosphere because rather than being posed, it seemed as though the image had been unexpectedly stolen, which enhanced its authenticity.

Laura was struck by how young and carefree everyone looked.

Only one person stared up at the camera, a young girl who stood in the foreground, just off centre. Laura stepped forward to observe her features more closely: she was wearing cut-off denim jeans and a bikini top; her face was framed by long hair parted haphazardly in the middle and she was looking at the camera almost insouciantly, hand on hip, with a vague half smile, as though she was the keeper of everyone's secrets.

Laura was startled to realise that she was staring at herself. It was a picture taken during a long weekend spent on a barge in Shropshire eleven years earlier. It marked a watershed: a month later Laura and Sam were married; Patrick left Janey for the first time and failed to turn up for Sam and Laura's wedding; Jonathan put in a bid for the premises that would become Eden and announced to the excitement of Luke, then almost seven, and his younger sister Gaby that he was finally going to marry their mother.

The photograph made Laura feel uneasy. She had never seen it before and struggled to remember who had brought a camera on board. Perhaps Hannah had unearthed the picture while moving house. The trip was memorable not least because it was one of Jonathan's earliest acts of ostentatious benevolence to his friends and the last holiday they all spent together. He was steering the boat. Hannah sat on the roof of the barge just behind him. On Jonathan's left was Sam, passing something to Janey that was too fat and smoky to be a cigarette. It was an image that would now make Janey wince.

It must have been taken on the last day of the three-day

trip. She remembered they had moored the boat illegally on the bank of a small channel in the evening, built a fire and partied through the night. Jonathan's dog was lying on top of her left foot. At the back of the boat was a friend of Sam's whom Laura recognised, although she couldn't remember his name. He had long hair and a honed upper torso that Laura appreciated more in her late thirties than she had in her late twenties. He was, she recalled, an old flame of Janey's who predated Patrick. Nothing about Janey back then was easy to reconcile with the person she had become, especially when it came to her choice of boyfriends. At the back of the boat was another couple whom Laura hadn't come across for years. That accounted for eight, but she was sure there was someone missing. She was of course forgetting to take into account the photographer, Patrick.

They all looked so young. Yet they hadn't really changed. How have we evolved? Who has changed the most? Laura wondered. She reached out to the photo and drew a line down the small image of herself, wanting to reconnect with the person she saw before her. She was surprised to find that she felt such a wave of nostalgia that her stomach ached as though she was winded. The sudden awareness of time passing was like a body blow. She sighed loudly and walked away quickly.

'What is it?' asked Sam.

'An old photo of us all, nothing really,' she said, feeling drained. 'You should check it out.'

Laura walked back towards their bag and pulled out a creased dress that he hadn't seen before. It was cream with thin grey stripes and broderie anglaise around the sleeves and the hem. She leaned over and precariously stepped into the dress, pushed her arms into the sleeves and struggled to pull it up over her thighs. Sam winced inwardly. Men of his age got off lightly really.

'Mind over matter, mind over matter,' muttered Laura, wriggling and squirming to force the dress towards her hips.

'Does it belong to Hannah?' Sam enquired. It was a reasonable question. The shoes almost certainly did.

'No, it's mine,' said Laura enthusiastically. 'A new purchase. What do you think?'

'Very Watteau. All you need is a yoke and you'd look like a milkmaid,' he said.

'Not a look I was hoping to achieve,' Laura replied.

'I've always had a thing for milkmaids,' said Sam appreciatively, reaching over to pull her towards the bed.

'I can't really move,' she said, remaining stiffly upright. 'I can only manoeuvre up and down.'

'That's all it takes,' Sam suggested hopefully.

'What do you think, honestly?' Laura asked again as the zip moved a couple of centimetres up her back.

'Difficult to tell at the moment,' observed Sam, knowing that whatever he said was liable to be misinterpreted. 'Maybe they sold you the wrong size?'

'I think I've got the opposite of anorexia,' muttered Laura, sufficiently buoyed by her progress to ignore Sam's comment. 'I think I'm smaller than I am.'

'Maybe if you lose the knickers you'll create more space,' suggested Sam helpfully.

'I don't think so,' she said firmly. 'Besides, they have a restraining influence on my stomach.'

'If you lie flat on the bed on your front and stretch your arms out in front of you, that might give you more purchase,' suggested Sam, patting the space beside him.

'As long as you promise not to take advantage of me,' she said. 'We must go downstairs otherwise Hannah will feel abandoned.'

'Hannah is used to being abandoned,' said Sam dismissively, taking another gulp of vodka and tonic. The prospect of analysing someone else's marriage was even more exhausting than considering his own. He wanted to forget life outside the confines of this bedroom in this house so familiar to him from his childhood and pretend that he and Laura were on a weekend away together.

'What kind of man is late for his own party?' Laura asked. The chance of a ramble around Jonathan's psyche was always irresistible to her. He was a complicated man involved in questionable patterns of behaviour. But she resisted the urge to tell Sam about what she had overheard in the restaurant in case she sounded paranoid.

'A busy man,' said Sam, still hoping to steer the conversation in another direction.

'You're so loyal,' groaned Laura, who was now lying on her front beside him on the bed, her hands adrift above her head. 'I wish I had your disposition.'

'Anyway she's not alone,' said Sam. 'She's speaking to one of their Slovakian farm workers.'

Sam was used to being described in terms better suited to a Labrador, even by his wife. People talked in front of him about his even temperament, his loyalty and his enthusiasm in the same way that parents talked about their children as if they weren't really there. It didn't bother him particularly. He accepted it as the corollary of being the type of person who seemed to want nothing more from life than what he already had. Until recently he was assumed to be content.

Sam ran a finger down Laura's spine, lingering at the base, but there was little possibility of creating any space where flesh and dress became one. He felt Laura shiver. When he was satisfied that there was no resistance, Sam contented himself with stroking a small patch of skin at the point where the crease in her buttocks began. He found the dimples either side of her spine and leant over to kiss them, gratified to find that the alcohol hadn't dampened his libido. But then libido wasn't the problem, the challenge was sustaining it. How to avoid that dangerous dip in nitric oxide.

Laura moved on to her side, her back towards him. Encouraged by her acquiescence, Sam slid his hand around her stomach and up towards her breasts. He pulled down the left sleeve of her dress and put his hand inside the unfamiliar purple and black bra. The lace scratched his skin and he pulled it away with more force than he intended to release the breast before Laura could protest. Then he began to trace small circles around her nipple until he felt it go hard between his fingers and Laura rolled on to her back.

From the bed Laura could see out of the long, generous window into the garden below. The first section consisted of flowerbeds designed to appear careless rather than crafted. Laura had spent enough time with Hannah to know that this was like assuming the ensemble she would be wearing tonight was in any way haphazard. The combination of artichokes, alliums and euphorbia would have been meticulously planned. The second part was still a project. There were plans for a wildflower meadow and an enormous vegetable garden with the potential to supply Eden.

'Do you think they can see us?' asked Laura, as Sam headed towards her nipple. She felt his other hand push the new dress up above her thighs and she wriggled to ease its progress over her hips.

'I don't care,' said Sam, glancing out the window to find the young man staring towards him.

His hand was now stroking Laura's inner thigh and finding its way past the forbidding knickers. Laura relaxed. The strangest thing about the long period of abstinence drawing to a close was that Laura always enjoyed sex with Sam when it happened. It reminded her of why she had been drawn to him in the first place: he enjoyed women with an unselfconscious certainty. Sam climbed on top of her, unzipped his jeans and pushed inside. This was more progress than they had made in months.

Laura glanced down into the garden and was pleased to see Hannah completely distracted by the gardener. She was gesticulating with her hands, trying to impress upon him the need to widen the raised beds and make them higher. His English was obviously limited. She held her hands as wide as possible and he walked over to her and carefully measured the exact span between the left and right hand. His left hand was pressed against Hannah's right to hold the end of the tape measure in place and he was forced to take a step towards her to keep it taut enough to reach the other hand. In its own way, it was a scene as intimate as that taking place in the bedroom.

Laura surrendered to the moment. The bed wheezed back and forth and the oak headboard banged rhythmically against the wall but there was synchronicity in their movement. Sam watched her, and the way her lips were half open and pouting and her breath came in small puffs reminded him of childbirth. Sam groaned and for a moment Laura thought that the pent-up frustration of the past six months had cost her an early orgasm.

'I can't do it,' Sam said, pulling out of her.

'What do you mean?' asked Laura.

'I'm defeated by your fecundity,' he said breathlessly, still lying on top of her.

'Don't be ridiculous,' said Laura. 'I'm not a fertility symbol.'

'I can't fuck because I'm too traumatised by the idea you might get pregnant,' said Sam, rolling on to his back.

'It's safe,' said Laura. Sam snorted.

'There's a mint-flavoured condom in that drawer,' said Laura, pointing to the other side of the room. 'You could use two if you're feeling unlucky. Double mint.'

'Ben is living proof of the fallibility of condoms,' said Sam, staring at the ceiling. 'Your desire to have another baby is stronger than my ability to prevent it. My sperm are in thrall to your eggs. And that has a catastrophic effect on my penis.'

Laura looked down and saw his erection deflate like a slow puncture. As she observed his penis wilting, a reel of inappropriate tangles played in her mind: in the church after the practice for their wedding; on her parents' kitchen table; at Sam's London flat after United lost to Everton in the 1995 FA Cup final; during the Oscars ceremony when *Forrest Gump* won Best Picture.

'Tell me about when you first had sex with the German au pair who worked for Jonathan's family,' said Laura, using a tactic recommended to her by Janey.

'Did I tell you about that?' Sam sounded worried and continued to stare at the ceiling.

'What is the worst thing that could happen?' asked Laura, using a method learnt during a cognitive behavioural therapy course that she had done to help patients overcome anxieties relating to their illnesses.

'You could get pregnant,' Sam said.

'But why would that be so awful?' Laura asked.

'Count the ways,' said Sam, struggling to zip up Laura's dress. 'We don't have enough money, we don't have a big enough house, we're as exhausted as a couple of old dogs and I don't think our marriage could take it.'

'That sounds pretty definitive,' said Laura. She felt curiously detached, partly because she knew she could only process the emotional implications of what Sam was saying when she was alone. What was more irrational, she wondered, her overwhelming need to have another baby when everyone around her advised her that it was folly or Sam's equally vehement desire not to?

'I sit staring at my computer screen every day, wondering "Is this it?"' Sam continued. 'I sat in meetings with other disappointed people wondering exactly when their life diverged from the script they had written for themselves. I saw the same lines on their faces, the same fear in their eyes, and the same sense of dread that their emotional wellbeing had become defined by their ability to pay their mortgage. And at these moments I thought, "Thank fuck we only have two children."'

'Then you should have the vasectomy,' said Laura, noticing his use of the past tense to refer to his job. 'I don't want any details or debate. Just tell me when it's over.'

She was now encased in her dress and stood up with difficulty. The overall effect was startling. She had the kind of deep cleavage best appreciated by teenage boys or very old men. The empire-line waist pushed the eye immediately back upwards. But the sleeves were long and the length of the dress made the rest of it almost coy. It was a schizophrenic outfit, he concluded.

'God,' said Sam.

'Is it a bit much?' asked Laura.

'It's a single-issue dress,' he conceded.

'I'm going downstairs. Why don't you try and get some work done?' suggested Laura tentatively as she headed for the door, hoping he might at least pick up the mystery film script. 'Then you can relax tomorrow.' It was the sort of thing she might say to Nell about finishing her homework.

It had been almost ten minutes since Sam last thought about the void he now faced since leaving his job, and the idea of being abandoned in this room with the re-writes to the final episode of *Do Not Resuscitate* playing on a loop in his head was so oppressive that there was little option other than to pour himself another double vodka.

As he took his first sip, he forced himself to replay his final script meeting with the production company, to reassure himself that he had made the right decision when he opted to commit professional suicide. He recalled one of the script editors putting forward an idea for a Christmas special in which an Al Qaeda cell was uncovered working in the hospital. Sam had tentatively suggested that it didn't sound either very festive or politically correct. But the spectacle of a hostage crisis and the possibilities for the special-effects team were too tempting. So Sam, partly in jest, suggested that an outbreak of Ebola would be a more realistic prospect. The producer drummed his fingers on the table.

'There's something there, Sam,' he said finally.

'I was joking. Ebola is only found in Africa, mainly in the Congo,' said Sam.

'And there's no budget for location work,' piped up an eager script editor.

'It's just not plausible,' said Sam.

'Since when did plots need to be believable?' said the producer, and Sam's fate was sealed.

Now Sam switched on his computer and the document that he had been working on late the night before immediately appeared. It was the Fidelity form. Impulsively, he deleted the file. What was the point in planning for the future when the present was so uncertain? Even Labradors get the blues. He got out of bed and decided to go for a long walk to clear his head, putting the bottle of vodka in his pocket in case he required further anaesthesia.

7

When did desire become so complicated? wondered Laura, as she closed the door on Sam and ambled back along the corridor, holding her shoes in one hand and a cardigan in the other. She shook her head in confusion at Sam's neurosis over his exaggerated sense of his own fertility. Did he think his sperm were different from that of any other man in his late thirties? Did he imagine them as all-singing, all-dancing sperm in primary colours designed by someone clever from Pixar? Did he think they had separate personalities with qualities of strength and determination that set them apart from everyone else's? That they could reduce condoms to dust and entice Laura's eggs away from her ovaries and into her fallopian tubes with charisma alone?

Some men had affairs and bought sports cars to suppress their subconscious fear about their diminished progenitive prowess, but not Sam. Instead he saw himself as Priapus. It struck Laura that if men were driven by the desire to impregnate as many women as possible, then what did this say about Sam? Perhaps he represented a new male species, higher up the evolutionary scale than those that had preceded him. It was his sense of responsibility that drove him towards the doctor's clinic to prevent his seed from spreading.

Laura followed a trail of dry muddy footprints along the

corridor to the staircase. This was, she calculated, the most efficient method of finding her way back to the kitchen at the back of the house in order to help get dinner ready. She felt guilty that she hadn't thought to offer before, ensnared as she was with her own preoccupations and the assumption engrained over the years that Hannah would have everything under control. She saw a light on in the children's bedroom and gently pushed open the door to find Nell sitting up in bed still reading and beside her Ben asleep in the same tiny single bed.

'He was scared,' Nell shrugged, looking down at her younger brother.

'That's so kind of you,' Laura said.

'No it's not. I was cold,' smiled Nell, benevolently accepting her mother's kiss.

Laura stepped out of the room and back along the mud trail, wondering at the length of Hannah's stride and the way the woven carpet was worn through to the floorboards. It was as far removed from the pristine beige runners and taupe walls in Hannah's former London home as could be imagined. The Jacobean house was an unruly, sprawling maze. The rooms were awkward shapes with wood panelling that made them dark and claustrophobic.

It was as though a scientist was conducting an anthropological experiment by plucking Hannah from her natural habitat and transplanting her to an alien environment to see how she would cope. She would be the anthropological observer, Laura decided, at least for the weekend. So far all the empirical evidence suggested a smooth transition, as witnessed by the lack of make-up, dishevelled clothes, flat shoes and dirty fingernails. Despite herself, Laura smiled.

At the top of the stairs, the mud trail unexpectedly split into two competing paths. The first, the main one, judging by the different qualities of mud and dust, led firmly downstairs. The other diverted towards a room on the left that Laura hadn't noticed before, because it was hidden behind an ugly mock-Gothic wooden archway that must have been added to the house at a later date. There was a small table outside with a china bowl containing ancient potpourri and a packet of tobacco that Laura lifted up to smell. This, at least, was fresh. Underneath the table was a pile of books: James Clavell, Brad Meltzer, John Grisham. Beside them sat a thick pile of well-thumbed comics. Laura picked one up. *Manhunter, Street Justice*, the title read. She opened it up and was startled to find the hero was a middle-aged divorced mother who worked as a lawyer by day and fought villains by night. Not even super heroines were allowed to sleep, she wryly observed.

Laura walked towards the door and slowly turned the handle. As she gently pushed it ajar a few inches, she could see that there was no bulb in the main light socket and no curtains at the window on the other side of the room. A shaft of light from the warm evening sun pierced the dark room and Laura blinked as her eyes adjusted to the contrast. In the middle of a surprisingly generous double bed Luke lay with his eyes closed listening to an iPod. In one hand he held a lit cigarette. The other was inside his trousers. There was a fine dust of ash scattered around him on the cover of the white duvet. A neat pile of books and essay notes lay untouched on the bedside table. Although he had been living here for almost four months, nothing was unpacked apart from a computer, which sat on a table in the middle of the room, surrounded by overlapping piles of paper. On the wall was a single poster of Jessica Alba wearing little more than a pair of bikini bottoms.

Laura had known Luke since he was a baby but his metamorphosis into a teenager still surprised her. He was like a familiar recipe whose essential ingredients had been modified over the years so that the overall dish looked the same but its taste was subtly different. She wondered whether he had a girlfriend and then realised that a steady relationship was not a prerequisite for a fulfilling sex life when you were a teenager. Laura thought of the condoms in their bedroom and speculated whether they belonged to him or even to Gaby, who was at a co-ed school.

Moving to Suffolk at this stage in his life, after a couple of years roaming London at night with friends, was not an ideal development for a sixteen-year-old boy in the midst of hormonal pyrotechnics. Still, Sam and Jonathan had spent their teenage years here and had emerged relatively unscathed, although Sam recently admitted that he spent rather too much time lusting after Jonathan's mother. From the photographs she had seen of her, Laura suspected Sam was not alone. She was the type of woman who attracted attention but repelled intimacy. In pictures she always seemed to be looking away from the camera with a half-smile on her lips as though enjoying a private joke with someone you couldn't see. Jonathan had told her that at his mother's funeral, men he had never seen before stood weeping at the back of the church. At the time, Jonathan considered this to be a response to his newly motherless status. Only many years later, during a drunken conversation with his father, did he discover that those men had been former and current lovers of his mother. A response, his father said regretfully, to his own peccadilloes.

Feeling embarrassed by her intrusion, Laura closed the door on Luke, who was still oblivious to her presence, and teetered downstairs into the oak-panelled hall on the ground floor. There was a flokati rug on the floor and hats that must have belonged to Jonathan's father hanging decoratively on the wall. Laura sneezed. A couple of corridors led from the hallway. She could hear music playing at the end of one. Talking Heads. That would be Jonathan's choice, not Hannah's. When Laura first met Jonathan, the same music was playing on a tape recorder in the kitchen. She could remember the way that the room smelt of joss sticks, and the unpacked suitcase in his bedroom. Jonathan had always been someone able to pack up his life in ten minutes if necessary. He was her introduction to Talking Heads; her introduction to her first and last line of cocaine; and most significantly, her introduction to Sam.

Laura reached the end of the corridor. There were no working light bulbs. She felt a door in front of her and another to her left, which opened into a large larder with a small window that looked on to the side of the house. When she pulled the switch a dull yellow glow of a bare light bulb warmed the room.

She could make out the shape of an enormous old fridge-freezer at the end near the window. The room was musty and there was a strong but not unpleasant smell, which Laura inhaled deeply. Feeling hungry and knowing that Hannah's fridge was generally well stocked, she headed across the cobbled floor. If she ate something now, she wouldn't have to suffer the ignominy of stuffing herself with crisps and nuts in front of Hannah, whose self-control was legendary. The heel of her shoe hit a particularly uneven stone and she put out a hand to steady herself. It landed on a soft, slightly hairy, clammy surface that Laura thought might be a cured ham. She opened the fridge hoping the light would help her to gauge her options.

When she gazed inside, Laura found herself face to face with the skinned head of a large animal, possibly a deer. Its glassy eyes stared at her from a plate where a pool of blood had collected. She could see two stumps on either side of the head where its antlers had been sawn off. On the shelf below, a collection of purple livers and kidneys were slumped in a bowl. And beside them was a dish containing a couple of pig's trotters and what looked like a pair of freshly cut testicles. They were perfectly round, smooth and pink. Laura recoiled, less from squeamishness than from the smell of raw flesh that filled her nostrils. It reminded her of open wounds she used to treat when she did her six-month stint in A&E, before she qualified as a neurologist. And it brought home the reality of Sam's vasectomy. A simple slice of the knife through the scrotum to cut the vas deferens.

As she stepped back on to the uneven floor, Laura again tried to steady herself by reaching out for the shelf that ran along the side of the room. She was relieved to find the same clammy surface to lean on. This time she bent down to see whether she had come across a ham. Instead she found herself holding on to the moist, hairy snout of an uncooked pig's head. She screamed, a short, high-pitched cry that was loud enough to send Hannah running in from the kitchen.

'You all right?' asked Hannah, glancing around the room to see what might have frightened Laura.

'It's like a voodoo chamber,' said Laura breathlessly.

'It's all organic,' replied Hannah, sounding a little defensive.

'It wasn't its provenance that worried me,' Laura said.

'We've farmed it all. I went with them to the local abattoir on their final journey,' explained Hannah enthusiastically, patting the pig's head. 'This was Clover. The other one,' she pointed to another pig's head in the corner, 'was Chester, Clover's husband.'

Laura's impressive cleavage heaved up and down. It would go down well with the hunting and shooting set, thought Hannah, not that she was trying to court that particular element of the Suffolk landscape. They liked a woman they could grapple with. Hannah's bony body and flat chest made her too exotic, particularly when combined with her short hair. It spoke of an abstemious nature.

'I'm sure that was very comforting to them,' said Laura.

'I'm experimenting with a new recipe.' Hannah laughed. 'It's a medieval English dish called headcheese. You boil a pig's head and feet to release all the gelatine and meat. Then you peel the skin off its face and dice the nose to make a terrine.'

'I can't see that going down well among the Islington crowd,' said Laura.

'Well, we thought we'd try it out on you and Sam first,' said Hannah generously.

'Who decapitated the pig?' asked Laura, appreciating the neat surgery.

'Jonathan gave me a chainsaw for Christmas,' explained Hannah. 'It has all sorts of uses.'

Laura peered more closely at the pig and admired its perfect long blonde eyelashes. It stared back at her reproachfully, its eyes bloodshot and swollen, as though it had been crying. Its mouth was half open and Laura could see a row of perfectly even, pointed teeth.

'You were a vegetarian when you left London,' said Laura, her appetite completely dissipated by the carnage in the larder.

'We're all allowed to evolve,' shrugged Hannah. 'And it's good to have an honest relationship with the food you eat. Jonathan thinks you show respect by using the whole animal. It's the natural course of things. People have been doing that for centuries. He even wants to turn the bladders into condoms and put them in display cases at Eden.'

'Sounds very Damien Hirst,' said Laura, but what she wanted to say was that Hannah's seemingly casual abandonment of her vegetarian principles was as significant as a loss of faith to a believer. Instead she unthinkingly stroked the pig's head.

She thought of Sam's impoverished penis lying on his thigh and her willing eggs condemned to a life sentence. And then to her surprise, she found herself laughing, because although she had seen many patients with impotence related to neurological conditions, she had never yet come across a case of someone who had developed a fully fledged phobia about making his wife pregnant. It was worthy of an episode of *Do Not Resuscitate*.

'Did Jonathan tell you that I thought Sam was trying to

find a dating agency for married people on the Internet?' asked Laura, surprised at how readily she could find humour in the situation.

'It's not that absurd,' said Hannah. 'That's how Janey met Steve, although obviously they don't really talk about it now.'

'You mean they met through a dating agency for married people even though neither of them was married?' asked Laura incredulously.

'I think she wanted someone to distract her from memories of Patrick, and Steve didn't want a relationship that would impact on his work,' said Hannah.

'I can't believe Janey never told me that,' said Laura.

'She probably thought you would disapprove,' suggested Hannah.

'But why would she think that?' asked Laura, who knew there was some truth in Hannah's observation.

'Because you would,' said Hannah. 'And people worry about your approval.'

'People always feel that around doctors,' said Laura.

'I felt that long before you qualified,' said Hannah. 'I knew I needed your approval if I was ever to get anywhere with Jonathan.'

'He was besotted from the moment he met you,' said Laura, who tried to imagine a period in her life when she might have been intimidating. 'What I thought was irrelevant.'

'Sam would always stand by Jonathan's decisions, but you were different. You're his moral compass. He still minds what you think. Do you know, I always wondered whether there had been something between you?' Hannah asked impetuously. 'I mean it wouldn't matter now obviously, but I always had this feeling that there was something unresolved.'

Laura was too taken aback to reply. How was it, she pondered, that after years of dormancy, this subject had suddenly become active? She wondered fleetingly if it was something to do with the photograph in the bedroom. It was a picture that posed more questions than answers. Like *The Arnolfini Wedding*. She tried to consider the photograph objectively. Did the way Jonathan stared away from the camera mean that he was angry with Patrick? A careful observer would note that although Sam and Janey appeared to be standing apart, in fact you could see that Sam's toe was nudging the back of her calf in that tender spot just above the ankle. And maybe they recognised something in the look in Laura's eye, but came to the wrong conclusions about the person responsible for this state of sated languor. Photographs were dangerous, thought Laura, because they told nothing of what happened before or after. That was why she liked medicine. A brain scan answered more questions than it posed.

She resolved to question Hannah more closely, but both of them became aware of a commotion outside the house. The Slovakian worker that Laura had last seen measuring the asparagus beds came to the open arrow-slit window at the end of the larder and called for Hannah to come outside. He pronounced her name with guttural emphasis on the first consonant and gave a friendly smile to Laura, but there was a sense of urgency in his tone.

'This is Jacek,' said Hannah.

He removed his hat and Laura was vaguely surprised to

see a full head of blond dreadlocks. Up close, he was older than Laura had imagined. He put a hand on the window sill and Laura noticed the scar from a burn on one knuckle and a couple of ugly red calluses on his fingers. Laura's habit of observing hands was one engrained since early childhood. Jacek's belonged to someone engaged in hard physical labour. They were so dry that deep channels had opened up in the creases around the joints. They were the same hands as those of the migrant workers who ended up at her clinic in London, after developing neurological problems following accidents on unregulated building sites.

Laura couldn't understand what he was saying but he pointed to a field beside the house several times and Laura thought she heard him say he would go and find a rope.

'Someone is in with the bull,' Hannah swiftly explained as she left the larder.

Laura stayed by the open window, trying to work out what was going on in the field and whether it warranted her attention. Already Laura could see Hannah heading towards the gate of the paddock about twenty metres away.

The narrowness of the window gave great clarity to the long thin scene taking place outside. So it was that she could see at the top of the frame a small figure in the field beyond the garden heading in a straight line towards the house, both hands stuck deep in the pockets of a coat. The person was walking intently, staring at the ground as though searching for the answer to a significant question in the boggy pasture. It was difficult to tell whether the figure was a man or a woman, because the undulating ground required the person to take deep, forceful, masculine steps.

As the stick figure reached the middle of the field, equidistant between the hedge that marked the boundary at one end and the gate that opened on to the driveway at the other, Laura noticed the bull appear at the far edge of the field, burly-looking even from this distance. It loped along, shuffling from side to side, its vast frame engulfing its tiny legs, as though it was propelled by the sheer force of its massive body. Its head hung low, but Laura put this down to the sheer effort it required to walk. It was the same mechanical instinct that her Parkinson's patients used to maintain momentum.

It progressed slowly, as though curious about the stranger in its midst. Even when it picked up speed it still seemed as though it was walking in slow motion. It headed towards the person with sluggish but meaningful intent. Hannah was nowhere to be seen. Laura guessed she had gone in search of the rope and began shouting out to alert the oblivious man, because now that he was closer, it was apparent the figure was male.

She glanced up and saw that the bull had broken into a lame trot and was lumbering towards the man, who seemed completely unaware of what was about to unfold. Laura saw it was possible to open the window wider if she leant over the ledge to push the rusty latch.

By this time the bull was only about ten metres behind the man. Its great belly swung from one side to another and it breathed deeply with the effort or perhaps with the rage of discovering someone trespassing upon its territory. It would have been a handsome specimen years ago but now, with its tangled thick white hair and faded brown coat, it resembled an angry old man.

'Watch out behind you,' she yelled out the window. Laura shouted at the figure in the field over and over again, gesticulating with her arm. And then in a matter of seconds it was too late. The bull stopped dead in its tracks just behind the man. It didn't touch him but the man fell dramatically forward on to his knees, and knelt in the mud as though he was praying. Laura felt a lurch in her stomach: it was Sam. What in God's name was he doing?

She stumbled out of the larder, still wearing Hannah's shoes, and found Gaby fumbling to open the stiff back door in the kitchen. Then both of them ran towards the gate.

'Do something,' Laura pleaded with Hannah.

'Don't worry,' said Hannah. 'I'll handle this. If he gets too excited it will reduce his sperm count and we won't get enough calves.' Out in the field, Sam remained on all fours. He stayed perfectly still, breathing deeply, before standing up to face the inquisitive beast.

'What about Sam's sperm count?' said Laura, astonished both by Hannah's protective instinct over her bull and by her newly acquired knowledge about the breeding habits of cattle.

Hannah didn't answer because she was mesmerised by Sam. Instead of retreating, he now stood up and edged towards the bull, his left arm stretched out at a right angle from the rest of his body. When he came to a halt in front of the animal he slowly stretched out his hand, held it horizontally in front of the bull's furry face and unfurled his index and middle fingers to point at its eyes. When he had the bull's full attention he started making tiny rotating circles with his fingers. The bull stood perfectly still, seemingly transfixed.

'What's he doing?' asked Laura.

'I think he's trying to hypnotise the bull,' said Hannah in disbelief. 'He's been watching too many wildlife programmes.'

'Drinking too many vodka and tonics more likely,' said Laura.

Then Sam surprised them again by slowly rotating his shoulder to shrug off an arm of the jacket and then in a single flamboyant gesture catch it in his right hand. He dropped his left arm and stood in front of the bull, waving the jacket at him like a matador.

Laura didn't know whether to laugh or cry. Sam shook the coat, gently at first so that only the seam at the bottom quivered slightly. The bull stared at the coat, lowering its head. She could see Sam's lips moving and wondered what he was saying.

'I'm going in to help,' said Hannah, taking stock of the situation.

'The only person who can save Sam is himself,' muttered Laura, with utter conviction.

'I mean I'm going to save the bull,' said Hannah, as she jumped down into the field. 'Sam is really going to unsettle him. He's completely harmless. Even when provoked.'

'Bloody hell,' said Jonathan, who had just appeared beside Laura. 'Is he having a Hemingway moment?'

'Something like that,' mumbled Laura.

'Someone needs to act as a decoy,' Jonathan said as he climbed up the gate. 'Then Sam can run for it.'

'How about you?' Hannah yelled. Jonathan pointed at his shoes.

'These are my new trainers,' he said, shrugging his shoulders apologetically.

'Isn't there a bull keeper?' asked Laura.

'Like a gamekeeper, you mean?' countered Jonathan.

'A dedicated bullish person,' said Laura.

'That's Hannah. He's really docile when she deals with him. She has a naturally soothing nature. The bull is sensitive to Sam's mood.'

'It's got nothing to do with Sam's mood,' said Laura. 'He's drunk too much to feel anything.'

'I've been with Sam many times when he's pissed but he's never shown any matador tendencies,' said Jonathan. 'He doesn't even get argumentative. Don't worry, Laura, here's Jacek, he'll sort everything out.'

Jacek had a rope and halter slung over his shoulder. He walked with an easy rolling gait, like a cowboy. His jeans hung off his hips and his hair swayed from one side to the other as he strode towards them. Laura tried to open the stiff iron handle of the gate but it wouldn't shift. Jacek stood beside her and bent down to examine the rusty bolt. Laura leant over and found her nose level with his hair. She tentatively breathed in and was surprised that apart from a trace of oil, possibly almond, it smelt not unlike the hair of her own children. She was seized with the urge to touch it and hold it in her hand to feel its weight. What must he make of us? Laura wondered. For a moment she envied the simplicity of his life. He was here to earn money to send to his family in Slovakia. He would earn in a day more than the average Slovak made in a week back home. He would work hard: his honed body was testimony to physical labour, not hours spent in a gym. He must look at us and wonder at the trivia of our lives, sighed Laura. She envied him, though, not for his youth or his good looks. She envied him his detachment.

'You'll make him angry, Sam,' Laura shouted over the gate, but Sam either couldn't hear or wasn't listening.

When the bull realised that the coat had been pulled away at the last minute, it stared at Sam.

'This is all your fault,' said Laura angrily to Jonathan.

'How can it be? I've only just arrived,' Jonathan said bemusedly. 'You're always so hard on me, Laura.'

'I don't mean directly. I mean indirectly.'

'What are you talking about?' asked Jonathan, genuinely perplexed at her tone. 'Well you can't blame me for that. It's the red lining of the coat that's provoking the bull.'

'Bulls are colour-blind,' said Laura.

Sam was seemingly oblivious to anything taking place outside the confines of the field. Now that he held the bull's attention, he began to flap the coat more vigorously. The bull pawed at the ground with one leg, sending small blades of grass into the air, slowly dropped its head until it almost touched the grass, and then stood still. Everyone was transfixed.

Sam felt adrenalin coursing through his body. He quivered with anticipation, resisting the urge to move until the bull was upon him. He felt something close to ecstasy and for a second allowed himself to close his eyes to savour the moment. Then it ambled towards him and stood stock-still.

'Olé,' shouted Sam, trying to provoke the bull. But it was

unmoved. In a fit of pique, Sam threw the coat at the bull and it caught on its horn. Unperturbed, the bull shuffled away, its vision restricted by the coat's lining. Everyone gasped as it lumbered aimlessly away from him. Sam sat down unsteadily on his haunches and remained in the same position.

He checked over his shoulder and saw that the bull had retreated to the far corner of the field. It was trying half-heartedly to shake off the coat. Sam was pleased to see Laura climb over the gate into the field and run towards him.

'Sam,' she cried. 'Are you all right?'

'Brilliant,' he shouted back. 'Never better.' He half wondered why she was running when the drama was over. But that was Laura's style. She managed to hold things together in a crisis but fell apart when it was resolved. He smiled because he found it reassuring to be married to someone with such a transparent nature. He should have told her about borrowing money from Jonathan. Mostly he should have told her that he had resigned from his job to finish the film script that he had started writing more than six months ago.

She was waving her arms like a windmill, Sam thought with amusement, as she drew closer. She had taken off her shoes and he could see even from a distance that the front of her new dress was filthy. The shoulder had slipped down over the top of her arm and below that he spotted the bra strap. He could see the bulge of her left breast threatening to pour out of its broderie-anglaise tether. He thought about the holiday Jonathan planned and for the first time in many weeks found himself looking forward to something. By then the vasectomy would be over. Their children would be with Laura's parents and for the first time in seven years they would get to spend time alone together. It didn't really matter where they were going. All that mattered was that for seven nights they would get to sleep in the same bed without any interruptions and, unfettered by worries about making her pregnant, he could finally capitalise on the fact that he still found his wife attractive.

8

The trouble with knowing something is that you can't unknow it, thought Sam, as he sat at the breakfast table the following morning. His eyeballs felt like prunes, shrivelled and dry with tiredness. His mouth tasted of stale alcohol and cigarettes and his throat burnt.

He was reading one of the Sunday papers but the words kept blurring before him. He read the same sentence over and over again, as though by repetition the words would diffuse into meaningless fragments. *Jonathan Sleet explores new English dish*, the caption read, beside a small grainy photo of Jonathan leaving a private members' club with a woman with short black hair.

It was a tabloid story that Sam would generally dismiss out of hand. But as he contemplated the picture, he knew it was the same woman who had sat beside them when he'd gone to the theatre with Jonathan the previous week. Even with her head turned away from the camera he was certain it was her. The short, scruffy, dark hair, the mouth that made a man think of one thing, the almond-shaped, almost oriental eyes, were all familiar. Sam shook his head at the irony that he'd been the one forced to deny to a marriage guidance counsellor that he was having an affair, when Jonathan was the one engaged in multiple deceptions.

'You got the wrong man,' he wanted to tell everyone seated around the table. Because although there was no evidence to build a case against Sam, some people might consider there was no smoke without fire. 'It's the one outside sending texts on a Sunday morning that you should keep an eye on,' he wanted to say, as he saw Jonathan stroll past the kitchen window intently punching the buttons on his mobile phone.

Sam looked up and met three pairs of concerned eyes. He must have been mumbling out loud. He could tell from the range of expressions around the table that talking to himself was viewed as just another symptom of his now very public midlife crisis. Itself another irony, because since he had decided definitively to go ahead with the vasectomy, he had felt a vague sense of equilibrium return.

He got up to slice a piece of bread. It was wholemeal and organic with seeds and nuts and although his hand was shaky, he managed to cut a reasonably straight line through the middle. As it browned in the toaster, Sam leant over to feel the heat from the filament. His face burned but he wouldn't allow himself to move until he could provide a reasonable account of events the previous evening.

He remembered standing in the field with a bull, feeling inexplicably elated, and then nothing until he woke up at five thirty in the morning in bed with Laura. The bit in between was lost. To Sam it was simple: he had gone for a walk to clear his head, unexpectedly encountered a bull and decided that it might be entertaining to provoke a fight. Now he could see that rather than a sign of his recovery, his behaviour was being interpreted as further evidence of an emotional decline.

The feeling that he might have done something regrettable he couldn't remember was exacerbated by the fact that he had got up in the same clothes he had worn yesterday, to be met by fixed smiles from Laura and Hannah when he came down into the kitchen at ten o'clock in the morning. It should have been his turn to get up with Ben and only something serious would have derailed Laura from a lie-in. Especially given the protracted negotiations during the car journey over who exactly had had the most sleep the night before.

The toast popped up and hit him in the face. He saw Gaby furtively observe him from over the top of a magazine and smiled at her. She looked down a little too quickly. She was wearing several long tops, the sleeves pulled down to cover her hands, and a denim miniskirt with black leggings, the uniform of the brittle London teenager. But in rural Suffolk, way beyond the sartorial radar of even the Home Counties, it marked her out as someone ahead in the style game.

The teenage thermostat must be permanently set lower, thought Sam, because they were shrouded in so many layers. Perhaps it was because they were always too thin. Although Gaby didn't appear hungry. She was long-limbed and athletic, unfashionably voluptuous even. There was nothing skeletal about her body. Sam noted that her black leather ballet pumps were covered in mud and guiltily recalled that Gaby was among those who had come into the field to try and persuade him out. How old and ridiculous he must seem to her. He wondered how much she knew about what was going on.

'Coffee?' asked Hannah from the other end of the table.

Sam felt a stab of guilt as he considered what he had read in the newspaper. It was swiftly followed by a sense of rising panic that he couldn't remember what he might have said the previous evening. Perhaps he had told Laura what happened at the theatre. He caught her eye, but her expression revealed nothing, so he quickly returned to his seat and flicked through the newspaper to the sports pages.

'Fantastic,' said Sam, spreading a thick layer of marmalade on the burnt piece of toast.

'What do you fancy?' asked Hannah. 'Espresso, latte, macchiato, Americano or cappuccino?'

'I think a double espresso would probably be a good idea,' said Sam.

'I've got the most amazing Matari beans from the Yemen,' said Hannah enthusiastically. 'They are really difficult to get hold of. Or I could do you a blend of Brazilian Santos and Ethiopian mocha? Or if you fancy something with a hint of chocolate then you should try some Guatemalan maragogype. Have you ever seen an elephant bean?'

'Er, no,' said Sam, as Hannah opened a cupboard dedicated to different types of coffee and pulled out various brands. She was wearing a pair of denim shorts and from behind she looked no different from when Sam had met her seventeen years earlier, when Jonathan had brought her to Oxford for the first time.

'It's the biggest bean in the world. I don't buy any robusta,' she said. 'The Colombian Medellín is a little less acidic, which might be better for you given the excesses of last night. But the Nicaraguan makes really good espresso. I'll take that to Scotland with us.'

'You know what, Hannah,' said Sam apologetically. 'Do you have any Nescafé?'

He carefully folded the newspaper in half and leant on it with his left elbow. But as Hannah approached him with a couple of different bags of coffee beans, he picked it up again and turned to the first page.

'I never had you down as a *News of the World* reader,' said Hannah, skim-reading a story about a footballer involved in a threesome over his shoulder. 'But then I had no idea about your matador tendencies either. It's wonderful to think you can know someone for so many years and still discover new things about them, isn't it?'

'How is the bull?' asked Sam, quickly moving on to the next page.

'Fine,' said Hannah, a little abruptly, as she went back to her chair. 'The vet's coming later.'

'God, did I hurt him?' asked Sam.

'He ate your coat,' said Laura, staring hard at him from the other end of the table. It was the first thing she had said to him since he came downstairs. 'And zips aren't widely acknowledged as a staple food among organic cattle.'

He could see Gaby smile. Sam grimaced and turned once again to the incriminating page to stare at the grainy photograph of the woman. He had only seen Jonathan once since the evening at the theatre and neither of them had alluded to what had happened. Instead they had covered the litany of injured players at Arsenal, how businesses were going to function now that the Poles were heading home, and whether other banks were going to fall in the wake of Bear Stearns.

Sam's strategy had been to obliterate the evening from

his memory and he was fairly confident that Jonathan felt the same way. His behaviour was an aberration, rather than part of a pattern of infidelity, Sam concluded. And any further discussion made Sam more complicit than he already was.

Being married to a neurologist, Sam understood better than most how memories are laid down. Endless analysis and repetition of detail was an irrefutable way to ensure they became embedded in your limbic system, ready to creep up on you in moments of doubt. Sam was determined the evening should be confined to his short-term memory, but the picture in the newspaper fired up those synapses. As he sipped the exotic blend of coffee that Hannah placed beside him, he remembered what had happened at the theatre with such startling clarity that he wondered whether it qualified as a flashback.

The evening had started with promise. Unusually, Jonathan had suggested they see a play together. Of course now, the idea that he might have selflessly organised a trip to the theatre to shake Sam out of his mood seemed ludicrous. He had known Jonathan long enough to understand that apparent acts of benevolence often contained a rich seam of selfishness. Even the holiday in Scotland was part of a self-serving publicity campaign. It was all part of a plan.

Sam had initially resisted the theatre offer because Jonathan was incapable of sitting still for any length of time. But he changed his mind when Jonathan explained that one of his kitchen staff had secured a minor role as a waiter and given him a couple of free tickets. Besides, it was a Pinter play about adultery, and Sam thought the subject matter might hold Jonathan's attention, although not for the reasons that were subsequently revealed.

Unless his own work was involved, Jonathan's powers of concentration were notoriously fickle. Sam recalled the first time that he had articulated the general parameters of his crisis to him almost a year earlier. Jonathan had given the subject his full attention for all of five minutes, during which he barely drew breath while he expounded on what he thought Sam should do (give up the soap, write something of his own, as it transpired). He then turned the conversation to the subject of his father's farm in Suffolk and whether he and Hannah should take it over to supply Eden. Actually, Sam reflected, one of the great things about Jonathan was that he allowed little time for introspection. He lived firmly in the present. By never taking Sam's problems seriously, he generally managed to marginalise them.

When Sam collected his ticket at the door of the theatre in Covent Garden, he wondered whether he would end up watching the play alone. He went up to wait in the bar and managed a couple of vodka tonics. Vodka was less soporific than wine and Laura couldn't smell it on his breath. He was pleased when Jonathan sent a text announcing his imminent arrival. Because there had been a couple of times, more recently, when Jonathan had failed to turn up and Sam had spent the evening drinking alone. As someone who could rarely use work as a legitimate excuse for cancelling anything, Sam was inclined to believe Jonathan's excuses that an unexpected crisis had arisen: stroppy chefs, unreliable suppliers, drunken restaurant critics had all featured in the past year. That evening, Jonathan eventually appeared just as the one-minute bell rang. Sam got up to go into the auditorium, carrying his drink in a plastic cup, but Jonathan pulled at his arm.

'Do you fancy a quick toot?' he asked.

'No,' Sam told him firmly, but still Jonathan had disappeared to the toilet.

The usher needed a little persuasion to let them in so late and the people in their row at the back of the balcony muttered as they clambered across bags and legs to reach seats that they should have negotiated from the other end. It was a small theatre, which highlighted the sense of intimacy between actors and audience. They sat at the end of the back row. As they settled in their seats, Sam closed his eyes and breathed deeply for a couple of minutes. He clenched and unclenched his fists until he felt the muscles in his arms finally relax. He felt resolute: he would go through with the vasectomy. There would be no further discussion, nothing that might divert him from this course of action. And he would tell Laura at a later date. Fortunately the elderly doctor he had seen came from an era where fathers were discouraged from being present during childbirth and decisions concerning the male reproductive organ were taken unilaterally. Unthinkingly, Sam put his hand over his crotch and concentrated on the stage.

The play was divided into nine scenes and at the end of each the lights went down for a couple of minutes. Sam tried to remember at which point he first noticed Jonathan fidgeting beside him. At the end of scene one Jonathan had asked him if the actress was the woman from *Ballykissangel* and Sam had confirmed that it was indeed Dervla Kirwan. Somewhere in the middle of scene two Jonathan's left leg bumped his knee. Sam thought he was trying to indicate to him that the man who worked at Eden was about to appear and told him that the restaurant scene didn't occur until scene seven. At the time, Sam had thought this was a good thing because it would force Jonathan to stay beyond the interval.

Sam scrutinised Jonathan and was surprised to see him staring unblinkingly at the stage. His facial muscles were taut with emotion and he was breathing a little unevenly. Small beads of sweat laced his upper lip. For a moment Sam assumed he was moved by the events unravelling on stage. He even wondered fleetingly whether the adultery plot-line resonated with him. Jonathan had a brooding vulnerability that made women want to save him from himself. If there were indiscretions, Sam didn't know about them. On balance, this meant there probably weren't, because Jonathan wasn't good at keeping secrets. Sam smiled benevolently.

The lights dimmed for another scene change and Sam was aware of the quality of Jonathan's breathing again. When the third scene began, Jonathan lifted his left leg and rested his foot against the seat in front of him. Sam knew this would irritate the person sitting in the next row and put out his hand to push down Jonathan's leg. In that moment, Sam noticed that not only was the top button of Jonathan's jeans undone, but that the left hand of the woman sitting on Jonathan's other side was deep inside his trousers. Sam breathed in sharply. Apart from the rise and fall of his ribcage, Jonathan remained completely still, staring resolutely ahead. He made no eye contact with Sam, even when Sam nudged him.

Instead, Sam tried another tack and leaned forward to observe the woman sitting next to Jonathan. When she realised that he had noticed what was going on she would become embarrassed and remove her hand. Sam couldn't understand how Jonathan had allowed this to happen. It was unbelievable. More unbelievable, in fact, than the fictional copulation taking place on stage.

But far from being embarrassed when Sam caught her eye, the woman sitting next to Jonathan continued to rub inside his trousers. She was gorgeous, Sam conceded, holding her stare. She gave Sam such an insouciant smile that he was forced to look away. As the lights came up for the interval, Jonathan leant over to Sam and whispered in a strained voice, 'Sorry. I've got to go.' They quickly got out of their seats and that was the last he had seen of Jonathan until this weekend.

Sam shook his head, partly in disbelief, but mostly to rouse himself from his hangover. His priority right now was to remove the incriminating page from the newspaper before anyone else saw it. It was less to protect Jonathan than to save Hannah from the humiliation of discovering her husband's duplicity exposed in such a public way.

Perhaps Jonathan had only seen this woman a couple of times and Hannah never needed to know.

As he nonchalantly thumbed through the newspaper in search of the photograph, he felt a growing sense of rancour towards Jonathan. Sam tried to rationalise this feeling of simmering contempt. Was it the fact that

Jonathan was having an affair that bothered him? Or was it because Sam was now implicated in the deception? Perhaps it was because at their age there was more invested in friendship with other couples than he had anticipated. If Jonathan's marriage with Hannah fell apart then who would they spend the New Year with? Who would they go on holiday with? But his sense of unresolved anger was more complex. It thumped in his head like a drum roll until finally it found resonance with other ancient resentments that Sam thought had been buried long ago.

He wished he could unburden himself to Laura, but until he knew the facts it seemed a little premature. And in any case, he didn't want to upset their shaky progress.

He carefully opened up the page in front of him and separated it from the rest of the paper. Then he folded it over and over again as though he was making a complicated origami model and stuffed it in his back pocket. He wouldn't destroy it quite yet.

'So, how are you adjusting to country life?' he heard Laura question Gaby.

'It's pretty crap,' replied Gaby smiling cheerfully. 'No one's interested in politics. And they all have those patio heaters. The worst thing is the constant introductions to local teenagers. It's all a bit Jane Austen. Too much wisteria and talk about dynasties.'

'Friendship is definitely a chemical thing,' Laura concurred. 'It's a bit like marriage really. Not something you can force.'

'I know,' said Gaby. 'Dad always says that Mum and you would have been a match made in heaven.'

'He does?' said Laura, a little taken aback.

'You've never had an argument,' said Gaby.

'We're very comfortable with each other because there's nothing unknown,' agreed Laura.

'Mum and Dad never argue but that's because Mum spends a lot of time anticipating Dad's needs and subjugating her own,' said Gaby, adding by way of explanation: 'I'm studying psychology.'

Laura wondered how many years she had until Sam and she were called to account by their children. She imagined it would be a slow process of disenchantment. Or perhaps there would be one defining incident. She tried to imagine what they would say about her. Perhaps the labels that friends had attached over the years would be the source of their disillusion. A tendency towards overanalysis, coupled with a desire to impose order that could make her seem rigid; her inability to dissimulate; and a degree of certainty about everything that made her seem more confident than she really felt. Laura would agree with all these descriptions.

She hadn't always been like this. If she had chosen a different man then perhaps there would have been different labels. It wasn't always easy being married to someone who was incapable of planning his own life beyond the next day. Who couldn't hit a deadline until it hung over his neck like a guillotine, and who was incapable of performing the simplest administrative task. Niceness was sometimes an overrated virtue.

She observed Sam, who was busily folding a piece of paper over and over again. He seemed preoccupied. Unlike Hannah, she found Sam's new unfamiliarity disconcerting.

This was a time of their life when they needed to be certain of the ground beneath their feet. Laura peered at the cover of the book that was lying upside down beside Gaby's plate of toast. It showed a girl holding a knife towards her wrist.

'Gosh, what's that about?' she asked.

'A girl who self-mutilates,' explained Gaby in a matter-of-fact tone.

'That sounds a little heavy,' said Laura, trying to sound less taken aback than she felt.

'There's a girl at school who does it,' Gaby said. 'I tried it once but I passed out.'

'Well that's probably a good thing,' said Laura.

'She did it when she was stressed,' continued Gaby, pulling down the sleeves of her top until only her fingertips were visible. 'Maybe moving here will drive me to it. People who say the countryside is relaxing just don't know what they're talking about. Having nothing to do is really stressful.'

'Where's Luke?' asked Laura, wanting to steer the conversation on to more comfortable terrain.

'He's on Facebook,' said Gaby.

'Is that a horse?' asked Laura.

'No, it's an Internet thing,' laughed Gaby.

'Of course it is,' said Laura, sounding embarrassed.

'He's got more than a hundred friends,' Gaby continued. 'It's because he's very funny. He's much better virtually than he is in person, if you know what I mean.'

'Are they real people?' asked Laura. 'Are the friends human beings?'

'Some of Luke's friends are a bit on the strange side, but mostly they qualify as human beings,' said Gaby, smiling.

'They're not a bunch of men masquerading as teenagers if that's what you mean. You can only get on his site if Luke approves.'

'I mean are they playing themselves?' asked Laura. 'Or do they take on other personalities?'

'I think you're getting confused with Second Life, Laura,' said Gaby, trying hard not to sound patronising. 'His friends are who they say they are.'

'Well that's quite interesting in itself,' responded Laura, hoping to redeem herself. 'Because I guess that the information you include is indicative of the image you want to project of yourself.'

'That's true of everyone,' agreed Gaby. 'Consider Dad. Everyone thinks that he is an amazing chef because he owns a restaurant and is about to publish a cookery book. But anyone who has eaten a boiled egg cooked by him knows the horrible runny undercooked truth.'

'I wonder how he's going to get round that when he's got a journalist hovering over him when we're in Scotland?' smiled Laura.

'He'll gloss over the facts,' said Gaby. 'Dad has a loose relationship with the truth. You've known him long enough to be aware of that.'

Laura stared hard at Gaby wondering whether there was a subtext to the conversation that she was meant to access. She observed her jawline and searched for the small muscle below the eye socket that revealed the authenticity of a smile. The body was like a map if you knew how to read it properly, she thought to herself. She spent a lot of time staring at her patients looking for clues. The pupils of the eye could reveal a problem in the brain; wastage in the tiny muscle between the thumb and index finger pointed to damage to the peripheral nervous system. She was relieved to find that Gaby's smile was sincere.

Jonathan came into the kitchen through the back door.

He went over to Gaby and ruffled her hair.

'How is my little revolutionary this morning?' he asked, as he kissed Gaby on the back of her head. 'Did you know Gaby wants to go to the next G8 summit with the anti-globalisation protesters, Sam? Would you agree that finishing her education should be the priority?'

'You might laugh, Dad, but one day you'll thank me,' said Gaby, quickly sliding *Grazia* under the *Observer*. 'From what I can see, it's not as though you guys are exactly engaged with the issues.'

'What do you mean?' said Jonathan.

'Well, I would say there is a definite emphasis on the personal rather than public interest,' said Gaby emphatically.

'What exactly are the issues?' asked Sam. 'I mean it used to be fairly simple in our day: if you bought Nicaraguan coffee and boycotted South African wine you could go to bed with a clean conscience.'

Gaby threw him a scathing look. 'Child labour, the West using a disproportionate share of the world's resources, multinational corporate power, destruction of the environment . . .' she listed.

'My business has impeccable environmental credentials,' protested Jonathan.

'You wear Nike trainers, Dad,' said Gaby scathingly.

'What's wrong with that?' asked Sam, glancing down at his own mud-covered trainers.

'They use child labour,' said Gaby.

'Don't be absurd,' responded Jonathan.

'And we're doing everything organically on the farm,' said Hannah.

'But who is doing all the work?' asked Gaby. 'Underpaid Eastern Europeans who have left their wives and children at home to be exploited by people like you.'

'I don't think Jacek feels exploited,' said Jonathan. 'He could have been picked up by a gangmaster in Lincolnshire and be living in a Nissen hut with a bunch of Albanians. He's got a good gig here.'

'Do you know there are forty-one brothels in Peterborough?' said Gaby.

They were interrupted by the sound of fighting on a monitor that Laura had set up so that she could hear Nell and Ben in the playroom at the top of the house. The red light flashed continuously, and as Laura turned up the volume she could hear they were in the midst of an argument that would inevitably end in violence.

'I'll go,' said Gaby, jumping up from the table. 'And leave you to your navel-gazing.'

'Sorry,' apologised Hannah, as Gaby left the room.

'If you can't be like that when you're fifteen, then when can you?' Sam shrugged his shoulders. 'It's good to have a belief system, even if it's incoherent.'

'I'm sixteen, Sam,' Gaby shouted back through the door, 'and that is a very condescending thing to say, especially from someone who gets his kicks out of provoking geriatric bulls.'

Jonathan strolled over to an old pine dresser at the other end of the kitchen and pulled out a plastic folder stuffed with papers. Sam wondered at his ability to compartmentalise his life. How could he manage the subterfuge with such ease and apparent lack of conscience? Although, of course, Sam now had a bit part in his parallel universe. How long had he been seeing that girl? Sam wondered.

'Great news about Coll,' Jonathan said, enthusiastically waving the plastic folder. 'BA's agreed to sponsor all the plane tickets to Oban. It's completely free.'

'Don't you think flying undermines your environmental credentials?' asked Laura.

Jonathan stared at Laura in surprise. 'That didn't occur to me,' he said. 'But you're completely right. We should go by train. Or maybe you could all go by train and I could fly later? I just can't afford the time.'

'Janey and Steve might baulk at a day on a train with a new baby, a travel cot and all of us,' said Hannah calmly, as she piled cups and plates into the dishwasher.

'So what exactly are you going to talk about in this magazine interview?' asked Sam, suddenly aware that he hadn't added anything coherent to the conversation since he stepped into the room.

'Well, obviously what people will be really interested in is how I developed my passion for food and cooking,' said Jonathan thoughtfully. 'And they'll want to photograph us all eating a meal cooked by me.'

'That will be one of the highlights,' teased Laura.

'I'll have it all worked out beforehand,' insisted Jonathan. 'I'll be prepared. They want to include the recipes as part of the piece.'

'And I'll be on hand to help,' reassured Hannah.

'They also want to know about how we all met and

how our friendship has evolved over the years,' said Jonathan. 'That whole business about how success doesn't change your essence and my loyalty to my old friends.'

'You can talk about your obsession with music trivia,' suggested Hannah.

'How about references to food in songs by Bob Dylan?' proposed Sam.

'Now that's a tough one,' said Jonathan closing his eyes to think in mock earnestness. 'How about "Country Pie"?'

'Not bad,' said Sam. 'Or the reference to having your cake and eating it in "Lay Lady Lay"?'

'Very good,' said Jonathan, conceding early victory.

Jonathan was trying to bolster Sam, thought Laura. But when she looked up she caught Jonathan's eye and realised that he was the one who needed reassurance. Maybe the contradictions inherent in maintaining his culinary deceit were beginning to wear him down. Jonathan shifted uncomfortably in the seat he had taken next to Sam. It was as though he saw something barbed in Sam's comment. But this was the kind of banter that both had enjoyed for years. Even Laura, who professed to find it boring, found the repetition comforting.

'I've got one,' said Hannah. 'How about that song "Only a Prawn in Their Game"?'

'It's pawn, not prawn,' laughed Jonathan.

'Or what about the reference to pizza in "Silent Weekend"?' suggested Sam.

'You've got me there,' said Jonathan, holding his hands up in defeat.

'It's the one about the guy who gets down on his knees

to beg his wife for forgiveness after cheating on her,' said Sam benignly.

Jonathan shot another look at Sam and this time even Laura saw in his eyes a hint of reproach.

'It's his girlfriend, not his wife,' he said.

'Does that make a difference?' asked Sam.

'Well there are degrees of infidelity,' said Jonathan.

'As defined by Bill Clinton?' Hannah joked.

'Or on a sliding scale, perhaps?' interjected Sam.

'On a scale of one to five, there's thinking about doing it in the abstract, there's fantasising about someone else while having sex, doing it before you get married, doing it after you get married, and the nuclear option, doing it after you get married and have children,' said Hannah.

'That's an interesting thesis,' said Jonathan calmly. 'Now tell me what you think of this invitation for my book launch.'

His voice was drowned out by the sound of Nell and Ben arguing. The situation was deteriorating fast, Laura gauged. An angry row of red lights lit up the baby monitor again. She couldn't hear whether Gaby had reached the room.

So Laura turned up the volume to try and work out the nature of the altercation in case she was required to mediate. There was nothing subtle about a row between children, no undercurrents or hidden messages. Their fights reminded her of cartoons with speech bubbles that said things like 'Kapok!', 'Bang!' and 'Zip!' as superheroes fought their enemy. Sam and she used meteorological terminology to describe them. 'Nimbus approaching,' Sam would say, as he saw Ben's face darken. They would use the

Beaufort scale to gauge their intensity, force twelve being a row that could wreak havoc.

It was almost impossible when things had reached this stage to judge who was in the wrong. It was simply a question of who would resort to physical violence first. Laura heard Gaby come in the room and the argument immediately abated.

'What's up?' everyone heard Gaby ask Nell and Ben. 'You shouldn't argue. It wastes a lot of energy.'

Jonathan and Hannah snorted at the irony.

'Parents do,' said Nell defiantly.

'They do,' agreed Ben.

This was going well, decided Laura, who had discovered recently that if she became the enemy then it could defuse even a force-eight argument.

'Mum and Dad argue,' Nell insisted.

'Everyone argues sometimes,' Gaby said diplomatically. 'Sometimes it's good to disagree.'

'Shall I tell you what they argue about?' Nell asked Gaby. Everyone stared at the baby monitor in interest.

'Dad's willy,' Ben triumphantly interrupted.

'Oh God,' groaned Sam, leaning over until his forehead touched the table. They could hear Gaby laugh a little too loudly.

'Ben got his caught in the kitchen drawer once,' continued Nell, 'and the tip went completely black.'

'It can be very dangerous,' said Ben earnestly, as they heard Gaby smother a laugh.

'There is an important artery running through the middle,' added Nell.

'Crucial,' Ben agreed.

'Do you know what Dad wanted to do?' asked Nell.

'He wanted to chop off his willy,' said Ben seriously. 'In true life.'

'To decapitate it,' said Nell dramatically, 'like Henry VIII and Anne Boleyn.'

'And Mum wouldn't let him,' said Ben.

'Why?' asked Gaby bemusedly.

'Because of the fish,' explained Ben. 'We need the fish.'

'Otherwise they can't sex each other,' said Nell.

'And that is that,' said Ben. 'He's gone to the Dark Side.'

9

The status of lawyers in Janey's office could be measured in terms of their upholstery. In her glass cabin somewhere off centre stage there was a chocolate-brown leather sofa, an Eames executive chair with pneumatic lift and adjustable seat back and a blind on the window. There was a small Abusson carpet on the floor under a low glass table with an assortment of magazines carefully fanned out each day by her secretary. These included *Practical Law Company*, *Legal Week*, *Acquisitions Monthly*, *The Economist* and *Private Eye*. There was also an enormous beech desk, a lamp with a heavy metal base and a mahogany cabinet that she had inherited from a partner who hadn't returned from maternity leave.

All this marked out Janey as one to watch. Another partner, one who wore flamboyant ties to express his individuality, had a chaise longue, and the only openly gay partner, a Lalique vase. But a woman couldn't get away with that. It was too domestic. And while it was no longer professional suicide to have a picture of your husband on your desk or tasteful black-and-white portraits of your children shot by someone like Guy Hills on the wall, Janey had already decided that a small photo on the desk would suffice.

Working in a company like Foss and Spring was

generally about neutralising your sexuality. Unless you could keep up with the boys, go out drinking at night after work, and didn't baulk at lap-dancing clubs. But Janey wasn't one of those. It wasn't a morality issue. It was more that she didn't feel comfortable hanging out with her colleagues. And it didn't matter as long as she was careful to adopt the correct camouflage: repressed patterns in unthreatening colours, hard angles, and nothing that made you stand out from the crowd.

You could lie on your sofa to recover from a hangover but not because you had stress-induced Braxton Hicks contractions that made your stomach as hard as a football. She would keep the breast pump, the nipple shields and the haemorrhoid cream locked in the bottom drawer of her desk. This kind of schizophrenia was the price working mothers paid for breaking through the glass ceiling. That's where feminists got it wrong: they shouldn't have focused on being equal in a man's world; they should have tried to make the world of work more female. Where was the equality in watching your colleagues drool over an Eastern European girl winding her way around a pole when you couldn't admit you were taking the day off because your child was sick? It was like thinking that Madonna's body at fifty represented progress for womankind.

But the real problem with being pregnant was that it made you potent in the wrong way because it highlighted your femaleness. Initially when people urged her to finish work a month before the baby was due, she assumed it was a benevolent gesture to give her time to rest. Now she realised, just before her due date, that it had more to do with the sight of her swollen belly and enormous breasts.

People averted their eyes when she stood up, as if trying to block out the incontrovertible truth that everything about Janey was now round edges and soft focus.

The problem for Janey was that even though she could give up her job, she loved it too much. She loved the rationality of law. She loved the intense detail of a legal document in the same way that someone might appreciate the exquisite geometry of an old Persian tile. She loved the logic of legal argument. She could cast her careful eye over a draft and winkle out its inconsistencies better than most of her colleagues. She was adept at finding solutions to tricky problems. Most of all she loved the adrenalin rush of a big deal.

She had been in the office until 2 a.m. the past four nights, and although her associates and trainees had carried around the boxes of legal documents, held the door open for her and generally tried to make life easy, elation was now tempered by exhaustion. So she turned to the bits she didn't love: the uncontrollable elements; the unpredictable hours; the tricky personalities; and the egos bumping together. The way no part of her private life was sacrosanct.

Janey pulled herself out of her chair and stood up in a pair of high-heeled Christian Louboutin sandals, and headed towards the filing cabinet. She felt like a cruise ship coming into dock. A potential new client was scheduled for a ten o'clock meeting. Given she was going on maternity leave in two weeks she should have got someone else to sit in on the meeting, but then she would never have any chance of keeping the client afterwards, so she'd decided to go it alone. Besides, if Steve's doom-mongering was correct and double-dip recession was inevitable, then every client counted. His fund was fine, he insisted, because most of their positions were shortened. But if the rumours about Freddie Mac and Fannie Mae were true, then turbulent times lay ahead.

Janey opened a file marked *Limitations of Liability* and glanced inside without pulling it out of the open drawer. It was where she kept all the details about nanny agencies. Roughly speaking, they could be divided into three categories: those with posh-sounding names like Regency, Burlington or Knightsbridge, which inspired images of Norland Nannies in neat uniforms pushing old-fashioned prams; those that engendered feelings of security like Blossom, Buttons and Cosy Toes; and those that sounded rigorously efficient, like Clockwork Care. The one you chose would define the type of mother you intended to be. So Janey went for the one that promised confidentiality clauses in contracts and sent its nannies on resuscitation courses and training in how to deal with threatening situations, including kidnap and Al Qaeda attacks.

The search for a full-time nanny and someone who could offer weekend cover had begun shortly after the search for a maternity nurse had successfully ended. When Laura had phoned to tell her about their weekend in Suffolk, she had also advised against recruiting someone from the moment the baby arrived home, with a persuasive argument that motherhood was a job best learnt at the coalface. Janey had argued that it would make it easier to go back to work if someone else was already involved and that maternity nurses always got babies into good routines.

'You have to accept there will be an underlying sense of chaos, Janey,' Laura had suggested at the beginning of the phone conversation, trying to work out how she was going to tell her that after over nine years without any meaningful contact, Patrick had returned and wanted to get in touch with her.

'You're good at managing spontaneity, Laura, I'm not,' Janey had said.

'I have no choice,' Laura had replied.

What Janey didn't tell Laura was that having someone to help from the outset was also a preventative measure. She wanted to inoculate herself against the contagion that inflicted other mothers: loss of professional drive. She had seen it happen time and time again. If she could have perspective, then perhaps she would be able to keep her hormones in check. Then she could resist the lure of her baby.

She didn't want to feel like Laura, who, in her unguarded moments, admitted to Janey that full-time work had failed her. Part of Laura's desire for another baby was simply to have what she didn't have when Ben and Nell were born. Laura wanted open-ended maternity leave. She wanted to flirt with the possibility of breastfeeding for a full year and to spend her days discussing the relative values of sweet potato over butternut squash when weaning. And this was someone who went to America to lecture on new techniques for early identification of Parkinson's patients. Just recently Laura had said she would happily forsake the possibility of research, topple over the career ladder and simply see patients if it meant she could work part-time.

The phone conversation had then turned to Sam's contretemps with Hannah's bull. Janey wished she had been there. She had told everyone that it was too uncomfortable to travel, but the reality was that Steve didn't want to go.

'It sounds like an attempt to assert his masculinity,' joked Janey, 'a physical manifestation of his mental grapple with the vasectomy question.'

'He was pissed,' said Laura.

'Laura, maybe you should consider the upside of Sam's decision to have the snip,' suggested Janey.

'There is no upside, other than the fact that he'll no longer have this neurosis about making me pregnant,' said Laura, who had now forgotten the reason why she had called Janey.

'It shows commitment to you,' interrupted Janey. 'He's rejecting the possibility that he might want to have children with another woman.' This thought hadn't crossed Laura's mind. 'And if you really don't want him to go through with it, then move to France because under the Napoleonic Code vasectomy is considered an act of self-mutilation.'

'Tell me, what am I doing?' said Laura abruptly, in a tone so fierce that Janey wondered whether she had offended her.

'You're just trying to find the best way through a tricky situation,' said Janey soothingly.

'I told you, he was hit with an arrow,' said Laura, sounding a little impatient.

'Sam was?' said Janey, in confusion, wondering why Laura hadn't mentioned this at the outset. 'Where? How?' She presumed it was connected in some way to the bull-fighting incident.

'Hastings,' said Laura.

'But that's miles from Suffolk,' said Janey. 'Were you doing a historical re-enactment or something?'

'It went straight through his eye,' said Laura in a matter-of-fact tone.

'Oh my God,' said Janey.

'And before you ask, an injury like that causes irreparable damage to the front part of the brain, so it's probably a good thing that he died,' said Laura. Was this how she delivered bad news to her patients? Janey wondered in shock. 'And that is how William the Conqueror became King of England. Henry I died of a surfeit of lampreys,' she continued in a more emollient tone. 'They belong to the eel family. Janey, sorry, are you still there? I'm really sorry, Nell has got to finish this project before tomorrow. Can I call you back later? There is something I really need to speak to you about.'

Where did all the unfinished conversations go? Janey now wondered as she flicked through the nanny file at her desk. She imagined lost strands, half arguments, solutions to great philosophical questions stranded in space, floating aimlessly through the stratosphere hoping to regain contact with their missing half. Once you were a parent there was too much unfinished business.

Janey returned her attention to the nanny file. Pregnancy was making her dreamy. She focused on the latest crop of CVs in her hand, wondering how she could recruit someone for a job that she knew nothing about. She noticed that one of the nannies gave Jerry Hall as a referee. Was that a positive or a negative point? Janey wondered. Did the fact she had cared for the children of one of the Rolling Stones mean that she would look after Janey's baby better or worse than the comfortable-sounding Australian girl under her in the pile? It was impossible to know. The phone on her desk buzzed. The client had arrived. Janey asked the receptionist to give her ten minutes to allow her to reach the sixth-floor meeting room. It was essential to be sitting down when she met people for the first time. That way she won a few vital minutes of reprieve before they realised she was pregnant.

Seconds before he came into the room, Janey understood that there was no prospective client coming to visit her. Even before he nervously poked his head round the door, some instinct told her that it was Patrick. Perhaps his pheromones preceded him, Janey wondered, anxiously sniffing the air. One of the most remarkable side effects of pregnancy was the way that it induced an animal sense of smell. During the first three months it was so acute that Janey could close her eyes and understand the essence of another human being simply by inhaling their odour. She remembered sitting next to the CEO of a big property company during a takeover, noting the scent of fear that hung over him and wondering why this wasn't obvious to his overconfident underlings. Another time she noted the perfume of one of her female assistants on the sweater of an allegedly happily married father of four. It was the closest thing to having occult powers that Janey had ever experienced. She sniffed Steve's shirts every night and was relieved to find that they only ever smelt of him. The urge to mistrust was a reflex learnt from the years with Patrick.

The unexpected appearance of Patrick in her office was the sort of unfulfilled fantasy that had sustained Janey through the difficult days following his departure for Afghanistan and the definitive end of their relationship. She had envisaged this moment of happy reunion like a scene from the end of a Richard Curtis film. There would be passion, laughter, a thick layer of sentimentality and music by Dido playing in the background. As Patrick stood before her, however, none of these emotions stirred. Instead she felt consumed by a hormonal rage that started deep inside and rose within her like molten lava. How dare he unexpectedly turn up unannounced after so many years of silence? Had Jonathan not thought to warn her that Patrick had come home? And surely Laura had known when they spoke last week? She felt her face redden, until even her lips, ears and the tip of her nose were aflame. Thanks to the layers of restraint built up during her sixteen-year legal career, Janey's features, however, remained composed.

Patrick came in tentatively, shut the door behind him and then leant against it with his hands behind his back. Janey realised that he was holding the door handle shut. Was he worried that someone might spot he was an imposter or that she might try to leave? She leant forward, her forearms resting on the table, and waited for him to speak, a tactic she had learnt to disarm angry clients.

'God, it's easier to arrange a meeting with the Taliban,' Patrick said finally. He was wearing an expensive suit that Janey recognised as one of Jonathan's cast-offs and a carelessly knotted tie. In the five years that she had been with Patrick, Janey couldn't remember a single occasion when he wore a tie. She wondered what the receptionist had made of the long dark hair rolling towards his shoulders and how he had convinced her that he was legitimate. He was smaller than she remembered, a combination of the suit consuming his small frame and the fact he had lost weight. His eyes darted across her face, as though trying, but failing, to read her expression.

'Clients are only allowed on the sixth floor,' said Janey coolly, 'and never alone. It's to avoid financial espionage.'

'All very cloak and dagger,' said Patrick nervously. There was a slightly dismissive tone in his voice that Janey recognised. He had never really understood the point of her job, beyond the fact that she earned embarrassingly large bonuses and still worried that she was getting less than her colleagues. 'I want you to know that you can tell me to fuck off at any point and I will go straight out the door. I just want you to hear what I've come to say. Please.'

Janey knew that she should tell him to leave. But now that he was standing here before her, she couldn't bear to let him go. She just wanted to watch him for a while. She noticed that her anger was not contaminated with any of the pain of the first year following his departure and her body began to relax. She tried to remember the list of questions she had composed in her head in the long trough between Patrick's departure and her first meeting with Steve. Why did he leave without saying goodbye? Why did he never respond to her letters or emails? Why did he abandon not just her, but all his friends, including Sam, who more than anyone tried to persuade him to re-establish contact? The questions now seemed irrelevant, she had just the ephemeral curiosity you might feel flicking through a piece about Angelina and Brad in a glossy magazine.

'I saw the photographs in the *Sunday Times Magazine*. Very impressive,' said Janey, trying to keep her tone neutral. Patrick had never made much effort to read her emotions and this gave her an important advantage over him now. She pushed the anger back inside her. 'How did you get in?'

'My interpreter organised it. We walked for days. I couldn't use my mobile phones in case someone tried to track me. And then I couldn't get out because the Americans kept strafing the area I had to cross to get back into Afghanistan,' said Patrick quickly. He clearly didn't want to talk about work.

'So were they in Pakistan?' persisted Janey, with a mixture of genuine curiosity and pleasure at his discomfort.

'Difficult to tell,' mumbled Patrick, stepping from one foot to the other. 'But most probably.'

'I knew you were back when the pictures dried up,' said Janey. She was now smiling, but it was a difficult expression to read because it spoke of politeness rather than warmth.

'So you've followed my progress?' asked Patrick hopefully.

'No,' said Janey bluntly. 'Sam kept me posted. Periodically. If I asked.' There was an uncomfortable silence. The mention of Sam was pointed.

'You should try and see him,' Janey suggested, 'he's feeling very gloomy.'

He looked up now and caught her eye. Janey remembered a conversation they had once had about what they would do when they retired. After much discussion, they had resolved to travel around India together on a motorbike and experiment with hallucinogenic drugs. At the time it had seemed like the promise of a future together. Less than six months later, Janey had turned thirty, and Patrick was gone.

During the period immediately afterwards, Janey thought about Patrick so much that she felt as though he was in the room with her. She appreciated work as never before, as the only distraction that could temporarily obliterate him from her thoughts. Then one day she checked her watch and saw that it was almost midday and realised that she had managed to get through a whole morning without thinking about him once. For the first time she saw the possibility of recovery. There followed years of unsuitable couplings: the television producer with a cocaine habit; the advertising exec who couldn't have sex without watching porn at the same time; the bisexual estate agent; and the married woman. During this period Laura and Sam joked that her only prerequisite for relationships was that they wouldn't work. Janey didn't tell them about the website to meet married men, but two weeks after she first logged on in March 2007, she met Steve.

Apart from posing as a married man, from the outset of their relationship Steve had been utterly straightforward. Over dinner the first time they met he was the one who confessed that he was single but enjoyed being with 'attached women' because they were generally less demanding about relationships. After coffee, Janey had told Steve that she was physically single but still mentally attached to her previous boyfriend. He had smiled and told her that it was too late because he wanted to see her again anyway. He said he would call the following day and that they should go and see a film at the weekend. The next morning he called her office, even though she hadn't given him the number.

*

'I knew you wouldn't take my calls,' said Patrick. 'I couldn't think of any other way to see you alone.'

There was another long silence. Janey directed him to the seat opposite, wondering why she still wasn't asking him to leave. Perhaps it was a combination of impulses: curiosity mingled with a heavy dose of nostalgia, the lure of flattery steeped in anger, or the dangerous heat of unresolved desire.

'You'd better come and sit at the table,' said Janey, 'otherwise it looks a bit odd.' She pointed at the long glass window that ran the length of the office in case Patrick hadn't seen. Her acquiescence now gave him the upper hand, she thought, as did the fact that he had the advantage of anticipation. She sat very still and breathed deeply, partly to induce calm but mostly to prevent herself saying anything that she might regret later.

He walked towards the table and his lopsided gait was so familiar that it made Janey want to laugh. It seemed absurd that you could know someone so intimately and then they could disappear from your life without a trace only to emerge years later and dissolve the intervening years with a single action.

As if he knew what she was thinking, Patrick started nervously running his hand through his hair in the way that he did when he was about to formulate an argument. It was a gesture that made her solar plexus ache. This was why people who had lived with each other for years and then split up never saw each other again. Sometimes it was too painful to confront all that familiarity with the knowledge that you could never rekindle the intimacy.

She noticed Patrick staring at her hand and realised he was studying her wedding ring. She started to fiddle with it, trying to move it around her swollen finger as if to underline her marital status.

'I heard,' Patrick said, pointing at the ring and nodding his head slowly. 'Jonathan told me.'

'What did he say?' asked Janey, inwardly cursing Jonathan again for not warning her that Patrick was home.

'That you've married a really nice guy who you met through work,' said Patrick.

'I don't believe you,' said Janey, grateful for Jonathan's uncustomary discretion. 'Jonathan pretty much loathes Steve, partly because he's not you, but mostly because of his absurd and irrational prejudice against anyone who works in the City. Although he's always pleased to take their money in Eden. Especially now.'

'He blames me for him,' said Patrick. Janey looked puzzled.

'Jonathan says that if you'd never gone out with someone like me, you'd never have ended up with someone like Steve,' Patrick continued. He was watching his hand as his index finger made small interlocking circles on the table.

Janey couldn't resist the urge to inspect his hand. It was tanned, she noticed, and there were liver spots around the knuckles. He flexed his fingers and she began to consider the trajectory they had taken around her body the last time they saw each other. She remembered him lying beside her on one elbow drawing circles around her hip bone. She now unconsciously touched her left hip as if to confirm the memory and eventually found the bone amidst the expanse of belly.

'That is a little patronising,' said Janey, trying to sound less angry than she felt.

'I made that bit up,' Patrick admitted. 'What he said was that Steve is a bit of a control freak, and is slowly diluting your essence.'

'What is my essence?' questioned Janey.

'Essentially, you're a free spirit, Janey,' said Patrick, crossing his arms and leaning them on the table. 'You're like me. You like the trappings of stability because they insulate you against the vagaries of your childhood, but sooner or later you'll want to break free again.'

Janey struggled to remain silent. Patrick had inadvertently exposed the underlying problem in their relationship. He only wanted the parts of her that absolved him from responsibility. The other bits, the need for definition, the desire to make plans, to be able to talk about the future without an argument, were ignored by him.

'Janey, I know you never have any time, so I won't procrastinate,' declared Patrick suddenly. 'I've come to ask if it's too late.'

'Too late for what?' asked Janey, sounding confused.

'Too late to ask you to reconsider,' said Patrick slowly, his voice filled with emotion. 'Leaving you was a huge mistake.'

'It's taken you nine years to realise that?' Janey said, her voice taut with emotion. 'I know that you never wanted to rush into anything, but even by your standards that's quite extreme.'

'There were things I needed to exorcise,' said Patrick. 'I've been seeing a therapist since I came back and I've been doing a lot of thinking about our relationship. I think basically we needed to be apart so that each of us could grow alone. We were too codependent. But now I'm ready for you again. My therapist thinks it's the right decision.'

'So you're here on the advice of your therapist?' said Janey, now openly outraged. 'You only want me now because I belong to someone else,' she continued angrily. 'I was there for the taking for five years and you could never make up your mind if it was the right thing. Then you walked out the door without any explanation and now you expect me to just fall back in line? I'm married now.'

'You could leave him,' pleaded Patrick. 'You could take a sabbatical from work and come with me back to Kabul for six months.'

'Kabul?' said Janey in astonishment.

The baby started to kick and she saw two dark circles on her black silk shirt as milk began to leak. Her jacket was on the back of the chair. She reached back with one hand but it was clear from the expression on Patrick's face that he had noticed.

'What's that?' he asked, pointing at her shirt.

'Milk,' she said calmly. She couldn't feel embarrassed about something like this with a man who had once taken long and slow pleasure in hours of worship between her legs.

'You mean I've made your breasts leak milk? Isn't that a bit Oedipal or something?'

'It happens towards the end of pregnancy.' She leant back from the table and for the first time Patrick caught a glimpse of her stomach. He stood up so fast that his chair tipped over.

'Oh fuck,' he said.

'What's wrong?' asked Janey.

'I didn't know,' gasped Patrick, stabbing his finger towards her stomach. 'Jonathan didn't tell me.'

'I assumed you realised,' said Janey, wondering why Jonathan wouldn't have told him this.

'How could I have known?' demanded Patrick, who couldn't take his eyes off Janey's stomach. 'Couldn't you have let me know?'

'You didn't leave a forwarding address,' said Janey. 'And to be honest, it came as a bit of a surprise to me.' Her voice was softening.

The phone on the table began to ring. Janey was grateful for the opportunity to escape Patrick's wild eyes and picked up the receiver. Her secretary was primed to interrupt any meeting that went on longer than half an hour.

'There's someone on the line for you,' the secretary said.

'Thanks,' said Janey, 'I'll be right down.'

'Janey, there really is someone,' insisted her secretary. 'His name is Sam Diamond and he says it's urgent. He sounds quite distressed.'

Janey hesitated. The baby kicked against her ribs again and she winced. She wasn't sure that she could cope with the dimensions of Sam's current crisis. What was the remedy for systemic gloom? She felt a wave of nostalgia for the calamities they faced in their twenties: the hours spent advising Sam on how to tell Victoria that their relationship was over; the drama when he left the laptop containing the first script he had written for *Do Not Resuscitate* in the back of a cab; and the excitement and then the disappointment when his third film script was optioned for a couple of years and never made. Their relationship was always an easy one, which was why some evenings in their twenties they had ended up sharing a bed together and why there was never any emotional recrimination the following morning.

'Put him through,' Janey said in an even tone.

He was probably calling to warn her that Patrick was back. Her gratitude that at least someone was watching out for her was tinged with a familiar sense of irritation that Sam's intervention was too late. She turned her back on Patrick. When Sam spoke it was immediately apparent that he wasn't calling about Patrick.

'I'm in hospital,' he said dramatically. Janey could hear him pushing coins into a pay phone.

'What's wrong? Is it your eye?' asked Janey unthinkingly.

'My eye?' repeated Sam. 'No, I'm worried I might have a haemorrhage. Did you know that one of the body's main arteries is located in the penis? Hang on a moment will you?'

Janey could hear him breathing heavily into the receiver resting on his shoulder as he rustled around in his pockets for more loose change.

'Will you come to Queen Charlotte's and then help me home afterwards?' asked Sam. 'Otherwise I don't think I'll be able to go through with it on my own. I know men have been doing this for two hundred years and that I'm in good company if Yeats and Freud both had one, but I read a testimony on the Internet this morning from a man who had such post-operative pain that he had both bollocks removed. And I don't want that.'

'Sam, you've lost me,' said Janey.

'I'm about to have the vasectomy and I would really

appreciate some company,' said Sam. 'I can't phone Laura because she's too angry about it. She only wants to know when it's over. I've tried to call Jonathan, but I can't get hold of him.'

Janey studied her schedule for the rest of the day.

'I'm on my way,' she said. When she turned around again the door of the meeting room was open and Patrick was gone. That would be the last time they would ever see each other, Janey concluded, as she picked up her handbag and headed out of the office towards the lift. She couldn't have been more wrong.

10

When Janey arrived at the hospital an hour later, she found Sam deep in conversation with a nurse. The door was half open and he didn't notice her appear because his line of vision was obscured by a large fan that sat on the table beside him, whirring wildly and making his hair stand on end. Sam's face leaned towards the fan and the nurse was focused on fixing the screen that separated Sam's upper body from its lower half. It looked as though he was about to participate in a magic show where he would be cut in two.

The room smelt of disinfectant and fear, thought Janey, as she paused at the door, sniffing the air. It still wasn't too late to retreat. This was a situation that Steve would disapprove of. And how could she explain her presence at Sam's vasectomy? It was difficult to justify even to herself. But he had called her and asked her to come and she couldn't refuse because Sam was an undemanding friend and everyone knew he was immersed in the midst of an ill-defined midlife crisis. Besides, if he was having second thoughts, then she owed it to Laura to hear him out. Just because he was trapped on a hospital bed with a screen preventing him from escaping, didn't mean he had to go through with the operation.

Janey resolved not to say anything to Steve about the strange tangent the day had taken. Firstly it would fuel his misconceptions about her friends and secondly it would further harden his resistance to the idea of going on holiday with them in a couple of months. Still less would she mention Patrick's surprise appearance at her office. Even if Steve believed that she knew nothing about his return to England, he would assume that either Jonathan or Laura had engineered the meeting.

It was an unexpectedly sultry day in early May. Janey used the sleeve of her favourite cardigan to wipe beads of sweat from her brow. The cardigan sat atop her belly, its diminutive size completely disproportionate to the rest of her clothes, with their extra panels and carefully cut folds. But it provided her with a valuable link to the wardrobe she used to wear and therefore the person she used to be before the baby had taken up residence.

She could hear Sam firing off questions to the nurse. How many hours do you work? Do you get overtime? Where do you live? He couldn't be doing research for *Do Not Resuscitate* because Jonathan had told her that Sam had given up his job. The nurse patiently explained to him that she usually worked in the eye hospital but came to the vasectomy clinic one afternoon a week in order to earn some extra cash and learn a new procedure. Sam asked whether there were any similarities between eyes and testicles.

'They're both round,' she said drily.

'And you've done this before?' he asked anxiously, gripping her hand.

'Seventy-eight and a half times,' she said reassuringly,

releasing his grip and rubbing the red marks that Sam had left.

'How do you account for the half?' asked Sam.

'One patient couldn't go through with the other testicle,' she explained, shrugging her shoulders. She was so young that she couldn't possibly empathise with the situation of a thirty-nine-year-old man who was so terrified of impregnating his wife that he could no longer have an orgasm. Sam looked at her as she bent over to check the screen again. Her poorly cut trousers couldn't disguise the richness of her body with its satisfying curves and promise of comfort. For a moment Sam wondered whether he could persuade her to remove her clothes and straddle the part of his body below the screen to see whether the same thing occurred if he had sex with a woman who wasn't his wife. Just for research purposes.

He waited, half curious, half worried, to see if he felt anything that might qualify as arousal, feeling strangely detached from the bottom half of his body. It was covered in a green hospital sheet with a strategically placed square hole over the groin and a towel to protect his dignity. To his relief nothing happened. One of Sam's anxieties, not one he expressed to Janey, had been that he might get an erection when the doctor stretched his hand through the gown to make the incision in his first testicle. This at least now seemed highly unlikely.

Janey put her bag of legal papers on the floor and Sam looked up. He was so pleased to see her that he moment-arily forgot about the screen and tried to get up from the bed to greet her.

'Janey, Janey,' said Sam, his voice taut with emotion.

'Are you all right, Sam?' asked Janey.

'God, it's good to see you,' said Sam.

'Just try and stay still, Mr Diamond,' said the nurse. 'The doctor will be here very soon and he can answer any last-minute questions. He's very experienced. One of the best. His nickname is Zorro.' She smiled. Pretending her hand was a sword she drew three swift cuts in the air, making a whistling noise for each slash.

'I'm not sure about the sound effects,' said Sam, looking pale and worried.

The nurse went to the corner of the room to fetch a chair for Janey and brought it round so that she could sit beside Sam's head.

'Here you go, Mrs Diamond,' the nurse said. Neither of them corrected her. Janey carefully lowered herself into the chair. Sam tried to look up at her face as he spoke but he couldn't see past her stomach.

'I've taken a Xanax to calm my nerves,' Sam explained to Janey. 'But I don't think it's kicked in yet.'

'Are you sure you want to go through with it?' asked Janey, wondering whether Laura knew that Sam was here.

'It's non-negotiable,' said Sam seriously.

Relieved that someone else was willing to take responsibility for Sam, the nurse put on a pair of surgical gloves and began to lay out the instruments the doctor would need on a spotless silver table at the bottom of the bed. There was a scalpel, a pair of scissors with flat ends and something that looked suspiciously like a blow torch. Janey picked up some pieces of paper from the bed and began fanning herself with them.

INT. COMBE GUEST ROOM. LATER, the top of one

of the papers read. It was a page from one of Sam's scripts. She marvelled at its neatness as she read a few lines. Each character's name was written in capitals, the dialogue beautifully centred with all the correct punctuation and each scene neatly numbered on the right-hand side. Janey appreciated its pared-down beauty. It spoke of a punctilious nature that was so at odds with Sam's general demeanour that Janey felt as though she had accessed a previously hidden part of his personality.

'What's this?' she asked Sam, hoping to distract him. The edge of the scalpel caught the sun. Janey winced as she imagined it cutting through raw flesh and wondered if this was an instrument her consultant would use for the Caesarean in two weeks.

'It's something I've been working on,' Sam mumbled. 'It's almost finished.'

'That's great,' said Janey. 'What's it about?'

'I find it so difficult to describe what anything I write is about,' said Sam. 'But very loosely it's about what happens to a group of friends when a secret from the past is revealed when they go on holiday.'

'Sounds good,' said Janey. 'Can I keep reading?'

'Sure,' said Sam. 'How are you feeling by the way? It must be so hot for you.' It was a perfunctory question. People with older children were inured to the side effects of pregnancy. If she had sensed Sam was genuinely interested she would have told him that the latter part of pregnancy was probably not dissimilar to the post-operative discomfort of a vasectomy. Both made you walk with your legs apart and both required well-engineered underwear. In her head Janey listed her ailments in alphabetical order: haemorrhoids, heartburn, heat rash. They all began with the same letter.

'Good,' said Janey, wiping another film of sweat from her forehead.

She picked up a newspaper and absorbed alarming headlines about inflation and interest hikes, the prospect of world recession and the typhoon in Burma, even though she knew they would fill her with an ill-defined anxiety that would make her breathing shallow and her ribs ache. Before, Janey could have ingested such news with empathy but without feeling that it bore any relevance to her. Now everything seemed relevant. She wanted to know that children in Burma were being helped by aid workers because she needed to believe in a world that was essentially good.

'How's Steve?' Sam asked. He didn't wait for an answer. 'I am so grateful to you for coming,' he said, gripping her hand. 'I should never have looked at the Internet this morning. There were some very graphic images, including one of a man performing his own operation.'

'Look, what's the worst thing that can happen?' asked Janey in her most soothing tone. 'Apart from castration of course.'

'There's some research that suggests keeping the sperm in perpetual captivity can trigger an autoimmune disorder,' said Sam. 'And of course one in a hundred men becomes impotent.'

'That's worth considering,' conceded Janey.

'But that's why I'm here,' said Sam.

'What do you mean?' asked Janey.

'I've become phobic about sex because of unresolved

fears about having another baby,' explained Sam. 'I've talked to the doctor about it. It's not uncommon in men of my age apparently. I thought maybe Laura might have mentioned it to you.'

Sam could see the nurse was listening but he assumed correctly that such stories were too commonplace to hold her attention. The drama at the vasectomy-reversal clinic was undoubtedly more compelling.

'We don't talk about that kind of thing,' said Janey a little primly.

'I thought that women talked about sex all the time,' said Sam.

'Not once you're married,' said Janey. 'Unless it's very good or very bad or something really dramatic happens, like your husband impales himself on your Mirena coil. And our, er, history makes it less likely.'

'Laura doesn't know about that,' said Sam staring at the ceiling.

'Actually she does,' said Janey apologetically. 'When she came to see me after the fiasco with the marriage guidance counsellor, she asked me if we'd ever slept together and I couldn't lie.'

Sam could see that although the nurse was still fiddling with the exact placement of the surgical instruments, she was now obviously engrossed in their conversation. He tried to move towards Janey.

'Why didn't you tell me?' whispered Sam, sounding panicked. 'She hasn't mentioned anything. And why did you tell her now, when everything is so precarious?'

'I assumed you told her years ago,' said Janey, fanning her face with Sam's script. 'And since it was never mentioned,

it was as though it never happened. I thought it was
something you would rather forget. If it's any consolation,
she didn't seem to mind.'

'I intended to tell Laura, but the more time passed, the
less important it seemed,' said Sam.

'It was irrelevant,' agreed Janey. 'I can barely remember
the details.'

'You can't remember sleeping with me?' asked Sam.

'Well, the earth didn't exactly move, did it?' said Janey.

'That's because the earth was moving around us. We'd
taken too many psychotropics,' said Sam. 'And my technique has probably improved since then. Was I really so
unmemorable?'

'It was a long time ago,' smiled Janey.

'Do you ever wonder what might have happened if you
hadn't met Patrick and I hadn't met Laura?' asked Sam. 'Do
you sometimes imagine other lives with other people,
maybe people you haven't even met yet?'

'No,' said Janey calmly.

Her answer wasn't entirely honest. Women were prone
to making up endings for even the most unlikely couplings,
thought Janey, and she was no exception. If Patrick hadn't
come along and overwhelmed her, then her occasional
forays with Sam might have evolved into something more
domestic. They might have started eating cornflakes in bed
the morning after the night before or borrowed each
other's clothes or started to read more into the psychology
of those late-night clandestine encounters.

That possibility vanished the day Janey walked into
Laura's bedroom in the Shepherd's Bush house to find Sam
squashed into her single bed. Even though Janey and

Patrick had been going out with each other for three years, Janey still sensed Sam's unresolved need for her. His relationship with Laura, however, altered that dynamic and allowed them all the possibility of uncomplicated friendship.

The doctor came in through the door. Sam and Janey caught each other's eye and started laughing at the improbability of such a conversation in these surroundings. The doctor was taken aback to see Janey sitting beside Sam and asked whether she was really sure that she wanted to stay while he performed the procedure.

'Do you know that in the early twentieth century men thought vasectomy would heighten a man's intellect and sexual performance and control excessive masturbation?' asked Sam.

'I can see you've done your homework, Mr Diamond,' said the doctor. 'Now do you want me to quickly run through everything again?'

'No, thanks,' said Sam. 'I think I'm abreast of it all.'

'Do you have any new questions or want to discuss anything we have gone over before?' the doctor asked.

'What happens to the sperm?' Sam asked.

'Your body still makes them but they can't get out,' he said, poking his head around the screen.

'You mean they are imprisoned forever in my scrotum?' said Sam, sounding worried again.

'Yes,' said the doctor. 'They pile up behind the cut ends of the tube and are mopped up by scavenger cells.'

The doctor handed Sam a consent form and he swiftly scrawled a signature.

'Mrs Diamond, can I propose that you step outside and stay in the waiting room until we're finished?' the doctor suggested. Janey looked blankly at the doctor as it dawned on her that he assumed she was Sam's wife.

'Please don't go,' begged Sam. 'You're such a good distraction.'

'I think I'll stay,' said Janey resolutely.

'Well, can I recommend that you don't look beyond the screen,' the doctor said. 'Even though it's a tiny operation, it can be a little graphic for some people, especially in your condition.'

Sam focused on the ceiling light. He felt the towel being removed from his groin and wondered whether it was the doctor or nurse who had lifted it up. He imagined his penis, limp and flaccid, clinging to his thigh in fear. As instructed, he had shaved his balls in the bath this morning. The doctor had said to do a small area at the front of the testicle close to where the vas deferens lay. Sam had erred on the side of caution and shaved almost three-quarters of the pubic hair from each testicle until the skin had the goose-pimpled texture of a plucked turkey.

It had taken him almost half an hour. At first he had treated it like a regular shave, lathering up his balls with shaving foam. But he had quickly discovered that the hair was so long that it was clearly worth a quick short back and sides with Laura's nail scissors before embarking on the more intricate close shave. Even then he had snagged his right testicle.

He felt the doctor put his hand through the hole in the sheet and gently tug at this same testicle. There was a cold sensation as he sterilised the skin where the incision would be made. The doctor then felt for the vas, near to the neck of the scrotum, and squeezed it as close to the skin as possible. He asked the nurse to pass him two millilitres of lignocaine in a syringe. She pressed the plunger in slightly and a small stream of anaesthetic spurted from the end of the needle.

'Is that going in my bollocks?' asked Sam nervously.

'It's the anaesthetic,' said the doctor reassuringly. 'Believe me, it would be far worse without it.'

'What happens if I scream?' asked Sam.

'You won't because I've applied a bit of local to the scrotum,' said the doctor calmly, perching on his stool, legs slightly apart, waiting for the right moment to plunge in the syringe.

'This is the worst bit,' said the nurse reassuringly.

'I don't know if that makes it worse or better,' said Sam.

'All fine, Mr Diamond?' the doctor asked, peering round the screen.

'Never better,' said Sam, 'just stick it in.'

Sam felt nothing. He closed his eyes and saw thin spaghetti of vas deferens floating before him. But it was better than focusing on the centimetre-long scalpel incision that the doctor was now cutting through his left testicle. He felt a tug and guessed correctly that the doctor was pulling out a long loop of vas through the incision. He was aware of Janey's hand on top of his own, but couldn't say how long it had been there.

'It's surprisingly long,' Sam told Janey. 'He's going to remove about a centimetre, burn the ends and then retie them.'

Sam found it oddly comforting explaining the operation to Janey. He imagined he was doing research for *Do Not Resuscitate* and tried to detach himself from what was going on. He felt no shame at Janey's presence. Instead fear was replaced by guilt at making Janey sit in this hot, stuffy room. He knew, however, that he couldn't get through this without her.

He tried to imagine Jonathan sitting in the seat beside him, because, like being best man at their wedding, this was a role he should have performed. Jonathan might not be a good listener but he always rallied in a crisis. Sam had told Janey that he couldn't get hold of him. But he hadn't even bothered because he was still too angry with him.

'I know I'm being totally irresponsible,' Jonathan kept saying to Sam during their last phone conversation. 'But I've been responsible for years. It's a lust thing, Sam.'

'It's a middle-aged-man thing,' said Sam. 'And you have free will.'

'There's a sense of destiny about it,' said Jonathan, as though this absolved him of any responsibility for his actions. 'I feel as though I'm destined to be with Eve.'

'So when you got married to Hannah, did you think you were destined to get divorced?' asked Sam in exasperation at Jonathan's hackneyed attempt to invest the relationship with a romanticism it didn't deserve.

'God, Sam, aren't you ever tempted?' asked Jonathan.

Lying on the hospital bed, his eyes still closed, Sam thought about Eve's dark eyelashes and the tilt of her chin and the way that her body swung when it moved past him in the theatre. She might as well have been naked even when she was dressed. He started to sketch the outline of her body with his finger on the sheet beside him. He imagined how she would taste. Not sweet, more spicy, he decided. He imagined running a fingernail down the side of her arm and between each of her fingers. She was the sort of woman who made you want to draw blood, he thought, moving his hand from beneath Janey's and gripping the side railings of the bed. They were too old for women like that.

Sam tried to imagine what it might be like if Jonathan brought Eve on holiday to Scotland instead of Hannah. He conjured up various scenarios: Eve sitting on Jonathan's knee watching television with Luke and Gaby at the other end of the sofa, her hand tucked inside the top two buttons of his shirt; Eve debating with Laura the historic inevitability of her relationship with Jonathan as though all the years he spent with Hannah counted for nothing; Eve on the beach with Steve, his new baby in one arm and BlackBerry in the other, extolling the virtues of working for a hedge fund over life in an investment bank. Sam shook his head. It was implausible.

The smell of burning flesh made Sam open his eyes again.

'What's that?' he asked.

'I'm just burning off each end of the vas and then I'm going to tie the knot,' said the doctor.

'Just relax,' said the nurse.

'I'm done,' said the doctor a few minutes later. He instructed the nurse to make sure that Sam left with two small plastic pots. 'You need to make absolutely sure that you empty your tubes of all remaining live sperm and then send these back so we can check. Do the first one in four weeks and the next one the following month. And make sure you use a contraceptive until you've had the all-clear.'

'Remember your scrotum might be black tomorrow,' said the nurse in a kindly tone. 'It's the bruising.'

'These might contain the last sperm I will ever produce,' Sam said dramatically, looking at the pots.

Janey sat on the chair, trying to maintain an upright position, shoulders pulled back to help her breathe more deeply. Using the full force of her diaphragm to encourage her lungs to work at full capacity she took a deep breath. The smell of Sam's singed flesh filled her nostrils until she could taste it at the back of her throat. She tried to distract herself. She imagined going to the party to launch Jonathan's cookery book with her newborn baby in a sling. Despite the incontrovertible visual evidence, she still couldn't imagine holding her own baby. She then started to play a variation on 'I Packed My Bag', visualising all the things she would need to take for the holiday in Scotland laid out on her bed in alphabetical order. Curiously, there was nothing belonging to Steve.

This might have worried her but the stench of burnt flesh was a more compellingly immediate problem. Her mind kept returning to the smell of cooked meat. Since she became pregnant Janey had stopped eating red meat. The fibrous texture, the smell, the way it looked made her feel nauseous. The odour of Sam's burnt vas reminded her of all this. And it was exacerbated by the fact that it was distinctly the stench of burnt human flesh. She felt herself gag. It was an involuntary move from deep within and once she started she couldn't stop. She pulled herself out of the chair and was violently sick. And as she stood up she saw a burst of water pour on to the floor.

'I think my waters have broken,' said Janey in wonder.

'Well at least you're in the right place,' said the nurse.

'I'm meant to be having an elective Caesarean in two

weeks at a different hospital,' Janey said, pointing at her stomach. 'I haven't even got the birth plan with me. Or the baby clothes. Or the car seat. Or my husband. This isn't part of my schedule.' She opened the diary on her BlackBerry.

'Children don't always conform to our expectations,' smiled the nurse.

Sam lay on the bed, vaguely wondering how to respond, but unable to react. The Xanax made him feel one step removed from what was going on. He felt a pleasant sensation, like warm oil being poured over his body, as he finally relaxed. He was vaguely conscious that his timing was wrong. He should have taken the pill an hour earlier. But it wasn't simply the way the drug had taken the edge off the fear and neutralised the stress hormones that should have been coursing through his body. It was also the relief that now he could get on with the rest of his life. Sam was reborn. He looked at the film script sitting on the table. This was the one. That is what his agent had said and for the first time he believed it.

11

Five minutes after she rang the bell for the first time, Laura dropped to her knees on Janey's doorstep and wedged open the letter box with a rolled-up copy of *The Lancet*, in order to work out exactly what was going on inside. She hitched up her skirt over her thighs so that it wouldn't trail on the ground and fray the hem. The skirt was a designer hand-me-down that Janey had bequeathed to Laura when she discovered she was pregnant. Janey had already berated her for putting this skirt in the washing machine and since then it had lost a significant tussle in a grey wash. But Marc Jacobs wasn't here to register his disapproval and Laura was counting on Janey's mind being too occupied by the unexpected early arrival of the baby to notice its transition from pale blue to mud.

As she bent forward towards the letter box, Laura felt the wind glance the back of her upper leg and it reminded her of the days when she wore miniskirts, before her thighs had developed the depth of character normally used to describe faces.

She peered through the opening into the hallway of Janey's house searching for signs that someone was there. A huge pram dominated the space, but Laura could see there was no sleeping baby inside. An expensive leather sling lined with sheepskin lay on top of a car seat that matched the pram. *Bill Amberg* it said in big letters on the side of the sling. Big name for a small baby, thought Laura. At least they had stopped wrangling over what to call him. The baby must surely be in the house because all his favoured modes of transport were lined up before her. She called Janey's mobile phone and heard it ring in the hall.

What struck Laura most was what she didn't see. There were no milk-encrusted white muslin squares stranded on the stairs. No nappy sacks in disorderly queues hoping to be taken outside. No hillocks of Babygros waiting to be washed. No half-eaten bars of chocolate. In the same way, Laura realised, there would never be tummies spilling over baggy tracksuit bottoms worn three days in a row; or arguments over the ethics of going to church to secure a place in a good primary school; or jars of baby food for those days when climbing Everest seemed a preferable option to the endless puréeing of vegetables. This was a sanitised version of the kingdom of new baby. This was how the very affluent had babies. Up and down this road in central Notting Hill babies would be born into similar orderliness. Laura envisaged newborns cooing contentedly in identical wrinkle-free, bright white outfits, beside shiny Poggenpohl kitchen units in cool colours, while their mothers expressed organic milk from pale breasts before their morning Pilates class. There was no grey wash in W11.

Laura put her mouth to the letter box and shouted a couple of times. Then, getting more frustrated, she decided to use the rolled-up magazine as a loudspeaker, bellowed as lustily as she could and put her ear to the end. She was trying to remember the noises of a newborn baby: the high-pitched mewing cry for milk, washing machine on endless rinse cycles, the sound of Mother sobbing as oestrogen levels plummeted and prolactin spiked, the humming of whales communicating under water on that CD that claimed to soothe even the most colicky baby. But there was nothing. Just white noise. She held her breath for a moment to sharpen her senses and listened out for signs of someone either walking upstairs from the basement or downstairs from the top of the house, because anyone in the sitting room would surely have heard her.

Placing the palms of her hand flat against the door so that her mouth was as close as possible to the letter box, Laura yelled Janey's name so loudly that it brought the next-door neighbour to the front door. Laura thought she saw the sitting-room curtain move.

'What sins are you atoning for?' an amused voice unexpectedly asked. Laura turned her head and saw a tousled-headed man of indeterminate age addressing her. She must have looked puzzled because then he added, 'You remind me of those Catholic ladies crawling on their knees during pilgrimages to Lourdes. Except their dress code is a little more sober.'

'Gluttony mostly,' joked Laura, pointing to the large panettone sitting beside a huge bunch of peonies. She stood up and started to pull down the skirt.

'In my book, appetite isn't a sin,' he said, appraising Laura's body with a lascivious sweep from top to toe.

Laura was a little taken aback. She couldn't remember the last time a stranger had flirted with her so obviously.

'If she doesn't come, you can always wait at mine till she's home,' the next-door neighbour said. 'I've finished work for the day.' It sounded a well-rehearsed line.

'Do you work from home?' asked Laura, not wanting to be rude.

'Mostly,' the man said. 'Compared to Janey and Steve I guess I do. Until she had the baby I don't think I'd ever seen her during daylight hours. Now I see her, but I can't speak to her because I can't get past the guard.'

'Steve?' asked Laura, a little taken aback at his direct manner, but quietly reassured that it wasn't just Janey's old friends who found Steve overly possessive.

'No,' the man laughed, 'Mrs Doubtfire,' and then when Laura still seemed puzzled, he added, 'That woman they've got in to help with the baby.'

Laura heard a noise inside the house and knelt down to continue her vigil. This time the view in the hall was obscured by a piece of brown material. Laura stretched her fingers through the letter box and tried to grab at the heavy gaberdine fabric, wondering whether a curtain had fallen in front of the door from the inside. Drapes were not really Janey's style, although she had become obsessed with blackout blinds after reading some baby book. Laura's hand flailed around. The letter box was too narrow and she could only pull the material using a pincer movement with her thumb and middle finger. Then the door opened so forcefully that Laura found herself tumbling over the doorstep on to the floor in front of a doughty sixty-year-old woman who must have been peering through the spyhole as Laura was looking through the letter box.

'Can I help you?' the maternity nurse asked imperiously,

as she smoothed the wrinkled piece of skirt Laura had been clutching.

'Sorry, I've come to visit Janey and baby Bill,' Laura explained, getting up from the floor. 'I rang the bell but no one came.'

'Baby is asleep,' the woman said, defiantly blocking Laura's way into the house. 'Baby always naps between one forty-five and two thirty every afternoon.'

'Gosh, what a compliant little fellow,' said Laura, impressed. 'Still, at least Janey is awake.'

'She's expressing milk for the feed tonight,' said the maternity nurse firmly.

Laura pointed to the staircase as Janey appeared from upstairs and tentatively began her descent into the hall. Janey held the banister tightly and put both feet on each step, as though trying to conserve energy. When she reached the landing between the first and ground floors she stopped to smile at Laura, but it was more grimace and grit than relaxed bonhomie. The discomfort of childbirth was certainly democratic, thought Laura, recalling the soggy experience of leaking milk, unexpected gushes of blood and bloody craters in her nipples that meant her babies burped up pink milkshake when they had wind.

Janey's gait reminded Laura of Sam, who was sitting at home watching daytime TV, wearing two pairs of white Jockey Y-fronts and holding a packet of frozen peas over his groin with one hand and a can of beer in the other. When Sam had showed Laura his testicles the morning after the vasectomy, she put her hand over her mouth in a silent cry of shock, not because she was surprised that he had gone through with it, but because his testicles were coal-black, as though frostbitten. He said it would take weeks for the bruising to subside. Then he casually mentioned that he had sent off a finished film script to his agent and wouldn't be working any more that week. *Do Not Resuscitate* had expired, Sam explained, as if he was talking about something trivial like reaching the end of the cornflakes packet. Laura hadn't reacted. Her relief at Sam's honesty outweighed her concern over what he might do next. It seemed a sign of hope.

There was a strange symmetry in the fact that Sam had had his vasectomy and Janey had given birth on the same day, thought Laura, remembering Sam's panicked phone call from the hospital. But perhaps no stranger than Sam's recent admission that he had slept with Janey the same evening he thought he'd first met Laura over dinner at Jonathan's house. Laura tried to imagine Janey seeing Sam through his operation and then both of them going up in wheelchairs to the maternity ward on the fourth floor of Queen Charlotte's after Sam had passed out. Sam had eaten Janey's Dextrose energy tablets and stayed with her until she was almost eight centimetres dilated, when Steve finally arrived back from a business meeting in Frankfurt. Steve's biggest concern, said Sam, was that he hadn't brought the iPod with the music for the pushing stage.

It was unorthodox that Janey had attended Sam's vasectomy, Laura concurred with Steve when he called her the following day to announce the birth of a baby boy, name undecided. And most unfortunate that he was flying back from Frankfurt through most of Janey's labour. An image of Janey, feet in stirrups, lying on a hospital bed wearing nothing more than a stiff gown while a midwife examined her in front of Sam, momentarily seized their collective consciousness and they both fell silent.

Laura then hurriedly explained that she had told Sam she didn't want to be involved with his operation and couldn't really blame him for contacting Janey instead of her. Steve reluctantly agreed that he was grateful for Sam's presence at the hospital.

'At least their historical familiarity should neutralise any potential embarrassment for them,' Steve said stiffly.

'God, what have you done to my skirt?' Janey asked Laura as she finally reached the bottom of the stairs. This type of comment might once have irritated Laura as faintly patronising, but she recognised it as Janey's attempt to convince herself that she would find these things important again one day.

'Now, remember that at quarter to four you need to feed baby again and then play with him for twenty minutes,' the maternity nurse advised. Janey meekly nodded.

'Are you doing Junior Monopoly already?' Laura asked quizzically, as she walked over to give Janey a careful hug.

'Don't make me laugh, it's too painful,' said Janey, who couldn't remember being more pleased to see Laura.

'Which bit?' asked Laura, wincing in sympathy.

'It's very fickle,' said Janey thoughtfully. 'It alternates between the haemorrhoids, which require heat, and the stitches which require frozen peas, until it's time to breastfeed and then it transfers to the cracked nipples. Why did no one tell me to save the epidural for afterwards?'

'It gets easier with each baby,' Laura reassured her.

'Well I'll never know because I'm not having another one,' Janey said emphatically. 'Do you want something to drink, Laura?'

Laura waited for the maternity nurse to offer to put the kettle on but instead she headed upstairs stony-faced, after informing them both that she was going to wake up the baby.

'No one wakes a sleeping baby,' Laura blurted out in astonishment, immediately forgetting her promise not to interfere.

'If I can stick to the programme laid out in the book, then the baby will be sleeping through the night within three weeks,' said Janey, sounding as though she was reciting a mantra. 'It's a bit labour-intensive at the moment, but I'll reap the benefits later.'

'Well, it should make it easier when we go on holiday,' said Laura, trying to be encouraging.

'I don't think we'll be able to come to Coll,' said Janey apologetically. 'I haven't even made it to the shops yet.'

'Two months is a great age to go away with a small baby,' insisted Laura. 'They are so portable. And we'll all help.'

'It's not that,' muttered Janey, glancing around the room to check the maternity nurse had left. 'It's just that the book says the baby should always sleep in the same room.'

'So you're never going away again?' asked Laura.

'And there's the question of the blackout blinds,' sighed Janey. 'The book says babies should always sleep in a room with blackout blinds and they almost certainly won't have any in a rented house on a remote Scottish island.' The book didn't say anything about how to persuade recalcitrant husbands to go away with their wife's friends, but Janey didn't mention this.

Laura remained silent. Everyone found their own way in the end. Instead she wandered into the kitchen, hoping Janey would follow her. She put the cake, the bunch of flowers and a present on the kitchen island in a careful row. A new piece of intimidating gadgetry sat there glinting in the sunlight. Laura stroked its shiny steel exterior and picked up a plastic suction pad that attached to the machine with a long tube. It was a breast pump, she realised, but not like any she remembered. It conjured images of intensive milking parlours in Eastern Europe where cows stoked by hormones and growth stimulants produced unimaginable amounts of creamy milk from engorged swollen udders.

'That's quite a piece of kit,' Laura said, eyeing Janey's impressive cleavage.

'I express milk every morning at six forty-five,' explained Janey. 'And then I freeze some of it and the maternity nurse uses the rest for the night feed so that I get a full night's sleep.'

'God,' said Laura, impressed.

'Except I can't sleep when I hear him cry,' admitted Janey.

Laura tried to remember the aftermath of Nell's and Ben's births, the struggle to get dressed before noon and the way that having a bath assumed mythical proportions because it was the only time she was on her own. Sam would watch BBC World at three o'clock in the morning with Ben, wide-eyed and unable to sleep, lying in his arms. Days and nights were seamless.

'Baby Bill,' exclaimed Laura, as she walked over to take the tightly swaddled baby from the arms of the maternity nurse, who had just appeared in the kitchen. His eyes were tightly shut, like a tiny rabbit. Laura put out her arms to hold the baby for the first time. Reluctantly the maternity nurse handed him over, instructing her how to hold him.

'I've had two of my own,' smiled Laura reassuringly as she placed a firm hand behind his head.

'Bill?' questioned Janey from her pile of carefully positioned cushions on the sofa.

'I thought you had called him Bill Amberg Dart,' said Laura.

'That's the brand of baby sling,' said Janey, crossing her legs to prevent any pressure on the stitches as she started laughing. 'He's called Jack Oberon Henry Milo Dart. It's our compromise solution, we each chose two names. No prizes for guessing mine.'

'Baby needs to lie in his play gym for twenty minutes,' the maternity nurse instructed Laura, as she removed Jack Oberon Henry Milo Dart unceremoniously from her arms and laid him beneath lions and tigers in exuberant primary colours. The baby lay there sound asleep, legs straight, arms above his head. Laura admired his tenacity as the maternity nurse tickled his feet and blew in his face to try and wake him up.

'Shall I look on the website to see if it says what to do?' asked Janey anxiously.

'Perhaps if you show him those black and white patterns, that will stimulate him,' the maternity nurse insisted, pressing a pack of cards into Janey's hand.

'Isn't he a bit young for snap?' teased Laura.

The doorbell rang and the maternity nurse gave Janey a disapproving look.

'You'll miss your afternoon nap,' she said, heading towards the door.

'The book doesn't recommend guests,' said Janey, shrugging her shoulders as she struggled to pull herself out of the sofa. 'It will be either Hannah, who is already four hours later than scheduled, or Pete from next door, who is worried that I've joined a cult for mothers of newborn babies.'

'I met him on the way in,' said Laura, urging her to stay still.

'Did he flirt with you?' asked Janey. Laura nodded, annoyed that she was disappointed to hear that she hadn't been singled out for special treatment. A few years ago, she would have been irritated by a man like this. Now she was flattered by his attention.

Hannah breezed into the room without any explanation for her lateness. Laura and Janey knew better than to question her. Ever since Laura first met Hannah it was apparent that she was someone who liked to do things on her own terms and in her own time. Although Janey was the one who had grown up on a commune where self-expression was revered, it crossed Laura's mind that Hannah was the true free spirit among them. For years Laura had assumed that Hannah stood in Jonathan's shadow. Now it occurred to her that shadows were a good place to hide from the well-meaning scrutiny of friends. Hannah might be adept at pleasing Jonathan, but she was not immune to pleasing herself.

Laura had considered Hannah's decision to go through

with her pregnancy with Luke when she was just twenty years old as a sign of self-sacrifice. Yet it was this decision that had propelled Jonathan to formally end his relationship with Victoria in order to move in with Hannah. Similarly Laura had pitied Hannah for her failure to forge any meaningful career after she abandoned her university degree when she discovered she was pregnant. Laura had always assumed her dilettante approach was a sign that she lived in Jonathan's professional wake. Yet as she now pushed bags of muddy vegetables and a big bunch of alliums into Janey's hands, Laura realised that Hannah was happy to watch her friends bump their heads on glass ceilings and that flitting from one job to another suited her better.

'What's with the battleaxe?' Hannah whispered, as the maternity nurse headed back upstairs.

'She's an acolyte of Gina Ford,' explained Janey in hallowed tones.

'Well she's not wearing any Gucci,' said Hannah. She headed towards Jack and gently picked him up off the floor, ignoring Janey's instruction to wash her hands. She began the eulogy of the newborn baby, commenting on his looks (Steve's mouth, Janey's eyes), his sweet smell, the tininess of his hands, and the way he still behaved as though he was not yet quite of this world, with his aversion to light and the odd way his fingers traced patterns in the air even as he slept.

'Not Tom Ford, Gina Ford,' whispered Janey.

'Who is Gina Ford?' asked Hannah. Janey stared at her, open-mouthed.

'She's the baby guru that those mothers wanted to fire

into the Lebanon on rockets,' said Laura, forgetting that Hannah rarely read the papers. 'She has all these rigid routines.'

'Everyone swears by her,' said Janey. 'She gets babies to sleep.'

'Babies don't need gurus and manuals to get to sleep,' said Hannah, shrugging her shoulders. 'They do that anyway.'

'Can you switch on the *Baby Mozart* please?' asked Janey anxiously.

'Definitely beats Bruce Springsteen,' said Laura, as she tried to remember where the CD player was hidden.

No one realised what it was like to grow up without any foundations for parenting, thought Janey. Her only real conviction was that whichever route she chose, it should be as far removed as possible from everything her mother had done. Demand feeding, babies in the bed, sex education at five years old, lengthy discussions about the exact nature of the female orgasm, home education, primal screaming, rebirthing, none of these would have any place in the life of the baby lying asleep on the floor in front of her. Janey would never take magic mushrooms or smoke home-grown grass with her children as her mother had done.

She remembered describing these experiences to Patrick and his laughter at the absurdity of it all. It had made her attractive to him because it marked her out as someone who had grown up outside the boundaries of middle-class convention. But he ignored the fact that many of the fundamental decisions she made about life were because she wanted the orderly existence in adulthood that was denied to her as a child. She might have felt the pull to be reckless in her twenties but she chose friends who wouldn't exacerbate that urge.

It wasn't that she had had an unhappy childhood, thought Janey, as she shifted uncomfortably from one buttock to the other. It was a commune, not a cult. There was no dark underbelly of child abuse, although benign neglect certainly played its part. There were strong personalities who had an unhealthy influence over the way things were run, even though they were democratically elected. She remembered an American woman who was obsessed with the idea that everyone should have a bowel movement each morning. Then there was a Scottish man, with whom her mother had a two-month relationship, who lectured Janey and her teenage friends on the importance of free love. But many of the obsessions were harmless, even educational: how to grow enough food to be self-sufficient; how to earn money that wasn't tainted by association with exploitative capitalist practices; how to live a life where emotions were freely expressed and nothing repressed.

It was more the disorderly and unpredictable nature of the experience that unsettled her. The way she and her younger brother would unexpectedly be left at the home of another family for a few days while her mother explored a new relationship unencumbered by small children. Sometimes it was a good experience. She remembered a Canadian woman who introduced them to the joys of chocolate brownies. Other times Janey would be left to comfort her brother, who often sobbed himself to sleep imagining their mother, like their father, was gone forever. Despite the best efforts of the psychotherapist she had seen briefly after Patrick left for Afghanistan, Janey didn't blame her mother for these failings. Her mother's only crime was to believe that she should share her husband with another woman. It was a bad call because the woman didn't show any reciprocal generosity.

When her mother had offered to come to London from Lyme Regis last week to help with Jack and cook energy-inducing vegan dishes, Janey politely explained that she had recruited a maternity nurse who would help her get the baby into a good routine so that she could go back to work in twelve weeks. And her mother, who had finally found happiness in a relationship with a Norwegian Rolfer ten years younger, sounded relieved.

'My one piece of advice is not to fall for that old adage that you can't get pregnant when you're breastfeeding,' said Hannah, who got pregnant with Gaby when Luke was just four months old. At the time it hadn't seemed odd that Hannah was breastfeeding nine-month-old Luke with her pregnant stomach already pouring over her jeans. It was simply impressive and incomprehensible that at twenty-three years old Hannah and Jonathan were parents of two small children.

'I cannot imagine ever having sex again,' sighed Janey.

'Well you shouldn't anyway for at least the first six weeks,' said Hannah.

'Why not?' asked Janey with consternation, because this was not something Gina Ford had covered.

'Something to do with air bubbles,' said Laura vaguely.

'There was the case of that mother who died after she had sex because her uterus hadn't sealed and a pocket of air entered her bloodstream,' Hannah explained.

Janey looked even more concerned. Mothers wrapped apocryphal stories around themselves as though they were an invisible cloak that might protect their own children from similar danger: the child who choked to death on a cherry tomato; the toddler who suffocated after a Hama bead travelled from its left nostril into its right lung; the boy who contracted MRSA from a public swimming pool. Someone had even told her about a maternity nurse who fed their newborn baby Calpol to get it to sleep through the night.

It seemed incredible to Janey that less than a week ago such stories slipped through her consciousness with barely a trace. Now a rich bed of anxiety had developed in her subconscious, waiting to fertilise such tales until they assumed distorted proportions in her head.

Janey had prepared for childbirth in the same way she had prepared for her law exams. The pile of books on the kitchen island bore testimony to the breadth and depth of her research: Dr Spock, in the revised eighth edition, sat beside Sheila Kitzinger. Gina Ford straddled Miriam Stoppard. She had read widely and conscientiously. But what none of the books had told her was how her once even temperament would alter overnight. Janey found herself buffeted by alternate waves of utter bliss and utter anxiety that left her feeling seasick. The sense of responsibility for this small person lying on the floor in front of her was almost overwhelming. You could read every single book in the parenting section at Borders, but none would adequately explain the oppression of having a baby. You could try and resist it, or give into it, but you couldn't avoid it.

Not for the first time, Janey wished the baby was still in her stomach where she could best protect him from the vicissitudes of the world. She would have liked to explain this to Laura and Hannah, but their experience inhibited her. They made it seem so easy.

This was the problem with modern-day motherhood. Everyone did it at different times. So instead of sharing this anxiety with close friends whom she had known for years, Janey would more likely tell people from the antenatal yoga class whom she had met less than four months ago. She glanced over at Laura, who was staring into her mug and probably thinking about something completely different.

'I just don't know how people do married sex,' said Laura so abruptly that her tea slopped over the edge of her cup and on to the floor.

'What do you mean?' asked Janey, adding another subject to her rapidly expanding list of new worries.

'I just don't understand how something that starts out being so compulsively physical and straightforward evolves into something so compulsively psychological and complicated,' said Laura. 'Where is the tipping point?'

'Sam is a particular case,' said Janey, wondering whether she was trying to reassure Laura or herself. 'Most men run a mile if their wife even suggests a vasectomy.' She found herself ignored by Laura, not wilfully, but because what Laura really wanted to broach was the subject of Jonathan and Hannah's marriage, held up by most of their friends as an exemplary relationship.

'Children,' said Hannah authoritatively. 'That's when things become more complicated.'

'You and Jonathan have managed that conundrum for years,' said Laura. 'I saw that half-used packet of condoms in our bedroom in Suffolk. How do you do it? How do you do long-term lust?'

'Porn, threesomes and the odd line of coke,' smiled Hannah without missing a beat. 'That was a joke,' she added. 'Mostly.'

'We can't talk about sex in front of Jack,' said Janey, taking Jack from Hannah and putting her hands over his ears. His fingers made soft curls in the air, as though he was performing a complicated t'ai chi movement.

'Janey, don't worry, he's too young for opinions,' smiled Laura.

'It might irrevocably affect his emotional development,' said Janey disapprovingly.

'Well make sure you don't get a nanny who watches *The Jeremy Kyle Show* then,' said Hannah. Janey looked worried.

'He is sound asleep,' said Laura gently. 'His only interest is whether a nipple is approaching.' Laura had released her inner perfect parent when Nell's tantrums began at around two years old, but her children were young enough that she could still remember those early days when every tiny decision assumed monumental proportions.

'I can't believe that someone who has told us that she once had sex with her boyfriend in the loo at Eden can be so puritanical,' laughed Hannah.

'That was before I got pregnant,' said Janey, beginning to smile. 'It's the missionary position in our own bed from now on.'

Married sex, Laura was thinking, was like a huge

country with different tribes, each living by their own set of customs and rules. Some people spent a lifetime skirting around the issue of their sexual incompatibility with vague excuses about tiredness and headaches, their early compatibility just a mirage. Others, like Sam and herself, propelled by nothing loftier than a vague sense of unhappiness, tried to peel back the layers to expose the problems that lay beneath or just took the easy option and had sex with someone else. Then there were those enviable people like Jonathan and Hannah whose desire timelessly rose above the domestic quagmire to make everyone else feel inadequate. God, they even bothered to specify mint-flavoured condoms.

'There's going to be so much pressure when Sam finally decides that the time is right,' said Laura, unwilling to reveal the exact nature of their problem. 'It seems incredible that we spent so much of the first half of our relationship consumed by passion and so much of the next part of it trying to manufacture it.'

'You should try it somewhere away from home,' suggested Janey.

'When you're in Scotland away from the children, maybe,' said Hannah. 'Anyway, I wouldn't worry about it. I've got a couple of friends who haven't slept with their husbands for years.'

'So what do they do?' asked Laura.

'They accept their sexless status or they sleep with other people,' smiled Hannah.

12

Sam lay on the bed having just enjoyed yet another post-operative ejaculation. He hadn't masturbated so much since he was a teenager. He marked down this latest session in the notebook he kept beside the bed and was pleased to see that he had hit the maximum target of twenty-five recommended by the doctor to purge his testes of any stubborn sperm. He had taken a similarly bureaucratic approach to the subject of fantasy to sustain this strike rate, allowing Eve to feature in exactly five, Laura in ten, both of them together in five and random women in the remainder. He was generally impressed with his rigorous approach to his post-operative deadlines. His only days off had been when United qualified for the Champions' League and the evening they beat Chelsea in Moscow.

Now, exactly two months after the vasectomy, Sam eyed the small transparent plastic pot in his hand, searching for any signs of life. It was a long time since he had studied O-level biology and he couldn't remember exactly what a sperm looked like. When he heard Laura approaching from the bathroom, he abruptly put down the pot on the bedside table, pondering the tiny amount of liquid that came out during a single ejaculation. For a moment, he wondered whether he should show Nell and Ben the source of their evolution.

After the weekend in Suffolk three months earlier, Laura had tried to steer them away from further musings about their father's genitalia. On balance, Sam decided this probably wasn't the best moment to introduce serious biology into the equation because his parents-in-law were downstairs in the kitchen and they were already late for the launch party for Jonathan's new cookery book, *Back to Basics: Recipes from Eden*. Besides, Nell and Ben would probably think the liquid was sea monkeys and want to pour it in the fish tank.

Laura walked into the room with a hairbrush in one hand and nail scissors in the other. She was wearing the same outfit and shoes she had worn in Suffolk, except that she was holding pieces of the dress in her hand.

'What are you doing?' she asked, an exasperated tone entering her voice when she saw Sam on the bed with a towel wrapped round him. Then she noted the pot stranded amidst the rubble of half-filled coffee cups, half-read books and half-filled notebooks on Sam's side of the bed. Since Sam had decided that the bed was the most inspiring place for him to write, their room had evolved into a bachelor pad. The pillows were stained with ink; the carpet was hidden with a confusion of dirty clothes, old tissues and biscuit wrappings.

'Oh God, not more,' Laura complained.

'This is the big one,' said Sam, tapping the lid. 'If we're given the all-clear then we can resume sexual relations.' He raised an eyebrow.

'Have you considered that I might have chosen a life of

celibacy by then?' teased Laura, as she picked up an assortment of socks from the floor.

'What's that?' asked Sam, pointing at the pieces of
material in her hand.

'I've customised my outfit, by removing the lace edging,'
said Laura. 'It's just not me.'

'I liked the way it defined the frontier between flesh and
dress,' said Sam thoughtfully, as Laura turned her attention
to the hem. Once she was satisfied with her handiwork, she
walked towards the bed and for a moment Sam thought
she was going to kiss him but instead she leant over to
remove five coffee cups and put them on the bottom shelf
of the built-in wardrobe, behind a couple of pairs of shoes.

'Why are you doing that?' Sam asked. 'I thought you'd be
pleased that I've substituted caffeine for alcohol?'

'I can't face my mother coming into our room and
finding these here,' she said.

'Then tell her she can't come in,' replied Sam.

'She'll ignore me,' shrugged Laura. 'It's the quid pro quo
for babysitting. We have to give her free rein to tidy the
house.'

Laura bent down to look at her face in the mirror that sat
atop the chest of drawers. But each time she tried to focus
on applying a layer of foundation, her attention was swayed
by the view of the bedroom reflected back at her. All she
could see were uncompleted tasks. She did a brief
inventory: the mirror, which had sat on the chest of
drawers for three years waiting to be hung on the wall; the
door that had fallen off one of the cupboards and was now
leaning against the window; a couple of boxes that still
hadn't been unpacked from the move; and most signifi-

cantly, the crack that had appeared at the top of the wall by the ceiling. Marriage is nothing more than the sum of unfinished business, she thought.

'Don't leave that pot on the table,' Laura urged, as she made a few cursory sweeps of her eyelashes with the mascara. 'Mum might think it's face cream.'

'I'll put it in the fridge,' said Sam, getting up from the bed, 'they need to be kept cool.'

'Who?' asked Laura.

'The sperm,' said Sam, pulling on a pair of jeans. 'These could be the last ones ever released from captivity.'

They went downstairs into the kitchen and found Laura's mother, Elizabeth, sweeping the floor. She did it in the same methodical way that someone might mow a lawn, moving up to the end of the room and then down the other side, in perfect straight lines, ensnaring anything that stood in her way with the broom. Nell stood compliantly at the end of the room with a dustpan and brush, waiting for the next pile of rubbish to arrive. A small collection of objects retrieved from the floor sat on the corner of the kitchen table. They included the upper body of a Thunderbirds character, two tiny plastic sheep with horns missing, a silver earring and an Oyster card.

Sam watched all this with fascination. He was particularly taken by Elizabeth's hair, which remained in the same position even when she leant over at a ninety-degree angle to examine a piece of food that refused to shift. It defied gravity. He could smell the hairspray from the doorway. She had sported the same style, straight with lots of volume on top, since Sam first met her. On special occasions she would use Carmen rollers to turn up the ends, applying even more spray to fix the curls in position.

'I can't sit here staring at that mess,' Elizabeth said apologetically, using the back of the broom to dislodge a couple of petrified Cheerios stuck on the floor.

'Fortunately we eat off the kitchen table,' said Sam, winking at Nell. After a week with her grandparents when Laura and he went to Scotland Nell would be completely indoctrinated. She would have a GCSE in micromanaging dust, a degree in cleaning fluids, a PhD in ironing and insist they buy things like antibacterial wipes.

Elizabeth gave Sam the quizzical look that she used when she wasn't sure whether her son-in-law was taking things seriously enough. It was half-frown and half-astonishment. Sam dutifully gave her a kiss on each cheek and inhaled the fumes from the hairspray, wondering if it was something she had bought in the seventies that contained a banned substance, like Agent Orange or paraquat. He waited for her to ask how work was going, knowing that she viewed his job as something between a hobby and an indulgence. Elizabeth liked people to have professions that you didn't need to explain. Laura's sister was married to a lawyer, her father had been an accountant, and her grandfather a doctor. Sam's job was not only mysterious to her, but more significantly, it didn't make enough money to allow her eldest daughter to employ a regular cleaning lady.

'How is work, Sam?' she asked.

'Ticking over,' he replied, putting the pot with the sperm in the fridge door.

'Sam's just finished writing a film script,' explained Laura, as she pulled on an old jean jacket over the top of her dress.

'Hasn't he done that before?' Elizabeth asked rhetorically. 'Tilt the dustpan, Nell, then it's easier to sweep all that dirt in.' Nell obeyed.

'This is great fun, Granny,' she said.

'Sweeping the floor is obviously a bit of a novelty in this household,' said Elizabeth. She threw a disapproving look at Laura's jean jacket.

'I'm not going to say anything,' she said, staring into the middle distance, as Laura and Sam left for the evening.

Jonathan's book launch had turned into an excuse to celebrate his fortieth birthday. This came as no surprise to Laura and Sam, who from the outset had doubted that a holiday in Scotland with friends would satisfy either his ego or his desire to party. But the dimensions of the celebration weren't completely obvious to Sam and Laura until they arrived at Eden to find the restaurant closed for the night and a couple of burly men checking names against a guest list that ran to at least three pages. A phalanx of waiters and waitresses stood in a semicircle with trays of champagne and cocktails. As she handed over her coat Laura could see that the restaurant had been transformed. The tables and chairs had been cleared and the benches around the edges turned into intimate spaces where people could sit and talk if they tired of the fray in the middle of the room.

Someone Sam knew from the BBC came in the door behind them. Sam waved at him and elbowed Laura gently in the ribs. It was the signal he used when he couldn't remember someone's name. But the man, a commissioning editor from the drama department, was clearly hoping to avoid Sam because he was in turn propelling his partner past the trays of champagne towards a group of three people at the edge of the room.

'We don't know them,' the woman said, sounding slightly irritated as he urged her away.

Laura winced on Sam's behalf. His currency must be running lower than she thought. Sam, however, was unmoved and turned around to say hello, thereby closing off their escape route.

'Sam, Sam,' the man said, putting an arm round Sam's shoulder and urging his wife back towards the drinks tray. 'Great to see you. I hear you've written the last episode of *Do Not Resuscitate*. End of an era.'

'I know, I know,' said Sam, shaking his head in disbelief.

'Is it in production?' he asked.

'They've almost finished filming,' said Sam.

'Did you go along?'

'I didn't think I'd be very popular,' said Sam. A waitress came over and offered them slices of Norfolk smoked eel harnessed to carefully sliced pieces of smoked salmon that she indicated should be immersed in the pale horseradish dip in the centre of the tray. She was wearing a maxi-dress and Laura realised that the party had a loose seventies theme. Laura took one but the eel fell off in the dip and she found herself floundering with a cocktail stick trying to catch it again. She smiled at the waitress hoping for encouragement but there was none.

'Odd choice, Ebola,' the man said. 'Why not bird flu?'

'I wanted an incurable pandemic,' said Sam, shrugging his shoulders. 'A couple of the doctors and the nurse with the long blonde hair who's having an affair with the heart surgeon escape to North Wales, so I guess that leaves the path open if they want to do something else with those characters in a rural location.'

'Sounds like professional hara-kiri to me,' the man said, looking over Sam's shoulder to scan the room for someone else to talk to. 'And are you working on anything else?'

Laura aggressively stabbed the slice of eel, finally pinning it to the cocktail stick, but spilling the horseradish over the edge of the small bowl on to the decorative bed of lettuce leaves.

'I've got a couple of ideas,' said Sam vaguely.

'Anyway, it's great to see you, Sam,' said the man, edging away. 'I didn't realise you knew Jonathan.'

'We grew up together,' Sam explained. 'I met my wife through Jonathan.'

Laura smiled dutifully as Sam introduced her, wondering why he was bothering when the man so obviously wanted to extricate himself from their conversation. Sam explained proudly that Laura had played a pivotal role over the years, casting her expert medical eye over his scripts. He then mentioned, almost casually, that she was a neurologist and the man's eyes lit up. Even before he spoke, Laura could tell from the expression on his wife's face that he was a hypochondriac.

'I've been having these headaches . . .' he began. Laura looked over his shoulder to the side of the room beside the window where neat piles of Jonathan's book were stacked on a long table decked out with vines and fruit to resemble the Garden of Eden. Her eyes narrowed as something on the cover caught her attention. The man was busy telling Laura how the headaches were worse in the morning and that everything he researched on the Internet pointed to a brain tumour. Then he waited expectantly for her response.

Sam touched Laura's lower arm.

'Sounds nasty, I'd get it checked out,' she said. 'Sorry, I've just seen someone I really want to talk to.' She pulled away from Sam's arm towards the piles of books without saying anything. Clutching her champagne glass by the stem, she picked up a copy and felt its weight before turning it over to admire the glossy quality of the cover.

Back to Basics: Recipes from Eden, it read on the front. But it wasn't the title in discreet black lettering that commanded her attention. It was the black-and-white photo that spread from the front to back cover: it was the same picture that hung in the bedroom in Suffolk. She held the book tightly in both hands, as though she was holding a baby for the first time, and stared at the cover. The photo had been cropped so that the people at the back of the boat were cut from the image completely. But this meant even more focus was drawn to the face of the girl standing in the foreground, staring at the camera, hand on hip. You could even see her freckles and the necklace that Janey had brought back for Laura from a trip to Vietnam.

'Fuck,' said Sam, shaking his head in disbelief as he came up behind her.

'How could he do that?' groaned Laura, putting the book face down on the table and then immediately picking it up to stare at herself again.

'Fuck,' repeated Sam, picking up another copy, as if to check the first wasn't an elaborate hoax, and holding it at arm's length. 'Do you think your legs have got shorter?'

'It's a proportion thing,' mumbled Laura. 'My thighs

have got fatter. I can't believe he did that without asking.'

Sam didn't say anything but Laura saw his mouth harden until his upper lip was a tight mass of wrinkles. He was making jokes about her legs, but his eyes were firmly fixed on her face.

'That's because you'd have said no,' interrupted Jonathan, coming up behind and putting an arm around each of them. 'What do you think?' He leant over to kiss Laura on the cheek but she turned away and instead his lips landed on her neck.

'An official request would have been nice but at the very least I think you should have warned me,' said Laura tightly. She stretched over Jonathan to put a hand inside Sam's jacket to see if he had a packet of cigarettes hidden in the pocket. Someone she knew from Manchester held the book up, pointed at the cover, and waved at her. Laura realised that she quickly needed to devise an appropriate public reaction to the picture for anyone who might recognise her. She stared at the cover again. Her attitude reminded her of a Guatemalan Indian woman who had cried when Laura and Sam had taken a photo of her on their honeymoon because she thought the camera had robbed her soul.

'I showed the image to my editor and he said it was perfect,' said Jonathan, stroking the cover lovingly. 'It conjures up images of England in all its languid summer beauty. Once we'd seen it we couldn't let it go.'

'You do look wonderful, Laura,' said Sam appreciatively.

'Come on, Laura,' urged Jonathan. 'Isn't there any part of you that is secretly pleased? Is there no hint of vanity beneath that Presbyterian exterior?'

Laura didn't say anything. She shifted silently from one foot to the other. Sam watched her face closely. He could read her effortlessly. Her lips were pressed together, her eyes were aflame and, most significantly, her nostrils were flaring slightly, not unlike the bull in the Suffolk field. Laura was angry in a significant way.

A waitress passed by with a tray of food and Sam grabbed a couple of small biscuits with cheese on top and half a grape on the peak.

'That's Cornish Yarg on top of a Bath Oliver,' explained Jonathan. 'It's my version of those cheese and pineapple sticks we used to have when we were at children's parties. Do you remember? The biscuits are named after William Oliver, a doctor from Bath who wanted to devise a healthy biscuit for people who came to take the waters.'

Laura and Sam didn't say anything. Laura asked Sam to get her a glass of water and he headed towards the bar. He distracted himself from the drama unfolding by the book table by surreptitiously scanning the room for the girl from the theatre, justifying his interest by arguing that he was trying to protect Hannah, and then finding himself disappointed when he couldn't see her. Of course, it would have been ludicrous for Jonathan to invite her, especially after the photograph in the newspaper, but Jonathan's mood was so reckless that Sam couldn't discount the possibility.

'Can you believe she's called Eve?' Jonathan had asked a couple of weeks ago when Sam's anger was sufficiently submerged to contemplate lunch together again.

'Why is that so significant?' Sam responded a little too quickly.

'Because I have a restaurant called Eden,' Jonathan explained emphatically.

As he waited at the bar Sam wondered what he would say to Eve if he met her again. Would he adopt an avuncular tone and try to convince her that married men never left their wives, and if they did they brought too much baggage in the way of children and old friends with them? Or would he be more belligerent and try to appeal to her conscience? He couldn't really imagine either scenario. In fact he couldn't really imagine talking to her at all. He could only imagine having sex with her.

Not surprising, given his lunch with Jonathan earlier in the week. It had taken a superhuman effort on Sam's part to get Jonathan off the subject of Eve. The graphic conversation had reminded him of their early teenage years, when they had discovered that both of them had lost their virginity to the German au pair brought to Suffolk to deal with Jonathan's younger sister. Sam remembered how Jonathan confessed to him she liked having sex outdoors where people might catch them, and Sam, bruised by the discovery of her treachery, told Jonathan that he could make her come by burying his face between her legs. Jonathan had stopped gloating and looked at Sam with new respect.

Having not had sex for almost nine months, Sam contributed little to the conversation in the pub, although he felt an encouraging stirring in his loins as Jonathan outlined the key moments in the short history of his relationship with Eve. The adjectives he attached to her now slewed around Sam's head as he waited at the bar. She was high voltage, electrifying, supercharged, disorientating, Jonathan had said, checking his phone for messages while Sam tried to convince him to give her up. It sounded as though he was describing something elemental, like an electrical storm.

That's what happens when you sleep with someone different after seventeen years, Sam tried to persuade him. It was the lust equation. Sam felt torn between pity and envy as Jonathan outlined a couple of encounters that left a cloud of heavy languor hanging over them. He told Jonathan that he was acting like a self-centred teenager and Jonathan had replied acerbically that he couldn't simultaneously be having a midlife crisis and be behaving like a teenager. Sam said it was more tautology than contradiction. Jonathan insisted that Eve understood him like no other woman and Sam countered this argument by telling him that he was simply trying to invest the relationship with romance to disguise its essentially tawdry soul.

Sam then tried to persuade Jonathan that the longer the relationship continued, the less likely it was that he would be able to mend his bridges with Hannah. He also pointed out that if he simply stopped seeing Eve then he wouldn't have to confront the impossibility of resisting her. But it wasn't until Sam suggested that it might undermine his business if the affair was uncovered that Jonathan allowed a hint of doubt to enter the general tone of the conversation.

Of course married men contemplate infidelity, Sam thought, as he headed back towards Laura with a bottle of fizzy water. But most don't go through with it and those that do manage to remain detached. The trouble with Jonathan was that his sensibility was female. He seemed to think he was in love.

'So what do you think?' a voice said behind him. Sam felt

someone touch his shoulder and turned to face Hannah.

'I think you should move back to London right now,' said Sam, smiling with his mouth but not his eyes.

'What are you talking about?' asked Hannah. 'I love it in Suffolk. Nothing could induce me to come back. Not even you.'

'We all miss you,' said Sam. 'And I'm not sure it's good for Jonathan to be on his own so much.'

'It might be good for me though,' laughed Hannah.

They walked back towards Jonathan and Laura, who were still standing uncomfortably beside the rapidly diminishing piles of books. Laura absorbed Hannah's appearance. Flat shoes, gladiator style. No discernible make-up. Sun-streaked hair. Other women instinctively checked themselves against Hannah, not in a competitive sense, but to gauge whether they had got it right. And Laura knew immediately she had got it wrong. She looked too formal, despite the frayed hem. Her lipstick was a shade too bright and her shoes a shade too dark.

Hannah put her arms round Laura to hug her hello and tipped fizzy water down her back. The ice-cold sensation helped Laura collect her thoughts.

'Did you know?' asked Laura as she disentangled herself.

'Of course,' said Hannah, 'that's why I hung the picture in the bedroom, to subconsciously prepare you. What do you think?'

'It's a little exposing,' said Laura. 'What do you think my patients will think? I don't suppose that had crossed your mind.'

'They won't recognise you,' Jonathan reassured her, 'and in any case the book might not sell.'

'It's great,' said Sam, stroking the cover of the book with one hand and Laura's shoulder with the other. 'You're beautiful, other-worldly.'

'It's the look in your eye, Laura,' explained Jonathan. 'It's so post-coital. It makes people instantly equate food with sex and what better way to sell a product, especially in an economic downturn. Advertisers do it the whole time. I thought you would be really pleased.' Laura felt her face grow hot.

'And what better memory of that month before you got married?' said Hannah, glancing from Sam to Laura, feeling tension but misunderstanding its origins.

Sam put his hands deep into his trouser pockets, like a recalcitrant child. Jonathan had pushed things too far this time. How can she not know? he thought to himself, as he caught Hannah's eye.

Sam stretched out towards Laura as if to reassure her but Jonathan was pulling him away by the elbow into the centre of the room where he wanted to introduce him to someone who did film finance. The circle of people opened to let him in and Sam was swallowed up.

Laura didn't want to be at this party any more. Snatches of conversation buffeted her until she felt giddy. Someone described how they were at a party where Gordon Brown appeared and stood awkwardly in a corner all evening. A couple earnestly debated how the world had to choose between alleviating poverty and saving the environment. Non-doms. Oil price hikes. Stagflation. Organic denim. Negative equity. Laura wanted to put her fingers in her ears and shout like Nell did when you tried to tell her something that she didn't want to hear.

Hannah opened a window behind the table of books and pulled out a packet of cigarettes. She lit one and blew the smoke out of the side of her mouth.

'I get fed up with regulations,' Hannah said, smoking the cigarette a little too quickly so that billows of smoke obscured her face. 'Don't you sometimes mourn the loss of freedom?'

'What do you mean?' asked Laura, fanning the smoke out of the window.

'The sensation that nothing matters but the moment,' said Hannah. Her right hand propped up the elbow of the hand holding the cigarette.

'You mean living in the present?' said Laura.

'Exactly,' Hannah concurred, nodding her head a little too vigorously. 'The way you could smoke without worrying about your next mammogram or fly to New York for the weekend without considering your carbon footprint or take Ecstasy without worrying about your serotonin levels dipping. Now everything is about long-life light bulbs and pension plans and mortgages that will be paid off just as we're being packed off to an old folks' home.'

'But you never took Ecstasy,' said Laura, mystified by Hannah's diatribe, 'you can't miss something you never experienced.'

'You're being too literal,' retorted Hannah, a little impatiently. 'You can mourn the loss of what you haven't done as well as what you have done.'

'I thought it got easier as the children got older,' said Laura. 'Don't you rediscover yourself and start to relax again?'

'Less breadth, more depth to the worries,' said Hannah,

sucking on the cigarette. 'Meningococcal rashes and paedophiles recede and skunk and binge drinking emerge from their shadows. And I have no idea what Luke is doing on his computer. He's got a blog or something. I long for a life without consequence.'

'There is no such thing as an inconsequential existence,' replied Laura, scrutinising the book jacket again. 'Everything has consequences, even the stuff we did that we thought didn't matter. It all catches up with you in the end, and it shapes the present, because it defines who you are now.'

'That photograph is dangerous,' said Hannah, pointing her cigarette towards the cover of the closest book, 'because it's an image that makes people want to take risks. You understand that, don't you? You know what I'm talking about.'

As Hannah spoke, Laura wondered whether Hannah knew and was surprised to feel a vague sense of relief. Secrets were a burden. The fear of them unravelling a constant companion. She wondered how Hannah had discovered. Whether it was intuition or a process of elimination, because once you knew that it wasn't Sam who had reduced her to that state of spent languor, then there were a finite number of men and women on the boat trip who could have been responsible.

They leaned out of the window, Hannah blowing smoke on to the street below. A couple of men in suits sat at a table drinking beer, talking about work. The problem with being forty, one was explaining to the other, was that you could no longer pretend to yourself that you were going to suddenly become an Oscar-winning film director, play cricket for England, or climb the seven peaks. The licence to dream became the province of the deluded. It was facing up to the prospect of your own mortality that was hard, countered the other wearily. But if you made it to seventy then you were meant to be as happy as you were in your twenties. Long time to wait, they both agreed.

A fierce summer storm was brewing. A reproachful breeze blew the ash from Hannah's cigarette back into the room, where it settled on the piles of books. The sky was going through changes, like the colour of a bruise, starting out yellow then turning deep purple before finally settling on a murky grey colour. There were seven flood warnings in the West Country. People were filling sandbags in Tewkesbury. Digging ditches in Aylesbury. She took the cigarette from Hannah's hand and took a deep drag, enjoying the way it hurt her lungs. Her messy little secret was out.

Inside, the atmosphere at the party was also evolving. There was a sense of growing expectation as guests began to congregate in the centre of the room, wondering when Jonathan would stand up to make a speech. It sounded as though someone was slowly turning up the volume. Laura could hear Sam laughing but couldn't see where he was standing. She found herself missing him. Laura turned towards Hannah and focused on her mouth to force herself to concentrate on what she was saying. Gaby was right, she decided, they were all becoming more and more self-indulgent and insular.

'I'll try and distil everything into a single sentence,' began Hannah slowly. 'When I told you the other day that I had friends who hadn't slept with their partner for years, I was being economical with the truth.'

'You're losing me,' said Laura.

'What I meant to say was that I hadn't slept with Jonathan but that didn't mean I hadn't had sex with someone else,' said Hannah.

'Too many double negatives,' said Laura, taking a deep drink from the avocado-green cocktail she was holding.

'Laura, I've done something completely irrational,' Hannah said. Her tone was precise and even.

'Something inconsequential?' teased Laura.

'Difficult to tell at the moment,' said Hannah. There was a long pause. Music drifted between them and Hannah unconsciously swayed to the rhythm, her eyes half closed. Laura thought she had never seen her more beguiling. She was unreachable. Laura put out a hand to touch her shoulder, feeling a stab of envy for her detachment.

'I've slept with someone,' Hannah said as she opened her eyes, sounding surprised, as though she had only just grasped that this was something out of the ordinary.

'Someone who isn't Jonathan?' said Laura, wanting to be sure she understood her.

'Who is most definitely not Jonathan,' said Hannah.

'Who is he then?' asked Laura.

'He works on the farm,' said Hannah. 'You met him.'

'The boy doing the asparagus bed,' said Laura. It was more statement than question, because as soon as she replayed the scene in the garden in Suffolk, Laura knew exactly who Hannah meant.

'God, please don't call Jacek a boy,' sighed Hannah.

'That is a blinding piece of news,' said Laura, shaking her head in disbelief. 'How old is he?'

'Thirty,' said Hannah. Laura raised an eyebrow.

'Twenty-eight,' said Hannah.

'I don't believe you,' said Laura firmly.

'OK, he's twenty-five,' Hannah conceded. 'Just.'

'You're having sex with a twenty-five-year-old Slovakian boy,' said Laura in astonishment. 'God, he's only nine years older than Luke.'

'Enough maths,' pleaded Hannah. 'I feel like I'm playing the main role in a cross between *The Graduate* and *Lady Chatterley's Lover*.'

'And he's got dreadlocks,' said Laura in disbelief.

'You're beginning to sound like your mother,' said Hannah. 'Why is his hairstyle relevant?'

'Less than a year ago you were having your highlights done by Nicky Clarke,' said Laura. 'Now you're inseminating bulls and decapitating pigs.'

'Does that make it better or worse?' asked Hannah, puzzled by her scattergun response.

'It simply underlines your recklessness,' said Laura in astonishment. 'Fuck. I can't believe you've done that.'

'Fuck indeed,' said Hannah.

'So how did it all happen?' asked Laura, hoping to win a few minutes' reprieve to process this information. She noticed a symmetrical line of bruises that ran up the line of the humerus on each of Hannah's arms. Small, perfect circles, the same colour as the sky. She looked closely and saw the imprint of Jacek's fingertips. She put out a hand, tenderly touched one of the marks and Hannah winced, less from any physical pain than the fact it reminded her of Jacek's absence. This sort of carnal knowledge always demanded a high price, thought Laura. She imagined the boy on top of Hannah, fingers digging into the soft flesh of her arms, their limbs enmeshed, as the bed in the room where she had slept with Sam bumped the wall so hard that it left deep wells in the plaster. Flesh wounds were secrets best kept between lovers.

Objectivity was out of the question, so Laura tried to work out how this situation might impact on her. There was the extraordinary revelation that the monolithic edifice of Hannah and Jonathan's marriage had cracks. Not superficial fractures that would mend in time, but a major fault line running down the middle. Laura shifted uncomfortably as she realised this discovery gave her a kernel of hope for her own relationship. However bad things were, and at least from Sam's perspective they seemed to be improving, they weren't that bad. She pulled herself up. Schadenfreude was an unattractive response.

'You've got it bad,' said Laura, wanting to shake Hannah out of her state of listlessness. She glanced over at Jonathan and saw him laughing at something with Sam. If his ego wasn't so demanding then he might have noticed what was going on earlier.

'It started properly at the end of last November,' said Hannah slowly, taking another cigarette from the packet. 'Although of course it began improperly before that. He wanted to learn to speak better English so we talked a lot while we worked. He told me about his life in Slovakia and I described my life in London . . .'

'And you discovered that you had a lot in common,' said Laura. 'Similar taste at the organic counter at Fresh and Wild, identical Volvo estates and mutual affection for anything by Marc Jacobs.'

'I know, I know,' said Hannah, holding her hands up to

concede defeat. 'Superficially we have nothing in common, but there was a definite connection. I related to the way he has had to struggle to make something of his life because I've done the same thing.'

'Just because you connect with someone doesn't mean you have to end up shagging them,' said Laura, taken aback by Hannah's logic.

'And there was this underlying attraction which became more and more difficult to shake off,' said Hannah, ignoring Laura. 'Then one day I was in the larder, the light wasn't working and I didn't notice he had come into the room. He came up behind me, put his arms around me and kissed me almost imperceptibly on the side of my neck.'

'And you felt as though you were drowning,' said Laura, staring at the front of the book and understanding perfectly what Hannah was saying.

'I felt almost nauseous with desire,' said Hannah. 'It was visceral.'

'Probably all the dead flesh in that larder,' said Laura, trying to imagine what it might be like to have sex with the smell of freshly slaughtered raw meat as the main olfactory backdrop.

'He said he wanted to fuck me,' said Hannah, looking around to check that no one was listening to their conversation.

'No room for misinterpretation there,' said Laura. 'Did he say it in Slovakian or English?'

'English, of course,' said Hannah, 'otherwise I wouldn't have understood. Six months and two weeks later and I'm lost. I'm one of the drowned.'

'Hannah,' said Laura, gripping her arm below the

bruises. 'You have to remember that you're undergoing nothing more than a complex chemical reaction.'

Relieved at her response, Hannah began to giggle.

'I love the way you always try to find a scientific explanation for everything,' she said. 'Your belief that the world is an essentially rational place is so comforting.'

'Lust can drive you temporarily insane,' said Laura, in the same practical tone that she adopted when dealing with patients.

'Well that's a comforting thought,' said Hannah.

'The chemicals released when you have great sex with someone have an almost identical effect on the brain as cocaine,' said Laura. 'Scientists have done brain imaging proving this. It's very interesting. Dopamine, norepinephrine and serotonin are a powerful cocktail. You are at the mercy of your biochemistry. You think you are having a profound emotional experience but really it's no different from adding water to sulphuric acid.'

'So what's the antidote?' she asked.

'And I haven't even mentioned oxytocin,' continued Laura.

'What does that do?' asked Hannah.

'When you have an orgasm you both release oxytocin and it has a binding effect on you both. The more sex you have with someone, the deeper your bond becomes. That's why Sam and I need to sleep together, to bind ourselves together again.'

'So what should I do?' repeated Hannah helplessly.

'You need to go cold turkey,' said Laura. 'Stop seeing him. When we go on holiday, tell Jacek he's got to find another job somewhere else and you start sleeping with Jonathan again.'

'I don't want to go to Scotland. I'll miss him too much,' said Hannah.

'Don't be ridiculous,' said Laura. 'You can't let down Jonathan like that.'

'I can't be apart from Jacek for a whole week,' said Hannah dramatically.

'You've got to get a grip,' said Laura, 'you can't walk away from a nineteen-year relationship because of an infatuation with someone fourteen years younger than you. Imagine telling the children. It's insane.'

'It's not easy living with someone like Jonathan,' said Hannah. 'I've been much happier since I moved away.'

'That's because you're having sex with someone else,' said Laura impatiently.

'Jonathan consumes me,' said Hannah, 'he requires a lot of attention. I feel more me without him than with him, if you know what I mean.'

'Even if that is true, and remember you might be rewriting history to suit your current situation, then you shouldn't make any decisions when you're having a relationship with someone else,' said Laura. 'You're not in your right mind.'

'I think I'm in love with Jacek,' sighed Hannah.

'You have a chemical dependency on him,' said Laura firmly. 'And you're nearly forty. You'll find yourself wanting to get a tattoo and start wearing miniskirts again soon. But you'll get over it. It's a question of mind over matter.'

'But what if your mind says it doesn't matter?' asked Hannah abruptly.

They looked up and saw Jonathan beckoning Hannah over to his side. Laura didn't recognise any of the people who stood in a semicircle beside him. This was not an unusual occurrence. Jonathan craved new people like some people craved new clothes, returning to the comfort and security of his oldest friends when people turned out to be less interesting or more demanding than expected. It was one of the traits that had driven Hannah out of London, Laura suspected. You didn't want to find strangers drinking Pétrus in your kitchen in the early hours of the morning when you were nearly forty.

Since he started filming his television series at the beginning of the year, Jonathan's time had become increasingly managed by other people. Last week Laura had dialled his mobile phone and someone else had answered it for him. Only a small circle of his closest friends had the number of his personal phone, the stranger informed Laura dismissively, before asking if she wanted to leave her name and number.

As Hannah drew closer, Jonathan held one arm open like a wing, ready to enfold her, and waved a piece of paper with a few hastily scrawled notes to indicate that he was about to speak. In his black T-shirt and jeans, Jonathan still managed to appear boyish at forty, despite the silver tinge to his hair and the lines around his eyes. He kissed Hannah for a little longer than was appropriate and Laura was surprised to see her emerge breathless but seemingly content to take her place beside him. Jonathan whispered something in her ear and then squeezed the side of her waist. It was a public display of unity. Laura watched people smiling benevolently at them and heard someone describe Jonathan and Hannah as having a near perfect marriage. For a moment she wondered whether she had imagined the recent conversation because the scene before her belied what Hannah had just described.

Sentences from Jonathan's speech drifted by. He compared Hannah to his favourite ingredients. She was a fusion of the exotic and sweet, a hint of cardamom rolled in honey. She wasn't an imposing or complicated dish full of loud flavours, but something that left a memorable aftertaste.

'I knew a lot of women before I met Hannah, yet until I met her I hadn't known women at all,' said Jonathan. 'Even after nineteen years she remains mysterious and uncompromising.'

He told everyone how much he loved her, what a wonderful mother she was to their children, and despite what she had just learnt, Laura felt herself swallow a couple of times. He then described a hard-fought battle for Hannah's affections at the beginning of their relationship, seeming to forget that he was the one going out with someone else, before describing how men still remained drawn to her.

It was strangely self-referential, as though Jonathan needed to emphasise that Hannah was irresistibly attractive in order to bolster his own ego and remind himself that she really was. At the end they kissed each other until everyone pleaded with them to stop.

Relationships were full of grey areas, thought Laura, remembering that four weeks before she got married, she had ended up sleeping with her best friend's boyfriend. And that when Sam had announced to everyone the following morning that he had finished his first film script, Patrick had been one of the first people to come over to congratulate them both and Laura had behaved as though nothing had happened. Nothing was mentioned again, even though Laura had on occasion tried to flush the subject out into the open. All friends had secrets. It was that some bore them more heavily than others.

13

It was one of those instances when, even years later, everyone would remember exactly what they were doing when the phone call came and they all first heard the news. The consensus that day was that it was a defining moment. This was partly because of the nature of how the news was delivered. The only working phone in the house happened to be in the kitchen, the housekeeper explained to them as they sat down for breakfast the morning after they arrived on Coll. And the line wasn't reliable if the wind got up or if there was a strong storm at sea. The mobile phone signal was at best erratic. If they needed an emergency doctor, and the phone was out of order, they would have to radio the mainland to send an air ambulance. Her eyes narrowed and the lines on her face concertinaed impressively as she suggested that they would get a more accurate weather report by listening to the shipping news. Coll was bang in the middle of Malin, she informed them. The prevailing wind was north-westerly, but a southerly could stop the ferry from running and it was important to keep abreast of the weather if they wanted to avoid being stranded. She paused for dramatic effect. She had seen Londoners reduced to tears in the face of such isolation. And it tended to be the high-flyers used to controlling their environment who crumbled first.

Luke's currency among the adults had risen immeasurably earlier that morning when he took Laura and Hannah to a small hillock fifty metres above sea level at the other end of the island, where he had worked out it might be possible to get a faint signal from the transmitter in Oban. Otherwise all communication from the island to the outside world was conducted from the single phone that sat in state on its own small table in the kitchen. The dramatic potential of the telephone had been forgotten, thought Laura as she listened to the housekeeper. For Luke, brought up in the era of mobile phones, call waiting, cordless handsets and Wi-Fi, it had never featured. He had never had the experience of overhearing an illicit conversation, or not knowing who might answer the phone, or trying to hold a private conversation with someone else in the room.

'Does this mean my BlackBerry won't work in the house?' asked Steve, anxiously holding his phone. His BlackBerry had stopped functioning a couple of hours out of Oban yesterday afternoon, as the ferry left the Sound of Mull, and he hadn't received any emails since, he explained, as though this news was relevant to everyone around the kitchen table. He had spent the rest of the three-hour journey out on deck, pointing the phone hopelessly back towards dry land, but the signal was lost each time the ferry cut through another wave.

Steve told the housekeeper, as though trying to underline the urgency of his predicament, that the collapse of the Californian lender IndyMac, combined with the hike in oil prices and rumours about Lehman's, meant that he really needed to keep in close touch with his office this week. 'It's a unique set of circumstances.'

'And this is a unique place,' said the housekeeper with a small smile.

'It's fantastic,' interrupted Jonathan, who always required absolute enthusiasm from those around him. 'We're very lucky because my son is a computer whizz who says he can hook us up to the Internet using the phone wire, and we've got our own medic on holiday with us.'

Luke smiled wanly. He was there under duress and he wanted everyone to know it. While Gaby had been granted permission to spend the week after exams with a friend in London, Luke's recent behaviour had undermined all possibility of similar freedom. What greater punishment could there be for his expulsion from school than a week's holiday with his parents and their friends?

'Brain,' smiled Laura, pointing at her head, when she realised Luke wasn't going to say anything. 'Not much use unless there's a head injury.'

'Shame you weren't here last year,' the housekeeper said ominously, but she was interrupted by the phone ringing.

'Hello, hello,' Hannah shouted into the receiver, but the line was already dead.

Unmoved, the housekeeper continued in the same even tone to explain that the bathwater would be brown with peat because all the water came from a well and the rip tides at Hogh beach and Feaull could carry a grown man out to sea.

'We nearly lost the vicar last year,' she mentioned casually. She advised them to get fresh water from the tap in the village at Arinagour each day, suggested that if they wanted to buy bread they should get to the shop by ten o'clock in the morning because otherwise it sold out, and explained that midges would only appear if the wind dropped, but since as well as being the sunniest place in Great Britain, Coll was also among the windiest, they weren't likely to pose a problem.

'Will you be requiring me to cook lunch and dinner each day?' she asked reluctantly before she left.

'I think we'll be fine, thanks, Mrs Buchanan,' said Jonathan, and everyone nodded in assent. As she reached the kitchen door, she stopped and turned around.

'Just one question for you,' she said, with a hint of a smile. 'Why have some of you brought your own sheets and pillows? I couldn't help noticing when I made the beds.'

Steve stood up abruptly. The draught from the door caught the front of his shirt and it billowed like a sail over his bright red corduroys.

'I always bring my own sheets,' he explained sheepishly, 'wherever I go. And my own mug.' He held up a large crockery mug with a hand-painted hedge around the rim.

'Ay,' she said, looking at him expectantly.

'He sleeps better,' Janey impulsively started to tell everyone, even as she sensed Steve's irritation. 'He likes to go to bed in his own sheets with his Tempur pillow.'

Fortunately the sound of Jack's cries at the top of the house drowned her explanation. Janey swiftly retreated upstairs to their bedroom, imagining them analysing how she could have married someone who took his own bedlinen with him on holiday. Going away with friends was an act of faith at the best of times, but going on holiday with Steve and her friends felt like a seven-day blind date. There was an unnerving degree of unpredictability to the enforced proximity.

She lay Jack on the pristine white sheet and slouched into a couple of goose-down pillows, feeling pleased that she had chosen a man who set such store by comfort, especially after the long journey by plane and ferry to reach Coll. Patrick would have argued about luggage and teased her about her tendency to hoard, she thought, as she eyed the packets of nappies, pots of nappy-rash cream and carefully ironed muslin squares that stood as sturdy as a sea defence on the dressing table. It was the first time she had thought about him for weeks. In the wake of childbirth, Patrick was forgotten.

Janey stared out of the bedroom window, absorbing the muted palette of soft purple heather, white fluffy meadowsweet and tangled silverweed as they blew in the breeze. The flowers of all these plants appeared so fragile and yet they must have strong roots to withstand the weather, she thought with a sharp intake of breath as she felt Jack latch on to her nipple. Everything on Coll was solid, from the hard grey rocks of gneiss scattered across the island to the sturdy Highland cows that stared at them as they drove from the ferry to the house the previous evening. For a moment she felt consumed by the landscape and her body relaxed. Then downstairs the phone started ringing again and, as she glimpsed the time on her watch, Janey noted with annoyance that Jack's feed was more than an hour before schedule.

The phone in the kitchen was an old-fashioned Bakelite one with a round dial and a curly black wire that attached the heavy handset to the base. It meant you had to be in the kitchen to use it, and had to shout to make yourself heard down the crackly line. Luke, who was closest, picked it up and heard someone with an American accent shouting back at him.

'It's probably my conference call,' said Steve excitedly, wresting the receiver from Luke. But the line was already dead.

Steve's BlackBerry, Laura's mobile and Jonathan's iPhone now lay on the second shelf of the pine dresser, as useless as a pile of decommissioned weapons. The others were mostly accepting of their incommunicado status. To Laura it seemed wondrous that a phone line worked at all. They were, she kept repeating to everyone, two miles west of Mull, in the middle of the Atlantic Ocean, in an area so far from the mainland that it merited mention on the shipping news four times a day. Over dinner last night, she had been the only one who could remember the name of every fishing area off the coast of Britain. Faeroes, Fair Isle, Viking, North Utsire, South Utsire, Cromarty . . . Laura muttered to herself when the sense of isolation from Nell and Ben became too overwhelming. It was like an ancient spell to ward off evil spirits.

Laura was sitting outside on a reclining chair struggling to read the first sentence of the same book she had started on the plane journey from London to Oban. It was an old-fashioned sunbed that groaned each time she moved and instead of reading she found herself anticipating the next crunch of flesh against wicker. She had envisaged devouring at least a couple of books while she was on holiday without the children, but had forgotten how the novelty of such proximity with friends could be every bit as compelling. So rather than travelling up the Congo with

Joseph Conrad, and then turning to Barbara Kingsolver, as she had planned, she was listening to Jonathan and Steve laboriously discuss plans for the evening meal. Once again she found herself putting the book face down beside her to stare out to sea.

She tried to shut out the entertaining but protracted debate taking place inside. They were discussing why Coll was the sunniest place in Britain. Jonathan argued that it was because there were no mountains to attract clouds, while Steve insisted he had met someone out running this morning who told him it was because the Gulf Stream ran down both sides of the island.

It was an exchange that wasn't really about the subject under scrutiny, but about the mutual antagonism of two men struggling for hegemony. Only instead of locking horns and physically fighting each other, the battle lines were drawn over issues like should the Federal Reserve have bailed out Bear Stearns, was *The Lives of Others* the best film ever made, and which beach they should visit next. It was a more sophisticated version of Nell and Ben winding each other up. Laura put her fingers in her ears and studied the sea for any change in the weather.

Everyone was instinctively drawn to the outside terrace that ran the length of the house because of the unrivalled views across the bay towards the Treshnish Islands. On a sunny day, they could be seen sketched against the horizon like four ghostly apparitions rising from the sea. Laura stared unblinkingly at the shoreline and found the same family of seals they had spotted at breakfast. They swam on their backs, flippers in the air, as though performing a well-rehearsed fly-past, thought Laura, resisting the urge to wave at them. But it was the rich turquoise of the sea that really captivated her. It sparkled against the white shell-sand beach like a precious stone. The waves seemed to break low and lazy along the shore, giving the impression that the sea was as still as a glass of water. Yet as they had discovered this morning, when you got to the water's edge it changed colour completely. And as soon as the sea lapped your calf, you could feel a dangerous undercurrent pulling you ever deeper into the water.

It was a bit like spending too much time with friends, thought Laura. The closer you got, the more evident their flaws, but the more beguiling their company. She removed her fingers from her ears and heard Jonathan and Steve still bickering in the kitchen.

Janey remained upstairs, struggling to keep Jack in the routine imposed by the maternity nurse in London. At the earliest opportunity this morning, she had gone to the only local shop on the island to buy Sellotape and bin liners to stick on the windows of his bedroom at the very back of the house. Jonathan had neglected to tell her that Coll was so far north that there were only five hours of darkness in the summer months and Jack had vocally expressed his disapproval at two-hourly intervals throughout the previous night. The walls of the house were made of material that reflected noise rather than absorbed it and only Sam had managed to get a full night's sleep.

At six thirty this morning, frustrated by her inability to sleep, Laura had come downstairs to make herself a cup of tea and had found Janey slumped over the breast pump, struggling to express milk. Laura casually suggested that perhaps Janey should try a bottle of powdered milk in the evening, to see if this would help get Jack through the night.

'I can't use formula milk,' insisted Janey angrily, switching the breast pump up to its maximum speed. Laura watched in shocked fascination as Janey's nipple was sucked in and out of the transparent tube with milk-curdling velocity. The machine threatened to suck in her entire breast. Her nipple was stretched as long and thin as her little finger. Lactating mothers were meant to be imbued with feelings of doe-eyed benevolence, thought Laura, remembering paintings in the National Gallery where dreamy mothers fed fat babies amidst bucolic scenes of sensual abandonment. Janey was as angry as a Tracey Emin installation.

'If I pump enough milk then Steve can do the five o'clock feed,' said Janey. Laura sighed with relief when she saw a small trickle of white milk start to drip into the bottle.

'Maybe you should relax the routine while you're on holiday,' Laura gently proposed.

'The maternity nurse warned me about people like you, Laura,' said Janey, only half joking. 'She said that you would try and tempt me away to the land of demand feeding.'

Laura started laughing.

'Are you the same woman that used to try and persuade me to have a line of coke before I went on duty at hospital because it would help to keep me awake through the night?' she asked. 'You're getting this totally out of perspective.'

'Look, I know that you breastfed your babies for eight

months because you couldn't afford private education and needed to maximise Nell and Ben's IQ,' said Janey, trying to be emollient, 'but I can only take off three months, so Jack won't get the full benefit.'

'What are you talking about?' asked Laura in astonishment.

'If you breastfeed for a year you can raise your baby's IQ by an average of six points,' said Janey. 'I've read all the literature.' She pointed to a book on child development that lay on the table. Laura paused for a moment. It had occurred to her a couple of times recently that her basic assumption about the correlation between scientific progress and the amelioration of the human condition didn't necessarily hold true for the mothers of newborn babies. For them knowledge mostly fanned the flames of neurosis.

'I know that at the moment this seems critical, but with the passage of time you won't even remember how long you breastfed,' said Laura, choosing her words carefully. 'You need to be a bit less fundamentalist.'

'I've got about a month's supply stored in the freezer in London,' Janey continued, 'so that means Jack will have breast milk for at least four months, but he'll probably lose out on at least two IQ points, because I'll only be able to do a couple of feeds a day. And even if wet nurses still existed, it wouldn't be the same because it is my milk that he needs. I have the antidote.'

'The antibodies,' corrected Laura, wondering whether she had been this volatile after Nell and Ben were born. Perhaps that was why Sam had baulked at the prospect of another baby. She buttered a piece of wholemeal toast and pushed the plate towards Janey, urging her to eat.

In a reflex borrowed from work, Laura checked Janey's face against her age. It was a gesture with no medical imperative, but it told you a lot about the stresses in people's lives that could account for their presence in her clinic. Not long ago Laura might have studied another woman and wondered whether she was more attractive, or more professionally successful, or more domestically capable than herself, and would usually have found herself lacking. But it had become apparent to her recently, as she approached forty, that the only thing that really mattered was how old you appeared. And in the past three months Janey had aged.

She was exhausted. Her skin was dry and drab, like an autumn leaf. Around her neck the skin puckered and there were tiny horizontal lines above her top lip that gave her a serious appearance, as though she was about to deliver another lecture on the importance of breastfeeding a baby for the first year. Dark circles gave her a wild-eyed look that was at odds with the listless way she was slumped over the table. It reminded Laura of Ben, when he complained that he hadn't enough diesel in his tank to walk to school and she had to pull him along the pavement like a spoon through treacle. Laura wondered, not for the first time, why there was so little research into the effects of prolonged sleep deprivation on the mothers of newborn babies. She knew the answer. It was assumed to be part of the female condition. If men had to endure similar conditions there would be government grants to investigate the subject.

'I can't go back to work, Laura,' Janey had announced, 'I

can't remember anything. I couldn't even remember the name of my assistant when she called up last week. I got as far as phoning the senior partner to tell him that I wanted to resign, but by the time I got through to him I had forgotten why I called. And I'd forgotten the most significant fact of all, which is that Steve's job could be on the line because the converts market is going through some drastic restructuring.'

'Why was your assistant phoning you on maternity leave?' Laura asked.

'Probably angling for my job,' said Janey. 'Do you think I might have premature dementia or the early symptoms of Parkinson's disease?' She leant her head on the edge of the breast pump and closed her eyes and still the pump sucked milk.

'In all my years as a clinician I have only seen two cases of Parkinson's in people under the age of fifty and both of them were men,' said Laura reassuringly. 'And people with dementia generally don't realise it. Someone else usually takes them to the doctor. You need to measure yourself by what you remember, not what you forget, Janey. You're probably subconsciously deleting all non-essential information so that you can focus on what really matters.'

That's what most mothers do for the rest of their lives, Laura wanted to tell her, but she held back. Instead she described the bare bones of a research paper that a colleague had recently published on memory and motherhood.

'The stresses of pregnancy and motherhood can cause a partial breakdown in the memory system,' explained Laura. 'There's an awful lot we don't understand about the brain but researchers think that having children may compromise the function of the hippocampus, which we rely on for short-term memory solutions. Then there is the impact of hormones on memory. Lack of oestrogen, for example, impairs memory . . . I think it's much more likely that you are suffering from a combination of this and severe sleep deprivation. All you need is a decent night's sleep and you'll be fine again.'

'I can't believe it's turned out this way,' sighed Janey.

'You'll learn to let go,' said Laura, 'in your own time. Everyone does. Just be gentle on yourself and can I have permission to toss these into the Atlantic?' Janey smiled weakly, one hand steadily protecting the pile of books.

That was this morning and since then, apart from a short interlude after breakfast when the baby finally slept for half an hour, Janey had remained upstairs. The holiday was characterised by this strange disjuncture, thought Laura, half closing her eyes as the sun came out from behind a wispy cloud. It was as though everyone wanted to avoid being in the same place at the same time. Apart from her. She was very happy to sit in this chair for the next six days.

Right on cue, Hannah appeared, driving up the track in the rental car. She was wearing tracksuit bottoms and trainers and told Laura that she had been for a run. Laura raised an eyebrow but didn't say anything. No doubt she had been at Windy Gap, perched on those gneiss boulders, trying to speak to Jacek. Her absence was marginally more comforting than her presence. Although Hannah hadn't mentioned Jacek since her revelation at the party a month ago, her silence on the subject spoke volumes. She clearly had no intention of ending the relationship. Laura noticed that she was carrying a large tin of formula milk for babies under the age of six months.

'We all need to sleep,' said Hannah, nonchalantly shrugging her shoulders and hiding the tin in the kitchen cupboard, 'otherwise we won't photograph well.' Jonathan appeared by the kitchen door.

'You'll be wonderful,' he said. Hannah gave a tense smile.

'She's homesick,' Jonathan explained to Laura. 'She misses the farm.' Laura gave what she hoped was an appropriately reassuring laugh.

The phone started ringing again and Jonathan went inside. For a moment Laura worried that it might be her parents calling about the children. But she remained still, arguing to herself that if something had gone wrong they would call again. Instead she turned her mind to Hannah's affair. The advantage of knowing was that it neutralised any residual preoccupation with the cover of the Eden cookbook. Sam hadn't mentioned it again and set against this compelling contemporary scandal, what Laura had done was ancient history. Everyone around her was looking forward rather than backwards. The weekend in Shropshire could finally be laid to rest.

Instead her attention switched to Jonathan. She turned to him in the kitchen and he waved happily back at her. How could he be so oblivious when the symptoms were so obvious? Hannah's new clothes, the hippy tops and denim shorts, the tiny tattoo that had appeared at the bottom of her ankle, the way she never brushed her hair. Most of all the way she moved, slow and languorous, like a cat. She talked to Laura and Janey about things like skin tone and elasticity, contemptuously pinching her stomach and the top of her arms in the way that someone might if they were intimately engaged with the smooth, hard body of someone in their mid twenties. She was affectionate to Luke, mentioning nothing of the scandal that had brought him at the last hour to Coll, and he appreciated her reticence. Hannah was on holiday with them but she wasn't really there. Even her cool green eyes were distant. She was going through the motions. Her detachment increased Laura's sense of responsibility for ensuring that Jonathan's interview went according to plan. Already she had persuaded Sam to drive to the ferry the following afternoon to pick up the journalist, and she'd helped Jonathan work out the menu for the meal that they would be photographed eating.

Laura felt herself relax, closed her eyes against the sun, and allowed her body to be overtaken by the lead heaviness of utter calm. This holiday was the best thing that had happened to her for years. Competing with books and the scenery for her attention was the irresistible novelty of having time for herself, the opportunity to drink a cup of coffee from beginning to end without any interruption, and the delicious indulgence of sitting completely still staring across the bay without having to move to wipe up snot, shit or tears, or search for the key that had mysteriously disappeared from the garden door, or deal with the vagaries of the new NHS computer system.

Far from missing Nell and Ben, as she had incessantly worried she would up until the moment she said goodbye, Laura was now wondering how on earth she would return to the status quo in London. That was the disadvantage of a holiday like this. It made you question the way you ran the rest of your life, or at least gave you the illusion that it was something you could recalibrate, which of course she probably couldn't.

Inside she could hear a heated debate underway. It was Steve's turn to cook dinner and judging by the ingredients under discussion, he was determined to trump Jonathan's meal the previous evening. Laura wondered what her mother would make of these men fighting for control in the kitchen, an irony compounded by the fact they had decided to dispense with the services of the cook who came with the house.

How people behaved in a kitchen revealed a lot about their personality. Jonathan was a classic glory cook, who wrenched as much drama as possible from rustling up a meal by choosing overly complicated recipes, using too many ingredients and creating too much washing-up that he then expected everyone else to do. Steve was simply someone who followed a recipe to the last letter and made it work through sheer bloody-minded force of will. Although Sam was probably the most consistent cook of the three men, he preferred to sit out this power struggle. Laura searched for him in the kitchen and guessed correctly that he was upstairs making further changes to the mysterious film script that he still refused to allow her to read, although Janey had let slip during the three-hour ferry crossing from Oban that she had read the opening couple of scenes. Laura pretended she had too, agreeing enthusiastically that the characters felt like people they knew and the dialogue echoed their own conversation, because it was easier than admitting that Sam wouldn't let her. Although their relationship had reached a happier plateau, he was still exacting punishment for her behaviour over the marriage guidance counsellor.

She glanced back over her shoulder through the open glass doors into the kitchen and saw Jonathan and Steve lining up bottles of olive oil on the kitchen table. It was the modern-day equivalent of a duel at dawn. They were being carefully observed by Luke, who was typing into his computer on a chair beside the table that housed the telephone. He was wearing frayed khaki shorts and a faded green T-shirt and his bare feet were resting on the back of an old armchair that sat beside the heavy mahogany dresser. His hair was so long it reached his shoulders. He hammered the keyboard, occasionally scrolling up and down the page to read what he had written. Everything about him was big and clumsy, as though he had found himself imprisoned inside the wrong body.

Laura wondered what he was writing. His verbosity on the computer was at odds with his otherwise monosyllabic approach to life. He wasn't rude. He simply didn't want to engage with the adults around him. Laura could vaguely remember this feeling herself. It was a sort of self-delusion, a way of reassuring yourself that you wouldn't turn into the kind of person your parents and their friends had become. It was born less of hatred and more of fear, decided Laura. Luke didn't know what he wanted but he knew what he didn't want and empathy wasn't a useful trait for a teenager. His silence was a vote against pointless arguments about the health benefits of a Mediterranean diet (Jonathan), the advantages of state education over private (Laura), whether late Nick Cave was better than early Nick Cave (Sam) and how making lots of money was the single biggest contribution someone could make to society (Steve).

Everyone was too polite to mention the circumstances surrounding Luke's unexpected arrival on Coll. The adults in the group behaved as though it was the most normal thing in the world to have a seventeen-year-old in their midst. Besides, nobody really understood exactly why Luke had been expelled from school. He had done an art project that involved morphing the faces of a couple of his teachers on to a Paris Hilton sex tape and tried to present it as part of his A-level coursework entitled 'Fifteen Minutes of Fame'. He was trying to comment on sex and celebrity, he told his parents during a tense phone conversation. The school hadn't seen it that way, even though his art teacher had tried to intervene in his favour. The clip made its way to YouTube where it had been viewed by almost half a million people and Luke's fate was sealed.

'This won the international prize at the 2008 Los Angeles Extra Virgin Olive Oil Competition,' said Steve, waving the bottle in his hand. 'It's all hand-pressed and bottled on the same estate in southern Calabria. Its acidity is 0.225 per cent. It's the oil equivalent of a fine Meursault. I brought it here especially for you, to help make your interview a success.'

The main difference between Sam and the other two men, decided Laura, was that Sam was competitive with himself. Steve's instinct to compete spilled over from work into home life with exhausting ease. He couldn't even allow Jonathan to be dominant in the kitchen. And Jonathan, who was ultimately unconfident about his culinary skills, took the challenge seriously.

'I'm really grateful but the point I'm trying to make is that if you are only using it to make the sorrel soup, then you might as well use a semi-fine virgin,' said Jonathan, taken aback at Steve's persistence. 'If you are really keen to try your olive oil, then you could use the sorrel leaves in a salad instead. There's no point in cooking such a fine olive oil. It's like drinking Meursault at a stag party. And don't keep it in the fridge. It will separate.' He was waving a well-thumbed copy of Richard Mabey's *Food for Free* a little too close to Steve's face.

'Are you aware that olive oil is among the most adulterated agricultural products in Europe?' asked Steve suddenly. 'You can make as much money from trafficking olive oil as you can from trafficking cocaine.'

'I wasn't,' sighed Jonathan. 'How do you know all this?'

'I was going to invest in an Italian olive-oil business,' explained Steve, as he began heating up the Il Casalone extra virgin olive oil in a frying pan. 'The American market alone is worth $1.5 billion, but then there was a huge case brought against the company I wanted to buy. It was trying to pass off soya oil as extra virgin olive oil.'

'Don't overcook the sorrel,' advised Jonathan, 'from what I remember it only needs sweating, otherwise it disintegrates.' He looked around for Hannah to back him up, but couldn't find her.

The sound of the phone ringing was a welcome distraction for Jonathan. He didn't have to worry it might be Eve, because she didn't have his phone number here. The biggest advantage of being on Coll was the fact that Eve couldn't contact him. The enthusiasm of the first five months of their relationship was beginning to dissipate and although he wasn't quite ready to give up on those afternoons spent in her Notting Hill flat, her function was now almost exclusively physical. He couldn't remember a woman who took a man's penis so gently in her mouth, exacted such teasing punishment with her tongue, and then so willingly swallowed his sperm. It had retreated into a one-dimensional relationship, he had proudly informed Sam the previous week. He had even let slip that he was trying to help her organise an internship at a magazine in New York for a year. Sam had never considered Eve in any professional light and was taken aback to discover that she was features editor of the same newspaper magazine that was coming to interview Jonathan.

'They would have done me anyway.' Jonathan had batted away Sam's questions about conflict of interest, reiterating the fact that their relationship was almost over. When Sam asked how Eve was responding, Jonathan replied curtly that everything was fine. He didn't want to talk about her any more. His loss of interest was in direct proportion to his increasing feeling of embarrassment, sensed Sam.

The call was also a welcome diversion from the discussion about olive oil. The debate with Steve added to Jonathan's growing neurosis that passing off soya oil as olive oil was little different from the deceit that he was a world-class cook, when really he was no more than an enthusiastic food pundit who knew how to recruit a good chef. It was nothing more than a question of semantics.

So with uncharacteristic intent, Jonathan strolled over to the phone and picked up the receiver to find Sam's

American agent at the other end complaining that he had been trying to call the whole day. Jonathan called upstairs for Sam to come down.

'Call from LA. It's your agent, says it's important,' shouted Jonathan in a tone laced with irony. It was a tired joke, made at Sam's expense, but still Laura smiled because its repetition recalled their historical ties. Everyone occasionally needed to be reminded of the reasons why they had become friends, thought Laura benevolently as she got out of the chair and wandered back into the kitchen. Later in the week, when everything had changed between them, Laura would wonder at this early mood of optimism and how she'd allowed it to cloud her judgement.

Sam came downstairs two at a time, less from enthusiasm than from the need to stretch his legs, clutching a sheaf of papers in his hand. Laura wasn't sure whether he was rewriting the ending of this latest film script or whether he had started work on something else. She felt a stab of guilt. She had stopped asking Sam about his projects years ago. As his confidence in himself dwindled, so did her faith in him. But this single, short phone call, during which Sam probably uttered less than thirty words, was to change everything. As Sam put down the phone, he faced the wall completely still, holding the receiver on the base, and for a moment Laura wondered if there was more bad news. Perhaps there were post-production problems with the last episode of *Do Not Resuscitate*, she thought. They were quite capable, even at this stage, of changing the brief. Maybe they wanted bird flu instead of Ebola. When Sam turned round, his eyes glazed and shaking his head, she could tell by the twist of smile on his lips that for the first time in years something good had happened.

'You won't fucking believe this,' said Sam to everyone in the room. He was still shaking his head incredulously. They all waited expectantly. 'I've sold the script in the States.' He shook his clenched fist in the air a couple of times and then apologised to Luke for swearing.

'That's awesome, Sam,' said Luke, who was the first one to react. 'Do you think I could get some work experience on the film set? I'm really interested in cinematography.' It was the most he had said since he'd arrived.

Laura was too shocked to say anything. For a moment she wondered whether Sam had got it wrong. Perhaps he had misunderstood his agent or was embellishing a less exciting, more prosaic truth. Laura understood enough about his business to know that he could be selling an option for a couple of thousand pounds and that the film would most likely never get made.

'What sort of deal, Sam?' asked Jonathan, anticipating her line of thought.

'Three hundred and fifty thousand US dollars for the rights, and then the same again if it gets made,' said Sam, shaking his head in disbelief, 'and Cate Blanchett has said she wants the main female part.' There was a long silence as they all tried to absorb the news and then everyone spoke at once.

'What's it all about?' asked Laura.

'It's about a group of friends who go on holiday together and discover they've all been hiding secrets from each other for years,' said Sam, shrugging his shoulders as though he couldn't understand what the fuss was about.

'Oh,' said Laura, looking for hidden undercurrents, but finding none.

'That's fantastic news, Sam,' said Janey, who had appeared in the kitchen from upstairs. She looked as though she was about to cry. 'You really deserve it.'

'God, so you've finally made some money,' said Steve with begrudging admiration, 'although I guess if you divide it between the number of years you've invested in all this then that's only £25,000 per annum.'

'It's not all about the money,' said Janey firmly.

'When you've waited this long, it is,' laughed Laura.

'Well I hope I get some of the credit for providing the office where some of it was written,' joked Jonathan.

'Laura gets most of the credit because she's the one who has held the faith for the past eleven years,' said Sam, aware that Laura was standing on the edge of the group gathered around him.

'And what's the likelihood of being able to raise finance?' asked Jonathan.

'It's a joint venture,' explained Sam, 'and with Cate Blanchett on board, that's not going to be a problem.'

'It's a question of instinct, isn't it, Sam?' said Hannah. 'You have to follow your heart not your head.' Laura caught her eye and Hannah smiled back at her, seemingly truly happy for the first time since they had arrived.

Jonathan pulled a bottle of champagne from the fridge. A sense of collective elation filled the room and for a few minutes everyone basked in the wake of Sam's success, delighted to be present at a moment of historical flux. Sam felt altered by the news in an irrevocable way. It felt as though a crucial part of him was missing, he tried to explain to Laura. The albatross of professional anxiety that had weighed him down for the past seventeen years had lifted. His chief emotion, however, was not elation but relief, as though he was the sole survivor of a fatal plane crash or the only person not to contract bird flu during an epidemic. He had survivor's guilt, he explained to Laura during a snatched conversation. He tried to persuade her up to bed, so that they could talk more, but she was too busy skim-reading the script that sat on the table to read the signals.

14

Everyone goes on holiday with expectations, mulled Sam as he gripped the steering wheel of the car and drove too fast down the windy road to the ferry port at Arinagour a couple of days later to pick up the writer and photographer. There is an excessive sense of entitlement: the right to happiness, to good food, to laughter, to sleep, to sex. By the time you've checked the toothpaste is packed for the final time, locked the dusty suitcase and glanced over departure times memorised weeks earlier, the sense of anticipation is almost overwhelming. Sam opened all the windows of the car and breathed in the sea air like a dog sniffing a scent, oblivious to the way the wind blew Luke's long hair uncomfortably across his face and into his mouth.

His fingers tapped the steering wheel in time to the music blaring from the CD player as he swung round the first corner past Ben Hogh, Coll's highest summit. On the map it looked like a mountain, but really it qualified as little more than a significant undulation in the otherwise flat landscape. Sam turned up the volume. The CD belonged to Luke, who had casually slid into the passenger seat as Sam was about to leave and asked whether he would mind some company.

'Beirut. Indie band. Quite recent,' said Luke, and then fell silent again. He rarely spoke more than a sentence and Sam felt flattered by his presence and his attempt to share his taste in music. Holidays are ultimately about wish fulfilment, Sam decided. But what people forget is that neuroses travel free of charge and without the structure of work and children to define the day, they can coalesce in your mind.

The day before they left London, Sam had received a letter from the hospital informing him that his sperm count was now negative. His main goal on Coll was therefore to resume sexual relations with his wife. But just as the right conditions materialised, he was thwarted from this end by his latest godson, whose high-pitched cries cut through the night and kept everyone awake, apart from Sam. It was like having a newborn baby without any of the benefits of ownership.

Every morning Sam woke up and was grateful to discover his nitric oxide levels undiminished by the recent vasectomy. Concerns about impotence became as distant and hazy as the Treshnish Isles, visible through the bedroom window. The heat, the salty taste of Laura's skin as he surreptitiously licked a shoulder blade while she slept beside him, and the possibilities posed by an exposed breast that peaked tantalisingly from her unravelled sarong, gave him an adolescent sense of erotic purpose. This morning Sam had looked down at the sheet and noted with pleasure that it was lifted a good seven inches from his groin. The satisfaction, however, was tinged with the knowledge that he was now halfway through the holiday with no measurable progress made.

At six o'clock this morning, when Jack woke for the fourth time, Sam had tried lifting the corner of Laura's sarong to draw a line from the inside of her knee up towards her hip, lingering over the soft flesh of her inner thigh before she rolled over on to her side. Then he held her from behind and whispered a detailed account of one of her favourite fantasies.

'Tell me what you'd like me to do for you,' he breathed heavily in her ear.

'Mend the leak in the bedroom, hang up that mirror and set up a direct debit for the phone bill,' Laura muttered. 'Sam, I'm sorry but I've got to sleep.'

In desperation he pushed her hand into his groin, but she was immovable. Finally he opened the curtains to let the sun pour into the bedroom. Laura had simply put her head under the pillow and fallen asleep again.

Sam tried to slow himself down by reciting the names of various beaches and bays around the island: Feall, Cliad, Crossapol, Gunna. They would make good surnames. He asked Luke, who was sitting beside him chewing a pen, if he wouldn't mind jotting some of them down for future reference. Luke obligingly scribbled a few down in the notebook that accompanied him wherever he went.

Everything Sam saw had erotic potential. The round rocks, sandpapered soft by the sand and sea. The pale purple harebells and bright red crocosmia; the way the horizon turned liquid at the point it touched the sea; the gear stick. Sam sighed and saw Luke watch him. He tried to give what he hoped was an encouraging smile but instead felt his face contort in a crooked grin that felt more leery than reassuring. The last thing Luke would want to know was that the rest of adulthood was a struggle against one's inner adolescent.

Sam would have liked to talk to him about what had happened at school, to tell him that it wouldn't define the rest of his life, at least not in the way he assumed, but felt inhibited by his silence and worried that he might disturb its dignity. He would have liked to learn how exactly he had managed to fake the image of the teachers and exactly what the Paris Hilton sex tape was all about, but it wasn't really godfatherly territory.

Sam had left the others drinking beer on the terrace and making plans for the meal that Jonathan would cook in a couple of days before the critical eye of the writer and photographer. A pile of books with dog-eared pages and paragraphs outlined with a pink highlighter pen sat on a garden chair. Some were cookery books. Elizabeth David, Hugh Fearnley-Whittingstall, Claire Macdonald. Others were about foraging for food and plant life on Coll. Steve obligingly offered to help with wine and olive oil. Janey said she would lay the table, and Laura, who in Sam's opinion was being irritatingly oversensitive to Jonathan's needs, helped him to draw up a plan of action. The first page included a list of ingredients that he needed to source today. The second a strict timetable for tomorrow. Whenever Jonathan asked Hannah for advice, she shrugged nonchalantly and said that everything would work out for the best. She had a glazed look in her eye that was reminiscent of someone who had joined an evangelical Christian church or was five months into a course of Prozac.

Most of the ingredients, Laura had noted with satisfaction, grew on Coll or were caught in the sea: lobsters, sorrel, kelp, mackerel, ceps, wild garlic. Forget organic food, extreme localism was the order of the day, Jonathan had announced excitedly. This should be the main angle of the story. People needed to wake up to the produce that lay at their own front door. He told everyone excitedly about a scheme in New York where people kept bees on Manhattan rooftops and chickens on their balconies. Then he talked about protein being the fundamental challenge on the road to true environmentalism. He mentioned an experiment in New Zealand that measured the average amount of methane produced by cows each day and talked about the huge distances covered by trucks transporting animals to meet demand for meat in Europe, India and China. Chickens were the way forward, he said. Cheap protein. Everyone could keep their own chickens. They could hatch eggs and give the chicks to their neighbours. When Sam pointed out that it might get a little unhygienic keeping Buff Orpingtons in a two-bedroom flat in Peckham, Jonathan bristled.

'It's a utopian vision, Sam,' he said, as though Sam moonlighted for Tesco, 'something to aspire to. We should export food to poor countries where people don't have enough to eat and produce what we can ourselves.'

'And the chickens would have a better life,' agreed Laura.

'Chickens don't deserve a good life,' said Sam, 'they're consummate bullies. Where do you think the phrase pecking order originated?'

'Maybe if teenagers had chickens to look after, there would be less knife crime?' suggested Laura enthusiastically.

'Or more dead chickens,' joked Sam. His cynicism was misplaced. The chicken scheme sounded good. It was this reignited closeness between Laura and Jonathan that irritated him. It reminded him too much of the weekend on the barge in Shropshire. He tried to banish from his mind the image on the front of the cookery book.

As they passed a couple of freshwater lochs, Sam took his foot off the accelerator. There was no point in arriving early. Jonathan had lost the details sent by the magazine and all Sam knew was that he was picking up a woman and a man carrying camera bags. Expediency rather than carelessness, thought Sam about Jonathan's disorganisation. He guessed that the writer's London credentials would make her stand out from the crowd. There would be no broken veins on her face, no wind tan, no dirty black rubber boots with salt-burnt holes. He imagined someone as poised and polished as the leather loafers that Steve insisted on wearing even when they went to the beach. He visualised her standing close to the end of the walkway, holding an enormous handbag of the kind favoured by London women.

The late-afternoon light was extraordinary, thought Sam. Different colours, a range of red and purple, bled through the sky and reflected in the flat surface of the hill lochs landlocked in the middle of the island. Everything was heightened by Coll's proximity to water. Wherever you stood, you could hear the ocean, even if you couldn't see it. In a storm, when the clouds hung menacingly low in the sky, it seemed as though Coll might go the way of Atlantis and sink into the water. What was holding it there? How was it attached to the seabed? That combination of strength and fragility fascinated Sam. It reminded him of Laura.

They were getting on much better. Her relief over the sale of his script was palpable. Her shoulders seemed to visibly relax as he told her the details. Already she was planning exactly how much of the money they should use to pay towards the mortgage and how she would work a three-day week. Although her faith in him had diminished over the lean years, she had never wavered in her loyalty and Sam was grateful for that.

Despite Steve's insistence over the best way to reach the port, as soon as Sam got in the car he ignored his written instructions and decided to take the route that would allow him and Luke to absorb as much of the landscape as possible. It was a ten-minute drive to the ferry and even if they took the longest route, driving along the track that connected Hogh with Feaull on the northern side of the island, it would take less than half an hour, Sam had tried to explain to Steve. Steve still insisted on unfolding the Ordnance Survey map on the kitchen table and estimating exactly how far it was to Arinagour from Acha, and exactly how long it would take to get there if Sam averaged a median speed of around twenty-five miles an hour.

'Eilean Cholla,' said Sam out loud, as they passed the sign outside Coll's only village. Was the letter 'h' silent in the Gaelic language? Sam wondered. It was odd to feel so foreign in your own country, but then the Inner Hebrides were remote to everyone but the people who lived there. And his Irish roots probably made him more culturally in tune with these parts than the Scots. Luke still didn't say anything.

The ferry had arrived early, Sam realised, as he drove down into Arinagour and parked the car. Luke got out the other side and they began walking down the hill towards the pier. Luke's trousers hung off his hips like a flag at half mast. His pants sprouted out of the top. Surely girls couldn't find this attractive? It shortened Luke's legs and elongated his torso, exaggerating the width of his shoulders and giving him a reptilian appearance at odds with his perfectly symmetrical face and open smile. Although it did give a satisfying insight into his well-honed stomach muscles, conceded Sam. Maybe that's why people over the age of twenty-five hated it, because it was a look they couldn't carry off. As if he could read Sam's mind, Luke hitched up his black drainpipe jeans. They immediately slumped back down again, resting on his narrow hip bones. Sam could see two people waiting and was surprised to see Luke lurch forward to greet the male figure on the right.

'It's my godfather,' Luke shouted back to Sam in surprise. 'It's Patrick. I recognise him from the picture on the wall of Dad's office.'

Sam squinted at the figure stepping to the side to greet Luke. Luke was right. Patrick's silhouette was unchanged from the first time Sam had met him at Oxford, with his round shoulders and Leica camera slung round his neck like a chunky piece of costume jewellery. Sam lengthened his stride and drew closer. He waved at Patrick and shouted a greeting that sounded too hearty, as though he was trying to simulate enthusiasm or stifle surprise. But what did Patrick expect? wondered Sam. He more than anyone had tried to defend the indefensible when Patrick left Janey almost ten years ago and Patrick had repaid this debt of friendship with inexplicably silent abandonment.

They had known each other for almost twenty years but it was a friendship that had suffered from drift the moment Patrick started going out with Janey. Patrick smiled at Sam and hugged him effusively but there was something restrained in his manner. In confusion, Sam turned his gaze to the woman, trying to work out whether she was the writer or Patrick's girlfriend, wondering whether her presence compounded or relieved the awkwardness of what lay ahead. He resolved to try and phone Janey to warn her about what had transpired and wondered whether this was part of a plan endorsed by Jonathan. But his resolution drained as he turned his attention to the woman and realised that he was staring at Eve.

'Hello, Sam,' she said confidently, kissing him on both cheeks. 'I decided to write this one myself.' She patted two large bags sitting on the ground and Sam could see a copy of *Recipes from Eden*, a couple of notebooks and a hand-held tape recorder lying inside one. She pointed at Patrick.

'I've done my research,' Eve said proudly. 'I can't believe that Jonathan never mentioned the man who took the photo. How did he think he was going to recreate the image without its original auteur present?'

'Interesting idea,' said Sam neutrally.

'She was very persuasive,' said Patrick. Sam gave Patrick a long even stare that was met equivocally.

'I'll carry your camera bags,' said Luke to Patrick, and started walking up the hill towards the car. Eve followed close behind, chatting to Luke and asking endless questions that he politely answered in sentences of less than five words. She was wearing a baggy shift top, a pair of shorts and rubber boots, looking more like a refugee from

Glastonbury than a broadsheet journalist. Her legs were tanned and when she bent over to put a bag in the boot of the car, Sam observed the rounded curve of her buttock. He caught Patrick's eye, and they shared the embarrassment of two almost middle-aged men appreciating the youthful curves of a type of woman they should have grown out of years ago. Sam picked up the other bag that Eve had left beside the open car and lifted it into the boot.

'God, what have you got in here?' he asked, struggling to lift the case.

'I've just done another piece in Hawick, the cashmere capital of Scotland, so one of the bags is full of dirty washing and the other full of knitwear,' Eve explained. 'And I'm on a fully organic macrobiotic diet and I didn't think the village shop would satisfy my needs.'

Does Jonathan satisfy your needs? Sam found himself wondering as Patrick and Luke unquestioningly climbed into the back of the car. Sam started the engine and stalled a couple of times until Luke pointed out to him that he needed to put it in gear. Sam decided he was in a state of shock. He turned on the engine again, went straight into second gear and stayed there to keep up his revs. He drove out of Arinagour even faster than he had arrived, hoping his passengers would assume his silence was justified by the need to concentrate on the road. He swerved to avoid a couple of sheep and felt guilty as Eve stretched out the seatbelt and strapped herself in.

'I didn't have you down as a boy racer,' she said to Sam, asking for permission to put on some music. Sam smiled stiffly in acquiescence.

'Great music,' she said appreciatively. 'Who brought this

with them?' Luke grunted affirmatively from the back of the car.

'They're playing at The Big Chill in August,' Eve said, turning round to stare at Luke.

Eve was still at a stage in her life where she seemed younger without make-up, thought Sam, as he glanced over at her. He couldn't remember whether Jonathan had ever disclosed her exact age. She must realise that Sam was shaken by her appearance but she displayed no sense of unease or guilt. She had the absolute self-assurance of a woman in her late twenties, decided Sam. She could ignore the ticking of her biological clock for a few years yet. There was lightness in her step, more physical than emotional: she didn't bear the weight of children around her neck.

The wind from the open window blew her dark hair towards him. Sam found himself unconsciously lifting his hand from the steering wheel towards her. He wanted to move the strand obscuring her face so that he could appreciate those lips again. But he caught himself in time and instead unsuccessfully tried to change gear again. He couldn't believe that Jonathan had the temerity to bring Eve on holiday to Coll with them. It was either an extraordinary lapse of judgement or a perfect example of his absolute arrogance.

He looked in the rear-view mirror wondering whether Patrick had noticed his own near catastrophic slip and didn't know whether to be pleased or annoyed to see he was fully concentrating on expertly rolling a joint. In Luke's eyes, this probably made Patrick the ideal godfather. He caught Patrick's eye in the mirror and tried to deliver a disapproving look but Patrick smiled back at him and lit the joint.

Sam was consumed with a sudden rage towards Jonathan. It was bad enough to bring this girl on holiday, but to do it knowing that Sam was complicit in the conspiracy was unforgivable. How was he meant to face Hannah? Duplicity wasn't his strong point, as he had discovered during his abortive attempt to have a clandestine vasectomy. And although Jonathan surely hadn't actively encouraged Patrick to come, he probably hadn't discouraged him either. At the very least he had indulged Eve's plan.

As they passed the hotel at the top of the hill, Sam seriously contemplated checking in there with Laura for the rest of the week. But how would he explain this? He could blame the crying baby, but then Janey would go into further decline, and Sam already knew he couldn't leave her to deal with Patrick alone.

Patrick passed the joint to him and Sam took a deep drag, hoping that the grass would shift his mood or at least deliver the necessary degree of detachment to get through the next hour of his life. His lungs burnt as he swallowed the smoke. He took another toke and was pleased to discover that it immediately soothed his jangly nerves. He passed it on to Eve, relieved that he didn't have to face the moral dilemma of handing it directly to Luke, although surely this wouldn't be his first time. But when Eve offered the half-smoked joint to Luke, he refused with such charm that Sam felt as though the seventeen-year-old showed better judgement than any of the adults in the car.

'I need to keep my head clear,' said Luke.

'To deal with the stress of being on holiday with your parents?' teased Eve.

'For work,' explained Luke apologetically.

Sam slowed down the car until they were travelling at exactly twenty miles an hour. He had forgotten how grass dulled his reflexes and increased his paranoia. He wasn't taking any unnecessary risks. It was as though they were now travelling in slow motion.

'From the sublime to the ridiculous,' said Patrick from the back.

'What kind of work?' asked Eve, turning round to face Luke.

'I have a blog,' explained Luke.

'How many hits a day do you average?' asked Eve.

'It varies,' said Luke, 'sometimes a couple of thousand, sometimes more.'

'How much more?' asked Eve. 'What is the most you've had in one day?'

'Half a million,' said Luke. 'That was when I got expelled from school.'

'Bloody hell,' said Sam, catching Luke's eye in the mirror. No wonder he was constantly making notes.

'What do you write about?' asked Patrick.

'My life as a teenager,' said Luke, 'there's a big demand for that sort of thing.'

'What's it called?' asked Patrick.

'*Keeping It Real*,' said Luke confidently. 'Actually, Sam, I wanted to talk to you, because someone approached me to see if I'd be interested in joining the writing team for *Skins*.'

'That sounds great, Luke,' said Sam, who couldn't recognise the funereal tone of his own voice.

Eve began rummaging in the bag that lay at her feet. As

she leaned over, the strap of her top fell from her shoulder down the side of her arm. 'Eyes face forward,' Sam repeated to himself a couple of times before he realised that everyone could hear him. He pulled on a pair of sunglasses from the pocket of his trousers, swerved into the verge and came to a complete halt as another car approached. He saw Eve line up the newspapers on her lap and worried about the print staining her long elegant legs.

'I've brought the weekend papers for you,' she said. 'I thought you might want to keep them.'

'How is Dad's book doing?' asked Luke.

'Number four in non-fiction hardbacks,' said Eve. 'But I brought these for Sam.'

'For me?' asked Sam blankly, making no attempt to steer the car back on to the road.

'Miramax issued a press release,' said Eve. 'Your film deal is all over the papers. All British cast, apart from Cate of course. British location. British crew. British director. It's a great angle.'

Sam felt her touch his upper arm. If he hadn't been expected to drive he would have closed his eyes. Instead he stared resolutely out of the front windscreen, not even reacting when he nudged the wipers on at maximum speed. Her finger was gently touching the soft fleshy part just below the sleeve of his T-shirt.

'It says you're Harvey Weinstein's wunderkind,' said Eve, sounding impressed, 'you need to get used to the adulation.' Sam couldn't speak. Instead he concentrated on the finger on his arm.

'I'm really pleased for you, Sam, but can we move please?' insisted Patrick from the back of the car. Sam fiercely pushed the car into first gear, but when he released the clutch it stalled. In the back, Luke and Patrick started giggling. Sam tried again and after a few abortive attempts the car stuttered back on to the road. He reached a T-junction, one of only three on the island, and turned left instead of right and discovered that he could no longer put the car into reverse.

'You'll be able to afford a driver soon,' joked Patrick. Luke leant through the gap between the front seats, touched Sam's shoulder and asked if he wanted him to drive. Sam stopped the car, slowly got out of the front seat until he was standing on the grassy verge and was violently sick. At least this completely neutralises my sexual potential was his first thought, as he leant over a ditch and watched first lunch, then breakfast disappear into the murky water. He retched a couple of times and felt Luke's arm around his shoulders.

'You are a great godson,' he said to Luke hoarsely.

It was ironic, thought Sam, that although he was the one who carefully organised the recycling into neat piles of glass, plastics and food waste every day, he was the one who would also pollute the water supply on Coll. The water in this ditch probably seeped down to the well at the house where they were staying and that well supplied a quarter of the island with its needs. At least Eve wouldn't write about something like this. She was resolutely on-message and undoubtedly this was why Jonathan had allowed her to come. It was his guarantee of a journalistic blow job. He looked over at Eve and saw her eyeing him with an expression that fell somewhere between sympathy and disgust.

*

When they finally appeared in the driveway back at the house, Sam was surprised to find everyone sitting in exactly the same places he had left them in. Wine had replaced beer and even Janey was holding a large glass, noted Sam. It was a scene stage-managed by Jonathan to give a good first impression to the journalist and Sam had to admit that by most people's standards it looked pretty idyllic.

A bowl of mackerel pâté made with fish caught by Steve sat on the table; Hannah lay on the wicker chair smoking a cigarette, simultaneously glamorous and picturesque; Laura was handing Jack over to Janey. Jonathan approached the car, the consummate performer, brimming over with confidence.

Sam could see that he was about to ask why Luke was driving, when he noticed Patrick get out of the back seat of the car. Jonathan stepped back appalled, as though unsure how to respond. He searched Sam's face for an explanation and Sam shrugged his shoulders, not wanting to speak in case Jonathan could smell his rancid breath. Really what he wanted to do was get to the top bathroom as quickly as possible and brush his teeth ten times in the way he used to as a child before a visit to the dentist. Then he would run a deep yellow bath, sink under the water, and hold his breath until he felt as though his lungs would burst.

Instead he stood like a master of ceremonies trying to direct a diplomatically challenging social event. It was as though the Chinese ambassador had walked into an event hosted by the Dalai Lama, or Gordon Brown had accidentally put Alastair Campbell on the guest list for a party.

Sam lifted an arm to warn Janey but he could tell by the look in her eye that she had already seen Patrick. She held Jack close to her, as though he would protect her from the unannounced visitor. Jonathan was about to intervene, to position himself between Patrick and the terrace, but he had just noticed the female figure unfurling her legs and clambering over her bag to get out of the front seat of the car. Eve stood still to appraise the scene and had the presence of mind to shake Jonathan's hand. But then she had the advantage of anticipation.

'Eve Bailey,' she said in an even tone. 'Great to meet you.'

Despite his tan, Jonathan went pale. He put a hand out on the bonnet of the car to steady himself, ignoring the heat from the overcooked engine, and in that sole gesture, that controlled resistance to pain, Sam understood that Jonathan had had no idea that Eve was coming. What was her game? wondered Sam incredulously.

Jonathan hesitatingly introduced her to everyone, including those who had travelled with her from the ferry port. But if anyone noticed anything strange it was instantly surpassed by the impact of facing Patrick for the first time. No one wanted to make a scene in front of Eve, who explained quite persuasively that she had forced him to come to ensure the absolute authenticity of the piece she was writing. But it couldn't have escaped Eve's notice, and it certainly harnessed Luke's attention, that Janey in her agitation had snapped the stem of the wine glass. A thin trail of blood ran down her hand and on to the back of Jack's white Babygro.

'I think', said Jonathan, eyeing Eve nervously, 'that once you're settled, of course, someone should show you around the island, so that you can get your bearings, and sort out what you might want photographed.'

'Right now, Jon?' questioned Eve, with so much familiarity that it made Sam wince.

'It will be good colour for your piece,' explained Laura, surprised to find Jonathan so discombobulated by the appearance of this woman. After all, he had been interviewed hundreds of times and completed a television series that had already involved live appearances on breakfast television shows. She found herself feeling almost maternal towards him. Perhaps he had searched Hannah's mobile phone and discovered the truth about Jacek, and from a misplaced sense of pride and desire that everyone else enjoy their holiday had decided to keep the discovery to himself.

It was left to Steve to instil some semblance of normality. As Patrick stood there awkwardly, shifting from one foot to another, he purposefully walked towards him and shook his hand, curious in part to finally meet Janey's most significant previous boyfriend. He then politely offered to show Eve to her room.

'Could you show me where the washing machine is, please?' asked Eve.

No one noticed Laura standing at the back of this tableau, apart from Patrick. She was never one to take centre stage. As he came towards her, Laura felt a nauseous lurch in her stomach. It was difficult to devise an appropriate response to a situation that she couldn't read. Patrick stood in front of her, scratching his unruly hair. He shrugged his shoulders apologetically and leant towards her as though he was about to kiss her cheek. Instead his lips stopped short of her ear.

'I'm not here to cause you any trouble,' he whispered.

15

Janey woke the following morning and sat up abruptly, hitting her head on the low oak beam stretched across the width of the bedroom. In the muddle between sleep and consciousness, she was gripped by a seam of anxiety that stretched from her upper intestine down through her stomach and into her colon, urging her out of bed and towards the bathroom. Something was wrong. As she pulled off the duvet, it stuck to her hand, damp and sticky with her own milk. Sometimes between the tears, the leaking breasts and the constant desire to pee, Janey felt she was no longer solid matter, but slowly melting, like the polar ice caps.

This morning her breasts had sprung a new surprise. They were as hard and cold as torpedoes, the nipples stretched so flat that she couldn't imagine how either the baby or the breast pump would get any purchase. She gently squeezed one and a perfect arc of milk spurted into the air on to Steve's chest, where it slowly snaked into the thick mass of hair. Jack must have slept through the entire night, Janey realised, trying to stem the tide of milk with the duvet. She looked at the notebook where she recorded the times of his feeds, nappy changes and mood fluctuations, and saw that for the first time he had slept for more than eight consecutive hours.

Janey slid out of bed and stumbled into the neighbouring room where the baby slept, cursing as she bumped her head on yet another beam. She checked the thermometer attached to the cot and noted that it was four degrees below the optimum temperature. One more degree and the alarm would go off. The black plastic bin liners lay in a pile on the floor. Light poured through the open window and the fresh sea air competed with the stench of stale alcohol. But Jack had slept through the night.

Janey could see someone asleep in the bed beside the travel cot. She vaguely recalled Steve waking her up with whisky breath and bloodshot eyes when he finally came up to bed in the early hours of the morning to tell her that he had put Patrick in with the baby. 'Keep your friends close, but your enemy closer,' Steve had slurred in Janey's ear as he slid in beside her. If he was feeling threatened by Patrick's unscheduled appearance then he wasn't showing it.

'We've been talking,' he had told her mysteriously, 'trying to work out what the fuck's going on. Patrick says that the girl persuaded him to come only a few days ago.'

'So that he could take the photo,' said Janey sleepily.

'He thinks there's more to it,' said Steve, leaning on one elbow.

'Unlikely,' Janey had mumbled, wondering whether Patrick had mentioned anything about his visit to her office.

'I'll say one thing for your friends,' said Steve, as he rolled towards her and kissed her on the lips, 'they're never boring.' It was the most positive comment he had ever made about them.

Janey tiptoed towards Jack and eased herself into the

narrow space between the cot and the bed. She put out a hand to touch the small mound and sighed with relief when she felt the short, swift undulations of sleeping baby. The ache in her stomach dissipated. Jack was in a deep sleep, hands lifted above his head, legs akimbo. Janey fought the urge to lift him out and sniff at the sweet, musty odour at the back of his neck. The desire for proximity was overwhelming.

She ignored the pins and needles in her legs and knelt there, her hand on his tummy, hoping that Patrick, who was snoring steadily just feet away, wouldn't wake up. Patrick was lying on his front, arms by his side and fists curled. He was wearing an old T-shirt with a Celtic symbol on the front that Janey had bought him before his first major journalistic foray into Pakistan. His long hair floated like a dark halo against one of the white cotton sheets that Steve had brought to Coll. It was more than ten years ago since they had last all been together like this, Janey calculated, recalling the weekend on the barge in Shropshire. It was after that holiday their relationship had imploded. Until his visit to her office, Janey hadn't seen Patrick for over nine years, and yet it seemed unexpectedly normal that he should be here with them now.

She took advantage to stare at him in a slow, methodical way that would be impossible if he were awake. His mouth hung open, slightly lopsided, and his features seemed to hang more loosely from his face, as though they had stretched and his skull had shrunk. His skin was tanned and leathery from so much exposure to the sun. She could see a small patch on the top of his head where his hair was beginning to thin. A bony knee peeked out from under the duvet. Knees always appeared so fragile when viewed in isolation, thought Janey tenderly. She found herself gently touching a scar beneath Patrick's kneecap. He flinched but he didn't wake up. She remembered the injury because it happened in a fall during a holiday in Morocco and she had had to drive at night through the Atlas Mountains to take him to hospital to be stitched up. She felt a lurch in her stomach but was relieved to discover it was nostalgia, not longing. Scar tissue: that was all that remained of their relationship.

She could have had children with Patrick. They had mulled over the possibility for five years. During the first part of their relationship, when Patrick was willing to talk about their future without complaining that Janey's demands stifled his freedom, it was he who made the prospect real. He envisaged a baby with Janey's angular face, perfectly pitched nose and generous mouth, and his dark eyes and gypsy skin. It would be serene, like Janey, not restless like him, he had said. Janey tried to explain that her serenity was a learnt condition, like politeness or the ability to cook, but he ignored the truth of this statement because it didn't suit him to believe it.

Throughout this period, however, he would lie in bed passively watching her swallow the Pill with her early-morning tea, sometimes only minutes after grand statements about how they would travel the world with their baby. The one and only time they had made love and she had forgotten to take her daily dose, it was he who insisted they go to the chemist to get the hormonal cocktail that would kill any prospect of an egg becoming a zygote inside her.

Now it was Patrick taking pills every morning, Janey noticed, as she picked up a half-consumed packet of antidepressants from the bedside table. Citalopram, the packet read. She turned them over in her hand and for the first time felt something close to compassion for him.

She considered the way his clothes were flung on the floor and the sleeves of his shirt stretched towards the open window. She used to think his constant momentum was a sign of ambition and superior self-knowledge. Now she realised that Patrick wasn't running towards anything, rather he was running away from himself.

Jack snuffled helplessly beneath her hand and her attention was once again diverted towards him. Sometimes she looked at the tiny space he occupied and felt panicked at how much was invested in that single square foot. No one could compete with him. Not even Steve. But fortunately he didn't seem to be someone who felt threatened by such devotion. He was as likely as she was to eulogise over any tiny new development. The way Jack started kicking both legs in the air or giggled wildly when Steve sang 'I can feel it coming in the air tonight' in a Welsh accent.

Tonight she would move Jack in with them, she decided. Laura was right, a new baby was like a love affair, to be indulged not controlled. Who knows, this might be her first and last child. Fertility at forty was not a given.

Janey heard a noise from the floor below like a lamp being knocked off a table and wondered who else was awake at six o'clock in the morning. She lifted her hand from the cot and was aware of the muffled sounds of two people talking, and then a stifled giggle as though someone was pressing their mouth very hard into the mattress to stop themselves from laughing. At least no one could blame Jack for waking them up today.

Then, after a short silence, the laughter turned to low moans and the regular beat of a headboard hitting a wall. Thud, thud, thud. Somewhere in the house someone was having sex. For a moment there was silence and then the noise started up again. This time the groans were louder, more constant, their rhythm echoing the pounding. The walls of the post-war house, built during a period when price was more important than privacy, were as thin as wafer biscuits. Oh God, Janey thought impatiently, let it be over quickly. If she added together all the years that she had known each of the people under this roof it would come to more than a hundred and still that wasn't long enough to overhear them having sex. Sexual intimacy was the final frontier among friends and, generally speaking, that was the way it should be.

She counted the times the bed pummelled the wall, imagining the dimples it would make in the plasterboard, until she got bored somewhere after fifty-seven. Whoever it was showed good stamina, Janey thought. She lifted her hand from the cot and found herself listening more intently, trying to recognise the male voice that occasionally said something that sounded like 'Is that good for you?'

'Not great for me,' Janey wanted to shout, less in condemnation than from the urge to let them know that everyone could hear. Given that at least one conversation over breakfast had already been dedicated to a discussion about whether the walls were made of anything stronger than cardboard, whoever was entwined below must be aware they might be overheard. Maybe they wanted to be heard, Janey considered, as they quietened down again.

Anything was possible. They were generation sex after all, born in the free love era of the late sixties, growing up through the swinging seventies, experimenting through the Aids-ravaged eighties, marrying in the Viagra-enhanced nineties and heading towards middle age in the no-holds-barred noughties.

In bare feet, Janey began making her way downstairs. She justified this decision on the basis that she needed to use the breast pump, but as she walked along the first-floor landing, she found herself slowing outside the various closed doors to see if she could uncover the copulating couple. But all was disappointingly quiet. So she continued towards the kitchen.

An empty bottle of whisky and a couple of glasses sat on the table beside a partially eaten summer pudding that Steve had made. She had tried to deter him from competing with Jonathan in the kitchen, but he was childishly obstinate. The summer pudding had marked a watershed. Steve had triumphantly tipped it out of the bowl and it had collapsed in a soggy soup of berries, the juice dripping over the side of the plate on to the floor, beside Eve.

'I think you went too long on berries,' Jonathan said, with a hint of triumphalism.

'He's trying to show you in a good light, Jon,' Eve had gamely suggested, as Steve sought his advice on how to redeem the pudding. Everyone had laughed in relief at his unconditional surrender.

*

It had been a strange meal, thought Janey, as she automatically began pulling out cutlery and laying the breakfast table, as she had done every morning since they arrived. People had come and gone so many times that Janey was certain there was never a moment when they had all sat down together. Sam's short walk with Eve took so long that when they finally reappeared with Luke, everyone else was already eating the lamb. Just as they sat down, Hannah had gone to make a phone call to see whether one of her cows had calved. Then the summer pudding collapsed. When Hannah returned, Steve had gone upstairs to give Jack his bottle of expressed milk. And when he came back down, Janey went to bed.

Years spent on a commune had equipped Janey better than most for living at close quarters with other people and she was tolerant of these idiosyncrasies. She methodically lined up the cereals on the wooden sideboard, noting on a piece of paper that they needed more cornflakes, and then turned her attention to emptying the washing machine. Janey was a creature of habit. This was something that Patrick had never understood. She had relished the boring domestic routines imposed by the community because they counterbalanced the uncertainties of the rest of her life.

Janey remembered breakfast well, because in all the years at Lyme Regis its time and essential ingredients never changed. At seven thirty every morning they had eaten dusty home-made muesli, with fresh unpasteurised yogurt, grown from a live culture by one of several Americans who lived there.

As she opened the washing machine, Janey was

surprised to see that all the clothes entangled inside were the same orange colour. Yet she couldn't remember anyone wearing anything orange since they had arrived. She unravelled a cotton shirt from the fray and recognised it as one of Steve's favourite white shirts. Then she pulled out a pair of formerly white trousers that belonged to Hannah and a couple of pairs of knickers and underpants. All were the same colour. Somewhere midway through this excavation she spotted a faded orange sarong and a couple of shift tops that she couldn't identify, and realised that in a bid to be helpful Eve had simply shoved in all the washing together with her own clothes and dyed everything. Even the jeans were tainted with an orange hue.

It reminded her of a week she had once spent with her mother and brother on a Rajneesh commune in Suffolk, when her mother was pursuing a love interest whom she had met during a six-week stint on an ashram in India. Fortunately she had decided to go back to Lyme Regis when it became apparent that the Rajneesh favoured separating children from their parents. But even after seven days, Janey had had her fill of sun-coloured clothing. Now, as she unfolded her beloved crêpe shirt and hung it over a chair, she was condemned to, if not a life, then at least three days in orange. All her clothes, apart from the pyjamas she was now wearing, had been in the dirty-laundry basket.

She laid the shirt flat and inspected the damage, inwardly cursing Eve and wondering what she would now wear for the photograph due to be taken later that day. But a small pile of white powder on the heavy mahogany sideboard distracted her. It was a tiny amount. No more than a broken line, concluded Janey, undoubtedly over-looked towards the end of Patrick and Steve's late-night binge. She felt angrier than she could remember. Her rage focused first on Patrick, for bringing the cocaine, and then on Steve, for consuming it with him. She railed at their collective irresponsibility and heard herself swearing not just at them, but at everyone in the house. She could have laid Jack on the table, his hand could have touched the powder and they would have been on an air ambulance to Glasgow, her legal career in tatters. She left the incriminating evidence on the sideboard, went to the bottom of the stairs and started calling Steve's name, her fury growing with each hopeless effort to rouse him.

Upstairs, Sam and Laura lay back in bed staring at the ceiling. Laura had a beatific look on her face, Sam thought, as he glanced at his wife. Her cheeks were flushed and her eyes had those curious flecks of grey that appeared when she was truly content. Sam swore that they changed colour according to her mood. He ran a finger across her eyebrow. She blinked slowly and closed her eyes as if the sun that rose through the window of the bedroom might blind her. A gust of wind lifted their clothes from a chair in the corner and on to the floor. Laura pulled up the covers until her head was the only visible part of her body.

A southerly had set in, Sam decided. He had spent much of the previous day reading a book about the weather that he had found on a shelf in the sitting room. It was literature best appreciated on holiday because when else would a person have time to consider the difference between a jet-stream cirrus and a cirrocumulus? Later he would examine the cloud formation and work out what weather they might expect on the ferry back to Oban, and when he got home he would amaze his children with his new-found knowledge about the secrets contained in clouds.

Neither of them said anything. Instead they basked in a shared but silent sense of achievement. It was official. At seven o'clock that morning, after exactly nine months and twenty days, they had resumed sexual relations. It was neither technically masterful nor stylistically perfect, but their timing was excellent. It was a better than average performance and there was room for improvement, which should certainly be exploited in the very near future. Possibly after a couple of hours' sleep, Sam thought optimistically. Being without children certainly liberated the libido.

Those who claimed that sex became less important in marriage missed the point. It was communication at its most visceral level, when all other forms were distilled into snatched conversations late at night and half glances across the dinner table. Sex was the most uncomplicated form of dialogue, Sam decided, as he rolled on to his side to stare at Laura, who was almost asleep again. Once the years of procreation were over, that was its point. As the drudgery of domestic detail sucked the oxygen out of passion, what else was left?

It was all so simple that Sam was bemused how only yesterday it had seemed so complicated. The timing was perfect, even though strictly speaking it wasn't their idea. It was a somnolent start, before they had really woken up, which heightened physical pleasure and reduced the possibility of anything cerebral interrupting the mood.

Although neither of them had said anything, both of them could hear the background noise of sex happening somewhere under the same roof and it provided both inspiration and good cover. But then sex always was half suggestion, especially where the male psyche was concerned. Sam thought of the women he came across on the tube, in his local café, on the school run. You didn't stop wondering because you were married. If anything, as passion became something that needed to be kindled, you wondered more. But it was essential to avoid situations where curiosity might get the better of you, Sam concluded, trying unsuccessfully to put yesterday behind him and focus on a possible new ending for the film script he had just sold. He sighed so deeply that even in her sleep Laura put an arm around him.

When Eve had asked Sam to show her around the island shortly after her arrival yesterday evening, Sam instinctively knew it was a bad idea. But he couldn't refuse. Relieved at the prospect of a couple of hours to acclimatise to Patrick's unexplained presence away from her watchful eye, everyone had greeted Eve's proposal with unbridled enthusiasm. Even Jonathan. Especially Jonathan: he couldn't even meet Eve's eye. It was impossible for Sam to say no. He had no baby to look after, no blog to feed, no meal to cook. He was the person delegated to deal with Eve, to charm her into writing a piece that would cast all of them in a favourable light.

'Take her, Sam,' Laura had urged. Even Steve recognised the need to discreetly shift Eve from the silent drama taking place centre stage. He undid his map of Coll on the table on the terrace and began plotting a route for them around the western peninsula of the island, using a pencil to draw a dotted line from the Hebridean centre at Ballyhaugh, across a stretch of machair, and down to the sand dunes and beach at Hogh.

'What's machair?' asked Eve, notebook to hand.

'It's a Gaelic word for the low-lying plains you find here,' explained Jonathan nervously. It was the first sentence he had addressed to her.

'It's one of the rarest habitats in Europe, there are birds and plants you won't find anywhere else,' continued Steve, sensing the need for someone to take control. 'It can be a bit rough on the legs, so you might want to put on a pair of trousers.' After a brief appraisal of Eve's legs, he went back into the house and came out with the set of car keys, which he pressed into Sam's hand.

'It's a long walk, an hour and a half at least, take your time,' he whispered in his ear.

They had set off by car and drove in silence until the asphalt road turned into rough track. Eve offered Sam a stale biscuit from the pocket of her coat as the car sputtered to an abrupt halt on the verge. He politely turned it down without making eye contact.

'God, it's so beautiful,' Eve had said as she climbed out of the car, still wearing shorts.

'The photos will be spectacular,' Sam conceded.

'Does anyone live there?' Eve asked, pointing to a building with her chin.

'Not all year round,' Sam replied, setting off across the machair without waiting for her. The marram grass scratched his legs, but the irritation was welcome because it helped to fuel his sense of annoyance. The sun hung low in the sky, still unwilling to let go of the day, its glare strong enough to make Sam push down his sunglasses on to his nose. A minute later, he pushed them back on top of his head because he didn't want to miss the spectacular infusion of orange and red that enveloped the sky as far as the eye could see.

'It's a landscape that swallows you up,' said Sam, staring at the sun until his eyes watered. Sometimes the red and orange wove curious bands together that produced a deep purple colour. And when the sun finally set, for a brief moment you could see a burst of green on the horizon. Sam guessed it had something to do with their latitude and the light refracting on to the great expanse of water.

'It's how the sky would look if the world was about to end,' said Eve dramatically.

Sam continued to stride over the machair. He spotted a wild orchid, yellow rattle and Irish lady's tresses and heard the sound of a corncrake, but pointed none of this out to Eve. His hands were sunk deep in the pockets of his shorts and his eyes stared firmly ahead, as though he wanted the walk to be over as quickly as possible. He strode onwards with silent purpose.

'I can't keep up with you, Sam,' Eve said breathlessly after ten minutes, as the machair gave way to a narrow path that bent down towards the beach at Hogh. It was a beautiful evening, thought Sam, perfectly still, as though the heat had sucked the energy from everything. The sky was now as red as a blood orange.

'We'll be late for dinner,' said Sam evenly, wiping a clammy hand across his forehead.

'Do you think it's a mistake?' Eve asked, as she struggled to match Sam's stride at the bottleneck at the beginning of the gentle incline down to sea level. The path was lined with high hawthorn hedges blown to a thirty-degree angle by the wind, which made Sam feel as though the world had turned on its axis. This angle and the way that the path curved and curled so that you couldn't see either back where it began or forwards made Sam feel almost seasick.

'Which bit?' asked Sam, increasing his speed around one of the curves. 'Your affair with Jonathan? Commissioning a piece about the man you're shagging? Coming here? Bringing Patrick? All of it or part of it?'

'Don't be so angry,' said Eve, half running to catch up with him as the ground gradually changed from dark peaty soil to sand, forcing Sam to slow down, 'it doesn't suit you. Jon was the one who wanted to bring Patrick. He's using me as cover.'

Sam ignored her and continued round the final bend before the path opened out towards the beach.

'I wanted to see him with Hannah,' Eve said as she drew up beside him.

'Why?' asked Sam, struggling to regain his advantage.

'To see how it works between them. And I wanted to write the piece,' said Eve simply. 'I'm trying to get a job in the States and I need to get a couple of profiles under my belt. Jon's becoming a significant public figure and he's got a group of interesting friends and I thought it would look good. I won't let my history with him cloud my professional judgement. I'm very discreet.'

'But don't you think the people here might notice a connection between you?' asked Sam in a tone laden with sarcasm. 'Particularly people who know Jonathan well, like his wife, his son and his closest friends?'

'Luke wasn't meant to be here,' Eve shrugged her shoulders, 'and Jon's relationship with Hannah was floundering long before I came along.'

'Married men always say that,' said Sam impatiently.

'I'm not the first one, you know,' said Eve.

'I had my suspicions but it's not the same as knowing,' said Sam brusquely.

'And Hannah's not entirely blameless,' said Eve. 'They have an arrangement.'

'What do you mean?' asked Sam, finally slowing down.

'There is a certain tolerance of each other's indiscretions,' said Eve precisely.

'I didn't know,' said Sam flatly.

'Well, it's probably not the sort of thing they want to let slip to a golden couple like you and Laura,' said Eve.

'There's no such thing as a golden couple,' said Sam finally. 'Relationships ebb and flow like the sea.' Sam fell silent. There was no way he was going to expose the inadequacies of his own marriage to someone like Eve and he was taken aback at her revelation.

He finally drew to a halt as the path opened out on to the beach. The contrast between the claustrophobia of the narrow lane and the open expanse of ocean was so dramatic that they both stood for a moment in awed silence. The sea exploded in front of them in a constant roar. Steep-walled waves crashed towards them as though trying to stretch towards the huge sand dunes on the shore.

Sam inspected his feet and noticed that he was wearing the same pair of leather boots that he had used to drive to the ferry earlier that afternoon. It seemed incredible that that had happened less than a couple of hours earlier. Only the dried vomit that he spotted on the side near the heel provided any temporal connection to that period. He decided to remove the boots, leaving them in the sand, and return along the same route instead of walking the loop suggested by Steve.

'I can almost understand why you came,' said Sam, still staring at the sea, 'in that utterly selfish, irresponsible, single, twenty-something way.'

'I'm twenty-eight,' said Eve, 'the trip to the theatre was a birthday present. I didn't realise you were joining the celebration until you both sat down beside me.'

'But you knew I was with Jonathan?' Sam asked, as he sat down abruptly in the sand.

'Yes,' said Eve, as she drew up beside him, 'don't you remember?'

'I do,' Sam nodded, as he undid his shoelaces, knowing that she was referring to the glance that had passed between them at the theatre. He saw her feet beside him and noticed a ring on one of the toes.

'You saw us,' said Eve, sitting down beside him. 'I've never done anything like that before, but at the time it felt good, as though I was touching you too.'

Sam knew at that moment he should have got up from the sand and continued with the walk but he was struggling against the undercurrents in their conversation.

'I even proposed to Jonathan that we should invite you home,' said Eve, smiling, 'but he was totally against the idea.'

Despite himself, Sam burst out laughing as he tried to

imagine himself in bed with Jonathan, Eve between them, sipping tea, the following morning. It was a ludicrous prospect and he could imagine Jonathan's outraged reaction to her proposition.

'According to the rules of heterosexuality, threesomes only work for men if there's another woman involved,' Sam said, hopelessly aware of the small hot body beside him. He half wondered whether he could suggest a quick swim and checked to see whether she was wearing a swimsuit under her vest top but she wasn't.

Eve sat down beside him and took off her flip-flops. She balanced her left leg across her right knee and started inspecting the sole of her foot. She brought the foot close to her eye and Sam could feel her thigh graze his own. He closed his eyes and took a deep breath.

'I've got a thorn,' she said, observing the foot closely and then squeezing the toe with the ring between her two index fingers.

In a situation where the ground rules were obvious, Sam, by nature both a kind man and someone whom people turned to for medical advice, would have taken Eve's toe between his hands and efficiently teased out the thorn. Right now, however, he felt as though he had fallen off the radar. He was flying blind in the outer boundaries of the Inner Hebrides, the hot red sky an accomplice rather than a friend. Yet to ignore the thorn was to concede that he didn't trust himself to touch her toe. He needed to get back to Laura.

'Let me see,' he said, determinedly avoiding Eve's gaze. He grasped her ankle with one hand and shifted in the sand until he was facing the sole of her foot and could locate the thorn. He rested her calf on his bare knee and squinted at the toe, lifting his sunglasses on to his head. Her foot was so narrow that he could fit his hand around all five toes. Maybe he could suck out the thorn, Sam thought pleasurably, squeezing her toes a little too tightly, until they curled up in resistance. They were now inches from his mouth. Sam could see the ring was obscuring the thorn's point of entry and he twisted the tight gold loop to see if he could shift it. But it was stuck fast.

'Is this painful?' Sam asked, as he tugged at the ring.

'There's a thin line between pain and pleasure,' said Eve, staring at him straight in the eye, 'you must know that.' Sam took a deep breath. His ribcage ached.

He noticed a small tattoo, three interlocked spirals, just above her ankle. Relieved to have an excuse to avoid her gaze, Sam stared at the tattoo, hoping for redemption. Instead he saw his index finger, as if it was detached from the rest of his body, move towards it and curl a slow, small loop around each spiral. There was no resistance. He could see the rise and fall of Eve's ribcage match his own. His hand slowly ran up the back of her calf and he removed her leg from his knee on to the sand.

'You go through a lot of gear changes in one day, Sam Diamond,' Eve said, leaning towards him. Sam's hand was now firmly around her ankle. He noted that he could clasp it in his fist. And then she was kneeling between his legs, pushing him back on to the sand, leaning over him so that he could see her small dark nipples and tiny breasts. He put a hand inside the leg of her shorts at the back and cupped the round flesh of her buttock, pulling her on top of him.

'You're a great guy,' Eve whispered in his ear.

I'm a total bastard, thought Sam, as he felt her fingers trail down his body towards his shorts. Sam tried to clarify the relationship between himself and Eve. He was almost certainly about to have sex with his best friend's mistress, who was here to write a piece about the bucolic life of Jonathan Sleet and his tight-knit, loyal group of friends, including his own wife, Laura. Things had gone so far that he might as well have sex with her anyway, thought Sam, closing his eyes in pleasure as he felt her hand move inside his shorts. But wasn't there a big difference between a few exploratory caresses and the real thing? It occurred to Sam that if he had sex with Eve now, after almost ten months of pent-up frustration, he might never want to stop. He wondered at the frailty of the line between total irresponsibility and utter reliability.

Sam took a couple of quick, deep breaths, almost hyperventilating, and pushed Eve away, groaning loudly, as though he was wounded. He pulled himself up and, without bothering to brush away the sand from his hair or his arms, walked fully clothed towards the sea, holding his arms out, as if in supplication, before stepping into the ocean. He continued to walk, without turning back, through the white froth where the waves broke on the shore, until a large breaker slammed over his head and he dived into its dark centre.

He swam underwater, diving down, his eyes tightly shut, heading out into the ocean until he felt his lungs were bursting. He was driven on by the certainty that the burning pain in his chest from holding his breath would eventually overwhelm the desire in his groin. Sam was struck by how free he felt and then remembered the uncomfortable relationship between detachment and danger. He decided to swim to the surface, but after a few strokes wondered if he was disorientated and was in fact going down ever deeper towards the ocean bed. He opened his eyes, wincing at the salt, and looked up, relieved to see shards of red light cut through the dark sea. As he broke the surface he gulped in air and trod water for a few minutes.

He swam through the waves again until Eve was a tiny figure on the horizon. As the tide swelled and the waves grew bigger there were moments when he could no longer see her. The water was freezing. Sam lay on his back, his arms outstretched, feeling the power of the waves below. He was only fifteen metres from the shore but he could feel the murderous quality of the sea numb his body. It was almost safe to come out, he decided. He began to swim across the waves, feeling the weight of his clothes in the water. He put down a hand and realised that his shorts were still half undone.

If he had planned to swim during this walk then Sam might have taken more notice of the housekeeper's warning about swimming at Hogh. The beach was not particularly narrow, but instead of tapering towards the ocean it embraced its reckless abandon in a generous wide arc that meant the sea was sucked from the bay like a centrifuge. Even from the beach, a careful observer could see fierce cross-currents competing for supremacy.

Sam started to swim into shore but after a few minutes had made only minimum progress. He searched for Eve and was startled to discover that he had been carried a couple of hundred metres away from her. He turned on to his back and resolutely cut through the ocean, increasing his speed to beat the current trying to push him back towards its depths. Then he stopped again and found that instead of swimming towards the shore, he was being carried along horizontally. He realised that if he continued the same trajectory he would leave the cove and slowly be carried westerly out to sea. He could see Eve running up and down the shore, her hands cupped to her face, shouting for him. He might be only fifteen metres from the beach, but he was as vulnerable as if he had been dropped in the middle of the Atlantic.

'I deserve to be punished, but I don't deserve to die,' he heard himself yell at the sky.

As the waves ebbed and flowed Sam saw another figure on the beach running towards him, carrying a length of rope. Sam put up his arm and signalled for help, trying not to expend too much energy. The man quickly peeled off layers of clothes until he was wearing only a pair of underpants, then began wading into the sea towards him. When he could walk no further without risking being tossed into the same current, he threw the frayed blue rope. The first time it barely made progress. The man, broad-shouldered and strong, pulled it back and held it aloft. He propelled it towards Sam again and it landed a few metres in front of him. Again Sam tried to swim to it, but the force of the current made him as helpless as a child. Sam saw the man's anxious face and recognised Luke. At the same time, Luke saw that it was Sam, and began pulling the rope back to him with renewed urgency. He used first one arm and then the other, building up an effective rhythm until the end was in his grasp again. This time Luke tied a couple of knots at the end, held it in the air and pumped his arms up and down before finally flinging it out into the ocean towards Sam with a guttural yell, like a shot-putter.

Sam lay on his back and felt his foot catch the edge of the rope. He managed to manoeuvre the knot between his knees and propelled himself towards it. He didn't want to risk diving underneath to try and move towards it or risk losing grip by trying to reach for it with his hand. Instead he grasped the knot with his knees and relied on Luke to slowly pull him into shore.

When he reached the shallow water at the edge of the beach, Sam finally let go of the rope. Luke put his arm round him and they walked towards the sand where Sam leant over and for the second time that day was violently sick in front of his godson.

'There's nothing I can ever do for you that will match this,' spluttered Sam, 'you saved my life, Luke.'

'I was searching for Mum,' said Luke, shrugging his shoulders. 'I thought she might be making a call. Then I saw you and Eve on the beach and thought I'd join you.' His voice betrayed nothing. Was he being deliberately sparse in his description of events leading up to the rescue to avoid mutual embarrassment or was it part of his normal manner? Luke gave him his own shorts to put on and Sam turned to face the sea again while he removed his wet clothes. The shorts that sat low on Luke's hips only just did up around Sam's stomach.

They all sat in silence on the way home in the car, between them a tacit agreement not to discuss anything. Perhaps they needed to process the drama of what had occurred before they could articulate it to anyone else. If anyone noticed when they got home that Sam was wearing

Luke's shorts and had removed his T-shirt, then no one said anything. They got back to find Steve unveiling his summer pudding. As it collapsed slowly on the plate, the sides of the bread unable to bear the pressure of the berries inside, Sam laughed louder than everyone else. He couldn't remember feeling so alive. He saw Eve glance over at him but she quickly looked away when he caught her eye.

Did he regret turning her down? This morning, any residual longing was far outweighed by relief that he could make love to his wife with a relatively clear conscience, even if his ardour was stoked by images of Eve's body that flashed before him when he closed his eyes. Even imagining a small part of how he might have felt if things had reached their logical conclusion was enough to make Sam swear to a life of fidelity. This is what happened if you kept secrets from your wife, thought Sam. If he had told her about Eve and Jonathan, this would never have happened.

'Laura, there's something I need to talk to you about,' he murmured in Laura's ear, pulling a strand of hair away from her lobe. He would have liked to have explained everything to her like this, in a half whisper, and avoid the recrimination in her eyes.

Laura's eyes remained tight shut. Far from being asleep, her whole body was alert to the serious tone in Sam's voice, but she wanted to win time to organise her thoughts. After years of waiting, why had he chosen this moment, above all others? Why would he want to rattle their foundations at the point where some hard-earned equilibrium had been regained? It was clear to Laura that Patrick's arrival must be the catalyst. He must have sensed something between

them. Laura wanted to savour the sensation of spent
energy and let the early-morning breeze lick her skin until
it was salty again. She wanted to live in the moment instead
of revisiting the past. For all his laid-back nature, Sam was
not one to compromise.

She also wanted to warn him that Eve had a crush on him.
Sam was oblivious to how women behaved around him. But
it was obvious to her, and even to Hannah in her distracted
state, that Eve was interested in Sam. There was the gleeful
moment when Eve discovered that they were both reading
Mother's Milk by Edward St Aubyn. The way she kept telling
him that she had watched every episode of *Do Not
Resuscitate*. The mutual appreciation of Elbow, followed
shortly by her offer to get Sam backstage tickets to their next
concert. At this point Hannah had winked at Laura, and
Laura had had to suppress a smile. Sam suddenly had the
scent of success, but he was completely immune to its effect
on other people. Mostly it established a light-hearted talking
point that created unity among them, the humour that
knitted together memories that would raise a smile long
after the holiday was over. Already Hannah did a fantastic
impersonation of Eve fawning over Sam.

Seeing her husband pursued by someone like Eve helped
Laura to unravel any outstanding erotic knots in her head.
Jealousy, or at least the awareness that your husband was
still attractive to other women, was an important
aphrodisiac, more effective than all the sea urchins that
Jonathan insisted they consume very publicly each evening.

'Sounds ominous,' said Laura, opening one eye to gauge
his expression. He gave nothing away.

'It is,' sighed Sam.

'Can't it wait?' asked Laura.

'It's too absorbing,' said Sam, 'it's about Jonathan.'

It was always about Jonathan, thought Laura. In some respects, given that everyone seemed to assume that something had happened between them, it would be easier if it was. But the truth was both more and less complicated.

'Can I put on my clothes first?' asked Laura.

'So you can make a quick escape?' replied Sam.

'I feel a bit exposed,' she said.

Then from downstairs they heard the noise of Janey shouting at Steve to come down. The yells slowly increased in pitch and volume until Laura saw the family of oystercatchers that normally waited for breakfast cast-offs each morning on the terrace turn tail and fly towards the bay. Laura and Sam stared at each other. Laura wanted to tell Sam to ignore Janey. That now was the right moment to talk about what had happened. But although Janey's ire was manifestly directed at Steve, it was evident that some of its force was intended for other members of the household. Steve couldn't be roused. Not surprisingly, thought Sam, given the state he was in when Sam had gone up to bed at two o'clock in the morning.

'Maybe someone drank the frozen breast milk?' said Sam, as he got out of bed and pulled on yesterday's jeans and T-shirt. 'You should come too. You're good in a crisis.'

They stumbled down into the kitchen and found everyone apart from Steve standing in a semicircle around the kitchen table. They were all wearing pyjamas, their hands clasped together, eyeing Janey so nervously that Laura stifled the urge to laugh.

'Who is responsible for this?' Janey shouted, and for the

first time ever Laura could see the hint of steel that made Janey such an effective lawyer. At first Laura thought she was talking about the rows of orange clothes neatly lined up on an old wooden clothes horse.

'I must have put in my sarong.' Eve spoke up eventually. 'I'm really, really sorry.'

'I'm not talking about the clothes, I'm talking about this,' said Janey. They all craned their necks towards the top of the sideboard to see where Janey's middle finger had come to rest.

All Laura could see was a tiny pile of white dust. In a move that won admiration from all those gathered in the kitchen Jonathan walked over, put his finger in the small mound and stuck it in his mouth.

'Sweet,' he said authoritatively, 'milky even.'

Janey noticed that a thin, barely visible trail led from this central mound of powder to the corner of the sideboard. She knelt down in front of the cupboard and opened its door. A tin of organic powdered milk for babies under the age of six months stared her in the face.

She pulled it out and saw that the seal had been broken. Then she opened the door of the dishwasher and found one of her baby bottles lying there.

'Who gave Jack a bottle of powdered milk?' asked Janey firmly. Everyone stared at their feet.

Steve emerged through the kitchen door, his hair on end, looking weak and pale. There was an even necklace of bruises across his forehead in various shades of blue and purple, not unlike the colours of the sunset in Coll, where he had bumped his head on the beam every time he'd leapt out of bed when Jack cried. Apart from last night. Because last night, under the careful tutelage of Hannah, he had decided to give Jack his first bottle of formula milk as an experiment to see if he would sleep through the night.

'God, Janey, what's going on?' asked Steve. 'A police line-up?'

'I thought you'd been snorting coke with Patrick,' Janey explained, as she slumped down on to the nearest chair.

'Antidepressants and cocaine aren't great bedfellows,' Patrick explained apologetically.

'And I've never done a line of coke in my life,' said Steve, running his hand through his hair in confusion. 'But I did give Jack the bottle of formula to see if he'd sleep through. We all deserve a good night's sleep. Hannah was only involved at the end when I couldn't work out whether to put the milk or the water in first.' To his relief Janey threw her head back and started laughing uncontrollably.

'Welcome back to the land of the living,' said Laura in relief. 'Let's have breakfast.'

Hannah sat down opposite Laura and began fanning herself with the financial section of *The Times*. Jonathan stood behind her. He tentatively put out a hand to rest on Hannah's shoulder, but in a gesture perceptible only to Laura, instead of welcoming its warmth Hannah pulled forward just as Jonathan was about to touch her so that his hand fell heavily on to the back of the wooden chair. Jonathan winced and rubbed his knuckles. Laura studied Hannah's face and knew that she had meant this to happen. The subtlety of such a gesture was in direct disproportion to its significance. It was a covert display of antipathy.

16

Eve's presence had a stupefying effect on them all. Over the next couple of days, the restless energy of the outset of the holiday was replaced by lassitude, as though everyone was waiting for someone else to take control. Meals became blurry affairs with breakfast taking so long it threatened to spill over into lunch. Instead of carefully grilled bacon, light fluffy scrambled eggs and field mushrooms triumphantly served by Steve on giant platters, leftovers from dinner the previous night sat in small pudding bowls alongside packets of cereal.

A plan hatched to pay an early-morning visit to the Celtic burial cairn and have an early swim at Cliad, when the light was at its best, was abandoned. No one got up to take the empty plastic water bottles to be refilled in Arinagour or began the search for lost sunglasses, swimming costumes, wetsuits and dry towels that marked the start of the day. Even the regular early-morning tussle between Jonathan and Steve to define the day's activities and discuss menu plans never materialised. For the first time, breakfast was dominated by the sound of the tumble dryer, furiously tossing dry another load of orange clothes.

Steve, unshaven and still wearing yesterday's clothes, sat at the table reading a two-day-old newspaper, having forsaken his early-morning run. Beside him, Patrick sat in companionable silence, meticulously cleaning camera lenses and endlessly checking his light meter. After her cathartic outburst a couple of days earlier, Janey was calmly breastfeeding Jack, his ten o'clock nap forgotten, and eating spoonfuls of summer pudding. Sam perused the cloud book. Only Luke remained constant in his rhythms, hooking up his laptop to the telephone wire for half an hour before making himself a thick black coffee.

In part the weather was to blame, thought Laura, as she walked towards the window that looked out on to the terrace. The thin trails of cloud that tried to impress themselves on the vivid blue sky struggled to dilute the heat of the sun. Whenever a breeze wheezed through the open doors of the terrace, everyone turned their face gratefully towards it, like sunflowers towards the sun.

'So what can we expect from the weather today, Sam?' Laura asked, anxious to break the silence.

'When Sirius is rising with the sun marks the dog days well begun,' Sam said, with mock seriousness.

'So we're going to go mad,' murmured Steve, without looking up from the crossword.

'It's a reference to the Dog Star rising in the summer,' said Sam, 'and the man at the village shop said the outlook was "blirty", which shows how much I've still got to learn.'

'What does that mean?' asked Eve from the stove at the other end of the kitchen. She was busy making her breakfast, stirring a bowl of wholemeal porridge mixed with miso soup and brown rice syrup that she ate at the same time every morning, and drinking a second mug of kuckicha twig tea.

'Changeable, uncertain weather,' said Sam, pointing at a bank of grey cloud so far in the distance that Laura thought it was nothing more than the frontier between sea and sky.

Laura glanced over at him. She felt compelled to ask Eve a question to compensate for Sam's curt response.

'So what constitutes a macrobiotic diet?' she asked, trying to ignore the collective groans from the other end of the table.

'It's all about balancing yin and yang,' Eve began. 'Yin represents the female force and yang the masculine. So yin people are more calm, relaxed and creative and yang people more energetic, aggressive and active. Like the difference between Sam and Jon, I guess.'

This comment caught Laura's attention and she turned her head from the window towards Eve. It seemed a little premature and overfamiliar to be drawing such conclusions about people she had just met, even if she was right. And why did she refer to Jonathan as Jon? Her expression was difficult to read. Laura couldn't really get beyond the curve of her generous mouth. There was something familiar about her.

'So there are yin foods, like tea, milk, herbs and spices, and yang foods like red meat, eggs, hard cheese and salt. Then there are foods where the energy is perfectly balanced, for example wholegrain cereals, fresh fruit, leafy vegetables and pulses and that's what I try to eat. It's mostly vegetarian, low-fat, high-fibre, with an emphasis on soya products.'

'It sounds a little bland,' Laura observed.

'You can add flavour with brown rice vinegar, umeboshi plum paste, or unrefined sea salt,' explained Eve, as she stirred her porridge.

'I'm surprised you're allowed salt,' replied Laura

amicably, trying to remember what she used to do with the extra hours in the day before she had children. Maybe Eve was trying to get pregnant, or the restrictive diet was a cover for anorexia, or women of her generation were simply more health-conscious.

'Unrefined sea salt has lots of minerals and trace elements found in the sea, whereas normal salt is about 99.5 per cent sodium chloride,' explained Eve. 'And salt is essential to digest food, enable muscles to work and ensure the central nervous system functions properly. That's why it was so important historically.' She turned to Jonathan. 'You must know all about this from that programme you made on Maldon sea salt? Didn't you say that the first records show salt was produced there in 1086 and that it cost the same as gold?'

'You've been doing your homework,' said Laura, sounding impressed. 'I didn't think the episode on Maldon was ready yet.'

'It hasn't even been edited yet,' said Luke, 'has it, Dad?'

'The publicist must have given Eve a rough cut,' he said, eyeing Eve expectantly.

'Precisely,' said Eve without flinching, as she turned back towards the stove to pour the porridge into a bowl before leaving the kitchen with a bunch of notes under her arm to eat alone on the terrace.

Jonathan remained silent. With Laura's encouragement, he was trying to piece together a final list of ingredients for the meal he planned to cook later in the day. His notebook was a mess of pencil scrawls and crossings out, like something Nell might produce, thought Laura, as she watched over his shoulder to see what he was writing. *Mussels, water mint, wild garlic, mackerel, nettles* . . .

He was insistent that, as far as possible, everything should be sourced locally, yet seemed unable to remember from one minute to the next exactly what he was meant to buy and what he could forage. Yesterday, Hannah had casually suggested he draw up a cooking schedule, but showed no inclination to help him.

'Where's the menu that you wrote out a couple of days ago?' whispered Laura, out of Eve's earshot.

'I can't find it,' said Jonathan, nervously pulling out hairs from his eyebrow with such force that it made Laura wince. Laura took the black leather notebook from his hand and immediately found his original menu plan squashed between a couple of pages at the back. She unfolded the piece of paper and spread it in front of him, pointing at the list. The contrast between the chaotic handwriting of his current list and the neat methodical scrawl of a few days earlier was more than an aesthetic issue, she thought. It was a reflection of his state of mind.

'Nettle haggis,' she said, tapping the first recipe on the list a couple of times to focus his attention. It was a tactic she used when conducting tests for patients with memory lapses. If it wasn't for the fact that the failure of his organisational skills coincided with Eve's arrival then she might be worried about the function of his frontal cortex. Instead she put it down to severe stress brought on by the pressure of cooking a meal that he wasn't competent to prepare and the fact that Hannah had silently withdrawn support.

'I've got the oatmeal and onions,' muttered Jonathan, flicking through *Food for Free*, 'but we need to pick the nettles. And they must be young. Old nettles taste revolting.'

'Bacon?' asked Laura, glancing down the list of ingredients.

'Yes. But I haven't got a tea towel to cook it in,' Jonathan said, in a panic-stricken tone, holding on to Laura's lower arm until it ached. 'Fuck, fuck. I've failed at the last fence.'

'Great alliteration,' said Sam, 'I'll note that one down.'

Laura resisted the urge to tell him that she wasn't sure he had crossed even the first fence, but he was in a mood that required gentle coaxing rather than forthright opinion.

'You can't eat a tea towel,' said Laura equably.

'She's right,' agreed Steve magnanimously, from the other side of the table.

'I need it to wrap up the ingredients and boil them,' explained Jonathan.

'Stop panicking,' said Laura firmly.

'How about one of Jack's muslin squares?' asked Janey. 'As long as you don't mind that it's orange.'

'Great,' said Jonathan, shaking his head with relief. Laura thought his eyes were welling with tears, but then realised that they were watering because he was once again plucking hairs from his eyebrows. Trichotillomania, a close cousin to OCD, Laura said to herself, gratified to remember the medical term for Jonathan's behaviour. Eve came in from the terrace and put her empty bowl and half-finished tea on the kitchen table.

'Does a macrobiotic diet preclude tidying up?' teased Luke, as he stood up with his laptop under his arm and made his way barefooted towards the table to pick up her dirty crockery and put it in the dishwasher. He smiled indulgently at Eve. Beautiful people were treated differently, thought

Laura, as she watched Luke's eyes devour her. She was misleading Nell when she said that looks didn't count. People's response to Eve couldn't simply be explained by her professional credentials, because even the elderly cleaning lady and the man they encountered in the village shop yesterday were mesmerised by her presence.

'That's a little hypocritical, Luke,' said Jonathan, his paternal reflex functioning for the first time in days. Luke raised an eyebrow and then walked over towards Jonathan, put a hand on his shoulder and asked whether there was anything useful that he could do to help.

'You could go and collect wild garlic,' Jonathan said.

'What does it look like, Dad?' asked Luke. Jonathan stared at him blankly for a moment.

'Dad,' said Luke gently, 'I need to know what I'm searching for.'

'You'll smell it before you can see it,' Jonathan said, covering Luke's hand with his own. 'Try the hedge at the end of the lane. It's got broad, bright leaves and there might be white flowers. Could you dig a few bulbs too? I need lots to make pesto to put on the fish.'

Eve was taking notes.

'The Latin name is *Allium ursinum* or bear's garlic,' Jonathan explained, carefully avoiding eye contact, 'because apparently bears waking up from hibernation want garlic to cleanse their metabolism.'

'So what exactly are you planning to cook?' Eve asked. Jonathan read through his notes. There was a long silence. Everyone stared, willing him to say something, and when he didn't, they waited for Hannah to intercede. Finally Laura stretched over the table for his notebook.

'Moules marinières, nettle haggis, mackerel pâté, monkfish with pesto sauce, and sorrel salad,' she said in the same slow, even tone that she used when trying to reassure patients.

'I'll only be able to eat the monkfish and the sorrel salad,' said Eve apologetically, 'but it will all photograph really well.'

'It will be great, Jonathan,' said Patrick reassuringly. 'Why don't we all go out together right away and I can get some shots of everyone foraging for ingredients?'

Grateful to Patrick for his intervention, Laura proposed that she and Sam should fish for mackerel and pick mussels. She caught Patrick's eye. They had barely addressed a word to each other since his arrival. Their silence went unnoticed. Everyone was too wrapped up in their own dramas, thought Laura. He was kind to her; neither of them sought to fuel their discomfort with words. She turned to the piece of paper in front of her and drew up a precise list of other ingredients for everyone else to find. Even Steve, who usually quibbled over any idea that wasn't his own, was relieved by the prospect of such focused activity. He laid Jack on the kitchen table and deftly poured him into his all-weather suit.

Laura collected plastic buckets, tackle and bait from the shed in the garden. Sam, who had learnt to fish for mackerel as a child off the Suffolk coast, pulled out a couple of blunt knives and a wooden priest to kill the fish because he couldn't bear to watch their slow suffocation in the bottom of the boat. As they walked out the door, first Eve and then Janey asked whether they could join them.

*

It would soon all be over. As she stood up in the back of the motor boat to pull the start cord, Laura counted how many hours stood between her and their departure the following afternoon. Twenty-six. She felt a surge of happiness at the prospect of seeing Nell and Ben and realised that for the first time in years she was looking forward to coming home from a holiday. As she clasped her fingers around the plastic handle of the start cord, Laura resolved to call her NHS manager as soon as she could on Monday morning to negotiate a three-day week, before she changed her mind.

Even though the main component of the holiday, the picture of them all together, loomed like the distant cloud on the horizon, Laura realised she was already beginning to consider the week in the past tense. She tried to decide where to hang a framed copy of the photo that would appear in the magazine and started to envisage other holidays together, perhaps even on Coll. On balance, it had been a success. She could euphemistically inform her friends that she and Sam were back on track. There had been no blowout with Steve. Her relationship with Jonathan was closer than it had been for years and Janey had found equilibrium with Patrick, even if Laura hadn't.

Laura took a deep breath and pulled the start cord as hard as she could, knowing that her first attempt would fail. She pushed her hand into her armpit until the ache in the socket dulled. As she waited for a moment, she allowed herself to imagine their reunion with Nell and Ben at King's Cross, visualising something akin to the closing scene in the film version of *The Railway Children*.

They had spoken to Nell and Ben every other evening

since they arrived. Last night, for the first time, Ben had asked exactly when they would be coming home, and made a few suggestions about the type of present that might compensate for their absence. Nell began telling her a long and involved story about how Laura's mother had washed the guinea pig and Laura had listened gratefully, savouring every detail.

She pulled the cord a couple more times to flood the engine with petrol and then had another rest to garner energy for the final haul that would start the motor. At the prow, Sam and Eve sat companionably on the wooden bench that stretched from one side to the other, baiting fish hooks with bacon. To Laura's relief, Sam was being more friendly, showing Eve the exact way to twist the meat on the hook so that it wouldn't fall off the first time a fish tried to bite, and answering questions about his memories of Jonathan from his childhood.

'Can I mention the story about the au pair?' asked Eve. Sam seemed a little taken aback. Eve reassured him, 'Only in the most general terms, to add a little colour.'

'Not sure even I know that one,' said Laura.

'You'd better check with Jonathan,' said Sam warily.

Laura might have taken more notice of this brief exchange if the engine hadn't spluttered into life. She put it in gear, grabbed the rudder and the boat bobbed gently over the break until they were heading out to an area east of the bay, where Laura had found mackerel before. She loved the rhythm of crossing the waves, their unpredictable undulations and the way the spray showered her face. The boat had become her domain. She was the one who had volunteered at the beginning of the week to walk down to the beach with the owner of the house to learn how it worked and everyone now deferred to her expertise.

Janey sat beside her, very erect, one hand on the side, as though she thought this might provide equilibrium if they hit a large wave. The breeze blew her hair back off her face, accentuating her aquiline nose. She insisted on wearing a life jacket. It was, she realised, her longest separation from Jack since his birth two and a half months earlier.

'Are you all right?' Laura shouted to Janey.

'Never better,' Janey called back to her. 'It's so exhilarating.'

They reached an area beyond the sandbank and Laura abruptly turned off the engine. She allowed the boat to drift in the water and instructed everyone to let go of their lines and wait for the fish to bite. Out at sea there was a pleasant breeze. Laura closed her eyes and savoured the moment, anticipating that this would probably be her last fishing trip. Sam pulled four bottles of Corona beer from a bucket and handed them round, giving instructions not to say anything to Jonathan, who favoured everyone drinking the locally brewed Fyne Highlander.

They began to talk. Eve asked Sam about his next project. He told her he was adapting a book about surfers written by an Australian novelist. Laura suggested, only half joking, that they might need to go to California for a couple of months for research purposes, and Sam smiled and said it was an excellent idea. Janey proposed that she, Steve and Jack could visit them and Laura happily agreed. Occasionally Eve interrupted with a question.

'Can you explain exactly when you and Jonathan met, Sam?' she asked, handing over her fishing line to him as she flicked back through her notes. Sam told her that they had met at school.

'Was Jonathan always interested in food?' she quizzed, chewing her pen and tilting her head to one side as she spoke.

'From the beginning,' said Sam emphatically. He didn't want to explain that Jonathan's parents were so busy pleasing themselves that sometimes, especially at weekends when the housekeeper was away, they forgot to feed Jonathan and his younger sister. He proved adept at concocting exotic snacks from the contents of the fridge but had never really progressed beyond an excellent club sandwich involving gherkins and salt beef.

Instead Sam described how he had first encountered olives in the fridge at Jonathan's parents' house and swallowed them whole, stones and all.

'One got trapped in my throat and Jonathan had to do the Heimlich manoeuvre to dislodge it,' said Sam.

'That is a great anecdote,' said Eve gratefully, staring at Sam until he could bear it no longer and turned away in embarrassment.

'He was always interested in wild food,' Sam continued, exaggerating Jonathan's strengths. 'They had a gardener in Suffolk who knew a lot about herbs and plants and he passed on his knowledge to Jonathan.'

There was another lull in the conversation. Janey's string began to jerk and she pulled out a large mackerel from the water.

'Where shall I put it?' she shrieked, as the mackerel squirmed at the end of the line. Laura took it from her hand, removed the hook from its mouth and threw it on to the floor of the boat beside her. Sam bent down and hit the mackerel on the head with the mallet. It lifted its tail one last time and then lay quietly on the deck.

'I'm going to stuff it and hang it on the wall of my office,' laughed Janey, bending over to admire its black and silver geometric pattern. 'I might be forgiven for taking three months' maternity leave if I can prove that I was doing something macho, like killing animals, rather than breastfeeding Jack.'

They began talking about the house on Coll, aware that it was secured free of charge in return for a mention in Eve's interview, stopping only when someone caught another fish. Janey described the decor as shabby chic and Laura extolled the virtues of the terrace overlooking the sea and described how she had seen a minke whale while she was in the bath.

'Its only drawback, and this, Eve, is completely off the record, is the soundproofing,' joked Janey. 'It's one thing to be woken up by a crying baby, but it's another thing completely to be serenaded by the sound of your friends having sex at six in the morning. It makes everyone else feel inadequate.'

'I assumed it was you,' teased Laura.

'God no,' said Janey, making a swift judgement call, 'it was Jonathan and Hannah.'

There was a long silence and Janey felt three sets of eyes on her. She grasped that she had said the wrong thing but couldn't understand their reaction. Surely it was a good thing that Eve knew that the subject of her story still had a close relationship with his wife?

'How do you know?' asked Laura finally.

'Because Jonathan told me,' said Janey.

*

Back on the beach Sam saw Jonathan picking mussels from the shallow rock pools scattered on the edge of the bay. Like Sam, he was wearing an orange T-shirt that made him stand out against the muted tones of the beach. They must look as though they belonged to an esoteric religious sect, Sam thought, as he deposited the bucket of mackerel by the path that led to the house and walked back towards Jonathan, waving his arms and calling his name. He didn't intend to take him by surprise. But as he walked and yelled, Sam realised that the offshore breeze had gained sufficient strength that the wind swallowed his words and deposited them somewhere deep in the ocean.

Jonathan was hunched over a small pool of water, busily chiselling mussels from the rocks. His bucket was almost full. Beside him were fistfuls of rock samphire that he had picked from the same area. Sam stood behind him, staring over his shoulder, knowing that Jonathan would eventually see Sam's reflection in the water beside his own. When he did, Jonathan jumped up so quickly that he knocked the bucket and sent a hail of mussels back into the rock pool, where they quickly sank to the bottom. For a moment they both stared in the water, each waiting for the other to speak.

'It's interesting the way that flavours that complement each other so often grow side by side, don't you think?' said Jonathan eventually, as he stood up. 'Like rabbits and dandelion leaves, field mushrooms and wild garlic, mussels and samphire.'

'It's the same with people,' said Sam, drawing lines in the sand with his toes.

'I'm not sure that I follow you,' said Jonathan affably.

'Some people bring out the best in each other,' said Sam. 'They make you feel that you're a better person than you really are. While others make you feel as though you're trapped in a negative force field where all your worst traits are highlighted.'

'You think too much, Sam,' said Jonathan, 'but it's an interesting theory.' It was a familiar refrain. The wind cut through the air between them.

'Jonathan, I want to know what's going on,' said Sam eventually. 'That noise the other morning . . .'

'If I'd known the walls were like transmitters then I would have sneaked off with Eve in the car,' said Jonathan apologetically.

'So it was Eve,' confirmed Sam. 'What about Hannah?'

'She's gone,' interrupted Jonathan, his voice taut with emotion, 'back home. She left on the boat this morning. I'm going to tell everyone later when I'm feeling less fragile.'

'Did she find out about Eve?' asked Sam incredulously.

'No. She left because of Jacek,' replied Jonathan, shaky-voiced.

'Who is Jacek?' asked Sam in astonishment.

'He's our new farm manager,' said Jonathan, shaking his head and laughing in disbelief. 'You probably remember him as the gardener, although now he's got a new role as my understudy or maybe I've got a role as his understudy. She thinks she's fallen in love with him.'

'I don't believe it,' said Sam, shaking his head vigorously as though his brain was struggling to absorb the impact of what Jonathan was telling him. 'What are you going to do?'

He put out a hand to touch Jonathan's shoulder. Jonathan shrugged him away.

'I don't know,' he said, 'we don't know. They don't know. It's a mess. And it's incredibly bad timing with the publicity for the TV series about to kick off.'

Jonathan stared at his feet and began picking bits of grit from his nails. 'I think I'm in shock. I've told Luke there was a problem on the farm,' said Jonathan. 'A breech birth involving one of Hannah's cows and I suppose that's what I'll tell everyone else. Hannah might remain in Suffolk for a while and I'll keep working in London. One way or another we'll muddle through.'

'Has this happened before?' questioned Sam.

'What do you mean?' replied Jonathan.

'Do you have a tacit agreement that allows the odd inconsequential affair?' asked Sam.

'Of course not,' said Jonathan, sounding surprised. 'There's been a couple of indiscretions, but nothing like Eve. You understand that I didn't know she was coming here, don't you?'

'What about Patrick?' asked Sam.

'I had no idea,' explained Jonathan. 'Of course I knew he was back in England and I spoke to him on the phone once to give him Janey's number, but bringing him here was Eve's idea. She persuaded him.'

'How?' asked Sam.

'She's a very persuasive personality,' sighed Jonathan. 'You can appreciate that.'

'Definitely one to watch,' said Sam, remembering a phrase from their adolescence.

'Sam,' said Jonathan evenly, 'Eve told me what happened

on the beach.' A flock of seagulls circled above them, eyeing the bucket of mussels and screeching loudly as though alerting others to their discovery.

'What did she say?' asked Sam finally.

'That things got out of hand and you frightened her witless by nearly drowning yourself in the sea,' said Jonathan. He bent down on one knee to examine the mussels, pulling off bits of weed and making sure there were no empty shells. It was activity that allowed him to avoid Sam's restless gaze.

'I don't know why you insisted on sending me off with her,' said Sam, unsure of what else to say and then berating himself for trying to blame Jonathan for his irresponsibility.

'You can hardly hold me responsible for the fact you couldn't keep your hands off my girlfriend,' said Jonathan bluntly.

'It wasn't like that,' insisted Sam, 'it was just a moment. It passed very quickly.'

'Its brevity doesn't dilute its significance. The assassination of Kennedy was just a moment in time,' said Jonathan bitterly. 'Eve told me it all started at the theatre.'

'She's exaggerating,' Sam said angrily.

'Why would she do that?' asked Jonathan.

'To make you jealous because she knows you're losing interest?' suggested Sam. 'So that you leave Hannah? To invest excitement into a flagging relationship?'

'Hannah has left me,' said Jonathan, as though it was a phrase that needed to be repeated until its impact was fully absorbed.

'It was a pretty innocent fumble in the sand,' said Sam,

walking over to Jonathan to touch his elbow, 'at least by your standards.'

In the distance Sam could see Laura walking towards them, her head down against the wind. He calculated that they had about three minutes to resolve the situation. Close behind her was Patrick, staring through the lens of his camera, poised to shoot a few long-distance frames of them set against the angry sky.

'What do you mean "by my standards"?' said Jonathan, his expression hardening.

'I've never mentioned this to you or Laura, and as far as I know, no one has ever spoken about it in a decade, but half the people here know what happened on that weekend in Shropshire, and I think that if I managed to subsume any residual feelings of bitterness over the fact that you slept with my wife a few weeks before our wedding, and then put that photograph on the cover of your book, I think you can get over the fact that Eve and I had an inconsequential entanglement.'

Sam lurched at Jonathan, lowering his head like a bull to ram him in the stomach with sufficient force for Jonathan to lose his balance and topple over backwards on to the sand. Sam fell on top of him and found himself lying across Jonathan's lower body, his head resting on the surprisingly comfortable mass of stomach. Laura was running towards them. Even through the wind, Sam could hear her shouting. She dropped the buckets she was carrying and threw off the jumper from around her waist. But she was too late.

'And then you tried to persuade me not to marry her,' Sam shouted breathlessly, grabbing Jonathan's T-shirt by the shoulders.

Jonathan didn't respond. It took Sam a moment to realise that he had fallen backwards on to a rock and knocked himself out. Sam gently slapped his cheeks with his hand, calling Jonathan's name, trying to remember the correct medical procedure from *Do Not Resuscitate*. Was it airway, breathing, circulation? Or should he put him in the recovery position? A steady trickle of blood streamed out of Jonathan's right nostril. Laura had almost arrived, Sam noted with relief, as he did nothing. Then suddenly Jonathan sat up.

'You've got it all wrong, Sam,' he groaned before turning on to all fours to push himself upright. Laura stood, her hands covering her mouth and nose, unable to speak but understanding immediately what had happened. She checked Jonathan's eyes and noted that neither pupil was dilated.

Jogging through the sand, hampered by cameras, bags and other paraphernalia hanging from him, Patrick progressed towards them. He arrived just as Laura spoke.

'It wasn't Jonathan, it was Patrick,' Laura cried above the noise.

17

Laura stared down into the bucket of mussels, shifting from one foot to the other and wishing all traces of that weekend could have disappeared as quickly as the footprints she had just trodden in the sand. A fierce southerly breeze had already erased her tracks across the beach from the other side of the bay. Sand whipped at her bare calves and the wind was now so savage it hurt to inhale. The mussels lay in a topsy-turvy muddle of grey-blue shells. They were tight shut, as though turning their backs in embarrassment at the scene unfolding before them. Laura envied their ability to close themselves off from the outside world.

She briefly glanced over at Jonathan, unsure what she was searching for, but when she saw the blood between his left nostril and upper lip she looked quickly away. His nose wasn't broken, she was sure of that, but his upper lip was already swelling, twisting his smile into a sneer. Laura removed her cardigan, dipped the sleeve in a rock pool and passed it to Jonathan, telling him that the cold and saltwater would reduce the swelling.

'I'm so sorry, Sam,' said Jonathan, as he pressed Laura's cardigan against his upper lip and then stared at the red stain on the pale green wool as though surprised to find blood. His voice was strained. Beside him stood Patrick, looking dazed, camera flapping around his neck, as though he was the one who had been hit on the nose. For a while no one spoke.

Laura became aware of Janey and Steve's presence, but couldn't recall when they had appeared. There was a long silence, interrupted only by Jack's gurgles, and Laura realised that everyone was waiting for her to speak. Sam was sitting on his haunches, trying to regain composure. His breathing was shallow and he kept pressing his right fist into his left palm and rubbing his knuckles. Laura noticed Janey's hand on his shoulder.

'I suppose, sometimes, in order to go forwards you have to go backwards first,' Laura said slowly. She had rehearsed this moment so many times that she now felt curiously detached from the words she heard coming out of her mouth.

'You don't need to, Laura,' said Sam, 'it's not what you think.' But Laura wasn't listening or if she was, she didn't want to hear.

Over the intervening years, Laura had managed to convince herself that excising memories of that weekend on the barge in Shropshire was a question of self-discipline. Right at the outset, even during the awkward train journey back to London from Telford on that August morning in 1997, Laura knew that the more she analysed what had happened, the more vivid the memory would become, so she tried to focus on what was going on around her. She had stared out the window of the train, feeling the cool glass against her cheek, watching as woods turned into fields, fields into rows of red-brick houses and then back into fields, until finally they reached London. The concept of motion was important because it gave Laura the sense that she could move forward, away from what had just come to pass between her and Patrick. Jonathan had lent her his new portable CD player and for a while she listened to Pulp, without hearing either the music or the words. She picked up a newspaper and was distracted by the account of Diana's holiday in the south of France with Dodi Fayed. There was speculation that she was pregnant. That she was going to get married. That he was already engaged to someone else. Tony Blair, elected eight weeks earlier, was on holiday in Tuscany in a house belonging to someone he had promoted as Paymaster General. There was talk of a new children's book about a child wizard called Harry Potter. Laura resolved to buy a copy for Luke, who was then almost seven years old. Patrick and Janey sat in front of her. When Janey got up to go and buy everyone coffee, shortly after the train left Telford, Patrick leant through the space between the seats and tried to reassure her that everything was going to be fine. Laura could see the tension in his jaw. She closed her eyes and moved away from him towards the window. Restless images of the previous evening filtered before her.

Laura knew that the same neural pathways would be reactivated every time she replayed the scene in her mind and, before she knew it, permanent connections would be formed and a long-term memory embedded deep in her amygdala, so that when she was ninety years old and had forgotten the names of her grandchildren, she would still be able to remember in perfect detail the way Patrick had casually tucked a finger in the back of her shorts and pulled her towards him as they searched for mushrooms on the edge of a small copse close to where the barge was moored.

Everything was crystallised in that moment. She remembered the sensation of being pulled backwards. How he pressed himself against her from behind. There was no mistaking the lack of platonic intent in that gesture. Why hadn't she walked away then?

Afterwards Laura had amassed an impressive file of literature on the subject of emotional memory, taking out subscriptions to magazines that her more conservative colleagues would have viewed with suspicion. *Journal of Experimental Psychology*, *Trends in Cognitive Sciences*, *Psychologica*. She pored over the findings in papers that might help her develop strategies for forgetting. 'The Cognitive and Neural Mechanisms of Emotional Memory', 'Sex Differences in the Neural Basis of Emotional Memories', and her favourite, 'Ageing and Emotional Memory: the Forgettable Nature of Negative Images for Older Adults'.

For a while, Laura had reread that last paper whenever she felt shaky. Its message was the most reassuring. It suggested that people got happier as they got older because they tended to remember more positive memories and discard unhappy ones. Then a dilemma presented itself in Laura's mind. Of course the main reason for forgetting was that she wanted to marry Sam, remain friends with Janey, and pretend to herself that nothing had happened. In those early days, confession seemed the nuclear option. Sometimes she was so consumed by guilt that she would lie on the floor, limbs outstretched, and breathe deeply until a shaky equilibrium was restored. Once or twice, when she felt she couldn't bear it any more, she had called Patrick and he had convinced her that there was nothing to be gained from disclosure. It was self-indulgent, he said, something that would make Laura feel better but everyone else feel worse. He had put it to the back of his mind and so should she.

Then just as she felt she couldn't bear it any more, the guilt started to retreat. But still Laura found herself treading over the same ground and she began to question whether instead of wanting to forget, she wanted to remember. The amygdala calculates the emotional significance of events. Even her colleagues were convinced of that. Perhaps the reason she kept returning to her encounter with Patrick that weekend was that it was more emotionally significant than she cared to admit to herself.

Although Patrick was careful to distil their relationship into nothing more than an ill-thought-out, ill-timed, mildly drunken entanglement, Laura knew that he found it equally difficult to escape its hold. It altered his relationship with Janey, because shortly afterwards she had begun to express doubts about Patrick's commitment. Certainly it affected his friendships. To Laura's relief, he didn't turn up to their wedding. Within a couple of months, Patrick completely disappeared from their lives. He ignored the phone calls, the emails and messages left with the picture agency that took him up in Afghanistan. And then after he vanished, the guilt crept back. Except now its focus switched from Sam to Patrick, as it dawned on Laura that he had sacrificed his friendships to secure her happiness.

Laura developed a successful array of strategies to foster

a long-lens view of that weekend. She didn't manage to obliterate the memories but their emotional resonance faded. She adopted methods developed by cognitive psychologists to train the mind to control reactions to emotional events. Whenever images of her and Patrick burnt into her consciousness, she recited the same sentence over and over again: 'A memory is nothing more than a series of neural pathways.' It was no different to the mantra given to people when they learn to meditate and it worked in the same way. She got rid of anything that reminded her of that weekend: she gave away her beloved shorts and the bikini she had worn since she was a teenager, she took the Pulp album to a second-hand shop, burnt the photographs. Sam didn't notice. He was too wrapped up in his new job writing scripts for *Do Not Resuscitate*. It didn't occur to Laura that he harboured his own suspicions about that day.

The most difficult part was listening to Janey talk about her problems with Patrick over the months before he finally vanished. He claimed that he wanted to get married yet was looking for work abroad, trying to get a job as a stringer in Kabul for a news agency. He kept getting angry and then telling Janey that it wasn't her fault. He criticised her for allowing herself to be in thrall to her job, mocked her when she earned a bonus that was almost double his annual income, despite the fact that it meant he could live free of charge in the flat she had bought in Notting Hill. Once Janey confided in Laura that she thought he was seeing another woman. Laura was simultaneously thrilled and appalled by her own duplicity as she found herself comforting Janey and suggesting that perhaps she should dump him.

*

As she stood on the sand, Laura closed her eyes for a moment and began to replay the exact sequence of events that night eleven years ago. When did it all begin? This was a question she had posed to herself many times, especially in the early years. Because it wasn't that moment in the tent when Patrick finally slid inside her and they began to lazily thrust against each other as though they were the only two people partying in a copse on the edge of the Llangollen Canal, and they had the luxury of a whole night ahead of them.

Then Laura remembered something that had happened on the first day of the trip, as they steered the barge out of Kington. Sam was annoyed because Jonathan had left his portable radio in the car and he couldn't listen to the cricket on long wave. They were bickering at the back of the boat over whose turn it was to steer. 'How can I trust you with the wedding ring if I can't even rely on you to remember a radio?' Sam niggled Jonathan. Laura retreated to the roof of the barge to be on her own. She lay down on a rug, closed her eyes against the sun, and listened to their argument, smiling at its familiarity. She could feel the heat of the wooden roof through the towel and for the first time in days she felt her body begin to relax.

The discussion distracted her from thoughts about her forthcoming wedding. They weren't the usual bridal concerns. Laura's main worry was whether her mother would be able to hold it together for the day. Gloves, thought Laura, sitting up abruptly. She must buy her mother gloves and then no one would notice the bloody trails across her finger joints and knuckles from the endless hand washing. A couple of months ago, Laura had written her mother a prescription for Prozac, and explained to her father on the way back from the chemist that there was a direct correlation between obsessive-compulsive disorder and low serotonin levels, and that he must make sure that she took them regularly. Her father had looked uncomfortably around the chemist as she pressed the pills into his pocket, warning Laura that he couldn't promise miracles.

'She's too old for change,' he said.

'How many years has she been like that?' Laura said, wondering why she'd never asked before.

'Since she had children,' her father said. 'Apparently pregnancy can trigger it.'

'Why didn't you talk to me about it sooner?' asked Laura, without stopping to wonder why she hadn't brought up the subject with her father.

'If adulthood appears too complicated, then children don't want to grow up,' her father said with a sad smile.

Laura could hear Hannah and Janey laughing at the front of the barge. They were discussing Jonathan's decision to launch his own restaurant. Hannah was telling Janey how a chef had asked him to go and buy some rosemary and he had come back with a lavender plant. She said that now both Luke and Gaby were at school she was going to try and help Jonathan out, because the concept of a British restaurant with environmental credentials was a good one, even if he had little idea of how to put together any of the ingredients. Laura switched on a CD player that Jonathan had given to her when she said that she might try and rest on the roof of the barge. It was an odd selection of songs that he had compiled for Sam to play at the party after the wedding.

Laura couldn't believe that in a month she would be getting married. Inside she still felt like the eighteen-year-old student who had arrived in Manchester, unsure of everything apart from an instinct that medicine would somehow provide her with the certainty otherwise lacking from her life. Her mother could face the world if she washed her hands five times before she left the house, tapped her foot on the doorstep exactly fifty times, and knew there was a packet of antibacterial wipes in her handbag. Laura, more like her father in temperament, knew there had to be an easier way. Her mother's condition was so familiar to Laura that she was surprised to find when she was studying medicine that it had a label, and even more that there were ways it could be cured. For years she had assumed that the reason her mother's habits had to remain secret was that they were peculiar to her. She hadn't even told Sam.

'Why do you do it, Mum?' she had once asked, as her mother tapped the doorstep on the way out to buy a pint of milk.

'To make everything fine,' her mother smiled.

Laura's eyes prickled with tiredness and she closed them hoping she could sleep. She was working as a registrar in a neurological unit at University College Hospital and the previous evening she hadn't got home until after midnight. On a drunken evening with Janey, they had worked out that Laura did almost the same hours as Janey for less than a quarter of the money. She had faith in the new government. New Labour would sort out the NHS. Tony and Cherie wouldn't worship at the court of the City fat cat. Everyone talked about them by their first names and surely that made them different from everything that came before. She was almost asleep when she sensed that she wasn't alone. She half opened one eye and saw Patrick staring down at her.

'Sorry, I didn't mean to wake you,' he said, sitting down beside her. Everyone was aware of Laura's brutal working hours. He offered her his bottle of beer and Laura took a deep gulp. Patrick held up a CD on the end of his finger.

'*OK Computer*,' he said, waving it cheerily at her. Laura must have looked at him blankly because then he explained that it was the new Radiohead album.

'I know the guy who does their graphics so I got an advance copy,' he said.

'I don't have much time to listen to music any more,' Laura said, as she sat up and stretched her spine, pulling her shoulders back. She spent so much time hunched over patients, writing up notes, studying images of the brain, that sometimes she felt as though her body was caving in on itself. She inspected her stomach and saw that it was already turning pink in the sun. Her hand touched her nose, and she thought she could feel freckles beginning to emerge. She wanted to go down into the tiny bedroom she was sharing with Sam and search for the sun cream, but was worried that Patrick might feel slighted. It was a widely held view among his friends that Patrick was going through another tricky period.

'Janey's the same,' Patrick said, as he pressed the eject button on the CD player, 'she works all the time.'

'Women have more to prove.' Laura shrugged her shoulders. 'We have to be twice as good to be considered half as relevant.'

'Not if you're a photographer,' said Patrick, offering her his beer as he rolled a joint. 'Pictures speak for themselves, as do patients, I imagine. Your gender is irrelevant when it comes to diagnosis.'

'Perhaps,' said Laura, but she still saw the disappointment on the faces of some patients when she pulled back the curtain around their bed and they realised they were being treated by a woman.

'In fact our jobs are remarkably similar,' said Patrick, warming to the subject.

'Because we're both trying to expose something, you mean?' questioned Laura, pushing back the joint he proffered.

'The constant tension between empathy and detachment,' said Patrick. 'You sympathise with your patients but you can't afford to become attached to them. It's the same for me with the people I photograph. We're probably different sides of the same person. We're both good at controlling our emotions.'

'I'm not like you, Patrick,' laughed Laura, lying on her front to enjoy the sensation of the warm wood of the roof baking her stomach through the towel.

'How do you think I am?' Patrick questioned casually, as he pulled off his T-shirt.

'Less cautious than me,' said Laura sleepily, 'and braver.'

'You could say that my inability to commit to Janey is more cautious and less brave than your decision to marry Sam,' said Patrick, lying on his front beside her. His head was facing away towards the riverbank, and she guessed correctly that his eyes were shut. Laura paused for a moment, wondering if he was going to be more expansive.

'You don't think I should marry Sam?' asked Laura eventually. 'You think it might be difficult being married to someone who writes for a living?'

'If I was a woman, I would marry Sam,' said Patrick.

'I thought you were going to get hitched after your next trip?' said Laura.

'People like me shouldn't get married,' Patrick replied simply.

'People like you shouldn't listen to music like this,' said Laura, stretching towards the CD player at her side and resting her finger on the stop button. 'It makes you too introspective.'

'You should face up to your uncertainty instead of trying to escape it, Laura,' said Patrick, 'go with it for a while. Don't be like me, always running. It's too exhausting.'

'I don't know what you're talking about,' said Laura, her finger pressing the eject button to cut off Thom Yorke midstream, 'and now probably isn't the best moment to explore the unknown.'

'Let yourself go, you might be surprised where it takes you,' said Patrick, leaning over Laura to press the play button again. The music started up. His arm remained on Laura's bare back to prevent her reaching towards the CD player again. It was a gesture that was difficult to interpret. It could have been playful, but there was too much mutual pleasure in the intimacy, a complicit desire to be close to each other. Recognising this, Laura lifted her shoulder blades, pushed against the pressure and urged Patrick to remove his arm. Instead he held her gaze and kept it there. She felt Patrick creep along her arm and down towards her hand until his fingers were curling around her own. The music came on again. She pressed stop, felt Patrick's middle finger on top of her own and felt a shudder of attraction snake through her body.

'Patrick, I'm about to get married to one of your friends and you're about to move in with my best friend,' said Laura with persuasive logic.

'I don't want to be your friend,' Patrick whispered in her ear.

Then Jonathan appeared on top of the boat. Laura saw him eyeing the arm across her back and the red imprint from Patrick's hand on top of her own.

'What's going on?' Jonathan asked disapprovingly. 'You'll break my CD player if you go on like that.' The sun behind Jonathan's head blinded Laura and she blinked without seeing the expression on his face.

Laura went further back in time. She remembered when she was living in London with Janey, the year after they graduated. Patrick had pitched up for dinner one weekend with Sam. His incipient relationship with Janey was already a curious muddle of disjunction. They were unofficially together living in her room at the flat. Then they were officially together but living apart. It was complicated. Laura and Sam were tentatively circling each other. After dinner Laura had slipped out on to the small balcony that looked towards the football ground and on the side furthest from her she spotted a bird nesting in the overgrown mess of thyme and rosemary that Jonathan had encouraged them to grow in large wooden window boxes. It didn't move when it saw her and so she put her head inside the window and called over to Patrick to come and see. He came out on the balcony and identified it as a thrush. They shared a cigarette together and she remembered their hands lingering too close together as they passed it to each other. Nothing was said. They went inside. It seemed insignificant at the time. But now Laura questioned why she had sought Patrick and not Sam.

Janey and Sam appeared on top of the boat and interrupted her thoughts. They all stayed there drinking wine and smoking until they realised that the barge had drifted towards the riverbank and that no one was steering any more. Relieved to have an excuse to leave, Laura went to the back of the boat. She was joined by Janey's ex-boyfriend, Tom, who was still unable to come to terms with the fact that Janey was about to move in with Patrick. She agreed with him that Patrick was dangerously unreliable but said that Janey needed to work this out for herself. That was why people got married. To have a structure to hang all these uncertainties on, thought Laura wearily.

She managed to avoid Patrick until much later that night. The day meandered by with the organic structure familiar from their days at Manchester. They moored the barge. A few of them drifted into the nearest village to find a pub. Jonathan and Sam took a couple of Ecstasy tablets. Laura helped Janey put up the tent she was sharing with Patrick in a field beside a small copse that overlooked the canal. Tom locked the door into their sleeping quarters and promptly lost the key. Hannah gave someone an impromptu haircut.

Sometime in the evening, as the sun started to sink towards the horizon, Jonathan announced that he wanted to cook a wild mushroom risotto and asked for volunteers to collect ingredients. He put his arms exuberantly around Laura, declaring that if the recipe was successful he would put it on the menu in Eden and name it in her honour. Laura greeted the idea enthusiastically because that was what was expected of her, knowing that by the following morning Jonathan would have forgotten his promise. She remembered Jonathan was wearing an orange tie-dyed T-shirt and sunglasses. On the basis that she was a doctor, and therefore both cautious and scientific in her approach to mushroom picking, and that she was neither particularly drunk nor particularly stoned, Laura found herself pushed out of the cosy kilim-covered armchair she had been occupying in the kitchen of the barge and on to dry land. She was still wearing nothing more than a pair of shorts and a bikini top, and was carrying a copy of *Food for Free* open on the page about field mushrooms.

'Don't let the evening end in dialysis,' Sam shouted after her. He should have gone instead of her, thought Laura. He was in the middle of writing an episode of *Do Not Resuscitate* about a group of people poisoned by mushrooms.

On the riverbank she found a pair of purple Converse trainers that belonged to Jonathan, slid them on to her feet and walked flat-footed on a natural path that led into the woods from the riverbank. She shivered as she walked under the trees and the coarse bracken tickled her legs. It felt good to be alone. Since her encounter with Patrick, she hadn't thought about her mother's bloody hands once.

Laura could see a field the other side of a barbed-wire fence that marked the edge of the wood. She opened the book and glanced through the list of edible mushrooms found in northern England in the late summer. Laura stopped for a moment to examine them. She said each name out loud, enjoying the exoticism of the unfamiliar words: bay bolete, bare-toothed russula, charcoal-burner, beechwood sickener, slippery Jack. Slippery Patrick, Laura said to herself a couple of times as she remembered the look in Patrick's eye. Should she tell Sam what had happened? Faithless was playing on the CD player back at the barge and she could hear Janey and Sam laughing. She envied their closeness. It was a more complex emotion than jealousy, less visceral and more wistful. Sometimes she felt that everyone was closer to Sam than she was. He would always belong to other people.

Behind her, Laura heard the noise of sticks being trodden underfoot, but before she could turn around she felt a finger attach itself to the belt loop on the back of her shorts and give a couple of gentle tugs. The force wasn't even sufficient to knock Laura off balance in the oversize trainers, but she felt every nerve in her body jerk to attention. The finger lingered in the belt loop. Then slowly it edged above her shorts and stroked a tiny line across her back. Even though he didn't speak, she knew it was Patrick. She didn't move and interpreting her silence as acquiescence Patrick found a gap at the top of her shorts and put his hand inside to stroke the dimple above her right buttock. Laura could feel the heat from his finger burning into her. They stood like this for at least a couple of minutes. Then Laura must have leant back towards him because she felt his breath on her neck, his belt buckle digging into her flesh and through his jeans the hardness of him pressing into her.

His other hand snaked around her shoulder, across her

neck, his fingers dancing slow circular patterns on her bare flesh. She found herself reaching for his hand with her own and their fingers restlessly entwined for a moment. Then Patrick's hand moved down Laura's stomach and pushed inside her shorts. Laura turned to face him, hoping one of them would decide that this was a mistake. Instead, Patrick loosened his grip on her shoulders and took advantage to manoeuvre his hand further into her shorts, towards her bikini bottoms, a half smile on his face, as though challenging Laura to reject him. Then, unexpectedly, he stepped away from her. Laura felt the despair of unfulfilled lust. She put up a hand to wipe her forehead. She could feel the heat from his fingers as though his hand was still inside her bikini bottoms. He held the side of her head in his hand and then they kissed each other, tentatively at first, as though trying to gauge whether they really fitted together, and when they were both reassured, they pressed against each other, his clumsily lifting his T-shirt to feel the heat of Laura's body against his own.

'Not here,' Patrick muttered.

He took Laura's hand and pointed towards the tent on the edge of the field. Without bothering to turn around to check that anyone had seen them, they crunched through bracken and ferns to the edge of the wood and clambered over the barbed wire into the field. Inside the tent, it smelt of mints and coffee and the musty odour of slightly stale sweat. There was no preamble. No talk. No need to discover that they had a mutual love of Philip Roth, or came from similarly dysfunctional families, or discuss whether their lives were heading in the same direction. Laura crawled to the other end on top of a couple of hastily thrown-down nylon sleeping bags. She could see a bag with Janey's clothes spilling out and covered it with a towel. Patrick fumbled with the zip of the tent, wincing as he caught his finger in its teeth. Laura took off Jonathan's trainers and threw them to Patrick, who put them neatly by the exit. Then she lay on her back and watched as Patrick came towards her. He straddled her, his arms and legs encasing her arms and legs. The zip of his jeans was stuck. There were plenty of moments like these, when Laura could have brought them back from the brink, but instead she impatiently pulled him towards her and helped push the jeans down towards his hips.

His hand tugged at her bikini top until the two thin strips of material parted like curtains. Laura wriggled underneath him until her shorts were down by her knees, slithering against the nylon sleeping bag and feeling hard stones and lumps of earth beneath the floor of the tent. Patrick pressed himself on top of her until Laura felt light-headed with the weight of his body crushing her chest and the sweet smell of his breath on her face.

His hands pulled at her shorts and bikini bottoms.

She tilted her head towards him to kiss him and was confused when he gently pushed her back down against the nylon sleeping bag and ran his finger tenderly across her lips and inside her mouth, indicating they should be quiet. Then he reached down with his mouth towards her nipple, and traced a circuitous channel down her body with his tongue. Laura's flesh shivered with pleasure. She glimpsed down at Patrick and was shocked by the black hair, so different from Sam's blond head, bobbing above her breast. She felt it between her fingers. It was rough and unwashed.

Then he was inside her. For a while they stayed like this, savouring their slow rhythm, looking at each other, waiting to see who would lose control and capitulate first.

Patrick looked away and she could see the line of his jaw and the way he chewed his lip as he began to thrust inside her. Then Laura thought of nothing.

Afterwards, Patrick lay on top of her, his head buried in her shoulder. They didn't speak. He gently bit her shoulder blade. Laura felt him stir inside her and even though she knew that she must have been gone for almost an hour she wanted him all over again. She closed her eyes and turned her head to the side. Patrick leant on his elbows above her.

'Let me see your eyes,' he said. Laura stared at him. She felt as though she had turned liquid. Beneath her the sleeping bag was soaked with sweat.

'If anyone looks at you, they'll know,' whispered Patrick. 'In a different set of circumstances, we could have been good together. Did that ever occur to you?'

Laura wanted to ask him what he meant but she felt Patrick's body freeze above her. His muscles tensed and when she rocked against him instead of responding he remained completely still. She felt something over her head. It smelt of chlorine and Laura guessed it was the towel. She opened her eyes but couldn't see anything, although she could feel its rough surface against her eyelashes. For a moment she thought that Patrick was going to smother her. She stuck out her tongue and pressed it against the towelling until it stuck to the surface. Then she felt him still hard inside her and wondered instead if it was part of a complicated sex game.

'Ssh,' he said, as he felt her wriggle. 'There's someone

here.' Laura heard the zip of the tent open and the noise of someone trying to get in. Perhaps it was an animal, thought Laura, her own body now rigid with tension. She heard a familiar voice.

'Patrick, are you there?' Jonathan asked. Then as he became aware that Patrick wasn't alone, Laura heard Jonathan apologise and beat a hasty retreat from the tent.

'Sorry, mate,' he said. Then he was gone.

They got dressed in silence. Laura stuffed things that had fallen out of Janey's bag back in and pulled on her shorts. For a brief moment, they were locked in a wordless embrace. Laura returned to the barge telling everyone that she couldn't find any mushrooms. No one seemed to have missed them. Jonathan said it didn't matter because he had managed to find a generous crop of field mushrooms, which had now been cleaned and chopped. When the meal was ready, Patrick stood on the bridge above the barge and took the photo now immortalised on the cover of Jonathan's book. Afterwards Jonathan asked Laura if she could please bring back his Converse trainers. He didn't look her in the eye.

The rain started to fall in an angry diagonal across the bay. No one showed any inclination to move. Sam stared at Patrick in confusion.

'I'm sorry, Sam,' Patrick said, but his voice was barely audible.

'So who brought Patrick here?' a voice asked. It was Luke. Everyone turned round to stare at him.

'It was me,' admitted Laura. 'When I knew we were coming here I contacted Eve at the magazine and put her in touch with Patrick.'

'But why would you do that?' said Janey in astonishment. Steve's arm was firmly around her shoulder.

'Because I felt guilty that he lost all his friends,' said Laura simply. 'I knew that Janey was happy with Steve. I thought enough time had elapsed that Patrick would be able to reintegrate. Eve liked the symmetry of having the same person take the photograph. I didn't mean for everyone to find out about what happened, I wanted to see if I could divert the flow of history and bring us all back to the point where everything started.'

'That is really fucked,' said Jonathan and a couple of heads nodded in silent agreement.

'I couldn't live with the fact that everyone thought Patrick had callously abandoned Janey when in fact he was sacrificing his friends to ensure my happiness,' Laura explained. 'I didn't want to live alongside the guilt any more.'

'Is this what it's like?' Luke asked. Everyone turned towards him.

'What do you mean?' replied Jonathan.

'Is this what it's all about?' Luke repeated urgently.

'I don't understand,' said Jonathan.

'Is this what middle age is all about?' asked Luke.

18

The photograph was never taken. The magazine piece never written. Notes for Eve's interview sat in the in-tray of her desk in Wapping until eventually they sank to the bottom, smothered by other bits of paper. None of her colleagues said anything because they all knew: the feature was pulled because Eve had become part of the story. Instead, she had hastily replaced the cover story on Jonathan Sleet with the first British interview with the new Venezuelan conductor of the LA symphony orchestra.

It didn't matter, because by the time the first programme of Jonathan's television series aired on BBC1 at the beginning of August, he was already a household name, although his notoriety had less to do with British cuisine and more to do with his private life. The series enjoyed consistently good viewing figures, partly because the credit crunch encouraged people to stay at home, and in the climate of austerity the idea of locally produced seasonal products appealed to the burgeoning ranks of the vegetable-growing classes. 'Doing a Bath Chap' passed into the lexicon as a euphemism for cheating on your wife. Jonathan's relationship with Eve endured another couple of months after they left Coll. It probably would have ended sooner, Jonathan had glumly explained to Sam in their most recent phone conversation, but they were stuck together by the glue of public exposure.

In his temporary home in LA, as he tried to decipher the latest round of notes from the team of script editors at the studio, Sam concocted a list of things that would never happen again because of the holiday. Janey and Steve would never go away with any of Janey's old friends. Apart from Patrick perhaps, but even that was unlikely because they spent so much time with him already, now that he was living with them in London in between photography jobs. He had even set up a studio in a room in the basement.

Steve had taken to periodically emailing Sam and Laura. He wrote in a formal manner with no effort to shorten phrases or sentences. It was a style reminiscent of those Christmas cards that people sent with news of their family, except Steve's news was invariably more downbeat. He had lost his job. Convertible bond arbitrage funds had gone 'tits up', he wrote to Sam in his most recent message.

His computer-generated models that spotted mispricings in shares were over-reliant on leverage and had suffered spectacular losses in the market dislocation after Lehman Brothers went bankrupt in mid September. The restrictions on short-selling bank shares had not helped either. 'If you trade volatility, then you're fine,' he told them. The crisis in the finance sector had contaminated the economy, and it was unlikely that he would find another job in the medium term. So, for the time being, the nanny had been dispensed with and Steve had become a house husband. There followed a long description of Jack's first attempt to crawl, an event witnessed by both Patrick and Steve, although not by Janey, whose workload had increased as the unravelling of banks generated ever more complex legal cases.

Jonathan and Hannah would never live together again under the same roof, at least not in the conventional sense. Jacek would never return to live in Slovakia. There was some doubt in Sam's mind whether strictly speaking Jacek's destiny had been shaped by what happened in Coll. It was collateral damage, decided Sam, because perhaps if Hannah hadn't missed him so much and prematurely ended her holiday, then at least their part in the story would have escaped the public eye.

Sam slowly stirred his lemon and slimline tonic water, a new drink he had discovered since they moved at the beginning of August. Although in the aftermath of the holiday Sam had taken up alcohol with meaningful intent, it had been easy to adapt to the curiously ascetic lifestyle of the people he was working alongside over the next year to develop his script. From Sam's perspective, California seemed the least hedonistic place on earth. Anything that undermined people's ability to work was rejected and that included alcohol. He had even taken up exercise.

For once, Jonathan had shown impeccable judgement, Sam decided, as he stared into the glass contemplating the bubbles and considered the content of their phone conversation earlier that day. American tonic water was definitely fizzier. The bubbles clung on to the slice of lemon like limpets. He closed his eyes, put his nose in the glass and felt the spray tickle his nostrils, enjoying the effect of imbibing a small dose of carbon dioxide. It was late afternoon and Sam had been up since the phone had rung at six o'clock in the morning. Ideally he would now take to his bed for a ten-minute siesta, but it would be another form of procrastination to avoid looking at the end of the script to discover whether his new ending had met with approval.

'She doesn't want me back,' a voice had said at the other end of the line in a flat tone, before Sam had a chance to say anything. Sam recognised Jonathan and understood immediately that he was talking about Hannah. Jonathan repeated the same sentence a couple of times, as though he was still trying to absorb its impact. Each time he said it, Sam could feel his fear. This was not the ending Jonathan had anticipated. He had promised to do anything to try and make their relationship work again. He had even offered to move to Suffolk. Hannah was adamant. He should remain in London, she was staying in Suffolk and Jacek would continue to run the farm.

'There's a euphemism if ever I heard one,' Jonathan sighed.

'Things might be very different in six months,' Sam reassured him, thinking of the unpredictable trajectory of his own life over the past year.

Jonathan explained that he had moved permanently back into his flat in London and had been joined by Gaby, who had decided of her own volition to return to her old school in west London, rather than stay in Suffolk to do her A levels. There hadn't been any stories in the newspaper about him for at least a couple of weeks. He was probably the only person in the country relieved about the meltdown in the banking sector. Bear Stearns had collapsed even faster than his marriage, he said, in a rare moment of humour.

Sam could hear someone firing questions at Jonathan and guessed that he was calling from Eden. There was a muffled discussion about whether they should buy organic celeriac from Scotland or more locally grown celeriac from Hertfordshire and Jonathan said categorically that given the current financial climate, they should go for the cheaper option. He said that a delivery of courgettes and squash from the farm in Suffolk should arrive tomorrow, although he needed to confirm the details with Hannah.

Jonathan turned his attention back to Sam and explained that the rich Americans, fund managers and investment bankers who used to eat conscience-free dinners on expenses at Eden were ordering in pizzas. If it wasn't for the fact that they could keep costs down because they owned the premises, produced a lot of their own ingredients and the television series had turned Eden into what Jonathan described as a 'destination restaurant', they would have been in trouble. There was a hint of the old arrogance and bluster in this statement that gave Sam hope Jonathan might eventually emerge intact.

'I offered to cut my bollocks off and cook them for her, Sam,' Jonathan sighed.

'How did Hannah respond?'

'She said remorse is a dish best served cold. She's worried sick about Luke and Gaby but says that she's happier without me,' Jonathan complained. 'The worst thing is Jacek's sympathy. He doesn't even feel threatened by me. And of course everyone thinks I brought it on myself.'

'What did you think would happen?' asked Sam. Perhaps if he had posed this question six months ago then Jonathan might have pulled himself back from the brink.

'I thought Hannah would never find out,' said Jonathan, 'and if she did I suppose I imagined a period of ugly recrimination and blind fury, during which we would attend Relate and analyse where things had gone wrong. This would be followed by an opportunity for mea culpa and the chance to put things right with regular deliveries of cut flowers, mini-breaks in Prague, maybe a brush with Viagra and then . . .'

'Back on the yellow brick road,' interrupted Sam, with forced cheer in his voice.

'Exactly,' said Jonathan. 'Instead I sit in my two-bedroom flat, eating Pot Noodles and facing the wall of savage wrath that is my daughter, and what's even worse is that I know it's no more than I deserve.'

'Do you love Hannah?' asked Sam.

'All I know is that I want my old life back,' said Jonathan glumly.

The conversation had turned to Luke. In the immediate aftermath of the holiday, there was much debate about what Luke should do. He had secured a place to read English at Bristol but there were enough people interested in advertising on his blog to turn it into a viable business. Hannah, who had never graduated from university, insisted he should take up the place, while Jonathan, who had scraped a second at Manchester, thought he should follow his entrepreneurial instincts, but develop a new business that didn't have anything to do with blogging. Instead, Luke had taken matters into his own hands and sent Sam an email saying he had deferred his university place for a year and could he come and spend an indeterminate period of time with them in

LA to do work experience at a production company and maybe help out with babysitting.

At first Sam had said no. He was enjoying the distance between this new life and his old one. Then after a couple of days' thought, he decided that he bore no ill will towards Luke and that it might be cathartic for them to spend time together. Laura was delighted when he told her about Luke's proposal. She said that Luke was the only victim of the whole sorry situation.

Luke seemed fine, Sam had reassured Jonathan. The worry etched on his face when they picked him up at LAX a couple of weeks ago had dissipated and playing with Nell and Ben, he seemed to have discovered a renewed sense of frivolity and lightness that he had lacked after the debacle on Coll. It had made Sam realise that Luke was little more than a child himself, he told Jonathan.

'I'm so sorry about the holiday. I just didn't anticipate that's how it would all end,' Jonathan sighed. 'What a fucking fiasco.'

'Nor did Luke,' said Sam, 'I'm sure he didn't realise the consequences of his actions.' Actually you could say the same thing about all of us, Sam wanted to point out before he put down the phone, but there was a tacit agreement between him and Jonathan that the less palatable details of the holiday, including Sam's encounter with Eve and their fight on the beach, were subjects, like the German au pair, that should never be revisited. The key to long-term friendship was knowing when not to say something. The key to long-term marriage, on the other hand, was full disclosure.

Sam stood up and wandered over to a leather chair by

the sliding doors that led from his office into the garden of the home rented by the film company in Santa Monica. He leant against the door frame and watched Nell and Ben playing in the garden. The sky was perfectly blue. The plants were as still as the heat. Nothing moved. The shocking pink bougainvillea, the cactus in the corner, the lemon tree and even the soft floppy leaves of the banana were motionless. Sometimes Sam felt as though he had accidentally blundered into a David Hockney painting. The only noise he could hear was the bubbles from his glass and the occasional flutter of papers, as the air conditioning filtered through the vent by his desk.

He opened the door and the sound of Nell and Ben arguing filled the room.

'I'm the Cheyenne Indian,' shouted Nell, 'it was my idea.' She was wearing a bikini and a feather headdress that they had found during a visit to a Native Indian reservation up near Sacramento.

'I've got the tomahawk,' said Ben, and in a swift move he brought it down on his sister's arm. He was obviously aiming for her head, but fortunately Nell was taller than him. Sam waited with bated breath. The longer it took Nell to cry, the more intense the noise when she did. A piercing scream came out of her mouth and Sam saw Laura rush into the garden as Nell threw herself on top of Ben.

'You can be a Pomo Indian, Nell,' Laura suggested as she pulled them apart. 'They're the tribe that lived closest to LA.'

Roused by the noise, Luke had also come into the garden from his bedroom on the ground floor.

'Who wants to listen to my iPod for a while?' he asked.

*

Luke was good at diffusing tension, which was surprising considering how much he had inadvertently caused, thought Laura. It was gradually dawning on the children, that if they didn't play with each other, there was no one else to play with until school started. Laura watched Sam close the sliding doors and return to his desk. They smiled hesitantly and waved silently at each other through the glass. Nell and Ben lay on the ground, a headphone in each ear, arms outstretched and their eyes closed against the sun. Laura found the grass coarse and prickly. But by the end of the day the ground was so hot that any discomfort was far outweighed by the sensation of warmth baking your body from the earth beneath. Sometimes she lay between them holding their hands and they would fall still and silent and Laura would feel a brief moment of timeless connection. It was easy to feel connected in LA because hardly anyone you met was from California, which meant you could define your own relationship with the city unhindered by the burden of history.

Some people might accuse them of escapism, Laura thought in her more self-critical moments. But it was easier to confront each other away from the gaze of well-meaning friends and uncomfortable family members, who had all read everything in the papers and decided it was best not to mention anything. She had never felt closer to Sam. Every time she spoke to Hannah, who was either euphoric or in the depths of despair, Laura was grateful for the slow day-to-day rhythms of her own relationship. She would go back to work when they returned to England. By then the fissures in their marriage would be repaired.

Time, money and history would once again be on their side.

She watched Luke at the other end of the garden, sitting in a chair reading *War and Peace*. He had asked Sam to make a list of twenty essential novels that he should read before he went to university and had decided to start with the longest first. He was wearing a new pair of shorts that he had bought with the money from his first week's wages. Luke had cycled to a shopping mall a couple of miles away, possibly the only cyclist on the road, and had come back with these shorts and a couple of sloppy T-shirts that he wore in rotation.

Nell was now lying directly under the palm tree in the narrow band of shadow thrown by its trunk. It was her favourite spot and already the grass there seemed rougher and drier than the grass in the rest of the garden. By the end of the day, when its shadow bisected the whole garden, Nell and Ben would have created rival camps with belongings patiently brought outside by Luke. On his forays into the garden during a break from work, a cup of tea in hand, Sam was careful always to stand with one foot in each camp.

Nell told Sam that she liked to lie under the palm tree in case a coconut fell down. She wanted to catch it so that the milk would be hers. Sam tried to argue with Nell that firstly it wasn't a palm that produced coconuts because the gardener had told him that it was in fact a Rio Grande palmetto and then, when she refused to listen to reason, he said that if a coconut fell on her head then she might turn into the sort of neurological problem that kept her mother employed. But she resolutely ignored him. The idea that her parents were fallible was slowly taking hold.

*

Sam was staring at the top of the palm tree from his office. He gave Laura a thumbs-up sign, which meant that work was going well. Even though he could only spot giant seed pods at its peak, he still worried that a rogue coconut might suddenly fall from the sky, because one thing that Sam had learnt over the past year was that you couldn't really take anything for granted. God, even his bank and mortgage company had disappeared. Metaphorical coconuts from the sky had rained down on everyone and he didn't want anything happening to Nell, certainly not on his watch. Then there was the question of the San Andreas fault, which could possibly run beneath the garden. You could never be truly certain of the ground beneath your feet.

Sam eyed the palm tree anxiously again and went back into his office, nervously chewing the skin around his nails. He paced around for a little while, picking up yesterday's *LA Times* and an old copy of *Screen International* that had belonged to the people who rented the house before. He opened another can of tonic water from the small fridge that sat in the office. When he first moved into the house, he had seen this fridge as a sign of decadence. Now he realised that keeping food and drink in your office was simply another way of avoiding distraction.

Finally Sam went to the last ten pages of the script, dreading what he might find in the notes, but instead he found lavish words of praise. The revised ending was *brilliant*, a short note from the director read. *Inspired. Cate will love this*, exclamation mark, exclamation mark, someone else had written in the margin on the final page. He recognised the writing. It was the stern woman with the red hair and half-moon glasses who got up at five in the morning so that she could do an hour of exercise before starting work.

He would show the notes to Luke later that day, when the children were in bed and they sat out in the garden sharing a beer, because it was Luke who had inadvertently provided Sam with the ending, although he didn't realise it yet. Of course it wasn't a complete account of what had happened on holiday. Sometimes the truth was simply too strange. But it had certainly provided useful source material. Sam still shook his head in disbelief whenever he thought about the last twenty-four hours on Coll.

After the fight on the beach they had all gone home together. They walked back towards the road, into the southerly gale, their heads bowed against the wind and rain, like a group of defeated soldiers in retreat in the Crimea, assuming that although something terrible had happened, the worst was surely over. A big mistake, it subsequently transpired.

As they reached the path that led up to the road Sam had glanced back and noticed the two buckets of mussels still sitting beside the rock pools. Although he knew the mussels would be there the following day and that under these circumstances it was now unlikely that any meal would be cooked or any photograph taken, Sam decided to go back to collect them anyway. Someone would find them and mutter about the wasteful Londoners with more money than sense, even as recession loomed.

Besides, the wind and the rain made it impossible to talk. And if he could have made himself heard, what would he have said? His reaction wouldn't have been appropriate. It didn't sound right to say that after so many years assuming that Laura had slept with Jonathan that weekend, it came as a relief to discover that it was Patrick, and that he didn't really mind. Nor was it appropriate to tell Laura that she had this ability to make even her friends feel inadequate and it was liberating for everyone to know that she was just as imperfect as the next human being. This wasn't the response that Laura wanted.

Mostly he wanted to avoid her because he couldn't face her contrition. He couldn't explain that her revelation about Patrick made him feel better about elements of his own behaviour. Sam had no appetite for full disclosure. In this, he was with Patrick. He reached the buckets and picked them up and then instead of walking back up the beach to the path, he headed towards the sea.

Sam found himself walking into the spray until his shoes and the bottom of his trousers were soaked. Then he stood in the water and watched it boil beneath his feet, not caring about his shoes or the way his feet and ankles were already numb with cold. He closed his eyes and listened more intently to its voice, distinguishing different rhythms and pitch. When he opened his eyes again, his trousers were wet up to his knees and he realised the tide must be coming in.

He looked towards the horizon, but could only find its narrow line in the brief moment between one wave breaking and another emerging. He decided to fix his glance on a single, perfect wave and then follow it in, watching how it gained force until it was as high as the house where they were staying. When it seemed as though it couldn't sustain the weight of its own energy it crashed down, violently spewing its burden at Sam's feet on the shoreline. Nothing would induce Sam to go in any further. When the numbness crept up to his calves he turned tail and walked swiftly back to the road.

He got back to the house to find everyone in the sitting room. There wasn't enough hot water for baths in the middle of the day and instead someone had lit a fire in the sitting room. There were neat balls of newspaper and on top a perfect circle of kindling that met in the middle like the frame of a tepee. Steve was kneeling on the floor aiming a pair of bellows firmly towards the centre of the fire. When Sam came in, he stood up to greet him and pointed to a space on the sofa closest to the hearth. Eve was sitting in the middle, looking preoccupied. Sam followed her gaze and saw that she was staring at Jonathan.

The room had a warm glow that Sam attributed to the fire and light from lamps on various low tables scattered around the room. But as he took in Laura's orange T-shirt, Janey's orange trousers and Steve's orange shirt, Sam realised that it had more to do with their clothing. It was like barging in on a Hare Krishna conference. Only Jonathan was still in the clothes he had been wearing on the beach and that was because Laura was tending to his wounds.

Jonathan sat on a sofa the other side of the room, leaning slightly forwards to stem the flow of blood from his nose. With one hand, Laura was pinching the top of his nose and with the other she was dabbing antiseptic on the cut above his lip. Someone had found a packet of small plaster stitches that Patrick held dutifully while Laura tried to clean up the wound. Her orange top was stained red. Sam noticed that Laura's first-aid kit was neatly laid out on the Eden cookbook. The picture of Laura in her shorts on the barge was partially obscured by a bloody handkerchief and a tube of Savlon that had leaked over her face.

'It's not as bad as it looks,' she said to no one in particular, although she was staring at Sam.

Sam went over to Jonathan to apologise.

'I'm really sorry, I don't know what came over me,' he said.

'I'm sure you've fulfilled a lot of people's fantasies,' Jonathan responded in a nasal drawl. He tried to lean back, but Laura urged him to keep his head forward.

'I used to get nosebleeds as a child,' said Jonathan.

'I remember,' replied Sam.

Patrick sat on the arm of the sofa. His nerves were on edge; his right leg jigged up and down so feverishly that Sam put out a hand to stop it. Patrick announced he was going to leave on the next boat, but Sam pointed out that the ferry wouldn't be running because of the storm.

'It can't dock in a southerly,' he said knowledgeably.

Patrick then said he would go upstairs to his room for the rest of the day, but Janey interjected in a surprisingly kind tone that Jack had gone to bed for his afternoon nap and that given the length of the journey the following day, she would really rather he didn't interrupt him.

'Patrick, it's fine, really it's fine,' Sam muttered a little impatiently, 'obviously it's not ideal, but it's not an unmitigated disaster.'

'What would qualify as an unmitigated disaster then, Sam?' asked Eve, a little too aggressively for Sam's liking. He ignored her.

'It's an interesting question,' said Steve, in between bellows.

Eve was nervously flicking through an old copy of *Vogue* that she had picked up from a pile of magazines on the window sill.

'Do you think the owners of the house kept this issue of *Vogue* because of the tartan logo?' she asked.

'Maybe there was something inside they wanted to read again,' suggested Janey, picking up an even more dated issue with a portrait of Diana the month she was married on the cover. '"The wedding of the century is now part of history, and like all true history, it will leave its mark on the future,"' Janey read out loud. 'There's a lesson for us all.'

It was a useful distraction, thought Sam, a laudable attempt to impose some normality on the situation, because they would need to be resourceful to get through the evening and next day.

'This page is dog-eared,' said Eve, as she flicked impatiently through the pages.

'There's your answer then,' said Janey, with satisfaction.

Eve read out the headline: '"Can friendship and sex mix?" There's a leading question for you all. God, you make life seem so complicated.'

Luke came into the room carrying a tray with a pot of tea and not enough mugs. He had opened a packet of digestive biscuits. He went over to Jonathan and put his arms gently round his neck from behind the sofa.

'Are you all right, Dad?' he asked.

'It was a misunderstanding, Luke,' said Jonathan. 'The stuff of life. A good lesson in the importance of honour among thieves.'

Then Luke disappeared to his bedroom. No one went after him. There was a sense of relief that he had left the room because his presence added to their collective shame. Sam couldn't remember at what point he found them tussling on the beach, but he could remember Luke trying to pull him off Jonathan and he knew that he would have to speak to Luke and apologise for his behaviour.

For a while they all sat in companionable silence, listening to the wood puff and hiss. Jonathan recovered sufficiently to be able to hold his head at the correct angle. Steve stopped niggling the fire. Janey talked to Laura about whether they should clean the mussels and cook them with chips for a meal later that night. Their proposal was greeted with enthusiasm, partly because it broke the stasis. Just before they left the room, Sam tentatively suggested that perhaps it was for the best if what had occurred over the previous forty-eight hours was something that could be buried on Coll.

'What do you mean?' Eve asked.

'I think we should agree to a pact of silence,' said Sam.

'No autopsy, you mean?' suggested Janey.

'I think that might be problematic,' said Laura, eyeing her nervously.

'What I mean is that it shouldn't go any further,' said Sam. 'There's nothing to be gained from telling anyone else what has happened. It's not in anyone's interests. Agreed?' No one contradicted him.

A little later Laura and Janey stood in front of the kitchen sink eyeing the buckets of mussels. Luke was sitting at the kitchen table typing feverishly on his laptop. Occasionally he stopped to run his fingers through his hair and read what he had written. They should show more interest in his blog, Laura thought. It was easy to ignore Luke because he was such an unimposing presence. They mistook his quiet nature for maturity when really what he needed was reassurance and encouragement, especially given his mother's unexpected and largely unexplained departure from Coll. When they got back to London, Laura would read it from beginning to end.

'How long have you been doing your blog, Luke?' she asked.

'Almost a year,' he said, glancing up from the computer, clearly hoping that Laura wasn't about to try and engage him in conversation.

'Can you tell how many people read it?' Laura asked. 'Or is it only for family and friends?'

'It's just there, somewhere in the ether,' said Luke. 'It's going very well at the moment.' When it was clear that Laura wasn't going to ask him any more questions, he smiled enigmatically and looked back down at his screen again.

'We need a system,' said Janey, clearly intimidated by the piles of mussels floating in the sink.

'Quite,' said Laura, who was perfectly prepared to spend the next four hours scouring shells and pulling off wiry bits of beard in penance. Janey decided that she should clean them up as much as possible with a nail brush and Brillo pad before passing them on to Laura, who would scrape them with the vegetable knife. They both spoke at the same time.

'You go first,' interjected Janey.

'I couldn't possibly,' replied Laura.

'Then I'll start because once you've heard what I've got to say then perhaps you won't feel so guilty,' said Janey, as she expertly pulled out mussels, examined them to check they were still closed and then began to scrub.

'Absolutely,' said Laura.

'The first thing is that Patrick and I would never have worked,' said Janey, 'so you did me a favour. And I don't hold you entirely responsible because I know you weren't the only one.'

Laura was about to respond, but Janey interrupted.

'The second thing is that Sam and I slept with each other more than once but not after you got it together,' said Janey, choosing her words with precision. Laura didn't ask any more questions because she didn't want to know the answers. Over the next couple of hours they discussed a variety of subjects. Janey asked Laura about how she felt when she went back to work after Nell was born. In the current economic climate, it shouldn't be difficult to find a good nanny, Janey said resolutely. They discussed whether Laura would move to LA with Sam and the children while he was contracted to work on his script and Janey suggested a couple of people Laura could speak to for recommendations on schools and where to live. Given the housing market in the States, rent would probably be cheap. Laura said that the film would probably never get made because no one was going to risk lending money to make films when the returns were so precarious.

It was a conversation you might have with someone you had just met, Laura thought. A sense of formality and politeness had replaced their easy intimacy. Eggshells, thought Laura, as she watched her hands pick up another mussel and begin the slow process of scraping tiny barnacles and stubborn bits of mud from its surface. They trod warily around each other. The activity was a relief. The conversation turned to the mussels. Why were they so small? Should they reject any that were open? Was it a good idea to eat them the day before a long journey? As the conversation threatened to dry up, Jonathan came into the kitchen and began a long explanation about how farmed mussels were much bigger because they were force-fed, like foie-gras geese, and that there was a growing body of opinion that thought a cooked closed mussel wouldn't necessarily lead to food poisoning. Neither of them listened but his explanation filled the silence and they were both grateful for that.

The first indication that something was seriously amiss came early the following morning. It must have been about seven o'clock when the phone rang for the first time. Janey was already in the kitchen and picked it up, holding Jack in one arm, trying to prevent him from grabbing at the curly plastic phone wire. When he caught it in his tiny but surprisingly strong little fist he pushed it greedily towards his mouth. She half hoped it was Hannah, calling up Jonathan to plea for clemency, but she didn't recognise the voice at the other end, although she sensed the tension in her tone when the woman explained that she needed to contact Mr Sleet as a matter of urgency. Janey unwound the wire from Jack's fist and called upstairs for Jonathan to come down, not really caring who she woke up. The house needed cleaning and there were bags to be packed. Janey wanted to go home.

After eating the mussels with bowls of chips as thin as matchsticks that Jonathan had cooked as an afterthought, they had all stayed up too late the night before. No one wanted to be the first to go to bed. It was part of a psychological effort to convince themselves that everything was fine, thought Janey, as she prised the wire from Jack's hand and examined the thin moustache of dust around his mouth. Only Eve was exuberant. As she trailed her arm carelessly around Jonathan's shoulder the source of her excitement became apparent. Janey berated herself for her lack of insight.

Luke, the only person obviously uncomfortable with the situation, had left early to watch television and seemed to have spent the night on the sofa in the small room beside the kitchen. Someone had thrown a blanket over him, Janey noticed, as she went into the room. His laptop sat on the table beside the small portable television. It was disconnected from the phone socket but Janey could see his last blog entry still on the screen. For a moment, she questioned the morality of reading it. Then she laughed at herself. It was a blog. Anyone could read it. She would take a look because she might learn something about up-and-coming bands, or whether Luke had a girlfriend, or what he might like for Christmas. At the very least, it would provide insight into the teenage psyche.

She could hear Jonathan's voice from the kitchen. Judging by the volume of expletives, something had gone wrong. A shudder crept up her spine. Jonathan expected a lot of his friends, Steve had said, when eventually they went to bed in the early hours of the morning. As she heard Jonathan shout into the phone, Janey ran through the possibilities. Salmonella poisoning at Eden. A legal problem with the television series. Another chef defecting to a rival restaurant.

She sat down on a cushion in front of the low table where Luke's computer sat and began to read his most recent entry. But after a couple of sentences and brief approval of his curt writing style and minimal use of adjectives, Janey's admiration began to curdle as she realised that she was reading an in-depth account of everything that had happened the previous day. Everything was there, from the fight on the beach, to Laura's confession about Patrick, to Hannah's relationship with Jacek. There were snatches of conversation between Steve and Sam that were repeated almost verbatim. It was well written. There was a level of dispassion that Janey found disconcerting. It was almost journalistic in style. Even her conversation with Laura and her admission that Sam and she might not have been entirely upfront about their relationship was recorded. One day Luke would go far, thought Janey, as Jonathan steamed into the room. Just not today.

Then the phone calls began in earnest, Sam remembered. This part was easier to remember because the facts were now familiar to everyone. They had been repeated over and over again in the newspaper until some essential truth emerged. Luke's blog, with its cast of adult characters observed from his teenage perspective, had become required reading on the Internet even before his holiday in Coll. The account of his expulsion from school had gained him a loyal readership. 'Hundreds of thousands,' Jonathan kept shouting at Luke as he snatched the blanket from him and pulled him off the sofa. But the account of what had unravelled in Coll had reached almost a million people because his blog had been picked up by a national newspaper and when it became apparent that the leading role was being played by Jonathan Sleet, it became required reading for anyone who wanted a little light relief from the mood of economic doom enveloping the country. When they disembarked from the ferry in Oban, a couple of resourceful tabloid photographers were waiting to take pictures.

'It wasn't vengeance,' said Luke. With his finger he stirred the ice in the tonic water that Sam had offered him. Then he tried unsuccessfully to catch it between his index finger and thumb. Sam waited for him to continue. It was as though he was writing a diary that no one else would read, Luke tried to explain to Sam. Of course, when his friends started to mention that they had seen his blog, Luke realised that there was an element of public exposure, but he couldn't imagine anyone who didn't know him truly taking an interest in the details of his life when the people closest to him barely took notice. And even when he knew that thousands of people were reading it, he still couldn't reconcile this with the fact that most of it was written in private in his bedroom. There was a degree of detachment that remained unfathomable to him, even now. He needed to be honest about his life to reassure himself that he really existed, Luke tried to explain to Sam. It was as though the words made him real.

'Sometimes I feel like the invisible man,' said Luke.

When Sam pointed out that he had a lot to contend with because his parents' marriage was going through 'a rocky patch', Luke stopped stirring the ice and said it would be self-indulgent to use that as an excuse. He didn't see himself as a victim. Luke briefly leaned over to look out the window to check that Nell and Ben were fine. Then he sat back in the chair again.

'I've destroyed my parents' marriage,' said Luke simply. 'I've turned our life into a reality TV show.' The heels of his trainers beat rhythmically up and down on the floor and Sam noticed that he was sitting on his hands. 'And yours too,' Luke added, shaking his head. 'I fucked it up for everyone.' His head hung so low that Sam couldn't see his face. A couple of tears fell on to Luke's shorts. Sam put an arm on his shoulder.

'Adults mess it up for themselves,' said Sam, 'they don't need any help. All you did was write about what you saw going on around you. It might have been misguided, but it wasn't done with malicious intent. Your mum would have found out about Eve eventually and your dad already knew about Jacek.'

'Laura would never have known about you and Eve, if it hadn't been for me,' muttered Luke, staring uncomfortably at his feet. That was certainly true, pondered Sam. He could still remember the icy look on Laura's face as they crowded around Luke's computer to read the entry for 15 July 2008.

Went to the beach to clear my head after finding messages from Jacek on Mum's phone. She had promised Laura and Janey that she would stop seeing him but it was pretty obvious from the content that nothing had changed. Scanned through a couple and then couldn't go on. Makes the stuff I look at on the Internet seem as innocent as CBeebies. I began to wonder if it was just my parents who were behaving like a bunch of hormonal teenagers. When I got to the beach I didn't know whether to be relieved to find Sam and Eve (yes, that is correct) getting some action. I was so close that I could see Sam's calves were red from the friction of sand against flesh. Not wanting to be accused of being a perv, I decided that I would backtrack around a sand dune and trek back to the house. I left my godfather writhing on the beach like an extra from Skins. *Just as well that I have already managed to get lucky a couple of times otherwise these guys might seriously fuck up my sexual development . . .*

Sam was a quick reader. He remembered calculating quite calmly when he reached the end of the screen that he probably had roughly twenty seconds of grace before judgement would be passed. He felt his throat constrict and swallowed nervously while the others caught up, watching Laura's eyes move from one side of the screen to the other. Laura read slowly and precisely, giving Luke's words the same careful consideration that she might apply to a medical paper. Sam watched her and saw how her facial muscles began to tense until it seemed as though her eyes, nose and mouth had all shrunk.

'If you hadn't been on the beach, then I would have drowned,' said Sam, 'and no matter what has happened, it is preferable to be alive.'

'I didn't mean to tell everyone what I saw,' insisted Luke. 'I had this urge to tell the whole truth so that it would at least be straight in my own head. When I realised what was going on between Mum and Jacek, I couldn't ignore it.'

'The eye of the storm has passed,' Sam reassured him. 'It was a very bad moment, but we're all coming out the other side. The advantage of having fifteen minutes of fame is that someone else steals the limelight pretty quickly.'

'Dad is still tabloid fodder,' muttered Luke. 'God, they even printed a photo of him outside the flat with Gaby trying to make out that she was a new girlfriend.'

'Well, thank God for the collapse of the finance system,' said Sam, 'because otherwise it could all have been so much worse.'

Epilogue

'So what brings you here?' The man peered over his glasses and smiled first at Sam and then Laura, before glancing down at his notes and turning on to a new page. He wasn't from LA. His voice had the slow soporific drawl of the South, possibly Arizona, decided Laura, wondering what it was about American accents that gave people immediate authority. Dr Lieber was older than them too, which helped, and Laura could see that he was wearing a simple gold band on his ring finger. His face was long and thin, his eyes a watery blue colour, and he had a long beard, giving him a quasi-religious look, like something El Greco might have painted, thought Laura. She wondered whether he was a medically trained doctor or whether he had a PhD in a subject like philosophy. Perhaps the title was bought from an Internet site. It was easy to do that in America. It was a place where reinvention was actively encouraged.

If she had been allowed to work, Laura might have considered a similar path, but for the first time she was taking a break and looking after Nell and Ben full-time. Except they were now at school most of the day, which gave her plenty of time to do things that she had never done before. Her fantasy of baking cakes and home cooking was already satisfied. She had joined a Pilates class at the local gym and every day she went running on the beach. Sometimes she contemplated herself and wondered whether she was observing the life of a different person. But even now, a couple of months into her new regime, Laura knew she wanted to go back to work. There was a financial imperative, because even if Sam's film project went ahead there was no certainty about his future. And given the current state of their marriage, it would be foolhardy to abandon her career. But notwithstanding all that, Laura found herself missing work in the same way you might miss an old friend. She had already diverted delivery of her subscription magazines to their Santa Monica address and during that void in the day when Sam was working, the house tidy and her emails answered, she found herself scanning the Internet for research jobs in the area.

Dr Lieber offered them a herbal tea and Sam pulled out a couple of Tetley tea bags from his pocket and asked whether it would be too much trouble to do a pot of English tea.

'I like it when the British conform to stereotype,' Dr Lieber drawled, as he picked up his phone and called in someone to prepare a pot with three mugs. He pulled a Mont Blanc pen out of his pocket and began tapping the piece of paper in a way that was thoughtful rather than impatient.

Laura looked out of the window at the blue sky and admired the carefully kept garden outside Dr Lieber's office. The plants and flowers in the semi-circular flower bed stood stiffly upright as a gardener doused them with water. He seemed to give undue attention to the cacti, thought Laura, who wished that he would turn the hose on her and Sam, as they both sat sweating on the worn leather sofa.

They were sitting so close that their thighs were stuck together and Laura could feel Sam's breath on her neck. He smelled of toothpaste and the idea that he had bothered to clean his teeth before the appointment made Laura want to laugh. Sam's arm slid down between them and she could feel his finger trace hot circles on the back of her hand. It struck her suddenly that marriage was linear, not circular.

'So have you done any therapy before?' Dr Lieber asked.

'By accident, not design,' said Laura. Dr Lieber looked at them in confusion under his bushy eyebrows.

'She gave me a session as a birthday present once,' Sam explained.

'Unconventional,' said Dr Lieber drily. 'So who is going to kick off?' Sam and Laura looked at each other. Laura raised an eyebrow.

'It's complicated,' said Sam.

'It always is,' said Dr Lieber.

Acknowledgements

I would particularly like to thank my editor Kate Elton, my agent Simon Trewin and my husband Ed Orlebar for their invaluable advice and constancy during the writing of this book. I am also extremely grateful to the following people who gave help and encouragement along the way: Emma Rose at Random House; Jim and Imogen Strachan for their hospitality on Coll; Carolyn Gabriel for sharing her neurological expertise; and my first readers Helen Townshend and Henry Tricks. Thanks also to Sarah Bell, Lorna and Simon Burt, Rosa Chavez, Becky Crichton-Miller, Fred de Falbe, Anne Dixey, Andrew Dodd, and the Chamomile Café in Belsize Park for allowing me to write there. I learnt about traditional English cuisine from a series of books on regional produce and recipes by food historian Laura Mason and food writer Catherine Brown. *From Norfolk Knobs to Fidget Pie: Foods from the Heart of England and East Anglia*, proved especially useful.

ALSO AVAILABLE IN ARROW

The Secret Life of a Slummy Mummy

Fiona Neill

For Lucy Sweeney, motherhood isn't all astanga yoga and Cath Kidston prints. It's been years since the dirty laundry pile was less than a metre high, months since Lucy remembered to have sex with her husband, and a week since she last did the school run wearing pyjamas.

Motherhood, it seems, has more pitfalls than she might have expected. Caught between perfectionist Yummy Mummy No 1 and hypercompetitive Alpha Mum, Lucy is in danger of losing the parenting plot. And worst of all, she's alarmingly distracted by Sexy Domesticated Dad. It's only a matter of time before the dirty laundry quite literally blows up in her face . . .

'This slice of angst and affluenza is several cuts above the rest . . . witty, observant and supremely intelligent.' *The Times*

'There is something of Bridget Jones's hopeless-but-adorable quality about Lucy . . . Neill's hilarious depiction of the manifold daily perils of stay-at-home motherhood is so convincing that it soon looks like the most challenging job in the world – and Lucy is all the more sympathetic simply for staying afloat.' *Daily Telegraph*

arrow books